Also by the same author:

Inheritance Lost
An Equal Judge

Ragged Cliffs

Julian Ruck

DINEFWR
PUBLISHERS

For Lynney, excuse me!

PROLOGUE

Denmark – February 1945

> *"To you in the Danish Resistance movement I say this: we know what price you have paid and are paying for refusing to be tempted by Nazi threats; we know something of your achievements in harrying and wrecking the German war machine which rolled across your borders nearly five years ago. We admire your steadfastness and skill. Your performance is a valuable contribution both to the Allied cause and to the future prosperity of a free Denmark . . ."*

Sixteen-year-old Lise Jacobson listened and tried to understand. Her young mind was unable to distinguish between war and hatred, but she knew that the words of Winston Churchill being broadcast by the BBC's Danish Service were the only true link to encouragement and hope for most of her countrymen. 'Hope'; the girl twisted the word around from each corner of her mind and tried hard not to despair. Tonight she was muddled and confused. She had been unable to hate the German conquerors who now occupied her country. Worse, she had become fond of a young German soldier who patrolled the small town where she lived.

The two had spoken with each other on a few occasions and had even enjoyed some short walks together. It was while the girl thought about these encounters with their timid silences and careful smiles that the piercing sound of shattering glass interrupted her innocent romantic fantasies.

The girl was alone, her parents had gone to some friends for the evening. Ignoring the efforts of Churchill at patriotic propaganda she left her chair to see what all the noise was about. Her hometown was a quiet place, crime non-existent; she had no need to fear anything untoward. The cat had probably knocked a milk bottle onto the floor and was now attempting to lick up as much of the creamy fluid as it could before human retribution arrived.

Walking into the kitchen, the girl was confronted by two men. Their heads were covered by woollen balaclavas; two eye holes had been crudely cut from the material. Masked anonymity inspired terror. They knew what they were doing.

Before the girl could utter any sound, any gasp of shock, one of the men grabbed her by the hair and slammed his hand over her mouth. He spoke quietly, the frustrated schoolmaster at the end of a long day, suppressed anger hurting the educated tone.

"Fornicate with the Nazis would you? You slut."

With that the other man pushed her onto a chair and gagged her with a stinking dishcloth. The girl was too terrified to understand what was happening. She had never experienced, never known such violence and hatred.

Her hands were tied tightly behind the chair. The teacher spoke again, the other smaller man having said nothing so far.

"Beautiful hair you have." He hissed into the girl's innocent face. "What a pity."

His eyes penetrated. They detested. She tried to turn her head away but there was no escape from the horror that stared at her with such disgust and venom.

The two men tugged and pulled her hair in all directions and began hacking it off with a blunt pair of scissors, cutting her scalp in various places at the same time. Within seconds the kitchen floor was covered with long, shining strands of childish innocence.

Tears poured down the girl's face and mixed with the trickles of blood from her butchered scalp. When the two men had finished cutting, a razor was employed to complete the mutilation. Their violent efforts at hairdressing completed they untied the girl's hands and hauled her onto the kitchen table. She tried to fight back but resistance was futile against the combined strength of her two attackers. She did manage though to tear the right shirt sleeve of the dumb, smaller assailant and see the dark brown birthmark on his shoulder that resembled almost exactly some preying eagle about to lift its prey off the ground, its talons outstretched and deadly, the wings spread ready for immediate flight.

The teacher began to undo his trousers, his excitement already apparent, his eyes mad with revenge and lust.

"Fuck with Nazis, you bitch! Well you should find us a luxury shouldn't you," he rasped.

His partner held her arms on either side of the table while the teacher carried out a savage punishment for her disloyalty. He wrenched her legs apart and thrust inside her. His eyes empty of mercy.

Her womanhood was ripped. Torn.

The girl passed out only to be brought round to consciousness by the smaller of the two. He had watched for long enough; he was already bitter at having missed the opportunity to devastate a young woman's virginity. His attack was frenzied and quick, his excitement too far gone to savour a long assault.

The girl neither heard the animals leave, nor their mocking laughter as they slammed the kitchen door.

The two patriots had made a loyal contribution to the freedom of Denmark.

Winston Churchill would have died of shame.

CHAPTER 1

Swansea, South Wales – 1952

Lise Jacobson listened to the detached ramblings of the decrepit Baptist minister as he committed her mother's body and soul to the hereafter. Her beauty ignored the morbid background of the ancient and neglected cemetery. Her unsure blue eyes and long, almost white, soft hair remained uncorrupted by the grief of black clothing she wore and the sin of death that surrounded her.

Her straight back and five foot six inches made her the ideal object of most mens' desire for the perfect woman. Breasts, hips, arms and legs had all been put together by a divine genius. The warrior spirit of her Viking father and the poetry of her Welsh mother also ran through her blood to create a face that was unspoilt by the bold tattoos of experience and the raggedness of too many years.

The minister finished reading from the Book of Revelations and rushed back to his chapel of fire and brimstone. Armageddon was an impatient Master; besides, it was starting to rain and he hadn't brought an umbrella.

Lise was left standing by the gaping hole, alone. She studied the mound of greedy earth which lay alongside the grave and bent down to pick up a handful; her small hand only allowed a token gesture as she dropped the soil onto the coffin lid that now covered her mother's lifeless face. The last time she had made such a gesture had been at her father's funeral. It had rained then too.

She remained standing and staring into the hole, oblivious of the rain that was quickly turning into a deluge. The coffin had been inexpensive; simple yet adequate for the purpose for which it had been made, there were none of the ornate trappings of wealth. Her mother would have been pleased, Lise thought, as she had always encouraged thriftiness in her daughter.

For a moment, guilt altered the serenity of Lise's face. There had been no tears. Until now they had refused a happy release; her mother's long illness had prepared the daughter for death. There was no shock, no surprise. Now, as she looked at the pathetic wooden casket, its poverty, its isolation, she cried. If only she had had the money to send her mother back to Denmark, to rest in peace alongside her dear father. It was not to be.

At last she stepped back from the hole of death as if frightened that it might not be satisfied with just one body. She looked around the cemetery one last time in the vain hope that maybe just one of her relatives had decided to pay their respects. There was no one.

The Bethesda Baptist Chapel was quiet and deserted. The rain had stopped pouring. It tumbled instead. Even the elements sometimes displayed a degree of respect for the dead. An irritated gravedigger coughed between a dampened Woodbine hanging from his lower lip. The lip was a richer brown than the tobacco he smoked or the soil that paid his wages.

Lise remained where she was. Alone. One woman amongst forgotten loved ones and dried-up tears. She looked out across the discoloured slabs In Memoriam and shuddered.

At last she braced herself and began the walk home. At the gates to the cemetery she took one last glance at her mother's final resting place, the cheap wooden cross not yet erected. In these last seconds of farewell all she saw was the impatient gravedigger, shovel in hand, drop himself into the grave. The dead never felt his muddy hob-nailed boots, what did he care?

She walked along the Hafod in Swansea town feeling miserable and lonely. The desolation of worked-out industries and empty, bankrupted business premises increased her feelings of dejection. It was a landscape of broken hopes and livid memories. Nature had long ago yielded to the power of man's desire for wealth and with it the dismal absence of any green or tree. She lived in the poor side of town, in a wasteland of unsightly tips and polluted water. The poor were always exiled to the blighted parts of a town. They grieved and wasted in dismal harmony with the rot that ignored their pleas.

She arrived at her own compressed terraced castle. She didn't use her key, the door was off the latch.

Bronwyn met her as she entered.

"Oh *Duw* (God), Lise! You must be soaked *mun*! Get them wet clothes off, quick now or you'll catch your death."

The young girl began removing the dripping coat; as this was being done Lise asked, "How is Kristian? Has he been good?"

"Lovely ee's been, good as gold. 'Ees fast asleep now. Now sit down and I'll make us a nice cup of tea. Take those wet shoes off too!"

"Oh, stop fussing Bronwyn! A little rain never hurt anyone."

"Never 'urt anyone! Did in my family it did, 'alf of them dead now, pneumonia or drink anyway. Evans the Milk is down with cold and Price the Coal. In 'ospital 'ee is. Mind you, maybe that dirty black bugger will 'ave a proper bath now, 'is missus 'as been tryin' for years *mun* to keep 'im clean. Now come on Lise give me those wet shoes. I'll dry 'em out in front of the fire."

Lise gave in, she always did. Besides she was too tired to argue. She allowed Bronwyn to fuss without objection, the girl was a treasure and the only person Lise would leave her son alone with. Whilst Bronwyn made the tea Lise thought back over the past six years. Reminiscing and death – what a happy pair, she thought.

The horror of that night in Denmark still haunted her. The violence. The hatred. Sleep sometimes chased them out of hiding, as dreams and their reality appeared from time to time. Lest she forget.

She had been so ignorant, so young. She had known nothing about the ferocity of nationalism. Of patriotism. Diseases that murdered and wasted all that was good in the human condition.

For years that night had seemed to be a part of her, a vivacious partner, a lover even. Now the sexual abuse of her womanhood was clouded by time and self-induced amnesia; her recall of the beasts who had ripped her open was now remote and distant, most of the time. She no longer tried to seek the kitchen table and the men who attacked her although sometimes she could still taste the filthy dishcloth that had been rammed into her mouth.

Kristian had been born and she still marvelled at how such a beautiful and gentle being could be created from such violence. When realising she was pregnant she remembered the devastation. The turmoil. The questions with no answers. The loneliness. She shivered when recalling her thoughts of murder and killing. She had heard of women destroying unwanted babies lying innocently in their wombs. How had they done it?

Her parents had stood by her, they loved their only child. For Lise the initial feelings of abhorrence and disgust at what was growing inside her finally vanished completely to be replaced by a deep and powerful love. How could she ever have considered killing this new life? The child would be hers, a part of her. She cared not who the father was, this fact only enhanced her exclusive rights to love the child. She would not have to share her motherhood or love. When holding the newborn baby in her arms she had whispered, "Kristian, my son," as though her heart were breaking. Stroking the delicate wisps of blonde hair, still wet from his entrance into a cruel world, Lise vowed to love and protect him for as long as she lived and had breath in her body.

The birth had taken place more than five years ago. Her joy at motherhood was short-lived. Once again patriotism held her in its jealous arms. Her father, whom she had loved and worshipped, was found drowned, his bloated body rising and falling with the river's current. It had taken two days to find him, two days of easy food for those fish not particular about their diet. The inquest had ruled accidental death. Lise and her mother had ruled otherwise. The shame, the poisonous whispers, the financial ruin had finally proved too much for her beloved father. He had succumbed to the postwar reprisal of his fellow citizens. Lise's 'crime' of friendship and the undoubted German father of her son had made his life unbearable.

In desperation and penniless from the ravages of war, her mother had brought Lise and grandchild back to the land of her fathers, back to the place where she had first met Lise's father, Swansea, South Wales. The mother had been a secretary in a shipping company of which her father had been a director. They had fallen in love, married and moved to Denmark, her father's birthplace and home.

Four years later to the day Lise was born. She was to be the only child and the pride and joy of both her parents. They doted on they newborn daughter and brought her up in an environment of uncomplicated love and happiness. Lise's childhood had been a secure and cheerful one.

Swansea, her mother's hometown, stood on Swansea Bay at the mouth of the River Tawe. Abertawe, its Welsh name, grew up around a castle, one of those built in the peninsula of Gower by its Norman conquerors. It was a borough in the twelfth century and a seaport then or soon after. In the eighteenth century the smelting of copper was introduced and about the same time coal began to be exported. Extensions and improvements of the harbour followed and canals were dug for the conveyance of coal. Industry had left its indelible mark as had the German bombs that had made a determined effort to flatten the docks and everything near them.

Lise now lived in the middle of one of its deepest, more livid scars; a far cry from the rural, agricultural world she had been brought up in. South Wales had always been a place faraway and unknown to Lise. A land of green valleys and coalmines, a land only read about in ink-splattered geography textbooks. Her mother had never spoken Welsh to her, neither had she ever said much about her place of birth.

On coming to Wales, the mother and daughter soon learned the futility of running away from people's bigotry and prejudice. They had hoped for a fresh start in Wales, far away from the self-righteous and judgmental accusations of their former countrymen. Their cowardice or perhaps courage had been in vain. The denizens of Swansea, though ignorant of their reasons for emigration, had shown only wariness and sometimes derision toward the two women from a foreign land. Relatives of her mother were nowhere to be found; letters sent were never answered. Her mother was a traitor, she had forsaken her Welshness.

The two women were again outcasts faced with cold looks and latent hostility. They were refugees, stateless and unwanted. The Welsh were not a cosmopolitan people, they tried and tested before giving and laughing.

Lise and her mother had to work hard in order to survive. Money was virtually non-existent, except for the bare essentials. They were both forced into a life of drudgery and backbreaking work with very little reward. The mother cleaned other peoples' houses whilst Lise took a job as a chambermaid in one of the grand hotels for the rich that settled sedately and with an eye for trouble in the main High Street of the town. They also took in other peoples' washing to gain a few extra shillings. Lise was determined that her son must never go without. She would starve herself in order that her child ate properly and wore warm clothes during the bitter winters.

There were times when she thought about the past. The once happy and plentiful existence. The safety. Before the war her family had been prosperous and content. Lise wanted desperately to embark upon a musical career and dreamed of being a concert pianist. A dream, she and others knew, that could one day become a reality. She had been blessed with a wonderful talent. But her hopes and ambitions, together with the life she and her parents had known, was shattered by the outbreak of war and its total corruption of human values. Now her fingers were hardened by coarse skin, abused beyond the sensitive touch of a concert pianist.

Lise's intelligence and cultured mind made her unique in the community where she now lived. Her quietness and reserve being interpreted as 'queer' and 'odd', she was never one of those standing at street corners gossiping. Her neighbours had never seemed capable of grasping the fact that their heavily accented English was not universally understood. At first Lise was constantly faced with weird looks and despair each time she spoke. Now though, despite her English being only slightly tinged with accent, she was still regarded with suspicion and treated like some alien interloper. There were the occasional smiles, though even these were tainted with narrowness and ignorance. She endured and hoped. The mocking whispers did not have her strength. She thanked God that Kristian did. Early on she had decided that her son would receive all the initial years of learning he required from her. Although she had little faith in the rough and basic schools on offer, she insisted he attend. His difference she knew would be bullied. He would fight. He would learn.

Her weekly day off was the only respite she received from the grey and mundane existence she led. It was a day when she could be with her son without clocks and babysitters. On this one day she would always try and take Kristian somewhere special and different. It was also a day when they would speak only in her native tongue.

Despite her Welsh mother, Lise considered herself a Dane. Her heart remained in Denmark, her birthplace and Kristian's. She never allowed her son to forget where he came from. She was also astute enough to recognise that his bilingual ability would give him an advantage in a rapidly changing post-war world. She encouraged the speaking of Welsh by Bronwyn feeling that this could only broaden his linguistic skills. Who knew where his life would go? Her thoughts were at last disturbed by Bronwyn handing her a cup of tea.

"Thank you," Lise said, looking at her almost permanently installed babysitter.

"There you are *bach* (dear), you will feel better after that."

Bronwyn still believed that a cup of tea was the miraculous panacea of all ills. The young girl sat down facing the woman she secretly hero-worshipped. Though the girl was only fifteen she was a capable young woman. Kristian adored her. Sometimes Lise would feel pangs of jealousy but this was quickly replaced by the need to earn money for food and clothes. Bronwyn shifted around uncomfortably for a moment, moving the last remains of puppy fat back and forth. Her pretty face showed genuine concern for Lise. She was opposite in looks to her friend and mentor. Where Lise was blonde, Bronwyn was the consummate Celt. Her hair was black and ferocious. Feral. Her dark brown eyes shone with an intelligence and independence that set her apart from her contemporaries. She had ignored the disapproval of her friends and family with regard to her friendship with Lise. Her self-willed nature rose above petty prejudice and tiny mind. Bronwyn maintained the Celtic fire in her blood and would follow her own path. She was slightly taller than Lise and bigger boned yet she moved with a grace that confounded her size. As womanhood gradually changed her body Lise could see that one day soon, men would be queuing up at the door for the privilege of courting Bronwyn.

"How did it go, the funeral?" Bronwyn asked. "Did that thieving bugger Thomas the Death give your mam a proper casket? You 'ave to watch 'im. Steals the pennies from the eyes I've 'erd. 'Ees 'alf dead 'imself most of the time and that's when 'ees sober! Couple of weeks back he lost a coffin' with the corpse still in it! They found 'im eventually in the local boozer, drunk as a navvy on a Saturday night and the corpse still in the Chapel of Rest! *Duw mun*, can you imagine it! The relatives weren't 'appy I can tell you! Don't suppose the corpse was too worried though, not in any 'urry was it?" Bronwyn laughed and Lise couldn't help smiling with her in spite of her grief. She was still coming to terms with the Welsh sense of humour that laughed at life and death in equal measure.

"The coffin was fine Bronwyn, so was Mr Thomas," Lise was used to Bronwyn colouring everything, it was the Welsh way, "not one whiff of beer on him either I assure you, the funeral was just like any other I suppose," Lise took a sip of her tea, it did make her feel better, "but more deserted," she added.

"Only you, was it?"

"Yes, only me. Nobody else turned up. I only wish I could have sent my mother home. To rest with my father, that's what she truly wanted."

"Never mind Lise, it's all over now. You don't 'ave to go to the 'otel today so put your feet up and relax. *Duw*, we all need to rest!"

"Yes, Bronwyn, I think I will. Perhaps I'll sleep for a while." Lise sank back into her chair and began to doze. As she fell asleep she thought of Bronwyn and realised that the girl was the only true friend that she had. She had been about Bronwyn's age when her body had been violated. Since then she had matured rapidly; adversity aged a person prematurely. She valued the young girl's friendship having learnt a hard lesson in Denmark. She now believed that if you could go through life and at the end of it count the number of true friends you had on two fingers, then you were indeed a fortunate human being.

With one last painful rush of grief for her mother Lise fell asleep.

The following morning she was up at 4.30. She started work an hour later at the Hotel Metropole in the High Street. Having scrubbed her face with cold water and soap she dressed in the black and whites of servitude. Any other woman would have looked drab and plain but Lise managed to maintain a shining presence when wearing even the bleakest of clothing.

Her long blonde hair reflected the electric light that shone down upon it from the ceiling. She sat in front of the battered dressing table mirror and began to brush her hair with an almost religious reverence. Every stroke was certain and thorough, as if she still had to convince herself that it was all hers and permanently attached to her head. She tied her hair in a bun at the back of her head; on most women this hairstyle would have created a picture of practical severity but with Lise it only accentuated her high cheekbones and beautiful face. Make-up was not required. Her twenty-two years of growing loveliness had made cream and paint unnecessary. On rare occasions she would sometimes apply a little lipstick but these were few and far between.

Satisfied with her hair she took one last glance at the mirror. Facial study of protracted minutes and fastidious vanity were not part of her character. One glance was enough.

Before leaving she crept into Kristian's room and kissed him on the cheek. He looked so like the fairy tale picture of a sleeping baby in one of his story books. Innocent and unspoilt. Her heart cried out with the love that always overcame her at moments like this. She traced her finger along his soft cheek, kissed him again then left the room that she had shared with her son until the death of her mother. Satisfied that her only priceless treasure was safe and sound she closed her front door, realising once again that for her, love was everything. It was all of life.

CHAPTER 2

It was still dark outside. The cold bit and tore but Lise was used to the far more penetrating coldness of Denmark and so the iciness of the air didn't concern her. She did worry about the dampness of the Welsh climate; it seemed to force its insidious way into everything, flesh and bone, clothes, bricks and mortar. It never gave up. The cold of Denmark was somehow cleaner, less offensive.

She walked past one or two men who lived in neighbouring houses and nodded, 'Good morning.' The men looked, their eyes saying far more than their tongues were capable of. Their faces reached out to Lise and begged. What had they done? What had they married? If only.

Although Lise was unaware of it, she was the cause of much comment and ribaldry in the local pubs which were dotted every few yards along the roadside, this being Wales. She walked along the Hafod making her way toward the railway station and then into the High Street where her place of work was situated.

Each morning, her eyes were met by the same spiteful dwellings. Small terraced houses all stacked together in opposite rows with a pavement as the front garden and some stubborn weeds as a flowerbed. Everything about these sorry streets was crammed. The bedrooms that wailed for space, the children who screeched for air in beds that overflowed with sibling rivalry and front rooms that stayed apart in superior isolation. She had become a prisoner of the two-up, two-down existence that dictated the lives of so many of Swansea's best. There were never ending rows of front doors and scrubbed steps acting host to empty milk bottles watching and waiting to be collected and re-filled, like the whores of the previous evening plying their sensual trade along Wind Street at the other end of town.

She saw a milkman listen to an old woman unable to pay her weekly milk bill having given her last shilling to the Catholic priest. The milkman had sneered his disgust; the lighting of Catholic wax was more important as food for the soul than milk! He told the old woman she could forget payment for this week. Torquemada and Ignatius of Loyola still roamed the streets ready to pounce but this was Chapel land. The Minister thumped and ruled. Papists rarely fought back, they didn't know how to.

High Street station came into sight and Lise noticed the London Pullman ready to speed off with hot coffee, bacon and fresh farm eggs for those who could afford it. The third-class carriages bore a marked resemblance to the troop trains she had seen bringing in the German invaders of her own county.

At last she came to her place of work. The heat from the kitchens was immediate and comforting. She went straight to her superior to find out her duties for the day.

Mrs Evans was in the staff room gossiping away in the lilts and tilts of the Welsh language to one of her equals in the hotel hierarchy. Lise couldn't understand or speak one word of Welsh; her mother had only reverted to it in times of anger. Vague memories of her mother shouting '*Cachi!*' and then being immediately contrite was the only Welsh she could remember and even this word apparently had some dubious meaning, something to do with human excretion Lise believed.

The language of ancient poets and legends stopped when she entered the room.

"Ah, Lise is it? Right *bach*, rooms 100–120 for you, see. Then come back when you've finished. There we are then. All right? Good."

Mrs Evans turned back to her Welsh and Lise left to begin her duties. When the door closed and Lise had gone Mrs Evans confided in her friend. "Funny girl that Mrs Thomas, bit simple if you ask me. Never says anything; foreigner see, still, fair play, does her work well enough mind, so can't complain."

"Yes, Mrs Evans, I've noticed she's a quiet one," her friend replied, "never seen 'er talking to anyone though. Bit funny. Got a baby 'asn't she?"

"That's right Mrs Thomas, mind you I don't think it's a baby any more. Little boy I've 'eard, five or six – husband killed in the war. If the boy is five or six makes you think doesn't it. That Lise must only be twenty something. Young anyway."

"Aye, Mrs Evans, does make you think. I don't know, young women today. The war has something to do with it, I suppose. Told me she was twenty-four."

"Ach, not likely *mun*, younger than that I'm tellin' you. Somethin' a bit fishy there if you ask me." Lise had raised her age by two years in order to avoid any embarrassing conclusions where Kristian was concerned. She hadn't counted on the searching, almost manic, curiosity of the Welsh.

"Any man there?" Mrs Thomas asked, feeding her instinct for the pursuit of exaggerated tittle-tattle.

"Not that I know of. Probably frightens 'em off. Never seen her smile or laugh, doesn't mix like, besides who'd want soiled goods, ay? Fair play though, she's a pretty girl for all that.'

"You're right there Mrs Evans, soiled goods or not, there's plenty round 'ere who would like to jump into her bed! Make no mistake!"

Their conversation continued along the further inanities of Jack's bad back and the new doctor up at Town Hill. There was talk or at least twitching curtain talk, of the doctor taking a fancy to a Mrs Williams who lived by Cwmdonkin Park. A war widow, or so she claimed, in her sober episodes anyway.

The Metropole Hotel was typical of its time. Flunkies and menials deferred and fawned. Chandeliers and silver plate ensured good manners, fine service and respectability. Understanding head porters ruled and turned blind eyes. They made unmarried sex an adventure. A piquant mystery. Anyway the tarts brought a jolly, understated colour to the male guests' crunched up notes.

Lise never showed any interest in the guests; they were part of a world she had once known, a world now forbidden to her.

She spent the morning as with every other, checking laundry and making beds. Ignoring always the roving eyes of some male guests and the occasional offer of money for goods so far undelivered. Grand hotels inspired grand prurience; she had been used once in her life, it would never happen again.

Despite what had happened to her, Lise didn't despise male kind. She had enough intelligence to realise that merely because two men behaved in a way that would shame any animal on earth, it did not mean that the whole male sex was the same. There were wicked and hateful women too. The rape had not turned her into an obsessive man hater, however, she was still mistrustful and cautious, even at times a little frightened when finding herself alone with a man. The German soldier had been the only 'man' that she had ever really come into any natural contact with and that had only been a brief innocent foray into juvenile romance. At twenty-two her interest in men remained dormant and subdued.

Lise did her work with total detachment. She had perfected this state of mind by becoming a willing automaton. When at work her mind closed down. She ceased to think. She took orders and carried them out, never complaining, never questioning. Her colleagues, like most of the hotel employees, regarded her at best with curiosity, at worst with ignorant suspicion and so she had never managed to find true friendship and had indeed never attempted to cultivate it. Her own genteel upbringing and education presented little common ground for conversation and now Lise simply did her work and dreamed of what might have been.

She came to suite 112 and knocked quietly. Her small hand seemed incapable of banging. The response from inside was a gruff, "Enter!" She walked in and found Mr Treharne grunting his way through breakfast. He had become one of the hotel's more permanent guests, refusing to render his independence to grasping children and servants – at least that's what he maintained. The truth was that he was waiting for building and restoration work to be finished on a property he had recently bought before being able to take up residence. Despite the old man's constant complaining Lise she liked him and always enjoyed their few daily minutes together.

As she walked in he looked up from his bacon and eggs and belched into his starched, white napkin. He wouldn't normally have bothered with the napkin but for Lise. He began his morning tirade of wanton verbal acid. "Good morning, my glorious Valkyrie! God but it's cold, and the bloody breakfast is too. Tell those lazy spivs in the kitchen to pull their fingers out! My God, the impertinence of it! I pay a fortune to stay here and what do I get? Bacon and eggs straight from the bloody *Titanic* – after it had sunk! If that cook, whoever he is, was employed by me I'd have the bugger out on his arse!"

William Treharne was a self-made man and didn't care who knew it. He had made a fortune from copper, steel, coal and numerous other business ventures. He was said to have a touch that would have exasperated King Midas and a fist in every business pie known to South Wales.

"Now, now, Mr Treharne," Lise replied calmly, "you know you're not happy unless something is wrong, you'd get bored." She knew her familiarity would not be received with any offence. The regular morning banter between the two had become an amusing ritual for both of them.

"Suppose you're right," Treharne conceded. "Anyway, tell 'em in the kitchen will you? Now then, how are you today, my lovely? You look a little pale, no on second thoughts, pasty."

"Well, thank you for the compliment Mr Treharne. Apart from looking 'pasty' as you put it, I'm fine. Yourself?"

His eyes twinkled, all thoughts of the cold breakfast forgotten.

"All the better for seeing you my lovely." His age hadn't yet made him impervious to young pretty females. "If I was twenty

. . . make that thirty, slip of the tongue . . . years younger you wouldn't stand a chance!"

Lise looked at him as she began changing the bed linen, she couldn't help smiling. "*If*, and it's a big 'if' Mr Treharne, you were thirty years younger." Her smile seemed to warm the whole room.

"I'm not past it yet you know. Fifty-four I may be . . ."

Lise interrupted, "Fifty-four? The other day it was fifty-three, make up your mind."

"Damn it, fifty-five then and that's the truth. When you get to my age birthdays are best forgotten!" If this was the truth then Lise was surprised, he didn't look his fifty-five years. "Too clever by half you are Lise, still you're better than most of the cretinous dimwits that seem to breed like rabbits in this place. Good to see a bit of spirit in a woman, you remind me of my wife, God bless her." He went quiet for a moment then added, "Haven't you got yourself a good man yet? A young woman like you on her own, it isn't right you know. What an appalling waste."

"No, there's no one Mr Treharne, and you know it, so stop being so nosey."

"Quite right, I'll mind my own business and drink this bloody awful coffee. Damn shame though, damn shame."

Lise ignored all the bad language; it was a composite part of the Treharne character. She carried out a pile of white sheets into the corridor and before closing the door asked if there was anything else he wanted being done. He looked at her for a while, his eyes deep in thought. When he spoke, there were no traces of banter in it.

"Yes Lise, there is something. You have a little boy don't you?"

"Yes."

"I was thinking, how about you giving an old man some enjoyment in his old age by coming with me to Langland Bay for the day? Bring the little one. Nothing improper, but I'd like your company. It would be a refreshing interlude away from most of the pea-brains I come into contact with. Well, what do you say?"

Lise was mildly shaken for a moment.

"Well, I . . . Mr Treharne, the hotel doesn't like staff to mix with the guests they . . ."

"To hell with the hotel," Treharne interrupted, "when's your next day off?"

"Thursday, but . . ."

"No 'buts'. I'll meet you at the station 9.30 sharp Thursday morning. That's the day after tomorrow. We'll take a taxi. Don't worry now, no one will be any the wiser, not from this place anyway. Some sea air will do the child good as well."

Lise stood in the doorway, not knowing what to say. It was the first time anyone had taken any interest in her as a human being for a long time, apart from Bronwyn that is. Before she could decline or even accept the offer Treharne confirmed, "It's arranged then, 9.30 Thursday morning. Wrap up warm, it will be cold down there. A good walk will do us all good and no bloody crowds either in the middle of winter. Perhaps we can walk round to Caswell Bay. We'll see."

At last Lise mumbled "All right" and left the room. When she had finished her work for that day she was still thinking about William Treharne and the promised day out. He hadn't given her a chance to refuse, bullying old man, she thought. She was worried about the hotel finding out but this anxiety soon faded as the prospect of Kristian breathing good clean air became more apparent. He might even get some colour in his cheeks, she thought.

She harboured no doubts where Treharne's intentions were concerned; like herself he was probably lonely, having been widowed himself quite recently. He had said little about his wife's death but sometimes when mentioning her, his eyes would change. Curtains would be partially drawn. Lise had experienced death, knew about it. She understood the emptiness.

Despite Treharne's cantankerous nature there was a kindness about him and he had always shown her consideration and thought. Although he was in his fifties, he was still a handsome man. He enjoyed a luxuriant growth of white hair and his teeth were brilliant white and cared for. They were definitely not of the false variety. Age had been kind to the man, it had refined him. His slim body still seemed firm and vital, his movements quick and easy. He was neither big nor small, he just seemed to hover between the two. His brain was always sharp and quick no matter what time of day, it was no wonder he was a successful businessman. He obviously took care of himself; every morning he would be sitting at his breakfast table immaculately dressed and groomed. Lise concluded that 'old' Treharne definitely didn't look his age. She would have described his physical appearance as one of distinguished maturity. The most striking feature of Treharne's face was his eyes. They were neither green nor brown; she had never seen eyes like them before. The colour seemed to change constantly from one shade to another. They seemed to soothe and placate. They were not the eyes of cruelty. These she had seen before and would never forget.

As Lise pushed the laundry basket into its last resting place her footsteps were lighter. The day out was something to look forward to for a change so she resolved to make the most of it. As she began to walk home she began to sing an old Danish folk song.

CHAPTER 3

Thursday morning arrived.

Lise and Kristian were waiting outside the main entrance to High Street Station. Another hotel stood directly opposite them making Lise feel nervous and apprehensive. What if she was seen by someone who knew her? That word 'fraternisation' again. Swansea was a village that had outgrown itself. Like a small boy with trousers at half-mast it continued to grow and ignore its size. In spite of this frantic post-war growth people still believed they had a right to know the ins and outs of everyone else's business. The local evening newspaper was more a confirmation of human foible than a delivery of 'news'. Neighbours knew their neighbours and these latter neighbours knew the neighbours' neighbours! And so it went on. Swansea Town was not a secret town. There were few dark corners or rancid whispers. Everyone knew who the milkman was supplying milk to and everyone knew when he was supplying more than milk. She remembered one of the waiters at the Metropole remarking rather crudely, "You couldn't fart in this town without someone raising a red flag."

Kristian stood next to her wrapped up in a mountain of wool with only his cheeky red nose and bright blue eyes betraying his membership of the human race. At 9.30 exactly Treharne arrived; immaculately dressed as usual and beaming good humour; he was drenched in Scottish cashmere from head to toe.

"Very good." He declared. "Punctual. I always say if a man can't be punctual then it means his life is a chaotic burden."

"I am not a man, Mr Treharne," Lise reminded him.

"True, true, all the more to your credit my lovely, women are usually the worst offenders. Privilege and all that, utter balderdash! Oh and enough of the 'Mr Treharne'. William will do, you're not in the hotel now. Now then, what have we here." He bent down to examine the small ball of wool, "And who's this, young Kristian if I'm not mistaken." He reached down and picked the boy up, "Kristian is it?"

The little boy nodded, apparently unperturbed by this man who had suddenly swept him up toward the heavens. Lise noticed the ease with which her son went to the man. The boy was normally cautious where adults were concerned, his innocent mind seeing through false emotion or dangerous intent. Treharne placed the child back on terra firma and said, "Right then, let's hail a taxi and enjoy ourselves. It's too cold to be standing around, so when we get to the beach we must move about." He took the hand of Kristian, who obliged without any hint of dissent. In a moment and following a wave from Treharne a car appeared out of nowhere.

Later as they walked along the beach, all they could hear were the waves reaching a state of panic as the shoreline announced another destination. Langland Bay was enjoying a lie-in. The winter months allowed it to rest in its natural state. Now and again one or two dogs would tramp along its shore and bark their objection to its ban on lively activity. Not all in the Bay were content. Rows of little green huts shielded each other against the cold and waited for the return of arguing couples and howling children with wasp-infested jam sandwiches and leopardskin bathing costumes. They missed the soothing whacks of tennis balls against wire and the occasional whimpers of randy youngsters leaning against their wooden panels.

Treharne broke the silence.

"I sometimes think, Lise, that modern man has a great deal to answer for. Not content with massacring his neighbours, he now seems obsessed with the obliteration of his natural habitat. Progress it's called, but I know that one day this progress will eventually bankrupt humanity. I often feel guilty about my own fortune, built as it is upon industrial waste – the end product.

How much can nature take I often ask myself? People seem to think that she is invulnerable, incapable of hurt or damage. One day I fear our complacency will turn round to strangle us in a cesspit of filth and poison."

Lise listened carefully to every word he had spoken and said, "Will . . .William," – for a moment experiencing difficulty with the informality of Christian names – "you do surprise me."

"Why?" he asked, turning to look at her.

"Well, one minute you swear like a trooper, the next minute you talk of nature's majesty."

"Yes, I suppose I do tend to be a little contradictory. Enigmatic even. But there you are. There have been many times in my life when bluntness and bad language have been the only means of communication left. Sometimes I know it gets the better of me. I'm too old to change now though."

They walked without saying anything for a little longer, both absorbed by their own thoughts. Then William broke the silence.

"I used to bring my children here years ago. Of course they are not children any more." As he spoke, Lise once again noticed a deep sadness pass across his eyes.

"How many children do you have?" she asked, wanting to know more about this human conundrum.

"Two now. One got himself killed during the war. Bloody fool couldn't resist the temptation to become a hero. Tried to take on a machine-gun single handed. He was the best of the brood too. 'Those whom the Gods love die young', Lise, at least according to Menander. I believe he had something there you know."

"I'm sorry," Lise said quietly.

"No need to be. You never knew him. I often wonder how others are able to be 'sorry' for another's grief. It's never made much sense to me. Be thankful you're alive and well; instead of apologies you should be saying, 'well at least it wasn't me'. Be grateful for the gift of living and enjoy it."

"That's a very cynical attitude . . . er . . . William, don't you think?"

"No, not at all. Realistic I call it, although I concede that age does tend to promote a degree of morbid cynicism. Certainly scepticism, its sleeping partner."

"What about your other children?"

"Welsh curiosity rubbing off on you is it Lise? Can't have that now, can we?" William teased. "My other son is a complete buffoon, a spineless waster. Spends his time drinking and gambling around various clubs in London. I believe he is what is called today a 'playboy', a whoring playboy at that. His mother left him a good stash of money but I should think that little oil well is about to dry up. My daughter, she is on her second marriage. God help her husband, the girl is a bloody disaster, a mercenary harpy if ever there was one. The only time I see either of them is at family funerals or when they want money. Doubt if they would make the effort to attend my funeral, come to think of it. The last time I saw them was at their mother's . . ." He stopped for a moment and drew in a deep breath. Lise decided to exercise a little tact, his wife's death still required some healing.

"Do you have any grandchildren?" she asked.

"No, I'm afraid not. I don't think either of my offspring are capable of procreation. Griffith is usually too drunk and Megan is too selfish and vain. Anyway, enough about me. You know Lise, you are a bit of a mystery. A Dane living in Swansea. Danish blood in the Welsh you know, so tell that to your fool workmates; it might make them think for a change."

"You are being unkind, William," Lise admonished.

"Unkind? Since when is speaking the truth unkind? I cannot bear people who live their lives with a fence post firmly embedded in their rectums; call a spade a spade and be damned, that's me. Anyway, never mind, I must admit I'm curious about you. You are an intelligent woman, educated. What the hell are you doing working as a chamber-maid? How did you come to be in Swansea? And how old are you?"

"My God William," Lise replied with a note of impatience in her voice, "I've heard of being frank, but this is an interrogation."

William smiled, unperturbed by the rebuke.

"Can't help it I'm afraid Lise, Welsh curiosity again. Tell you what, ignore the first two questions if you like, just answer the third. How old are you?"

"Twenty-four."

"Never, you can't fool an old boy like me you know. Try again. Truth this time," he persisted.

For some unknown reason Lise felt able to confide in this man, to trust him. Perhaps it was time to cast away the black cloak of deceit that sometimes seemed to smother her. William prompted a desire to speak about herself and her feelings. Her emotions had been incarcerated for so long. The need to talk, to confess was beginning to overwhelm. William noticed her reticence and the reluctant expression showing on her face. He stopped walking and looked at her. "I'm sorry Lise, I should mind my own business. Sometimes I know I am too blunt, too insensitive to other peoples' emotions. Forgive me please. Nevertheless, you are in a foreign land and the Welsh can be a narrow lot, insular, as you have no doubt already gathered. It must be difficult for you Lise, you seem to have an air of 'aloneness' about you. Or perhaps it's just plain self-inflicted detachment. I don't know, but you do seem so apart. So solitary."

Lise returned his look. She rarely looked directly into someone's eyes. Somehow William demanded honesty, even self-revelation. For once she made a rash decision; the sincerity in William's voice made her throw years of caution and subterfuge to the winds that raced around them.

"I'm twenty-two," she finally answered as if admitting to the perpetration of some heinous crime. William connected the age of mother and son but said nothing. "My mother was Welsh," she added, almost as an afterthought. This last fact seeming to explain everything.

"Was she? You must have a devil of a temper then. A combination of Welsh and Viking can result in some fairly combustible characteristics."

"Not at all, I'm very quiet."

"Precisely. It's the quiet, demure ones you have to watch."

"What do you mean?"

"Well, from my experience quiet women tend to have the most appalling tempers, but then, and again I speak from experience, they are also . . . er . . . I think I'll leave that." For a moment he actually seemed embarrassed.

"Leave what?" Lise insisted. "Come on now William, what were you going to say? I don't really see you as the bashful type." The growing familiarity between them was making Lise bolder.

"It's not important; besides you might be embarrassed or even offended."

"Embarrassed? You seem to be the one that's embarrassed not me, so say what you were going to say and stop being so evasive!"

"Now look here Lise, there's only one bully around here and that's me . . . if you don't mind. However, if you insist, I was going to say that I've always found the quiet ladies to be the most passionate in affairs of the heart and well . . . other related matters as it were." Lise couldn't help the sound of a giggle coming from her mouth.

"What's so damned funny?" William demanded.

"You . . . you look so awkward, even tongue tied. I would never have believed such a thing if I wasn't seeing it for myself."

"It's true, believe me."

"Oh, I do William," she said, thinking at the same time, 'if only he knew'. Passion was a word she could only fantasise about.

Lise wanted to end this particular topic of conversation before it went any further. She was on unfamiliar ground, not only where sex was concerned but also in the vague area of romance. They carried on walking, Lise never taking her eyes off Kristian. She was watching her son throw pebbles into the sea when William asked, "You haven't answered the rest of my questions. Of course you don't have to anyway, I don't want to intrude. I suppose I just want to know more about you, you are such a curious creature."

"That's all right William, you're not intruding. I've just been thinking about the answers, it's a long story."

"I understand, you are a sensitive young woman, I can see that. Wary too, although there's no need to be. Whatever you say will never go beyond the two of us."

"Yes, William, I believe you. Please understand that there are things that have happened in my life that have left deep scars. I don't know at the moment whether I am ready to talk about them. To satisfy part of your curiosity I can tell you I was born in Denmark, an only child. My mother was from Swansea. She met my father, a Dane, here. He was a director of a shipping company doing business here. They met, fell in love and moved to Denmark. I was born not long after. The war eventually arrived and with it financial ruin for my father. He wasn't strong enough to withstand the blow and eventually it killed him. After that my mother brought me to her place of birth. I've lived in Swansea now for some five or six years. Kristian has grown up here; even so, I still speak to him in Danish. I don't feel truly Welsh, I doubt I ever will. That's it William, put briefly of course."

"And your mother?"

"She died two weeks ago."

"I'm sorry. Oh dear, that was a little hypocritical of me wasn't it? Not practising what I preach."

"Never mind, I think we are all guilty of hypocrisy from time to time."

Lise stared down at her feet. She looked uncomfortable. Deception didn't come easily to her. She wanted to tell William everything but somehow her earlier resolve had dissipated. She was still frightened of the reaction from others. For his part, William had noticed the absence of any reference to a husband or father for Kristian. He decided to push ahead regardless, wanting to know what was troubling this beautiful, gentle, young woman. There was more for her to tell, much more, and he knew it.

"And Kristian's father?"

Lise sighed, "That's another story. Don't make me lie William, I'm not very good at it. Another time perhaps." He could see the struggle that was taking place deep in Lise's heart; he wanted to help but knew there was nothing he could do until she was ready to purge herself.

"Yes, alright my lovely, another time." He took her arm as a gesture of comfort, "No wonder you look so pale and drawn. Come on, let's go and get some tea and cakes. I'm getting a little cold now."

He took Lise and Kristian up to the hotel overlooking the bay. The place was empty but after sufficient bullying the manager was able to produce the promised tea and cakes. Kristian ate the cakes with childish gluttony and appetite. This was a rare event.

The rest of the day was spent enjoying the air and sea. William and Lise fenced with one another using words and innuendo as swords. Their intellects, well matched and sharp, forced them into a mutual respect and affection for one another. Although William's manner was sometimes abrasive even rude, he showed a genuine understanding and care toward Lise and her son. His sensitivity prevented any challenging of the huge gaps in Lise's life story. He had seen the agonies pursuing this young woman but relented in attempting to draw them from her. The pain inside her, he knew, must be revealed with her unconditional consent. For Lise the day had been new. Different. Intimate even. William had made her search within. To reveal, if only on a limited level.

That night, as she lay in bed, she thought about the day out and how enjoyable it had been. It had made such a change to speak with someone who would listen instead of walking away because her voice carried the tones of a foreign language. William had taken an obvious interest in her words and had not presumed her quiet disposition to be an indication of abject stupidity. She had actually managed to experience a full day of intelligent conversation. They had discussed music, literature and art, discovering that their tastes in these areas were similar. Not too similar though, that would have been tedious. Boring.

William, she thought, really was quite remarkable for his age. His body and mind managed to compete with the playful antics of Kristian's childhood. Wrinkles of age seemed to run away with the beach ball and her son's laughter. The boy had taken an immediate liking to the man, probably delighted by the unique experience of enjoying a father figure. She had always known that whilst she could only do her best for the child, she could never be a substitute for a real father. Sometimes it worried her that this essential balance was missing in her son's life. Single parenthood, she knew, was imperfect at best, and she was not naïve enough or foolish enough to ever believe otherwise. Every child demanded a father as well as a mother.

Before being dropped off at their little home William had suggested they do the same thing again next week. Lise had readily agreed.

She fell asleep that night still thinking about the old, young man whose laundry and bed linen she changed each day.

CHAPTER 4

Three months passed.

During this time William had taken Lise and Kristian out once a week, every week. For both, these days together brought a brief and cherished respite from loneliness allowing them to forget the vacuum caused by widowhood and the drudgery inspired by soiled linen and endless feather beds.

A friendship that was deep and affectionate had grown between the young and the old. Kristian had come to adore 'Willie' and Lise had grown to value and enjoy his company.

On one of their days out together Lise and William were sitting alone on a bench beside a duck pond in Brynmill Park. Kristian ran around feeding the ducks with stale bread purloined from the hotel's kitchen. The ducks darted this way and that unsure of which direction to take in order to avoid such uncouth enthusiasm. Lise's arm was entwined with Williams; it was a habit now.

As they sat together, she at last felt compelled to tell him the truth about her life. For Lise truth meant freedom. She desperately wanted to speak of her past. For weeks she had deliberated. For weeks she had explored her capacity to trust. To confide. William had been the only human being whom she felt could pull her to safety. Who could wash her tainted past clean.

She now felt that the time was at last right. She could trust the man sitting next to her. He wouldn't judge. He wouldn't blame.

"William," she began, "there are some things I must tell you."

Her voice was uncertain as she spoke. William noticed immediately that she was trying to unburden herself. He had waited for this moment but said nothing. He took Lise's hand and listened.

"Just before the end of the war I had been seeing a young German soldier. At least we had gone on some walks together. Two or three times if that, I really don't remember now. We were both young. I was only sixteen at the time. He wasn't much older. One night I was alone in the house when two men broke in."

She paused and gripped William's hand; she was trying so hard to keep back the tears. It had been such a long time since she had spoken with anyone about that night. That she had spoken about it at all. Her mother had been the only person that she had told about the exact events of that terrible night and even then she had refused to go into detail. Reliving the horror again still brought back a vivid attack of fear.

"Go on," William urged, knowing that she must exorcise this ghastly experience from her mind.

"They attacked me in the kitchen. They shaved my head and then . . . they raped me. Kristian . . ." Unable to go on or say any more, she buried her head in William's shoulder and cried. Relief and pain.

William held her close. Such cruelty and baseness directed at one so beautiful and innocent. His compassion and sympathy overrode the anger and helplessness that made him feel so useless. He said quietly, "My poor Lise, cry my lovely, cry."

Lise lifted her head and sniffed.

William handed her a handkerchief; she dabbed at the tears streaming down her face.

God, he hated seeing her so upset. War, he thought, does it never end?

"William . . . perhaps the worse part of it all was the fact that nothing ever happened between the soldier and me. Well, boy really. He was so young. Only a year older than me. We never even kissed. I don't think either of us would have known how to. We were both so shy and embarrassed . . . he was probably killed like so many other young men . . ."

When Lise had finally calmed down William lifted her tear-soaked chin with his hand and said, "Yes . . . so many young men . . ." He thought of his own son – the boy's blood given for King and country. Given for freedom. Given for everyone but himself. "There's no need to say any more, dear Lise, I'm glad you've told me. I've known for some time that there have been some awful devils chasing your spirit. Whatever you do, don't worry about our conversation going any further. It will remain with us and us alone. It's a wicked burden that you have been carrying all this time but you must let go and look to the future. We can never forget the past. Don't even try, it's what makes us who we are. Learn by it and use it to your advantage. Use it to shield you, not destroy you." Lise listened. The tears stopped. Release.

"Thank you, William, for listening. It has helped. I've wanted to tell you everything for some time, I just had to be sure."

"I know Lise, I know. Now then there is something I want to tell you . . ." For a moment Lise's vulnerable state imagined all kinds of retribution. William had been so calm. Was this the inevitable storm that followed? Was he indeed like everyone else? Had he judged her after all? "I'm leaving the hotel in about seven to ten days time. As you know, I've bought a house near the sea, good for my health so the quacks tell me." So, she thought, that's why he was being so kind to her. He was just preparing her for the blow. Like so many others he didn't want anything to do with her. For once her face betrayed the hurt. William had become her only true friend apart from Bronwyn. She had trusted him. He noticed her anguish. "Now don't worry, I'm not deserting you, quite the opposite. The house I've been waiting to move into has been having a lot of renovation work done. It's a big brute. All the work has now been completed. Anyway, it will need someone to run the domestic side of things. A home needs a woman's touch. I'd like you to run things, housekeeper if you like."

Before Lise could say anything he carried on, "This is a perfectly proper offer of employment. There are no strings attached. If you are worried about . . . well, er . . . anything improper, then don't. You're like a daughter to me and a very lovely one at that. One thing I do know, it will be better for you and Kristian than the hotel. Besides, I don't think I'm that bad an old curmudgeon really."

For the first time since they had sat down Lise smiled. This was certainly not what she had been expecting. William could have touched her relief. Still smiling she said, "No, you're not. Awkward maybe, but tolerable."

"Good, then will you think about it?"

"Yes William, I will." She wondered if she really needed any time to think about her answer.

"One more thing, Lise. We have come to know each other well. I want you to know that I treasure our friendship and I also want you to know that my feelings toward you are, like I say, that of father and daughter, God knows, I wish my own daughter was more like you.

"The point is, people sometimes talk. I don't suppose I have to tell you about that though Lise, I want to protect you and Kristian, I want to look after you both. There is very little left in my life now. You and Kristian give me purpose, a reason to be. Please accept my offer, Lise, and know that there is no ulterior motive on my part. I would hate it if you thought that."

He stood up from the bench held out his arm and said, "If you can cope with the sorry bastards I certainly can."

Lise stood up, took his arm in hers and for the first time in years she felt safe and loved.

CHAPTER 5

Lise stood on the pavement outside her house. Tea chests crammed with modest possessions and bits and pieces from another time stood next to her. Kristian kept pulling her arm. He was impatient and excited.

He couldn't remember the last time they had moved. He had been too young. It was just as well, Lise thought, it hadn't been a happy time. Thank God, on this occasion the circumstances were different. This time she wanted to move home and she wasn't leaving under duress. She didn't feel like some dispossessed refugee or an outcast running from malicious stares and verbal poison.

A battered blue van arrived, announcing itself as the property of Jones & Son. Mr Jones was to take them both and their few belongings to a new life in a small village overlooking the Gower coast where activity, so Lise had been told, was limited to a shop that sold everything from underwear to Brasso, a Post Office and of course, a pub.

Their new home was actually a mile or so away from those spots where human life could be confirmed. Apparently, so William had told her, the house had been used as a home for German prisoners of war. Not the rank and file. Officers only. Some of them had been known to frequent the local pub when given an easy parole. Why would they want to escape after all, their surroundings were far superior to anything back home and the Welsh were remarkably tolerant where an over-indulgence of strong drink was concerned.

Once the van had been loaded they set off.

Before long the roads started to narrow, twist and turn, marking their arrival in the Gower Peninsula. In the summer these slithering snakes of tarmacadam confounded the newly liberated enthusiasm of holidaymakers seeking lumpy sands, jolly ice cream and giggling swims. Oyster beds still flourished not far from fairy-tale caves and litter was only dropped under caution. The Gower held on to its innocence, there was nothing else it could do.

Eventually they turned off the road and drove along an even narrower track that seemed like a sinister tunnel without the manmade bricks and mortar. Shafts of sunlight battled their way through the foliage that overhung the only means of access to their new home. Hedgerows scraped the sides of the van although the silent Mr Jones didn't seem to care. A few more scratches on the peeling paintwork would add a little more character to his only means of income, and anyway at the moment he was more concerned about his absent son.

Jones the Removals sucked on his simmering pipe wondering what forms of punishment he could mete out to his son and heir – the bastard had gone out last night and hadn't returned home. Drunk again, Jones concluded, tucked up all nice and warm with some young filly no doubt – lucky bugger! The thought of his fat lump of a wife didn't help his already dejected mood. *Arglwydd Mawr*! (Good Lord!) Mrs Jones would need a team of navvies and a famous architect to put her face right. And her arse. Bloody 'ell, most nights he had to fight to find some space in their bed. Did the fat bitch care? Did she 'ell! Still kept stuffing her face with steak and kidney pie and bottles of stout, her pies being the best in Swansea mind, he had to give her that. These days that's all he did give her. Mrs Gwynne up at Tal-y-Bont farm received his favours now, grateful she was too. Winnie the Hay she was known as and her arse was just right too! Bit vintage but just right. *Duw mun*, nipples like Chapel hat pegs on it, lovely! Couldn't do a decent steak and kidney pie though, so fat-arsed Mrs Jones would always win in the end. Stupid cow.

The woman sitting next to him sure as hell didn't need any building work though. Beautiful she was and polite. Didn't treat him like dirt either like some of the people he worked for. Jones sucked harder on his pipe by way of distraction. *Duw*, what he couldn't do to this Mrs Jacobson! Mrs Jones, steak and kidney pie, Winnie the Hay or not!

At last they arrived at the gateway and entrance to the house.

Some 'ouse, Mr Jones thought, more of a bloody mansion. Be a good tip too if his passenger's smile was anything to go by. The van passed two sturdy white pillars with huge wrought-iron gates attached. A white sign with black lettering announced the name of the house: Ragged Cliffs.

It was surrounded by acres of green lawn and gardens that had been landscaped and created by a loving hand. Many beautiful houses have ugly and disquieting gardens for the reason that builders have indifferent ideas or none at all concerning horticulture. William had planned his garden.

To the east of the house the land had been altered and cultivated to provide a tennis court and croquet lawn. The sloping lawn to the south had been turned into formal gardens. He had created a combination of the old Dutch and mid-Victorian fashion of carpet bedding. These had been placed nearest the house and were laid out more or less geometrically. Where it was found necessary to terrace the land, formal bedding had been installed. William had kept to the rule that the fewer manufactured articles in a garden the better. The only man-made objects in sight were a sundial and the occasional stone seat. The formal beds provided a blaze of colour and beauty for about nine months of the year.

Lise stood in front of the house, absolutely still.

She wanted to absorb her new surroundings, her new home. It sat alone, overlooking a secluded bay that seemed untouched by human hand. The only noise in the air was the sound of sea and wind carrying the unique tunes of the Gower to all those who would listen. The Mabinogion, Dylan Thomas and the Morriston Orpheus Choir spoke and sang from the cliffs that overlooked a sea of ancient memories. The grey and green of rock, the cantankerous waves, the view of nature in all its anger and all its calm made Lise's Welsh blood simmer and subdue its Nordic partner. The Chapel Minister's power and glory, his *hwyl* (spirit) and battered Bible were all in this place. Hell had burnt itself out. Here was religion at its best and its most passionate. Lise had arrived at another home. A Welsh home.

After the crammed minuteness of a terraced existence she felt humbled in front of this huge house. She hadn't realised that William was capable of such wealth. He had never spoken about money with her, apart from remarking on one occasion that the "flouting of wealth was an insulting exercise in vulgarity."

As she stood alone, the house made her feel small, irrelevant.

At one time none of it would have bothered her. Her own upbringing had been privileged in many ways. Now, after years of tiny rooms, paper-thin walls and penny pay packets, she felt intimidated by the extravagance confronting her. Even Kristian had been silenced. His natural enthusiasm for once awed by the prospect of endless exploration before him. Stables, outhouses and gardens, all provided the essential elements for a little boy's childish adventures.

Both mother and son ignored the groaning wind that searched for every nook and cranny that may weaken the house. The wind seemed to fume with indignation at the hopelessness of its efforts. The house stood still and proclaimed its defiance.

In Lise's mind the house represented security, a new beginning. She believed that one had to suffer before ever being fully able to appreciate certain things. Her years of poverty, cold and damp, made her realise how lucky she and her son were to be given this new home, this world of certainty and comfort.

There was a shout behind them. They turned and saw William rushing up to them, a broad grin stretched across his face.

"Hello there, you've arrived without any mishap. What do you think of my new house then?" He waved an arm expansively at the house and didn't wait for an answer, "Big isn't it? I've been thinking of making it into a hotel; that's why I bought it. Give me something to do. Anyway, never mind all that, let's get you inside out of the cold wind. Not always like this by the way."

He turned to Mr Jones who was lifting boxes out of the van, "Hello, Mr Jones. Thank you for bringing Mrs Jacobson over. How is Mrs Jones these days?"

"Still talking Mr Treharne. Still talking."

"No harm in that Mr Jones. She keeps you in line and by God you need it. How are things up at Tal-y-Bont farm?"

"Er . . . fine thank you Mr Treharne." Mr Jones noticed the mischievous smile on Treharne's face. The bastard.

"I hear Mrs Gwynne's crop of cabbages are going to be the best on the Gower coast this year, is that right?" *Iesu*! (Jesus!) How did Treharne know about that! Last time he had seen Winnie the Hay he had been delivering some manure or so he had claimed, when her husband had turned up unannounced. Mrs Gwynne had sent the husband out to inspect the cabbage crop. The field lay just outside the kitchen window in full view. They had managed to enjoy themselves over the kitchen sink whilst keeping a close eye on Mr Gwynne inspecting the cabbages. Daft bugger was none the wiser.

"So I believe, Mr Treharne. Now I must go. Busy day, you now 'ow it is."

"Oh, indeed I do Mr Jones, indeed I do." Treharne was still smiling. "Here we are then," he said, handing the removal man a wad of notes. "Keep a careful eye on those cabbages now won't you?"

"Oh, I will Mr Treharne," and I wouldn't mind keeping more than an eye on your new 'housekeeper' either, dirty old sod, he thought. 'Housekeeper,' that was a bloody good one! "Now goodbye and pleasure doin' business with you." He couldn't get away fast enough, he had earned the generous tip though. Neighbours, again!

Treharne ushered them through the main entrance of the house into a large oak-panelled hall, octagonal in shape, with various rooms and corridors leading off it. Polished oak floors partially dressed with Oriental rugs that had been hand woven in the chaotic market places of Asia clashed with velvet sofas and easy chairs covered with battered hide. Round, square and in-between occasional tables of all shapes and sizes danced between the rugs as they listened to the sonatas being played by grand-father clocks and the gossip of vases and pictures from all corners of the globe. The house seemed to jostle, shove, banter and laugh at its own wonderful chaos with its explosions of Art Deco, dour Victorian, gentle Regency and the odd slice or two of cumbersome Tudor. There was life and excitement in every nook and cranny, in every creak and squeak and every squelch-ing inch of hide leather.

Two sets of French doors toward the back of the hall looked out onto a lawn that allowed light to shine and reveal. Sculp-tured privet hedges in the shapes of Disney cartoon characters could be seen through the windows adding to the interior's frivolity and comic charm.

William had made the house a celebration of human foible and immortal error and yet there was humour, optimism and style wherever one looked. Not one groan of misery or outrage could be heard from the ancient oak and copper pipes.

"Gwyn!" William shouted.

A man jumped out of the woodwork.

"This is Lise Jacobson, the lady I told you about. Would you start taking her things up to the new apartment please."

"Right away, Boss." The man disappeared as mysteriously as he had arrived.

"That's Gwyn, he's been with me on and off for years. Odd job man I suppose. He's a trustworthy fellow so if I'm not around he'll look after you. Devil when he's drunk though."

"Drunk?" Lise repeated.

"Yes, drunk. Don't worry though, when the alcoholic dogs start chasing him, which is usually every three months or so if past experience is anything to go by, he doesn't get violent or anything. Just drinks himself into a stupor for a couple of days then stops for another three months or so. He drinks in cycles you see. Predictable is our Gwyn."

"Well, that's all right then, I suppose." Lise said although her words lacked any real conviction. "Where is Kristian?" she asked, concern in her maternal voice, the boy had disappeared.

"Oh, he's around here somewhere . . . Ah! There he is." Kristian was standing by the French doors. His nose was almost poking the glass out. "Ah! You have discovered your very own cartoon world have you?" William said. He walked up to the boy and picked him up. They both looked through the glass, "There you are my boy. They are all yours. Mickey Mouse and Donald Duck. They will never grow old and they will always be willing to play. You must be kind to them though. When you grow a little taller you can give their beards a trim. How is that?"

"Beards Willie? Don't be silly! They don't have beards!" Kristian responded with a giggle.

"Oh, yes they do, at least Donald Duck does, look a little more closely." William put Kristian down and turned to Lise, "Well, I don't think young Kristian is going to be bored!" They looked into each other's eyes and saw only gratitude. "Now then, I'll take you to your own apartment. There's been a lot of work done on it so I hope you like it. Plenty of sunlight and a view of the sea. Once you're settled in we can have some tea and then I'll show you around properly."

He led Lise and Kristian along dark corridors and up flights of stairs, talking as he went.

"You are probably wondering what the hell I want with such a big place. Well, as I've already told you I might turn it into a hotel. I haven't made up my mind yet. There's still a great deal of work left to be done here, restoration and so on. I try to keep everything in its original state where possible. It's a good investment anyway, you can't go far wrong with bricks and mortar. Well, here we are." He stopped in front of a huge oak door and handed Lise a set of keys.

"This is your new home, Lise. It's all yours. Be happy. Come down when you're ready." With that he turned and left them.

Lise opened the door, took Kristian's hand and walked in.

Although the weather outside had turned grey and overcast the apartment seemed bright and spacious. There were windows everywhere. The door led into a sitting room with two bedrooms, a kitchen and bathroom leading off it. All the rooms were decorated with light pastel shades and colours. The furniture and everything else appeared to be brand new. Unlike parts of the house she had already seen, her apartment had been furnished and decorated in a modern post-war style. Everything was smooth and uncluttered. Thick pile carpet covered all the flooring, even the bathroom. The kitchen was stacked with all the latest domestic appliances, although Lise had no idea what some of them were meant to do!

Luxury was the only way to describe their new home. It was astonishing. William had obviously spared no expense.

She stood in the main sitting room and imagined sunlight pouring through one of the many windows. For some moments she felt confused. Overwhelmed. What had she done to deserve all this? Her genuine humility brought with it a unique sadness. Even fear. She was the recipient of a generous gift. She was unsure how to accept it.

She walked around the apartment touching everything, childhood joy and uncomplicated happiness moved through her fingertips and skin. The past was devoured for a few precious moments at least by the novelty of the new. She was a girl again, a child in a world of unknown reality and clocks that never seemed to exist. She found Kristian in a bedroom that had obviously been furnished and decorated with his age in mind. He was jumping up and down on a mattress that had been sprung by God Himself as far as her son was concerned. He could nearly touch Him and say 'Hello'. Imagine that! The boy was beside himself with all the space, the possibilities, the fantasies come true.

While Kristian explored and giggled, Lise went over to another set of French doors that opened out onto a balcony. As the apartment was situated on the first floor extra locks had thoughtfully been fitted to the doors.

When she stood on the balcony, colours reached up and bombarded her. In spite of the day's dull atmosphere that seemed to encourage yawns and bored expressions, yellow daffodils and wicked red tulips still swayed and moved with orchestrated precision as the wind tried to shake their beauty with awkward dance steps and tiresome clumsiness. Neither the sea with its surly motions nor the sky with its tired light were able to diminish the exuberance of the flowers. They danced and bowed their excitement, regardless of the dark moods above and below. Theirs was a short life of calm and reflection, their blooming the only brief opportunity to truly live. A time not to be wasted or squandered considering the future; it was now that mattered.

Lise looked at the flowers and wished that humans could be more like them. We waste so much precious time caring about an unknown future, she thought. So much time dwelling on times long past; she wished she could be more like the flowers and live for the day caring not a jot for tomorrow.

She returned to the sitting room and sunk into one of the armchairs. She wanted to gorge herself with the comfort around her. Her new position meant no more poverty. Now at last after more than six years she was able to provide Kristian with an upbringing that at least partly resembled her own. She was pondering her new life when Gwyn appeared at the door, she had left it open in her excitement.

"Where shall I put your things Miss?" he asked.

Lise had forgotten all about their luggage and few possessions, "Oh, I'm so sorry. Please just put everything on the floor in here for the time being. Oh and my name is Lise, we'll be working together so I hope we can be friends too. No need for formality."

"Right you are Miss . . . I mean Lise." The man seemed uncomfortable using her Christian name. Even embarrassed.

When he had left she thought about the 'odd job' man. There was an aura of brute physical strength about him, the tall broad frame demanded attention as did a face that was handsome in spite of the livid scar running from the corner of his left eye to the centre of his cheek. Jet-black hair matched a thick black moustache that appeared to cover another scar, although like the rest of his face nothing could be certain. His age was also difficult to calculate, he could have been anywhere in the twenties. For all his appearance of brutality Lise noticed that his hands were small even effeminate, and he spoke quietly, his voice releasing only deep tones of kindness and care. His green eyes too seemed to convey both inner hurt and compassion. The man seemed to brood. To fester. He intrigued Lise.

Having examined the apartment in every detail Lise took Kristian in search of their employer.

After numerous false turns they at last arrived in the main hallway. She called out William's name, not having the faintest idea of where he could be or indeed where to start looking for him. It would take her some time to orientate herself; the house was so vast. He eventually appeared from behind a door that faced them.

"Well then, are you pleased with the apartment?" he asked.

"I don't know what to say William, I really don't," Lise answered, still a little overcome by it all.

"Nothing to say, Lise. Now, come here young Kristian." William picked the boy up in his arms. "Do you like your new home then?" The child nodded, looked and then buried his head in William's shoulder." You know Lise, this child's big blue eyes are irresistible, God help the girls when he grows up."

Kristian pulled his head away from William's shoulder and said quietly, "For you Willie." His little hand unfolded to reveal a crumpled daisy.

"Well, well. A flower? For me? Thank you." He hugged the child tightly touched by his innocence. The boy must have picked it from outside somewhere and kept it clutched in the palm of his hand until now. The tiny flower was the best gift William had ever received.

"Now then Lise, how about some tea? There are a few things I want to discuss with you. I'll take you to the kitchen first and then, after we've talked, you can wander around and familiarise yourself with everything." He took Lise to an enormous kitchen which, like her own smaller version, had exhausted the post-war technology for easier cooking. It would take Lise weeks to learn how to use everything.

"I don't know where anything is Lise, so just rummage around until you find what you want. I'll be in my study – the room I came out from." With that he disappeared leaving Lise to her own devices. Searching for some tea leaves proved a task in itself. The cupboards were filled with all kinds of food, from the bizarre to the exotic. At last she had managed to fulfil the simple task and took the tray in search of William. With Kristian scampering at her heels, she headed for the only room she knew, the study. Knocking on the door and hearing a 'Come in' she entered.

The study was William all over. Refined, eclectic and gentle on the eye.

There were books everywhere. They didn't stand in uninterrupted lines of perfection instead they jumped, squeezed, pushed and shoved. Shelf space was at a premium. These books were for reading, for being used and their pages worn away.by constant turning. Two leather armchairs were placed in front of a desk that a cricket match could have been played on.

"Ah, Lise, good. You managed then. I apologise for dumping you in the thick of things as it were, still it's the best way to learn. Come and sit down. Kristian why don't you go outside to play for a while? Go and talk to Gwyn," he pointed through the window. "Look, there he is, go and say hello." The boy dashed off, glad of the chance to escape from adult nonsense. He couldn't believe the uninterrupted view of the sea through the windows of William's study; there were no grimy roofs, bleached long johns or filthy chimney pots!

"I wanted to have a chat with you, Lise, to discuss what your actual duties will be. Firstly though, you had better have this." William was all business and efficiency now as he handed her a large brown envelope. "In there you will find a domestic house-keeping bank account and chequebook plus your own personal bank account. I've arranged to have your salary paid into your personal bank account at the end of each month. I hope this is agreeable?"

"Yes, yes of course."

She had never had a bank account before or chequebook. She didn't even know how to write out a cheque!

"You know Lise, we didn't even discuss your salary, did we? I'm paying you monthly in advance so the balance you have in your account at present will be the amount you receive each month. Don't think about the figures right now, just let me know if you are unhappy about anything. You will be responsible for all household expenditure. You have managed to bring up a young child on your own and done extremely well if I may say so, therefore running this place should be easy. I have every confidence in you."

"I don't know what to say William, I mean Mr Treharne." Lise managed to mutter, still feeling a little overwhelmed by it all. "I must call you 'Mr Treharne' around the house, particularly when other people are present otherwise they will start talking. I shouldn't even be drinking tea with you should I? After all, housekeepers don't normally drink tea with their employers."

"Housekeepers maybe, but companions do. Don't even think about other people; consider them a constant source of annoyance, as I do. They are an irritation, nothing more."

He went on to explain that the house was to be Lise's sole responsibility. He was a busy man and totally uninterested in day-to-day domestic matters. These kind of things were best left to the experts, i.e. women.

"Well, do you have any difficulties with this arrangement?" William finally asked.

Lise made no reply, her determined expression enough.

"Good, then there's no more to be said. Take a couple of days to sort yourself out. It's Thursday today, so we'll start work proper on Monday morning. In the meantime try and see how many staff you will be needing and so on. You have a free hand. Gwyn is a permanent fixture. He has a small room he uses when he fights with his mother who has a cottage within walking distance of here. If you need anything on the domestic side he's the man to ask. Anything else you require, well . . . ambush me . . . if you must!"

"Just one thing William, would you mind if I ask a girl I know to come and work here? Her name is Bronwyn, she used to look after Kristian for me. They both adore each other and I'm sure she would welcome the opportunity of a decent job."

"If that's what you want, by all means. I've told you the domestic side of things is your responsibility now. Do whatever you think is best; I'm sure you will make the right decisions. Lise, I trust you implicitly, so carry on. Now then, I have some calls to make so I'll leave you to it."

"What time would you like dinner?" Lise asked. "I know how fussy you are about eating times."

"Quite so Lise," William smiled, "seven sharp."

"Very well then, I'd better go and see what's in the larder. Dinner at seven – that's if I can find everything I need."

CHAPTER 6

There was nothing more for Gwyn to do that day so he decided to go home. 'Home' was a short five-minute walk away. He stopped at the small post office and collected a newspaper and a packet of rolling tobacco.

As he walked he thought about the new woman in Treharne's life. She was lovely, a real picture. She looked so clean and unspoilt. Her skin and complexion was flawless; he had never seen anything like it. The little boy was a rare one too, looked just like his mother.

He had been embarrassed calling Lise by her Christian name, but he didn't quite know why. Perhaps it was because he felt that the two of them were like Beauty and the Beast. He, scarred, brooding and earthy, she seeming to be so innocent and defence-less. In spite of this he had noticed a determination and strength of will in her eyes that was inescapable. There was fire too and a sharp brain, she was no fool, for sure.

Before opening the gate to the small cottage he wondered if anything was going on between his boss and Lise. He doubted it but then he also knew that old Treharne had been a bit of a lad in his day. The man was still fit and healthy so . . . ach! What the 'ell, good luck to 'im, Gwyn thought as he walked through the front door.

"Hello, Mam, I've brought the paper for you." He looked at the old woman sitting in an armchair listening to the radio. The radio never went off unless there was some technical difficulty with the broadcasting. His mother would listen to the news a hundred times a day, regardless of repetition. The same stories being told time and time again drove Gwyn to distraction.

His mother looked at him, two beady eyes seeing everything despite the colourful crocheted bonnet and numerous shawls that engulfed her.

"Where 'ave you been then, you bugger? Out drinkin' again is it? You wicked swine!"

"'Ere we go again," Gwyn mumbled as he resigned himself to another onslaught.

The weekend before he had gone down to the local pub and got blind drunk. On coming home his mother had started her usual self-righteous performance, "I picked you up from the gutter, gave you a 'ome, a roof over your 'ed and look 'ow you treat me!" she had screamed. Gwyn had had enough of his mother's constant bawling. The booze hadn't helped his disposition either.

"Ah! Shut up Mam will you, you don't stop. Give me some peace for Gawd's sake!" he had shouted.

"Peace!" she had screamed, "*dammo di*, I'll give you peace." With that she had leapt from the chair with remarkable agility for a woman of her years and attacked him with a poker lying conveniently in the fireplace. "You wicked, wicked swine you! Talk to your mother like that would you. Me an old woman!" She nearly caught him with the poker but he ducked just in time, despite the slowness of movement inflicted on him by alcohol.

"Your wife couldn't stand you, you blackguard! Threw you out she did, quite right too, you drunken bugger!" Another swipe from the old woman just missed him.

"Right, that's it now, I've bloody well 'ad enough, you old witch!" he had yelled. "I'll swing for you I swear!" He had then stumbled into the kitchen and grabbed the chicken waiting to be prepared for Sunday lunch. Launching himself with slurring fury into the living room he threw the inoffensive bird with all his strength through the front window. Glass shattered and smashed.

His mother sat down but still kept the poker levelled at her miscreant son; silence prevailed for a brief moment.

"*Iesu Mawr*! (Oh Jesus!) What you do that for, you bloody fool?" she had asked calmly." The chicken hasn't done anything to you has it? It's dead *mun*!"

Gwyn had already fallen down on the settee. "Because it was there Mam," he slurred, "because it was there." He then began to lapse into an inebriated oblivion slurring as he did so, "Where would I be without my Mam! In the gutter that's where, in the gutter!" He had meant it too. An alcohol-soaked sob or two later he had finally fallen asleep.

His mother had carried on listening to the radio as if nothing had happened. She would collect the chicken in the morning, extract the bits of glass and cook it just the same. The cold air streaming through the window would sober her son up soon enough; he would have a cold arse too! Serve the drunken swine right! At least her bedroom would be nice and warm with the electric fire going full blast. Gwyn would repair the glass in the morning just as he always did; he had become quite a glazier. Plenty of practice. For some unknown reason windows and glass always seemed to have an irresistible attraction for him, particularly when he was drunk. Flying through car windscreens plastered was one of his specialities. He was famous for it!

Mrs Evans looked at her son snoring away on the settee. She lifted her eyebrows for a moment and nodded her head. Resigned. There's always a bad bugger in the litter, she thought, still his heart's in the right place. Secretly she enjoyed the rows. Life would be boring and lonely without Gwyn to spice things up. He kept her young.

Her other two sons and daughter had all left home and she was proud of them all. They were respectable, hardworking and caused her no trouble; now, she was alone with Gwyn. "Stupid sod," she mumbled to herself, smiling slightly as she thought about some of his previous handiwork. The front door for instance. It had once comprised a panel of square pieces of glass – all the same shape and all with the same design. Not anymore. Gwyn's unplanned arrival had seen to that. The door was now a mosaic;

the once uniform panels of glass had become a kaleidoscope of different designs and shapes. Lost keys, a drunken fist. Gwyn and glass again. It was a sorry day for Mrs Evans when Gwyn's wife finally decided she had had enough. Out he had to go. To his last place of refuge – his Mam's.

Gwyn Carwyn Evans was undoubtedly one of life's more colourful creations. Some might have said that he had been placed on this earth to remind those around him that human kind had simply evolved from a playful diversion of the Gods. His life to date, had been one of extremes. Calm periods never lasted long before some storm would explode and disturb the peace. He maintained the volatile temper of a Welshman, combustibility being an inherent feature of his character, although, where Gwyn was concerned, it had to be said that more often than not this fire was usually only ignited by the flames of alcohol.

He was a handsome, well-proportioned man despite the scars that criss-crossed his face. They added character he always boasted. His nose was twisted and turned in unnatural directions having been involved in many a direct impact. He wasn't sure himself how many times it had been broken. He did know that flying through car windscreens hadn't helped the noble structure. Indeed it was a wonder that he had any nose at all. The scars, or his 'battle trophies' as he liked to call them particularly when women were around, were all the result of drunken driving, PFO's (that's 'pissed fell over') and his natural affinity with glass.

Gwyn had grown up in a large family. One of four children to be precise, he being the second in line. Despite his roughness of nature, when adulthood beckoned Gwyn had shown a sensitivity far and above his siblings.

On the death of his father he had been the one most affected by the loss – indeed it had resulted in Gwyn being locked up in a padded cell for a few days to grieve. There were those who believed that he had never quite got over this tragic blow – thus his thirst for drink as soon as his hands could reach over the bar.

There were times, even now as a grown man, when he missed his father. He could still cry tears of grief – more so if he was drunk. His father had been dead for well over fifteen years, but for Gwyn grief was timeless. It was also a bloody good excuse to get drunk.

Apart from this one bleak period his childhood had been a happy one and innocent. There had always been plenty of food on the table and enough companionship to do a born-again Christian proud.

He and his brothers had always been in a perpetual state of war with a contingent of local gypsies. This never-ending theatre of hostilities usually involved Gwyn's natural antagonism and aggression. His once classical and refined Roman nose was softened up on many occasions. A necessary process he would have argued; at least it was fully prepared for the main events of later years.

On one such occasion the brothers Evans had decided to take on the gypsies at a game of cricket. They were to settle their differences in a gentlemanly way – at least that was the idea. The game had been friendly enough until Gwyn took up the bat and his position at the crease. He scored two runs and was given out LBW. At least that's what the gypsies claimed.

A great debate ensued with Gwyn yelling his objection to such a wrong and unfair dismissal of what he considered to be his outstanding cricketing prowess.

He adamantly refused to leave the wicket.

With characteristic stubbornness and pique he withdrew the stumps from the ground, the bails and the ball from a bewildered gypsy and stormed off, bat in hand shouting, "Right then, my bat, my ball and my bloody wickets, so fuck you!"

He hadn't gone far when a much bigger fellow from the Romany trail caught up with him and landed a weighty fist right on Gwyn's unsuspecting nose. This was the first nasal break in what was to become a history of many. Not shedding a tear, apart from a few hidden drops resulting from his broken nose,

Gwyn loped off mouthing all kinds of foul retribution on the perpetrator of his now painful nose. He would get even once he had grown a bit. Even at twelve years of age he had had enough intelligence to realise his physical handicap where the other boy was concerned – he was much older and bigger. More to the point, he was also fully aware that his impending manhood promised to be a good-looking affair and he had no desire to wreck his rapidly developing magnetism where the girls were concerned.

He did though eventually get even as promised. He was a man of his word – except in drink.

There was a cunning side to Gwyn. This part of his nature, certainly during his youthful days, cost him many a just hammering from his mother. His immaturity sometimes made him forgetful of the eleventh commandment, 'Thou shalt not get caught'.

A typical example of this arose, from of all things, a Christmas cake.

His mother had won the cake at the local Women's Institute whist drive. The cake was a veritable work of art.

Mrs Evans had placed the masterpiece on top of the sideboard so that all may see its festive glory and at the same time appreciate and congratulate her skill and dexterity at the whist tables. She was extremely proud of her prize which was not to be touched until Christmas Day. All in the house were warned.

The great day arrived at last.

Everyone sat at the dining table behaving themselves. The main meal was finished. It was time for the cake. The object of everyone's torment and greed was placed in the middle of the table.

After due ceremony and torture Mrs Evans hovered above the cake, knife poised. All the children sat wide-eyed and expectant; they had waited a long time for this moment. Turkey and Christmas pudding were as nothing to the fruity finale that had sat on the sideboard for two months sneering at their avaricious eyeballs.

They all turned into stone. Silent and still. They waited for the knife to do its work. They waited for the delicious explosion on their taste buds.

The knife went in – and the whole magnificent object d'art collapsed! All that was left of the tantalising cake was a crusty shell with icing on top.

Its guts had been eaten away – by Gwyn!

He never forgot that particular Christmas.

The next stage of note in Gwyn's charismatic life arrived in a flash of religious lightening. He forsook the evil drink and became a lay preacher of the old school, the Welsh school that is.

Many a small chapel shook with the storms of his Christian fervency and threats of Hell's flames to those evildoers fool enough to stray from God's righteous path. He pummelled his Bible in front of various unsuspecting souls and warned against the sins of the flesh and alcohol.

His own wedding was a non-alcoholic affair. His friends could only speculate as to its consummation. Gwyn was so close to God they wondered if he would be able to rise to the occasion!

He followed in the family tradition of farming the good land. When not showing people the error of their ways he tilled the soil and sowed the seed. He and his wife led exemplary lives of good honest labour and diligent, if not fanatical, attention to Christian morals. Then one day a property developer knocked on their farmhouse door. Gwyn sold his farm for a considerable amount of money; he also, some were later to maintain, sold his soul.

For the first time in his life he had money, real money. His world took on entirely new dimensions.

The Bible was hidden away to gather dust and preach to itself. He began to gorge himself with alcohol and women. Fast cars, luxury houses and bottles of Scotch turned him into a walking nightmare. Fortunately, God had not turned His back on

His fallen hero. He loved a sinner as Gwyn himself had often preached. He intervened in His mysterious way and saved Gwyn from an ignominious death. The money ran out, the wife booted him out and Gwyn ran to his last refuge on earth – his Mam.

At the time of meeting Lise, Gwyn had grown older and, he hoped, wiser. At twenty-seven he now took each day on its own merits and refused to look too far ahead. He had learnt the hard way that plans rarely worked out the way we wanted them to. He kept his drinking within reasonable limits, at least reasonable for him, avoided lustful expeditions into the unknown and generally tried to lead a quiet, sensible existence.

Treharne had offered Gwyn a job five years ago. This had been his own true Resurrection. No one had been prepared to offer the drunken ex-playboy work but for some unknown reason Treharne had seen some redeeming features in the man and decided to give him a second chance.

Gwyn had not disappointed his new boss. A versatile man, Gwyn could usually turn his hand to most things and over the years had become indispensable. He was a driver, builder, gardener, cook, and valet all rolled into one. Employer and employee had developed a strong and affectionate bond. Gwyn had found a father that he still missed so much, Treharne a son that he had lost. Both men held a high regard for the other.

Treharne never ceased to be impressed by the basic honesty and sincerity of his unfortunate helper.

Men like Gwyn were the salt of the earth, especially when they were not swigging out of a bottle.

CHAPTER 7

The second summer arrived at Ragged Cliffs.

The garden's soil had created a holocaust of colour having evicted the last grim remnants of winter. Lise stood alone in William's study looking at the vivacity and wilfulness of flowers suddenly granted a liberty that they knew would not last forever. Nature's ease and brash attention to the future was in sharp contrast to the serious erudition that surrounded her. All the walls of the study were lined with books from floor to ceiling. There were books on all subjects and disciplines, from the Hindu art of lovemaking to the philosophical rants of Kant. Peeling leather-bound volumes whiffed with time while newer tomes could only look on with envy. The sombre, masculine atmosphere of the room decided the character of the man who usually occupied it. Learned and yet humorous, a master of his own destiny and yet humble. So many contradictions, so many riddles.

A close and efficient working relationship had developed between Lise and William over the past two years. Lise had come to know and accept his irritating foibles and had learnt when to indulge his outrageous demands for perfection. For William's part he had learned both to respect Lise's sensible intelligence and listen to her opinions, while most of the time he even tolerated her admonishing and outspoken remarks with good grace; apart from anything else, when she did correct him on anything she was usually right. To begin with her astute mind had annoyed him; now he didn't quite know what he would do without it. She always brought him back to earth and had a subtle talent for calming his occasional irate nature.

As Lise looked at the floral scene before her, memories of another life came back to her. A life where her own father tended their garden in Denmark. A life of different tongues, traditions and people. Although eight years had now passed there were times when Lise still felt a certain yearning, a prickly homesickness.

She couldn't help it but the splendid beauty before her eyes threw her heart into a dark corner of sadness. Her life was full, she wanted for nothing and yet there was an emptiness. A place she couldn't touch. She knew what was wrong but always the truth would intimidate and force her to retreat.

Her physical experience of men had brought nothing but violence and shame and yet she remembered so well the delicate warmth of her first encounters with the young German soldier. Although so young, she could still recall the unpredictable rushes of excitement that flooded her body each time she saw him. The twists and turns of her stomach. Even now the memories of charm and innocent mystery brought on twinges of embarrassment and blushes from the past. She was not the whore that her rapists had charged her with, she was just a young woman trying to make the best of life. Fortunately for Lise her good sense had always prevailed and helped to save her from a destructive sense of guilt. She kept telling herself that she had done nothing to merit the appalling treatment of her body and mind. There was still a kind of hatred toward the two men who had savaged her and there were so many times when she wished that it would go away forever. But hatred she knew did nothing but poison and deny. It imprisoned emotion and prevented her from seeking the love she so desperately wanted to give and to receive.

She knew that her passions were being suppressed by fear and pain. This led to a crushing realisation that perhaps she would never be able to love or give herself to any man.

She was now twenty-five years of age. A beautiful woman with a smile and serenity that made men shudder yet she herself was naïve and oblivious to their reactions on sight of her. Her sexual attraction was devastating and yet she had no knowledge of this. Even her simple way of dressing failed to subdue the blazing sexuality that blinded men. This innocence added to her physical attraction made her all the more desirable. Lise had been born with a deep, inherent capacity to love, a capacity that knew no bounds or restriction. It was limitless. She knew this and accepted it; however, the conflict that raged deep within her prevented her from giving full vent to this most powerful of emotions. She was unsettled by the desires and thoughts that seemed to pass through her mind with ever-increasing frequency. Would this curse ever be cast from her?

She looked at the gardens, staring but not seeing, absorbed and distant, she whispered quietly to herself, "Sweet Jesus, let me find true happiness, help me to live, truly live again."

A door opened behind her, she turned around, a trifle startled.

"Lovely, isn't it Lise?" William stood in the doorway looking at her. His expression and voice hinted at concern.

"You didn't see me pruning some roses. I waved but you seemed to look right through me. Is anything wrong?"

Lise collected herself. "No, William, nothing is wrong. I was just enjoying all those beautiful colours. Can I get you anything?"

"No Lise, no more work for today. Come and sit down. I want to talk with you." They sat together on a leather sofa. William looked into Lise's eyes and his hand rested on hers.

"Memories, Lise. Memories can bring unhappiness and joy. Sometimes when we get older, they might be the only real things we have left. They may even give us wisdom. Most of us try to remember only the good things, but like it or not the bad intrudes from time to time. It may even gain sovereignty over the good. If that happens, then we as human beings become gnarled and unkempt in our sensibilities. Hope embarks upon a long journey to other places less fruitful. What happens to us then? We cease to live, to laugh, to cry. We become nothing, my lovely. We merely exist. You must not dwell. There have been many occasions when I have noticed your distant smiles, your retreats into the past. You must learn to smile more, to be kind to yourself. You have a long future just waiting to be used to the full. I don't like seeing you miserable Lise, please make an old boy happy and let me see your eyes as well as your lips smile at me. Smile from deep within and not just on the surface. No façades of happiness please, they really don't become you. You are a beautiful young woman, wallow in it!" He kissed her hand as he often did and hugged her.

She was grateful for his concern.

Over the years Lise had come to love her protector and saviour. Her love was borne of deep affection and respect. She knew that she could never leave him; she didn't want to. The love that had grown between them both was of a quality untainted by the romantic or amorous passions of sex and emotional turmoil. They had become father and daughter, not lovers.

Both were content with the relationship; there were no threats of unrequited love and rejection. They were able to express the close affection they felt for one another without having to fear where such affection may lead. They knew their respective positions. The awful uncertainties that prevailed upon those caught in a maelstrom of physical and mental desires were absent from the gentle and caring love that the two felt for each other. Their relationship had become a special and cherished one.

After absorbing William's words, he was rarely wrong about anything, Lise said, "I'm sorry William but a large part of me seems to be missing. I know this might sound a little self-piteous but there are occasions, especially at night, when I feel so lonely. Then I feel guilty. Here I am in a lovely home, I have Kristian, you. I want for nothing and yet . . ."

William finished the sentence for her, ". . . and yet Lise? I know deep down where the problem lies and so do you. You just won't face it because you are too frightened. Leave your fear in Denmark, Lise, where it belongs. You are a delightful young woman that deserves and needs the love of a good man. This is the most natural thing in the world, stop trying to fight against nature. It won't work my lovely. The powers of nature are far greater than we simple mortals. Let yourself be what you are, stop putting up barriers that keep you in and others out. There is a man out there somewhere, waiting just like you. Be patient, but Lise when the opportunity comes, and believe me it will, grasp it with both hands, don't hold back. Let your love possess you both. It is the most wonderful, glorious treasure that we are ever given. We don't often receive it. Some people go through life without ever knowing the experience of love. Real love. How sad and empty their lives must be. Perhaps in many ways love is all we humans really have. It's our reason for being. Our reason for going on. Mark my words, one day soon it will call for you and you must answer, for your own happiness you must answer."

"But can I William? I seem to be chained to the past. My life in its quiet moments returns to Denmark, to the good and the bad. I don't seem to be able to set myself free, I sometimes just despair."

"Well don't, you foolish girl. You have everything to live for. The key to the lock is out there somewhere, trust me. Be patient. You have everything to live for – like looking after me for a start!"

Lise smiled.

"Yes, I know, I suppose I'm being selfish."

"Not at all my lovely. We are all selfish. That's why mankind has endured for so long. I wouldn't worry about that if I were you. Damn it woman! Find yourself a man, get out more! A good man will sort you out believe me. Man and woman were made for each other you know, according to the Good Book anyway. Lise, I know what happened to you during the war has left deep and terrible scars, but even scars heal and fade with time. Don't imagine what might be, don't try and anticipate the future. Follow your heart and you won't go far wrong. Try not to dwell. Now then, you can hold my arm and walk with me around the gardens. I need the support you know, bones beginning to creak."

"Nonsense, William! You can probably outrun Kristian. Don't try to play on my sympathy, I know how crafty you are, you old goat!"

"Old goat! Be damned! I'll tell you this, if I was twenty years, no make that thirty years younger you wouldn't stand a chance. There I go again, wishing my precious years away. Come on, let's walk."

Lise took his arm as ordered and gave it a little squeeze as she said, "It's still thirty then? If you were twenty years younger William, I've no doubt I would be running around the gardens trying to get away from you!"

"You would too, I was a devil for the ladies in my younger days. Ah well, memories, ay? You see you're not the only one, Lise."

As they walked, Lise's black mood lifted, it always did when she spoke with William. His perception, his knowledge of her still surprised.

CHAPTER 8

Bronwyn sat at a huge pine table peeling vegetables while Gwyn sat opposite her drinking tea and recovering from the ill effects of his mother and strong drink. He couldn't make up his mind which did his body and soul more harm.

As a general rule he left alcohol alone but if he did touch the stuff he certainly didn't mess about with it. Not content with putting a foot into the shallow end of the alcoholic pool he would dive straight in at the deep end and make sure he was completely immersed.

Two or three pints of beer were a waste of time; he would rather not bother. If he were going to have a drink he would do the job properly and paralyse himself. His body, being usually unused to any form of alcohol, always reacted violently to the sudden deluge of poison.

Gwyn was ill. He suffered.

Looking at the vegetables Bronwyn was peeling with her small fingers was making his stomach turn in a merry go round of nausea.

Suddenly he leapt up from the table and dashed for the dilapidated toilet situated next to the stables. It had to be this toilet; it was reasonably sound proof and hardly ever used by anyone.

He reached the toilet door, yanked it open in a thorough state of panic and let loose a surging Niagara of vomit, at the same moment his bowels detonated and nearly lifted him off the ground.

For one hour his arse and stomach continued to ambush him. All he could do was sit on the toilet and wail 'Oh God! . . . Oh God! . . . Oh God! Over and over again.

He wanted to die.

Bronwyn carried on peeling the vegetables seemingly unaware of Gwyn's sudden exit. She hummed away to herself then got up to look for some bicarbonate of soda. She would have the drink ready for Gwyn when he returned.

She had seen it all before – and heard it! She was surprised at the fact that the toilet was still in one piece. Gwyn didn't fart, he exploded! And *duw mun* the smell! The stench hung around for hours no matter how much disinfectant she used. He would get better though as the day wore on, it was always the same. She had become fond of Gwyn and didn't like to see him suffering so badly even if it was self-inflicted. Fair play, she thought, stirring the brew, he doesn't often drink. Trouble is, when he does, look out!

A dishevelled Gwyn came back into the kitchen clutching his stomach; his face had drained of any colour and he was still pleading with God for salvation.

"Jesus God Bron! I thought I was givin' birth out there," he moaned.

"Sit yourself down *mun*, and drink this," she ordered as she gave him a hefty dose of the bicarb, "it will settle your stomach."

"Will it 'ell." Gwyn grumbled but drank it all the same, letting loose an ear shattering belch in the process. At least this time the wind had chosen a more socially acceptable orifice. At one point in the outside toilet Gwyn had experienced a sudden fear of cracking the toilet pan or at the very least shaking the foundations on which it stood. Bronwyn's fears were not unfounded.

"Serves you right, I don't know why you drink beer. You know it makes you ill. Look at you, good for nothing and supposed to be helping me!"

"Oh, Bron be quiet will you *mun*, you sound like that bloody old hag of a mother of mine! She drives me to drink she does. Drives me to it I'm tellin' you. Woman doesn't stop going on. Counts the eyes of a penny too she does, mean as 'ell and God 'elp me if I ever forget the bloody newspaper! She sits there in that sodding armchair like the Queen of bloody England she does. Deaf as a post too. I'm tellin' you Bron she would drive any sane and sober man to drink. The good Lord himself would be tempted if 'ee 'ad to live with my mother. Drink's the only comfort I 'ave."

"Maybe Gwyn," Bron scolded, "but it doesn't help does it?"

"No, I suppose not," he conceded quietly.

"There you are then, so why do it?"

"I don't really know Bron. Mind you, makes me deaf to my mother's bloody squawkin', which is somethin'." Before he could say anything else he suddenly leapt up shouting, "Oh, *Iesu Mawr*! Here we go again!"

All Bronwyn saw was Gwyn fumbling with his belt as he dashed for the door, an eruption of anal gas helping him on his way. In spite of the noxious miasma that engulfed and nearly flattened her, Bronwyn couldn't help laughing. Gwyn was a daft bugger but she liked him, and for a moment she thought that maybe her feelings toward him were a little bit more than just 'liking', farts or no farts.

Bronwyn Rees came from a family whose horizons were limited to Chapel on Sunday, hard work sixty hours a week and one holiday a year in Llandudno. She had been brought up on a strict Biblical diet of temperance in all things, sourness about everything and the belief that her sole purpose in life was to marry and have as many children as her belly allowed. She did not wholly agree with all these limitations on life or indeed her future, they suffocated, bored but more to the point they simply weren't Bronwyn Rees. She was far too lively.

She had more spirit in her than her mother and three sisters put together.

She wanted to find out as much as possible about the things life had to offer. Forbidden or not. A simple enough girl at heart maybe, but from time to time the Devil himself had a nasty habit of forcing 'Our Bron' to give in to temptation and each time she rather enjoyed the experience.

She also wanted to know how 'the other half lived' and wouldn't have minded some of it herself. The invitation from Lise to come and work at Ragged Cliffs had been a godsend – for once. The old bugger usually tried to make her life as difficult as possible. At first she had been overwhelmed by the luxury and opulence of her new home, her first night in her own bedroom being pestered by mischievous shadows and a fear of the unknown. *Duw mun s*he actually had her own room, her own wardrobe and her own chest of drawers too!

For years she had had to share everything, including clothes, with her three sisters and as for that strange word 'privacy', well what on earth was that? Whilst she had always yearned for her own room and her own private plot of living that first night had pounded her with loneliness and apprehension. Everything seemed so impossible, so apart and unreal. Dreams were only dreams after all; they weren't supposed to cross the barrier into reality were they?

At first she had found the vastness of the house with all its never-ending corridors, doors that opened into other worlds, Peter Pan nooks and creepy crannies all a little intimidating. This however hadn't lasted long. Now she loved Ragged Cliffs as much as everyone else did. She had also come to cherish her freedom.

Bronwyn had grown into an attractive young woman. The awkward puppy fat of pubescent angst had dissolved into a rounded figure of perfect womanhood. Her face seemed to move in gentle contours of whispered prettiness rather than raucous beauty. Her hair, as black as the coal that her ancestors had once transported along the canals of South Wales, continued to flop and flow around eyes that seemed to grasp all the subtle colours of autumn; one minute brown, the next minute golden red, or sometimes even a mixture of all three depending on where the sunlight shone.

She was typical of her Welsh ancestry. Her nature was warm and passionate, but there were occasions when, true to her blood, she was capable of erupting into a frenzied firestorm and God help anyone in the immediate vicinity.

She was still thinking about Gwyn when Lise came into the kitchen.

"Good morning, Bronwyn. Everything all right?"

"Fine Lise, just fine." She wasn't going to let on about Gwyn's troubles. She felt instinctively loyal to the man. "I've given Mr Treharne his breakfast and I'm doing the vegetables for dinner. I've left the beef out for you."

"Good, Bronwyn, we have got some fresh beans and sprouts haven't we?"

"Oh yes, picked them myself this morning from the vegetable garden. Nice and fresh they are."

"Right then, well I'll prepare the beef later on today. Where is Gwyn this morning, he's normally in here having his tea at this time?"

Bronwyn seemed to suddenly concentrate a little harder on the potato she was peeling. Avoiding Lise's eyes she said, "Well, he's not very well at the moment Lise. Bad stomach you know."

"Oh yes," Lise said suspiciously, "bad beer more like. Don't tell me, he's hiding in the toilet again."

"Er . . . yes, I think so." Bronwyn didn't say much but Lise knew all about Gwyn's drinking habits.

"Never mind, Bronwyn, it's not your fault. When he's finished purging himself tell him to come and see me, I'll either be in the study or the dining room. Ask him to bring his tools. One of the doors isn't closing properly. And Bronwyn . . ." The young woman looked up from the vegetables this time, "I don't know why you always try and cover up for the inebriated rascal." Lise smiled and added, "But then perhaps I do." She walked out of the kitchen leaving behind a blushing Bronwyn.

William was sitting in the dining room finishing his last piece of toast when Lise came in. Opened letters lay in front of him on the table.

"Hello there," he said, filling his mouth with copious amounts of thick cut marmalade, "you know this stuff is damned good, Lise. Best you've made yet. Come and sit down for a minute, have a cup of tea." He glanced at a letter he had been holding in his hand. "We are going to have some visitors soon."

"Oh yes, how many?" She was quite used to various people turning up at the Cliffs from time to time. Although William had disposed of most of his business commitments, people still sought his advice on various matters. He had also cultured friendships with a great many people from all over the world.

"Three to be exact; my son, daughter and son-in-law. I haven't heard a whisper from them in God knows how long, so why they should suddenly decide to descend on me in force I have no idea. Well, perhaps I do. I can't help feeling that the notion of strength in numbers seems to apply here."

William didn't seem overjoyed at the prospect of seeing his children. Lise had never met them and he rarely spoke about them. They had never been to the Cliffs but William did see them on the few occasions he went to London on business.

She knew that there was some deep hurt inside William where his offspring were concerned. She had always remained silent on the subject, never prying or allowing curiosity to get the better of her. Whatever troubled William he had kept entirely to himself. There were times when Lise wanted to reach out to him to help but he was a stubborn man and not one to flaunt his emotions. Despite this, she had always known that one day he would confide in her but that this would be in a time of his own choosing.

"It's my birthday a week Monday, perhaps that's got something to do with it. My sudden popularity that is. They've never bothered before so why should they now? Something is up."

"William, what is the matter with you?" Lise chided. "You are intolerable sometimes. It's your birthday, your children are coming to celebrate it with you, for heaven's sake. Honestly, you are too suspicious by far. Stop being so miserable about it will you? You might actually enjoy your birthday you know, you might even get a few pleasant surprises."

"That's what worries me Lise, you don't know my son and daughter. They are full of surprises believe me, and they are rarely pleasant."

"Oh, stop it will you, you're being silly. When do they arrive?"

"Next Friday. Probably want a couple of days to soften me up before the main attack."

"God William, you really are such a cynical man, now listen to me . . ." that's as far as Lise's admonishing went.

"Just hold on my lovely before you start the school ma'am act. You don't know my son and daughter – fortunately for you, I have to add. My son has turned drinking, debauchery and gambling into art forms. He was expelled from his prep school for blowing up the chemistry master's desk – while the man was sitting at it! He was expelled from public school for stealing all the lead off the school church roof and selling it for scrap . . ." William paused for a moment, ". . . got a good price for it apparently so he has a few chips of me in him. Anyway the list of his numerous unsociable misdemeanours is endless. I won't bore you with further details where that no-good boyo son of mine is concerned. Sufficient to say he is a total waster. And as for my daughter, well she's not much better. She eats men up and then spits them out when they can no longer afford her extravagant bloody tastes. She's already on her second husband, nice fellow too. Poor bugger. She'll bankrupt him before long. She's extremely selfish and thoughtless to the point of insanity, if that's possible. I really don't like her very much, daughter or not."

"William, that's an awful thing to say!"

"Yes, I know and I'm sorry, but it's true. I really do despair with both of them and there it is. Pair of useless damned parasites."

Lise had listened patiently to this tirade knowing that William must always be allowed to give full vent to his frustrations. After he had finished speaking she said gently. "I really wish you wouldn't swear so much, but apart from that I think you should make an effort to be pleasant when they arrive. They are your children after all."

74

"I sometimes wonder."

"I'm sure we will all have a lovely time. That's assuming, of course, that you can manage to raise the odd smile."

"Now, now, Lise, sarcasm doesn't become you. Leave that to me, I'm an expert."

"Being a crotchety old man doesn't become you either, so stop it! Kristian is very excited about your birthday, so at least try will you?"

This was a crafty move on Lise's part.

She knew full well how William had come to adore her child.

CHAPTER 9

William's son and daughter were due to arrive late afternoon.

The morning had gone off well enough with William as energetic and as lively as ever. He opened his cards and presents with juvenile enthusiasm and couldn't stop kissing everyone around him. As soon as the imminent arrival of his children was mentioned he skulked off to the study and hadn't been seen since.

Lise felt that it was best to leave him alone for a while and so she and Bronwyn busied themselves in the kitchen preparing dinner.

Lise wanted to be kept busy as she herself felt uneasy about the arrival of William's son and daughter.

In many ways her life at Ragged Cliffs had become a happy domestic vacuum. They lived apart from the rush and turmoil of busy town life and the irate tongues of people and gossip. Theirs was a world of smallness, of friendly intimacy and affection. Serious discord never arose and emotional battles were avoided. Peace and contentment were the only visible signs of the character of their lives.

Lise knew that perhaps this mode of existence verged on the ideal and like all ideals, if they existed at all, it would be transitory in nature. She would often shiver at the thought of their happiness being pulled away and drowned by the seas that raged against the cliffs outside. All their wishes and desires being swept away by the tides of fate.

How much had William told his son and daughter about she and Kristian? What were they both like? These questions kept racing through her mind, and the more she considered them the more unsettled and nervous she became.

At 6.30 that evening the familiar sound of car tyres squeezing the gravel on the forecourt could be heard. As the slamming of car doors echoed around the kitchen Bronwyn and Lise exchanged an agitated look.

"Well Bronwyn, they've arrived I think." There was a nervous twang to Lise's words. She hung her apron behind the kitchen door and smoothed down the conservative green woollen dress she wore.

Running her fingers through her hair one last time she turned to Bronwyn. "Do I look all right Bronwyn?" she asked. "I haven't put too much makeup on have I?"

"You look lovely Lise, you always do. Too much makeup? That will be the day *mun*. You 'ardly ever use any, don't 'ave to do you? Go on now, I'll finish things here. Dinner at eight is it?"

"That's right. I'll pop in later Bronwyn."

"*Dammo di*! I'd better get a move on then, now off you go; don't worry now they're only people, even if they are from up London!"

'Only people' Lise reflected; yes but what kind of people? The doorknocker resounded around the house, Lise waited for William to answer it but he didn't. So she was to meet the new arrivals alone, no doubt this had been contrived by William. She walked into the hallway and opened the huge oak door. Three people stood in front of her.

"Hello," she said, realising with a shock that she didn't know what to call them so she carried on quickly, "please come in, your father is in the drawing room, I'll take you to him." She hoped he hadn't remained brooding in his study. She wouldn't put it past him.

The new arrivals walked into the hallway after exchanging polite greetings and followed Lise. She knocked on a door and walked in.

William was standing in front of a marble fireplace warming himself. There was an austerity about his demeanour that tended to insult the comfort and heat from the log fire that crackled away behind him.

For a moment there was silence. A calculation of reaction. At last William finally broke the deadlock. "You've arrived then. Come in and make yourselves comfortable." His daughter rushed up to him enthusing love and emotion as she hugged and drenched with saliva; the look on William's face was one of pure distaste. Her husband stood back as if waiting for a train to arrive.

"Happy birthday, Daddy!" she handed him a small gaudily wrapped parcel. "I hope you like them. I searched all over London you know."

"Yes Megan, yes I'm sure you did. Thank you." William's voice was tinged with embarrassment; he was unused to his children being the providers. In the past his wife had always bought their presents to him for them. The dear woman had maintained this deception for years – or thought she had. The son came next. They shook hands as he wished his father 'Happy Birthday' and handed him another present.

"Good God," William muttered. "Why am I so popular all of a sudden?" He tried hard to hide his cynicism for Lise's sake.

"Because we love you of course Daddy, why else?" his daughter gushed. Her father grunted and looked over at Lise who was still standing ill at ease by the door.

"Now then my children, before we go any further I'd like you to meet the lady who looks after me and just about everything else around here. She has become a close friend too. Come over here Lise, stop hovering around the doorway, you are one of the family you know."

Lise felt awful as all eyes turned toward her. She walked up to William. There was both hostility and awkwardness in the air. The log fire seemed to crackle a little more loudly.

"Lise," William continued, ignoring the obvious atmosphere of enmity particularly from William's daughter, "this is my son Griffith, daughter Megan and my son-in-law, Hugh. All of you, this is Lise." Never one to miss the opportunity of devouring a beautiful woman, Griffith immediately stepped forward and shook her hand.

"How do you do Lise, I don't envy you the task of keeping the old man in line. Must be one hell of a job!"

As he spoke Lise noticed a roguish kindness in the green eyes. For some reason she instantly liked the prodigal son. He put her at ease. There was an openness about him. Almost honesty, in spite of what William had said.

She turned to Megan and Hugh. All she received from Megan was a restrained 'Hello', Hugh just smiled hopefully, as if his lips were trying to apologise for something he hadn't done. Hostility hung in the air like an executioner's axe.

After further exchanges of polite platitudes Lise prepared them all a drink and took her leave, using the dinner as an excuse.

The kitchen was a safe haven; it was warm and friendly, in total contrast to the drawing room.

William and his offspring had acted like strangers bumping into each other on some wind-blown pier, heads down, eyes attached to the wooden planks and legs hell bent on instant detachment. There had been no genuine affection between them, just the strained good manners of distant acquaintance. To Lise it all seemed unnatural, so forced. Where was the love, she thought?

Back in the kitchen Bronwyn said, "*Duw* mun, that was quick!" She couldn't hide her Welsh nosiness and added, "Come on, what are they like?"

Lise thought for a moment before answering.

"Normal . . . I think. Now then, never mind your Welsh curiosity, how is the lamb doing?" Knowing when to keep quiet Bronwyn decided against trying to glean any more information.

"There we are then! Fine Lise, everything under control. You need a drink if you ask me, bit haughty were they? Bit posh? Go on, 'ave a sherry, I'll see to things here."

"That sounds like the best idea I've heard all day. I'm going to my apartment. I won't be long." Was she being rude? Lise thought. Ill mannered? Companion, friend, housekeeper? She didn't know who she was sometimes or how she was supposed to behave.

Her own territory brought a few minutes of respite. She poured herself a large dry sherry and sat down, trying to make as little noise as possible. The last thing she needed at the moment was for Kristian to wake up and start asking too many questions.

She thought about the people she had just met. William rarely spoke about his children, so in many respects she was left to draw her own conclusions. She knew only too well how suspect first impressions could be. Appearances could be deceptive but also extremely revealing. The contradiction had always intrigued her.

Megan was a big woman, tall and sturdy. Hands and feet capable and large In spite of her size there was a trimness about her, there were no bulges of fat pushing her clothes in unsightly directions. Apparently horse riding was one of her passions, it certainly seemed to keep her lean and fit. In spite of her size the woman moved with an easy grace cultured by the best schools money could buy. Lise judged Megan to be in her early thirties. She was an attractive woman to those men who liked them big and busty. Long auburn hair rested on her shoulders; her face was strong, even masculine in some respects. She had a firm jaw, green eyes like her brother and a nose that had it not been for her general largeness would have been considered out of proportion with the rest of her face. Her physical features were neither pretty nor beautiful; it was the overall impact that created an impression of refined power. The clothes she wore were the best that London had to offer; her voice was cultured and educated without any trace of accent. She had been moulded and nursed by the top public school for girls, Roedean. It showed. Megan was self-assured, sophisticated and quite ruthless.

During the brief moments of their meeting it was obvious to Lise who yielded the power in Megan's marriage. She thought again of the way Megan had looked at her, the eyes had been so explicit; there had been no attempt by Megan to cloak the spite and nastiness that lay in the mind behind them.

Lise had observed rather unkindly – but then she herself was a woman – how Megan's teeth protruded. This was the only pronounced defect in her physical appearance. Thank God for small mercies Lise smiled, the woman's teeth were so obvious, so rude even by their intrusiveness they could guide the most distressed ship through any storm, day or night. Lise knew that some men found a large toothy mouth erotic, she couldn't understand why. How could the crashing of enamel against enamel be erotic? The woman couldn't kiss, could she? She could only devour.

Lise concluded that Megan was indeed a formidable woman. There was also an element of threat which made Lise feel decidedly uncomfortable. Taking another sip of sherry she turned her mind to the other family members.

Hugh, Megan's husband, was a different character altogether. Megan's size and dominant aura seemed to suppress the man. He appeared to dangle on Megan's will. He was her necessity. Another irritating bank account. He was small in build, a good head shorter than his wife in fact. His hands and feet were petite when compared to his spouse. There was nothing striking about him either in looks or in character. He wore the vacant expression of the cruelly oppressed. His eyes wanted to say something but he was never too sure what. With good reason perhaps. He said little, did little, except it seemed, to be led through life by the overbearing, big-breasted Amazon called his wife. He seemed dazed. Shell shocked. He was no longer allowed to think; he was dragged along by Megan's substantial body like a pampered poodle led by a silk lead. To add insult to this monstrous injury it was his money that had paid for the silk too – or at least his family's money. The poor man was thoroughly dominated. Any rebellion on his part would no doubt have been crushed by one swipe of his wife's expansive hand. Hugh was one of those men that women usually regarded as 'nice'. Like his character, his looks seemed to be a mixture of uncertainties. There was no one feature that particularly stood out. He was a shadow. There for all to see but only ever glanced at because there was nothing else to concentrate on. Like Megan he was well dressed, but even his clothes lacked any hint of panache or statement of individuality. Lise could just envisage him in a clothes shop; Megan would choose everything. The man would never voice an opinion; the shop assistant would deal with Megan only.

Hugh was a non-entity, the poor man.

Griffith. Round, fat and brash. These were the first words that came into Lise's mind. A rascal too, no doubt about it. She couldn't help but smile for a moment. His vain attempts at sartorial perfection had been demolished by food and drink. He was the classic example of the inability to make silk out of a pig's ear. Never mind the ear, Griffith was all pig.

No tailor, no matter how bespoke, could prevent Griffith's gut from overflowing with plenty. His face was inflated and full. Flesh hung everywhere, like the carcasses in a busy abattoir. It was impossible to discern exactly where his chin was situated. There seemed to be so many of them.

He must have been in his late twenties or early thirties. Lise remembered that he was a year or so younger than Megan. His age was hard to tell. Fat faces did that.

Griffith was without any shadow of doubt a distinguished drinker. Tiny red blood vessels burst along his cheeks to meet at the most outrageous feature on his face. His nose. It was a captivating, bright red bulbous beacon of nearly manic proportions that clung to the centre of his face like an over-ripe Mediterranean tomato about to burst. It was, he maintained, his most valued possession, an investment. It had taken a lot of years and thousands of pounds to culture and nurture.

He was proud of his nose. It had helped on many occasions to light his way through the murky paths of drunken darkness.

Griffith looked a depraved and utterly debauched character, a character that would have given more inspiration to Shakespeare's pen that Falstaff himself. Although he gave the impression of being an inebriated oaf or a court jester who had forgotten his riddles, Lise detected a sharp intelligence and a certain kindness and compassion in the man's eyes. She was also convinced that there was a latent strength deep within the man. It was there in his eyes for those who took the trouble to look.

He was an actor, Lise concluded, the true man rarely revealing himself.

Lise finally finished her drink and decided that perhaps she was being unkind; jumping to too many conclusions. After all she had only just met them all. She really didn't know anything about them so it was unfair of her to judge and criticise.

She must give them a chance at the very least.

She went back to the kitchen and told Bronwyn that she could now serve dinner. Making sure that everything was in order in the dining room, she went and told everyone that dinner was ready.

Griffith appeared reluctant to leave his whisky while Megan seemed delighted at the prospect of food. Hugh said nothing but trailed after his wife, knowing that she would, as always, do what was best.

Lise had gone to some lengths to ensure a successful birthday celebration for William. She had prepared a dish of mussels, cockles and white wine to start followed by Welsh lamb that had been marinated in herbs and red wine. The lamb had been cooked to perfection, rare in the middle and crispy on the outside. The vegetables had not been overcooked; they retained their crunch and taste. The main course was followed by a simple rice pudding made with lashings of milk and cream. Just the way William liked it. It was his day after all.

Throughout the meal conversation had been at a standstill. They all knew that William considered eating a serious business and not one to be interrupted by idle chatter.

Bronwyn cleared away all the plates; each one was stark naked, Lise had done something right at least. As she started pouring the coffee subdued tongues began to come to life again.

"Daddy tells us you are Danish," Megan said as she looked at Lise, having deliberately omitted to call Lise by her name. The taunt was ignored. Before Lise could answer, Megan continued, "How long have you lived in Wales? It must be very different from your native Denmark."

"In some ways yes, naturally," Lise replied cautiously, knowing that her responses would be carefully monitored. "Obviously there are differences in culture and tradition, but people are people the world over, the human spirit rarely changes despite nationality."

"Your English is very good, you must have lived here for quite a long time."

"About eight years now, I think."

Megan persisted with her interrogation. There was an edge to her voice.

"And what were you doing before becoming Daddy's housekeeper?" William glared at his daughter. "Sorry, I mean companion," she gave a little girlish laugh and added, "that was silly of me, after all a housekeeper would hardly be sitting down having dinner with the family now, would she? That wouldn't do at all, would it?"

"No, I suppose not," Lise answered, aware of the spiteful overtones in Megan's words. The woman had a childish high-pitched voice; she spoke like a little girl seeking sympathy and devotion. The voice alone irritated Lise. She couldn't help it but she felt like thrusting some adulthood into Megan's vocal chords. Not like her at all.

"So, what were you doing before coming to Ragged Cliffs?" Megan persisted, while almost blinding Lise with her row of brilliant white teeth. The predatory beast closing in for the kill.

"I was a chamber maid at a local hotel," Lise answered, there was no attempt at subtlety or subterfuge.

"Really? Well you have come up in the world, haven't you? Well done!"

The sarcasm bit all those sitting at the table.

"That's enough Megan," William's voice was hard, "Lise is not here to be interrogated by you. No more, do you understand?"

Megan went into a self-satisfied silence. Lise had never seen William look so angry. The contempt in his eyes when he looked at his daughter shocked her. For a brief moment she understood why he had managed to be so successful in his business life. There was a streak of metallic hardness in his character that she had never seen before. Had she not known the other side of him she would have been frightened. He looked at her and his face immediately softened.

"That was a wonderful meal Lise. Thank you." The others joined in the accolade; all that is except Megan who allowed a few mumbled and incoherent words to escape from her mouth.

"Don't mind Megs, Lise," Griffith said light-heartedly, "she lets her curiosity get the better of her sometimes . . . just as the drink gets the better of me on occasions." He laughed. "Would you pass me the brandy please, Lise?" Lise handed him the cut glass decanter. As she did so, his eyes looked straight into hers and held her for a few brief moments. She was used to men looking at her but usually their eyes contained threats of physical intent. Desire. Griffith's eyes told a different story. She detected only embarrassment and apology. Shame even.

Later that evening Lise and William were alone in his study.

"Please sit down Lise, I'll pour us both a drink."

"I don't really want . . ." she didn't get any further with her objection.

"Don't be such a puritan, woman. I should think you would need a drink after that little charade. Here we are." He handed her a brandy and sat down in one of the leather armchairs facing her. She could see that he was now more troubled than angry.

"I don't know what to say to you Lise. I'm so sorry for the way my daughter, God help me, treated you. I thought you were very brave remaining seated at the table as you did. Even I had no idea she could be so brutal. Griffith is just a drunken, prurient buffoon, there is no real harm in him but Megan . . . she's a different breed altogether. I am deeply ashamed Lise, more so because they are part of me. There are no excuses and I make none. Perhaps now you will understand why I tend to distance myself from them. I really don't know sometimes where the hell they came from. Their mother was a kind, gentle soul who harmed no one. Me, well I might be a cantankerous old man but there's no vindictiveness in me. I sometimes wonder if the Gods are punishing me in some way. The best of my children was snatched away by a bullet, God bless him. Look at the two I'm left with – an alcohol-soaked idiot of a son and a daughter who seems to have little feeling for anyone or anything – apart from herself, of course.

"I often wonder if the girl has the basic capacity to love full stop. She seems devoid of compassion or any warmth. She lives entirely for herself and money. Both her husbands were chosen for their financial worth not their worth as men, with hearts and emotions. God knows what either of them saw in her. Let's face it, she's no beauty. Take away the clever make-up and expensive clothes and what have you got, a bloody shock first thing in the morning I shouldn't wonder."

"Oh, William," Lise interrupted, "she is your daughter you know."

"Well . . . yes I suppose so, but that doesn't mean to say I have to like her does it? Hell, if her husbands hadn't been wealthy in their own rights I'd have to put their initial courting down to my money. But that's never been the case. Knowing Megan, she probably bullied them down the aisle or stuck a loaded shotgun up their arses."

"You're being crude again, William."

"Yes, I know, sorry, that's probably where my idiot son gets it from."

For the first time that evening William smiled, "Did you notice that Hugh hardly said a word all night? Probably too damned frightened. Megan even told him what to eat, did you notice? Damned idiot, more fool him though, he should have shoved her fork right up her arse if you ask me!"

"William! I know you're angry but there's no need for that! And yes I did notice." This was all Lise could say. She could see how upset he was and disappointed. All she felt able to do was to listen; she didn't feel it her place to voice an opinion of any kind, particularly where his children were concerned. She had to admit though that she couldn't quite understand how Megan and Griffith had turned out the way they had. They were both so unlike their father.

Megan looked nothing like her father and neither did Griffith although, where Griffith was concerned, there did appear to be traces of the Treharne blood; it was just that drink and gluttony had somehow managed to conceal them. The mystery was further compounded by the fact that there appeared to be little of the mother in them also. According to William anyway.

"I'd still like to know," William continued, "why they are here. Believe me, my birthday is just an excuse. Mark my words, before the weekend is out my chequebook will be red hot – at least so they think."

"William, don't you think you're being a little harsh jumping to conclusions like this."

"Lise, with all my heart I wish that were the case but I know my children. I've watched them grow up; studied what they have become. In many respects I suffer the guilt that many parents are plagued by when their children choose a path that is anathema to them. How many times have I asked myself 'Where did I go wrong?' How many times have I blamed myself? It never really stops you know. I suppose that's why, in many ways, I try to keep myself isolated from their lives. Keep them at arm's length. Each time I see them and see what they have become I am stricken by a terrible guilt. The questions never cease but worse still, there are never any satisfactory answers."

Lise listened and said carefully, "You must accept, William, that at the end of the day children are only with us for a short time. Eventually they grow up and leave to carry on their own lives and be their own people. Once they become adults they and they alone are responsible for their own actions. Not us as parents William . . . never us. All we can do is guide and help. Hopefully instil in them a basic knowledge of what is wrong and what is right. Once they mature, their decisions are theirs not ours. If they make a wrong one, we are not to blame; they are, and they alone must suffer the consequences. As parents we do the best we can. We give all the love we can, protect all we can, but sometimes these things are simply not enough. You cannot go on punishing yourself over Griffith and Megan. They are what they are, and you know there is nothing you can do about it. Stop trying William, let them go their own way and just hope that maybe one day they will see things in a clearer light and that life won't be too cruel to them. You cannot, like God, make a child in your own image you know. You are, after all, a mere mortal."

"A noble hope indeed, Lise. You are probably right though, as usual. Just take one piece of advice from a veteran father. Don't spoil Kristian. Don't give him too much. Make sure he learns to value things, all things. Teach him to respect people, no matter who or what they are. Teach him to understand the pain of others and to never turn his back on that pain. Most of all Lise, teach him to understand and to nurture civilised values. Do all these things and he will grow into a good and caring man. Neglect them and God help him . . . and you."

"Thank you for the advice. I will try, and I also have you to help me." She yawned and finished the remnants of her brandy. "Now I really am tired William, and must go to bed. It's been a long day."

"Quite right my lovely, I have been rambling on like some old woman. I'll just have another nightcap then go to bed myself. No doubt the others are sleeping the deep sleep of the innocent. Griffith certainly is, the alcohol-soaked bladder of lard."

"William! For heavens sake! Will you stop it!"

"My God, I love it when you get all lathered up," he laughed. "Now go on to bed and leave me to brood in silence."

"Don't stay down here too long now, will you?" She could never get seriously angry with him and he knew it.

"No Lise, I won't. I promise. Now off you go. I'll see you in the morning. Goodnight and sleep well."

"Goodnight, William."

CHAPTER 10

William sat behind his desk looking at his son and daughter,

"I was wondering how long it would take for the true purpose of your visit to be announced. Birthday my arse!"

"No need to be so coarse, Daddy."

"Shut up, Megan! I'll be as coarse as I like in my own damned house! And just remember that it is just that – my house! Money, that's what it always boils down to with you two, doesn't it? Bloody money!"

Griffith remained silent, preferring his sister to do the running; she was the eldest after all and he hated scenes particularly where money was concerned. Apart from anything else he was still suffering from the night before. The raw eggs and Worcester sauce had done little to settle his wrecked stomach. God though how he hated having to ask his father for funds; he had some pride, which was more than could be said for his sister. Their father's money was Megan's as of right. She owned the world and everybody in it. She was the centre of the Universe after all.

"Daddy," Megan continued in that voice that became even more annoying when it went into whine mode, "I've already explained to you, Hugh's company is on the verge of bankruptcy. Through no fault of his own I hasten to add. I'm not asking for a gift after all, just a loan. The money will keep the company going until things improve."

"What things?" William pressed.

"Well, we have plenty of orders, the trouble lies in keeping the creditors happy. Customers don't pay on time and so we have trouble paying the bills and so on. We just need some capital to help the cash flow."

"Cash flow be buggered! That's a good one! There's only one place the cash flows and that's into the Megan reservoir.

Another poor bastard going to the wall because of you. When I first met Hugh he was a prosperous young man, good business connections and an old family company behind him. Seems to me you have frittered all that away on big houses, fast cars and even faster delusions of grandeur. As usual I'm the one left to pick up the pieces. Hugh, the poor bugger, just isn't strong enough to say no to you, is he?"

"That's not true Daddy! Hugh and I discuss everything together. All our decisions are reached jointly. You are being unfair."

"Unfair am I? Well now I'm going to show you how truly 'unfair' I can be. I'm not giving you another penny. Not one solitary sou. This time the answer is no and there's no bloody chance of a reprieve. It's time you learnt to stand on your own two feet. I notice Hugh didn't come and talk to me himself, too damned ashamed I shouldn't wonder! At least he has some sense of propriety, and that's a damn sight more than can be said for you. Megan you are now a grown, mature woman, you can start behaving like one. Learn the value of money. Learn Megan, learn because I can tell you now there's no more from me. You still have a trust fund from your mother, which God knows is generous enough, so live on that. You have had far too much from me over the years, you and Griffith. And by the way Griffith, if you think you're in line for a fat cheque, forget it. Go and get yourself a job, you lazy good-for-nothing little shit – no, I take that back, you fat shit!"

"Steady on now, Dad!" Griffith objected. "No need to get personal. Jesus. A job? Are you serious?" The prospect of work made his bowels shake and his nausea take a turn for the worse.

"Yes, a job. You know work. Earn a living. You're as bad as your sister. A couple of useless parasites, a pair of bloody wasters both of you! Spineless. And while we are at it you can both bugger off to Woolworth's. I hear they have started a new line in mass-produced plastic spines – very durable apparently. Buy a gross each, you're going to need them. Use you're own money too. There is nothing more to say, except that I don't expect either of you to love me because of this – although I doubt if love is an emotion either of you are particularly familiar with. Perhaps one day you will thank me. I should have done this a long time ago."

Megan leapt up from her chair, her furious red hair seeming to get redder as her anger intensified.

"You realise what you are doing don't you?" she shouted, "you are ruining us, ruining me your only daughter. How can you do such a thing? How can you? You mean, nasty, old man! You just want to keep everything for yourself don't you? For yourself and that slut with a bastard son . . ." Megan's tirade stopped suddenly as she realised she had gone too far.

This time there was no turning back. A minute or two passed before William looked at his daughter and said calmly, "Leave my house now and never come back." The coldness in his voice was absolute; his eyes sliced right through his daughter. Megan couldn't face him, this was one man she could never dominate. Instead she turned and walked out.

Knowing when to run, Griffith quickly followed her.

William stood up from his chair and looked out of the window.

He had never been so hard on his children before. Children? Neither Megan nor Griffith were children any more. They were both in their thirties, adults, and yet neither of them had grown up. They were still playing at the serious business of living. They seemed to have no conception of life, no idea of its hardship, its tragedy. As long as there were chequebooks and signatures, all was well. How fickle and shallow they had both become. It saddened him that neither appeared to have any depth of feeling or emotion; they were both so appallingly unprincipled.

His heart didn't want estrangement; after all he had brought them into the world. Neither did he want them destroyed. And yet his own life had manoeuvred along a dangerous tightrope on more occasions than he could remember. Many times in the past financial ruin had been a near certainty and yet he had fought on. No one had given him gratuitous handouts. No one had helped. He had built his fortune up from nothing. He had been a penniless reject from industry's squalid might. He had known poverty, really known it. He had lived through the cold and hungry days and survived.

William's knowledge of abject destitution was not the superficial, smiling kind of the charity worker with a full belly and a warm home to go back to. His poverty in the early days had been real to the touch. He could still feel and taste the putrid corners of despair in London, the damp, freezing doorways of shelter and the kind, clean-shaven faces of the Salvation Army still haunted him. Perhaps it was because of all this that he had tried to spare his own children the crushing desolation of charitable rags and humiliation.

He had been wrong.

All he had done was to create a vicious monster and a useless overweight rake. Their only God was money.

What had he done?

This time he would not give in. He would not allow his love to weaken the resolve he felt. He must let his determined streak prevail and hope that his son and daughter might yet develop some notions of decency and humanity. All he could do was to hope and wait. He left the study and went to change into his gardening clothes. There was one place he could always find peace.

As he passed through the hall he saw Gwyn carrying some luggage through the front door. Megan was shouting at him to be careful. William paused listening to the verbal avalanche being heaped on Gwyn. She stopped in mid abuse and looked at her father, her face cast from iron, "I will never forgive you Daddy, never!" she spat. William said nothing but carried on walking to the rose garden, sure now that he had done the right thing. Megan continued to remind Gwyn of his stupidity as he put the bags into the boot of the car. Hugh stood by the passenger door like a bewildered mourner at a funeral not knowing what to say next. Eventually Megan and her monkey disappeared in a swirl of dust and screeching tyre rubber. Megan drove of course.

"Could I have a word, Dad?"

William looked up from the rose bush he was pruning. His son stood before him, bloated and painful. William and his wife had made a handsome couple; how had they nurtured two such chronic insults to the human race?

Their first son and first-born had been an exact replica of his father both in body and mind; that's what had probably got him killed, William often thought. Stubborn bugger.

"What is it Griffith?" William asked. He was still angry, only an hour or two had passed since the altercation in his study.

"Don't worry," Griffith said apologetically, although he hadn't actually done anything yet. "I'm not after any money."

"That's just as well then because I'm not giving you any."

"Straight to the point as always dad. Look do you think we could call a truce. I don't want to quarrel with you Dad, or have any more scenes. Life's too short and all that." Griffith smiled and William had to grudgingly admit that his son had still retained a certain amount of charm. At least he had inherited something from his father.

"Fair enough, I don't like quarrels either. So what is it you want?"

"You know Dad, you're not making this very easy for me." William sighed.

"I'm sorry, go ahead." At least his son was making an effort, although he couldn't be sure; Griffith could be a devious devil. Another less admirable inherited trait perhaps.

"I thought you might write some letters of introduction for me, you know plenty of companies in London. It's a start and I do realise that it's time I sorted myself out. Did something more um . . . respectable with my life."

William looked bemused as he said, "I'm in a state of shock, seeing a bit of sense are we?" Griffith ignored his father's caustic sarcasm. "How old are you now? – Thirty-two?"

"Yes."

"Thirty-two and never done an honest day's work in your life. That's got to be some sort of an achievement if nothing else."

"Oh, there's no need to labour the point Dad. I am trying."

"Yes, I suppose you are. I'll give you credit for that. However, you might start by getting yourself into some kind of physical shape. Look at you, you're a bloody mess. You look ten years older than you are. Pack up the drink and lose some of that blubber, you're a disgrace. The high living has had a detrimental effect on your sister too. She's getting to look like a constipated sow at the wrong time of the month." Griffith couldn't help but snigger at this last remark, his father hadn't lost his unique way with insulting words.

"Yes Dad, I know I need to start getting myself physically fit."

"And stop agreeing with me on everything will you? It's irritating. Oh yes, and while you're about this miraculous transformation don't forget to stop off at Woolworth's on your way back to London. I meant what I said, a new spine wouldn't do you any harm and that's a fact. Damned spiv. No decent company wants a fat, spineless shit on their books, so liven up. I'll do the letters for you but I'm not pulling any strings – so don't ask. You've embarrassed me enough in the past. Like your sister you're on your own now. It's a tough world out there and you have to fight hard to survive. No one is going to do you any favours and never forget that. When are you leaving?"

Ignoring his father's insults, Griffith said quietly, "I thought tomorrow morning."

"Good, that will give me time to write these letters. Now then go and amuse yourself somewhere and leave my whisky alone. And brandy and gin. Your sister has caused enough trouble for one day."

"Right, I'll see you later then."

With that Griffith walked off feeling quite pleased with himself. It didn't take much to placate the old man, he thought, he would soon come round. William watched his son roll back up to the house.

What a cretin! Does he honestly believe that I have fallen for that disingenuous nonsense? he thought. The trouble with Griffith was that he was a hopeless liar.

His eyes gave him away.

Every time.

CHAPTER 11

Shops of every description abutted the street.

Paris was a woman's dream and her male companion's nightmare. William had made a wise decision in leaving Lise alone to her own devices. Worn out at last, Lise had decided to stop for a while and rest at one of the numerous cafés.

She drank her coffee slowly and absorbed all the frantic activity that surrounded her. Life boiled and bubbled; she was still unable to suppress the constant flow of excitement. She thought back to the day William had suggested they go on a 'Grand Tour' of Europe; that night she had been unable to sleep. As a child she had always dreamed of travelling, seeing other worlds, new peoples and cultures. Now she was doing it and the wonder was as vivid as it had always been.

They had journeyed for two months from Vienna, the gateway of Europe, to Paris. With leaning towers and smashed plates in between.

It had been the most joyful time in her life.

She and William had been together now for more than eight years; she had broken the thirty-year-old barrier of age. He had given her so much and there were times when she just wanted to hold him in her arms and thank him. He had given she and Kristian life and yet had never asked for anything more than her companionship.

Often, over the years, she would fantasise about her mentor. In her secret moments she would wonder about a real relationship with William, his age belied his youthful physique and sense of humour. There were occasions when she would blush at some of the thoughts that entered her mind. She loved William deeply but somehow she had been unable to qualify that love or define its exact character. There was none of the juvenile infatuation she had experienced with the German boy so many years ago. With the passing of time both she and William had built up an emotional barrier, each wanted the other to be happy and yet they had both avoided using the key to unlock completely the door to this desire.

If love is blind, for William and Lise it had never even been born with the facility of sight in the first place. They both kept blundering on in a friendship that was screaming for more. They were two strong people and yet their courage wavered in the face of consummated love. Fear and trepidation kept the floodgates firmly shut.

Lise finished her coffee and decided to go back to the hotel. She missed William being at her side; the blaze of merchandise that chained her every footstep didn't seem so alluring without him. Besides they were returning to Wales the following day and there was a lot of packing to do.

That night at dinner they both drank a little too much wine and eventually arrived back at the hotel in the early hours of the morning. The food, drink and noise had left them both light-headed and happy.

In the corridor outside Lise's room William kissed her good-night on the cheek as he always did. He was about to return to his own room when Lise put her arms around him and pulled him to her.

Neither of them said a word.

They looked into each other's eyes and knew what was right.

Fear and reluctance cowered.

He kissed her again, but this time it was a lover's kiss, long and intimate. The years of latent courting and hidden thoughts vaporised into the air around them. Hitherto forbidden desire dissolved on their lips. Barriers disintegrated. Violence, rape and grief all made a final exit as their bodies demanded love.

William led her into the bedroom and undressed her with a slowness that was painful. He wanted to cherish every moment and to never forget. He wanted to give all his love to this beautiful woman. All of it.

Lise responded with a passion that had been suppressed and incarcerated for so many years. She was unable to resist, unable to stop.

At first their fingers stroked and touched.

William led. He guided.

Their bodies exploded with sensation and physical trauma as each kiss, each movement became an erotic voyage of discovery.

Their tongues searched and explored.

They both drank in the sexual aroma that fell on them like a mist and cloaked them from the vicious world outside. They became one and entered a paradise of pure sexual and loving insanity. Their mutual orgasm when it finally arrived created an emotional firestorm, a union of will and body that neither had ever experienced before. The years of neglected love and opportunity finally vanished into a past that was no more.

Later as they fell asleep in each other's arms tears left Lise's eyes and trickled down the smooth skin of William's shoulder.

He felt the release and said nothing.

Morning arrived.

Lise reached for William but he had gone. She opened her eyes and saw only an empty space in the bed. She could still feel and smell him. A wave of panic swept over her. Where had he gone? Had regret forced him away from her? Had some perverse guilt infected his mind? Just as she was about to pick up the phone to try his room a knock on the door stopped her.

She ran to the door naked forgetting all modesty.

"Who is it?" she asked, hoping with all her heart it was William and that her fears were unfounded.

"William," came the reply.

"Wait a minute." She quickly put on a dressing gown and opened the door. Before she knew what was happening his arms were around her once more and his lips were pressing against hers. All doubt melted away. He withdrew from her and sat down.

He looked at her. His eyes spoke a thousand words. There was a struggle within them.

"I've ordered breakfast for us up here. At the moment I don't feel like being surrounded by a lot of people."

"No, neither do I," Lise replied. She sat down opposite him.

"My God Lise, you look as lovely first thing in the morning as you do when you are dressed and about to go out. Lovelier in fact, more natural." She stood up and sat on the arm of his chair taking his hand in hers she kissed it. "What are we going to do, Lise? We really have crossed the Rubicon now. I love you, always have. It annoys me to think of all those wasted years. There were times when I would look at you and want you. I would go to bed at night wishing you were coming with me. Wishing so much that we could be together properly. I used to often wonder how I managed to restrain myself. The fear of making a fool of myself I suppose . . ." William paused, his eyes strained again. "Lise, I am an old man now, like it or not; you are young and so very much alive. I look at you as you experience this new and exciting world – you are so vibrant. I cannot impose on your life Lise, I want you only to be happy. I must tell you that I won't blame you in any way if you wish to stop things now. I'll understand. We are far away from Wales no one need ever know anything. It is enough that you have given me one night of yourself, a night I shall take with me to my grave."

Lise looked at the man who had become her life. "Oh William, don't you see that I too love you. I always have; it's just that time had to pass for me to fully recognise it. Last night was wonderful for me too, making love to you made me feel so alive, so human. You are not an old man William, neither in body nor in mind, particularly not in body." They both smiled. "Last night you cast away all the shadows and ghosts of the past. That horrible night in Denmark finally went away. You made my heart and body live. A resurrection of sorts if you like. You helped me to be my true self William, you helped me to love." She kissed him, "I love you William, your age means nothing."

At that moment room service arrived with the breakfast. When the girl had left, Lise took William's hand and said gently. "Leave the breakfast my darling. Love me instead."

CHAPTER 12

They were eating lunch in the dining car of the Pullman train taking them to Swansea from Paddington.

To the average onlooker they would have given the impression of a typical loving father and his adoring daughter. Had their true intimacy been known, then no doubt eyebrows would have risen in shock and lips curled in disgust. Even if this had been the case, they were both too absorbed with each other to have noticed and even if they had, neither of them would have been particularly perturbed by the jealous thoughts of others.

William had always maintained that hell usually emanated from other people and Lise had learnt long ago to ignore the malice of those incapable of anything else.

They had both led fairly insular lives at the Cliffs and had developed an armour-plated immunity to the vagaries of human kind. In spite of this, their love for each other was not obsessive in character. The physical bonding that had now taken place was merely an endorsement, a confirmation of the affection and love that had grown between them over the years. Their love was based upon solid foundations.

They knew each other.

They were comfortable with each other.

There could be no unpleasant discovery of past misdemeanour or vile inclination.

As far as love was ever able to be secure, then William and Lise had achieved it. Theirs was a matured and seasoned love.

A safe love.

When they had finished eating William took Lise's hand and said, "Lise, you know that when we return home, things are not going to be easy."

"No, I know," Lise replied. "I must admit I have tried not to think too much about it but I suppose we will have to face things now, won't we?"

"We will indeed. There will be a lot of talk, scandal even. Perhaps this time it will be justified."

"What do you mean William?" Lise asked with a note of concern in her voice. She had noticed that during the journey he had seemed withdrawn, remote even.

"Lise, we must face facts. There is one hell of an age difference between us, like it or not. You are thirty and I am sixty-three. You are still young."

"We have been through all this William, anyway I am not that young," Lise remonstrated. "I'm in my thirties now you know."

"Thirties! Good God woman, compared to me you haven't got out of your damned cot yet!"

Ignoring the outburst Lise said calmly. "William, why are you worried about the spiteful asides of silly gossips? Since when have 'people' ever bothered you?"

"Don't be silly Lise, you know me better than that. The point is that I probably don't have a great deal of time left on this beloved planet – certainly not as much as you."

"Ah, I see. I really don't see why that should be a problem," she smiled for a moment and tightened her grip on his hand. "Besides you're hardly bed ridden are you? You're probably healthier than I am, very active anyway." She smiled again and this time William couldn't help but return it. "I don't know why you should worry so much. Dear me William, who is to say that I won't have some kind of sudden accident or incurable illness and die before you? We must take what we have now William, grasp it with both hands. Each of us has had our fair share of pain and suffering. We must not let the chance of happiness slip past us. I love you William, and always will. Don't let an unknown future spoil what we have, please."

William looked into the beautiful face that confronted him, the blue eyes that seemed to defy adversity.

"You're right Lise, I know. Even so, it doesn't stop me worrying about the hostility that you will no doubt be confronted with. Neither do your feelings for me prevent me from thinking that you should be with a younger man – a livelier, more robust man. I don't want to hinder or spoil your life by imposing premature age upon it. Don't you see?"

"Yes I do, of course. You talk of hostility; well William, we have been receiving that for years – even though up until now our relationship has been perfectly proper. So what, for heavens sake, is so different now?"

"Oh God Lise. Don't you see that I worry about you and Kristian, after I'm gone. My son and daughter will crucify you, certainly my daughter. You will have few allies Lise, few friends. I am deeply concerned about your welfare. Your well-being after my days."

"I'll be all right, William. No one will hurt Kristian or me for that matter. I still don't see why you should be so concerned about my welfare after your death. Kristian and I will manage, believe me. We are both hardened veterans at the game of surviving."

William looked at the woman sitting opposite him and for a moment he couldn't say anything. Her loveliness entranced him; it was not just her physical beauty that paralysed his tongue, it was far more. Lise was totally unselfish and unspoilt by an appetite for material wealth. The practicalities of her future existence had simply not occurred to her. Security and money were only things to be considered at the last moment. They were not all important to her. He knew that to Lise, all that mattered were he and Kristian. He felt overcome by his love; he could not believe that the Gods had been so benevolent. He was almost frightened. What had he done in his life to deserve such unfettered happiness? Were the Fates playing one of their cruel games, giving with one hand only to take back with the other?

"What happens if I become an invalid, wheelchair bound or something?" William persisted, "I couldn't bear the humiliation of all that. My bones are beginning to ache now you know."

"William," Lise's voice became firm. "I've been looking after you for quite a while. There are occasions when it's easier to deal with Kristian; you can be extremely awkward and stubborn, sometimes downright rude and cantankerous. I know what I'm letting myself in for."

"Perhaps, but the age difference still concerns me . . . then again age only matters if you are a bottle of wine I suppose."

"Exactly, I love you and that's all that matters. Now be quiet, all this arguing is bad for your digestion."

"If you say so." He took her hand and looked at her, "Lise, will you marry me?"

"Pardon?"

"You heard. Will you marry me?"

"I . . . er . . . well."

"Don't dither woman. Yes or no?"

"Well . . . yes, I suppose . . ."

"My dear girl, supposition doesn't come into it. That's settled then. We'll do the deed as soon as possible. Don't look so shocked for God's sake. We've both had years to ponder the arrangement."

"Arrangement? Dear God William, you could try and be a little more romantic about it."

"Don't be silly woman, I'm too old for all that nonsense."

"Didn't take you long to get back to your usual domineering self now, did it?"

William smiled. "You know the quality of the goods you're buying. There are no latent defects I assure you. I may be approaching decrepit senility rather rapidly but I am not there yet. You know what you're getting into."

"Really?"

"Yes indeed. Besides you're the perfect spouse. You see a wife must be intelligent enough to recognise her husband's genius but stupid enough to be impressed by it. You're perfect."

"Thank you for the compliment William, I presume you're exercising that dry sense of humour of yours again."

"Something like that." Then he continued more seriously, "Never thought I would marry again, at my age it must be some kind of reward. All jokes aside my lovely; I will try and make you and Kristian as happy as I possibly can. I will care for you both with all the love a man can give. By being my wife, I know that you and Kristian will be secure should anything happen to me, which of course it will one day. I couldn't bear the thought of any harm coming to you both. But more than that I want you as my wife because I adore you. You are my life. I only wish that I were younger with more years to give you. I must love you tenfold to make up for the lost years. We must cherish what we have now, Lise, and never forget how ruthlessly life can snatch the good things away from us."

"I know William, believe me I know."

The train stopped at Neath, just outside Swansea.

"Well, we'll be home soon. Our home, we had better start getting ready Lise."

"Yes. Just one thing William. You know if you think that merely because I've agreed to become your wife, you can become more extreme in your bullying ways, well, don't delude yourself. And just because I happen to be your wife, does not mean either that you can rule me and do as you please. I'll fight you, William, if I have to, so don't forget it." Lise said these last words with the finality of a red letter threatening impending legal proceedings.

"Would I? Could I?" he laughed. "Your spirit is one of the reasons why I love you. Life would be very boring and tedious if you didn't give me what for now and again. You've always done that anyway, so hardly a novelty is it? I suppose as my wife you won't have to be as subtle about it anymore will you? God help me."

As the train approached Swansea all the decaying hopes of small industrialised people still echoed from the dismal mounds of waste and poor air. Time had betrayed this part of town. The exploited history still looked back and yearned. It still wanted more from nature and people's desire. Even the purest of loves was unable to ignite a spark of life into the bleak carnage that trespassed through the carriage window.

CHAPTER 13

As William and Lise approached the entrance to the Guildhall they were showered with confetti.

There were only three people at the wedding – Kristian, Gwyn and Bronwyn. This was enough. Sincerity and genuine blessing they both demanded; judgement and sour remarks could rot in Hell. Weak attempts had been made to inform William's son and daughter but neither had turned up. William had been unperturbed if not relieved by their absence. Their presence he knew would have tainted the day. Their lack of goodwill would have been seen and heard and there would have been nothing but ugliness in the waves of confetti.

Kristian had taken the news of his mother's impending marriage with a smirk and a knowing look. All his suspicions were confirmed once and for all. So his mother and William were 'at it' and had probably been 'at it' for a long time. He was delighted. Like any unspoilt and kind child his love for his mother was an unselfish love. Her happiness was more important than his.

He had seen the hidden tears.

He laughed and smiled with her and for her. He had not been ruined and corrupted by the deformity of parental over-indulgence and manic obsession.

Kristian looked much older that his fourteen years. His testicles had crashed into the ground and shaving had become an irritating necessity, at least every few days or so. He was tall and lithe, but muscular without being too heavy. He had grown into a handsome young man; some even said that his good looks were an utter disgrace. He had become the Wagnerian hero, with blond hair and striking blue eyes that would have made even

Lohengrin stop and look over his shoulder. There was a natural charm too, and a smile that could demolish and persuade in equal measure. At his young age he had already earned a reputation with the opposite sex, no matter what their age. Women found it impossible to resist the searching blue eyes, hardened muscles and deep soft voice. A voice, he had been told, that could serenade without the need of song or music. Many a young girl had thrown precaution to the winds when hearing the dulcet persuasions of Kristian's voice.

His entry into manhood had seen the boy develop into a caring and genuinely kind young man. There was no cruelty or belligerence in him. There was no obsession with himself. He had been born to give, not to take.

When they all arrived back at the house and started drinking champagne, Kristian realised that he had never seen his mother look so happy. Whatever had happened in Denmark all those years ago, and he had always known that there was something, seemed to have vanished. His mother seemed so content. It was as if some terrible weight had been lifted from her shoulders. He was not the only one to have noticed the transformation.

Back at the house the small wedding party gathered in the drawing room.

"Look at William and Lise," Bronwyn said to Gwyn, "they both look so happy. And Lise well . . . there's something different about her. Love I suppose. Who'd ever have thought it? I never realised that they were so close."

"Bloody 'ell Bron, you must live in a world of your own. I've seen this comin' for years. Surprised it's taken 'em so long. The way they've always talked to each other, looked at each other – Jesus, even going on holiday together. Housekeeper be buggered, good luck to 'em I say!"

At this precise moment in time it was Gwyn who was living in a world of his own; he failed to notice the way Bronwyn was looking at him. She wasn't the only one that day with adoring eyes but sadly Gwyn didn't notice and never had done.

"Another glass of champagne Bron?"

"No Gwyn, not for me. I'm feeling a bit tiddly as it is."

"Go on girl, enjoy yourself, if you pass out I'll make sure you get to bed safely."

I wish you wouldn't, Bronwyn thought. Get me to bed, yes – but safely, no. She almost blushed at the thought and put it down to the champagne. Gwyn was so handsome though, so manly. She couldn't help having these dirty thoughts from time to time; she was, after all, a young healthy woman. And a pretty one at that – at least if the sly looks and cheeky remarks from the local young men were anything to go by. She was in her early twenties now and had truly blossomed. All the puppy fat had disappeared to leave a sumptuous rounded figure with all the good things in the right place. Many a young man had wanted to get to grips with "That Bron up at the Cliffs."

So far she had refrained from giving in to their ardour; she did though wonder how much longer she could last out. She had her own needs after all and Gwyn just didn't seem interested. Admirers were all very well but none of them were Gwyn. It was so frustrating being around him all day and being unable to show her true feelings. The marriage today had brought all her emotions to a head.

She loved Gwyn and that was that. He was the only man for her.

How could she win him? He never seemed to take her seriously or even acknowledge her attempts at flirtation. Why was the silly man so blind? She was his for the taking. She knew there were no other women in his life – well apart from his mother that is, and she was no competition was she? What was the matter with the man?

"Oh all right then Gwyn, just one more glass." Bronwyn finally demurred. "It is a wedding after all."

"That's my girl."

She decided on a plan as the unsuspecting Gwyn went off to fetch another bottle. As he left the room William called after him.

"Gwyn, is Mr Pritchard still out there messing about in the greenhouse?" Mr Pritchard was the gardener, a wizened old man who was as dry and as wrinkled as the autumn leaves he swept up.

"Yes, Boss."

"Call him in then for a drink. This is a wonderful day and I want to share it. I hear he managed to get locked up last night, drunk and disorderly again – probably dying for a livener right now. Don't take no for an answer, you know what he's like."

"Leave 'im to me Boss, I know 'ow to 'andle the old devil."

"Oh Gwyn," Lise spoke to him this time, "tell that son of mine to hurry up and finish his cigarette – the one you gave him! He's being very rude."

Gwyn looked pained for a moment.

"Er, yes I will er . . . Mrs Tre . . . Lise . . . Oh 'ell, I don't know what to call you now."

Lise and William laughed while Bronwyn felt sorry for her unrequited love. There were times when the most masculine of men could look so childlike.

"Lise, as always Gwyn. Now go and bring that son of mine here, drag him in if you have to!"

"Right then Lise, won't be long."

The rest of the day was spent drinking and laughing. Only two well-wishers called: their solicitor Bernard John, and an old friend of William's. It had been a good day, one of warmth and true friendship. It was the most poignant day Lise had ever experienced. She felt whole again. A woman with a future.

Their lovemaking that night had been unhurried and calm. There was none of the rush and wild enthusiasm of youthful abandon. Their loving was of a more sophisticated, refined character. Gentle whimpers replaced carnal moans and shrieks of passion. The depth of love between them both placed their sexual union on a higher plateau than mere crude lust. During the weeks before their marriage they had thrown moral propriety to the seas outside their bedroom window. They had come to know each other's bodies, each other's likes and dislikes. Lise had wanted to try everything that her imagination could concoct no matter how outrageous. As far as she was concerned there was a lot of time to make up. Before William, her only knowledge of sex had been one of revulsion and pain. William had taught her otherwise. Now her inhibitions were gone, dissipated along with the heavy memories of guilt and horror. Her sexuality had received an explosive awakening, her orgasms leaving her totally drained and weak. She would tremble for minutes after, unable to sense or speak. At first the shock of her sexual enlightenment had almost frightened her. She had even wondered if her enthusiastic enjoyment had been in some way abnormal. After all, women were not meant to enjoy sex were they? Sex was there for the man to enjoy and to propagate the human race. William had reassured her and demolished all her unfounded reservations. His understanding and expertise had encouraged her to absorb and delight herself in the physical act of love so that she now knew that it was the most perfect, and at times awesome, way of expressing her love for the man she had married. When he was inside her she became part of him; she could smother and envelop him with her love. This was the one time when he was hers completely.

William woke first. Instead of getting out of bed immediately as was his normal habit he remained still, moving only his head to look at Lise. It was at these quiet, undisturbed moments that he loved her most. He would savour his wife, gorge himself with her innocent peace. When she slept her face receded into the utmost calm, her lips and eyelids remained so still, and yet an occasional secrecy would seem to move and molest her skin into a picture of the most impossible beauty. The slowness of her sleep allowed all the loveliness in the world to run across her cheeks and chin, making everything else seem so small and insignificant. Sheer wonder crossed lines that William couldn't even contemplate, the perfect face draining all words of any meaning, any force. The wicked demons of the past had been put to rest, shut away in their own fiery tombs. There were times when just looking at her like this would bring tears to his eyes. He had never thought it possible to love someone as much as he loved the woman beside him. He knew now that in the past his heart had only ever entered the outskirts of love, or perhaps once or twice a hinterland – a place that knew little and felt even less, a hard place that mocked the delusion of love with its tears and false promises. He had only ever dallied with love, flirted with it. Like an ice-skater avoiding thin ice and a cold death, he had always skated around the true depths of committed love. He knew about marriage to one woman, he knew about superficial infatuation, but it was only now that he was beginning to recognise the absolute power of a true and uncomplicated love. He had loved his first wife, she was the mother of his children, but his love for her was of a different nature to the love he felt for Lise. There had been none of the intensity that he now felt. The love for his wife had been habitual, necessary almost. There had been little passion. Her death had filled him with regret and sadness but it had not demolished him. It had not left him empty and useless. It had not ruined. He had often explored the character of love and had come to the conclusion that it was a million different things to a million different people. His love for Lise disturbed him in some ways because he knew that one day he would have to leave her. The hourglass of sand would need turning to begin another cycle. His life would end and another would begin. Could there really be anything in the unknown cosmos more heavenly than the woman beside him? Could there be another place more satisfying and happy than the one he occupied next to Lise?

He could never say yes to any of his questions and this would unsettle him.

CHAPTER 14

As Bronwyn sat drinking her tea all she could think about was Gwyn. She felt no guilt at all at the way she had planned to manoeuvre herself into his affections. Such ploys after all were a woman's prerogative. She had wanted Gwyn for a long, agonising time. Temptation by the exercise of her delightful charms had been the only weapon left to her.

The night before and at the end of all the celebrations, she had feigned speechless inebriation. She wasn't used to the bubbly bombshells, she wasn't used to alcohol full stop. The occasional glass of medicinal Guinness and that was it. But Gwyn had continued to persist and 'just one more glass' had turned into a few more glasses. At least that was what Gwyn thought. The truth however was rather different – most of her champagne had gone into Kristian's glass, who seemed over-joyed by the discovery of a never-ending supply of champagne. As the day drew to a close Bronwyn had slurred a request for assistance to her room. The request being aimed directly at Gwyn who was quite happy to oblige, he being the understanding type and fully aware of the frustrations that accompanied a total lack of co-ordination over one's limbs following an abuse of alcohol intake.

When they arrived at Bronwyn's door she decided to slide down the wall next to it.

"Oh, Gwyn, I'm drunk *mun"* She slurred. "Never . . . never ever . . . been like this before. Help me to my bed will you? I'll never make it on my own."

She had then let fly a lascivious giggle and to impress her point had allowed her rump to hit the floorboards with a loud thump.

"Jesus wept Bron!" Gwyn scolded. "Shouldn't drink if you're not used to it *mun*." Mind you, he was a fine one to talk he quickly thought. "Come on, I'll get you to bed. You can sleep it off." With that he hauled her into her room. He laid her gently on the bed and while his arms were firmly secured behind her back, she struck. Faster than any cobra. Gwyn had no chance. Before he knew what was happening his lips were being ravaged. Her legs quickly entwined around him to complete the body lock. He was helpless, a prisoner of flesh and blood.

"Duw Bron, what you doin' *mun*?!" was all Gwyn was able to shout. The next fifteen minutes would have done a knocking shop on a Saturday night proud. Here was lust at its very best, its finest hour. They tore, dug and pummelled each other with a wantonness that would have shamed an audience at the *Folies Bergère.* Bronwyn ate, nibbled and chewed, pinched, squeezed and poked with the ferocity of a wild boar devouring its last meal. When it was over and they were both equally spent, Gwyn in typical fashion got up from the bed, did up his flies and said rather distractedly.

"Thanks Bron, I enjoyed that." He then left the room without so much as a parting kiss.

Post-coital finesse had never been one of his strong points. A man of the earth was Gwyn.

Bronwyn was not in the least bit put out by this display of casual indifference – she had expected it. After he had gone she fell asleep with a self-satisfied smile on her face and knowing full well that Gwyn would be back for more of the same. Wedding bells would follow. A nice white wedding.

On arriving home that night Gwyn headed straight for the bottle of sherry hidden under his bed. He hadn't had much to drink during the evening, preferring to stay sober and thereby avoid making a total fool of himself. Besides, champagne was nothing more than a glorified version of Tizer as far as he was concerned. As it turned out restraint had been just as well; too much drink always affected his sexual performance and Jesus, with that Bron, did he have to be on form. To think that he had gone all this time without knowing what was really on her mind. Make a man happy that one, he concluded as he sat down in his armchair.

"Well, where 'ave you been then?" His mother asked, wrapped up in wool as usual. She had acquired a television now, so world events had aspired to the visual for her. Like the radio before, the television never went off.

"I told you mam, the wedding."

"Take all day did it then? Out with some trollop more like."

"No mam, don't be stupid. There were drinks and food after, you know how it goes."

"I know how it goes with you all right. Plenty of drink and no food."

He didn't answer, refusing to be drawn into another fight with his mother. He felt mellow and content. It had been a good day and one not to be spoiled. He was about to pour himself a drink when he looked at the bottle more closely.

"Mam, you've been at my bloody sherry again!" he bellowed. His mother's increasing deafness was very convenient at times like this.

"Are you listening to me you old witch? You've been thieving my drink. I know 'cos I marked the bottle. Do you 'ear me?" She kept on looking at the TV. It was loud enough to drown her son's shouting with or without impaired hearing.

"Mam, don't act deaf with me!" Gwyn shouted. "I know you can 'ear me." He was beginning to get into a right old state now. The hidden bottle of sherry was his passport to a proper night's sleep; without a few good shots he would be awake most of the night.

"How low can you get *mun!*" he continued, "buy your own will you? You've got plenty of money, more than me anyway you bloody old miser. Been lookin' forward to my couple o' sherries I 'ave before goin' to bed. You know it helps me to sleep."

His mother ignored her outraged son.

"Don't sit there pretendin' you can't hear me! 'Ell, if I rustled a five-pound note in Llanelli you'd hear it quick enough. Jesus you're the only bloody woman I know that can peel an orange in 'er handbag with a bloody boxin' glove on. Mean old bugger that you are. Ach! To 'ell with it. I'm goin' to bed with my sherry. I've 'ad a lovely day and I'm not going to let you spoil it. Goodnight!"

Gwyn stormed upstairs to his bedroom clutching the bottle like some desperate drowning man grasping a rapidly deflating Mae West. Mam continued to watch the television. Thinks ee's the only one entitled to a drink does 'ee? she thought. Well, I'm partial to a drop of sherry myself so bugger the wicked swine.

Tastes even better when ee's paid for it!

CHAPTER 15

Megan sat at the breakfast table smoking her first cigarette of the day. The ash at the end of the cigarette grew longer and longer but she didn't seem to mind. It would drop off eventually and land in some careless place, not an ashtray anyway. She would sometimes watch and wait for the ash to fall or see how many puffs it would take to send it on its way. There was nothing wrong with ash after all, it was so clean and sterile. So inoffensive. She didn't mind the smoke either, it could billow and smell to its heart's content as far as she was concerned. Megan had always found the smoky arms of a cigarette so wonderfully comforting and benevolent. She couldn't imagine a life without her cigarettes.

The passing years had not been kind to Megan. Without make-up she looked like some unkempt psychiatric patient in a mental home. As plumes of smoke tried to reach into every part of her body the hardness of her soul was stripped bare for all to see. Bitterness criss-crossed the skin around her mouth forcing her lips into a permanent sneer of contempt while her once large but unencumbered frame had degenerated into a monstrous temple of disinterested blubber. The elegant silk dressing gown she wore still tried to hold Megan's body together as a final act of loyalty, but its days were numbered and it knew it.

She looked at the newspaper for the umpteenth time and then ground her cigarette into the ashtray; for once she hit the target. Perhaps the anger and determined hatred in the plump hand had something to do with the sudden accuracy.

She looked around the small kitchen. Her face showed only disgust and genuine revulsion at the yellow Formica worktop, tiny cooker and fridge that wasn't large enough to chill a bottle of wine. Not that wine ever had a chance of being put in there anyway. It was too expensive.

She stood up and tore the newspaper into pieces; the news of her father's wedding had come as a shock. How could he?! Her mind raved. A foreign slut with no breeding and a bastard child to add even more insult! Megan had never believed the story of a dead husband.

How could he?

Megan kept asking the question over and over again. Here she was, alone, virtually penniless and shut up in a nauseating little flat in the centre of London. All her jewellery and valuables had been pawned and because her mother's trustees were exercising petty restraints on her spending, she had nothing. At least in Megan's world she had nothing. Even the flat was rented. She had stopped asking her father for financial help since the last time she had seen him, and that was years ago. Her pride would never allow her to suffer the awful humiliation of being belittled again. Neither she nor Hugh had had the wherewithal to recover from financial hardship. They were both idle by nature and used to having everything done for them. Money had always been available merely by flourishing a signature. They simply had no idea how to manage or control it. If it was there, it was spent. If it wasn't, the banks would always oblige. The combined wealth of their backgrounds guaranteed a smiling cooperation from financial institutions. Until, that is, the source of money was cut off. Hugh's family had lost patience just as William had. Megan, not being the loyal type, had divorced her second husband without a moment's hesitation and had then begun the search for a more suitable and wealthy mate. At the very least the unsuspecting victim would have to be able to keep her in the manner to which she was accustomed. Love did not form part of her avaricious equation.

Money came before love every time. After all 'love' was only a figment of some idiot's imagination and not to be taken seriously.

In her quest for the perfect bank she had failed to take into account two extremely important factors. Her age and her looks. Her calculating charm and wizardry with a make-up box had always subdued the effect of her horse-like face. However, time had pursued her like some avenging angel and its power had naturally prevailed. No amount of foundation cream and lipstick could hide the extended profile and cavernous mouth that threatened to devour everything in sight after crushing all signs of life with its formidable set of nicotine-stained teeth.

Megan was a mess, a physical disaster. Her flesh was a cruel warning to all who followed the path of intemperance and gluttony. Megan, of course, didn't quite see it like that. Desperation can often corrupt and annihilate sensible thinking. She was no Phoenix rising from the ashes of her life nor could she ever hope to be. Unfortunately for Megan men were of the same view, so she remained unattached in both the emotional and financial sense.

Her genteel poverty – as she saw it, the fact that her mother's trust fund would have enabled a more modest individual to live perfectly comfortably – fed her obsessive desire for revenge. It was all she could think about. For her, time didn't heal, it merely refined and cultured her ambition to see justice done. She was the first-born and therefore her rights to financial maintenance and inheritance were unassailable. It never occurred to her that maybe, just maybe, she was responsible for her own life and her actions; and that perhaps a job of work would alleviate her difficulties with money and self-support.

She had been educated at the best public schools and had obtained a History degree at Cambridge. Despite her education, she had never felt obliged to actually work; such a pastime was for the lower orders, not for Megan. Anyway, what could she do with a history degree except teach? The prospect of a schoolroom filled with demanding brats was too much to even contemplate. She despised children – it never occurred to her that she had been a child herself once.

When she had finally smoked enough – usually it took at least five cigarettes to wake her up – and finished her third cup of coffee, Megan began the tedious business of getting dressed. Tedious because like most women she never had anything to wear but *unlike* most women this was due to the fact that she could never find any clothes to fit her rolling waves of fleshy indolence.

As she heaved, huffed and puffed her way into a cotton girdle of dubious girth the seeds of a plan began to take shape. Further wriggling and gyrating of her formidable buttocks added substance to her plan and also did the trick where the girdle was concerned.

It was all so simple.

At their first meeting, Lise Jacobson had been far too reticent about her past.

Megan would destroy the bitch and her bastard son.

If her father became a casualty then so be it. He shouldn't have married the slut in the first place.

Griffith Treharne lay in bed absently stroking a rather large nipple. The girl next to him didn't move, she was fast asleep. He didn't know her name, neither did he care. She was just another strumpet to be recruited into his stable of obliging women who would in turn oblige his many but well-to-do customers seeking sexual satisfaction. Griffith had finally found a lucrative and yet undemanding profession – that of pimp extraordinaire.

He reached for the glass of whisky sitting on the bedside table and lit himself a cigarette. It was 9.15 in the morning. His hand shook slightly as he put the glass to his lips; not to worry, the shakes would subside after a couple more drinks. He accepted the fact that he deserved a knighthood for his alcoholism. However, an alcoholic he might be, a drunk he was certainly not. Alcohol had become an essential part of his existence, it was his life's blood. His celestial nectar. He drank heavily and consistently but he never lost control; a true professional and proud of it.

He stared up at the ceiling and wondered what his father would think if he knew that his son had now become a procurer of prostitutes. That was no doubt how his father would describe his corporate deliberations. Griffith preferred pimp, the word was much more succinct and certainly more depraved – depravity after all being his stock in trade as it were. He smiled to himself at the thought of his father's outrage. It would serve the old man right, having cut off both himself and his sister without a penny. Not at all obliging of him. Griffith's wily ways of persuasion had amounted to nothing; neither, come to think of it, had those 'Letters of Introduction". But as usual Griffith found it difficult to actually blame his father or to be even remotely angry with him. As for bearing any kind of filial grudge – well, that was definitely out of the question. The truth of the matter remained; Griffith had asked for it and had deserved all he had got. No question. His cheques had bounced all over London with more frequency than an athlete on a trampoline. He had been thrown out of his club, thrown out of his elegant town house and thrown out of the rarefied circles of a cherished society he had become a part of. Despite all this, his cunning and forced inclination toward the more prurient and exclusive side of personal services ensured his survival.

Griffith did not regard himself as a serious criminal. Apart from receiving two convictions in his student days for urinating in public places, he had a clean record. He knew that the law in its stupidity frowned on his living off immoral earnings, but as far as he was concerned he was merely providing an essential social service. Gentleman needed sex (as indeed did the occasional lady) in order to maintain happy and fulfilling marriages. All Griffith did was facilitate these noble aspirations, and what was so wrong with that?

He had built up a highly respectable 'Companion' agency, for that's exactly what his girls were – 'Companions'. Their friendship was the most erotic in London. Business was always brisk and profitable. He vetted the girls on his books thoroughly, very thoroughly. They were educated, clean, amenable and adventurous. The public-school variety were the best, class with the fingertips of a common whore when required. An admirable combination. His girls were also extremely attractive, both physically and mentally. More than anything else they knew how to keep their mouths shut. They had to. They looked after the best and highest in the land, from Royalty to Law Lords. Griffith's stable was renowned and so it should be. He personally rode all the fillies to make sure they were up to scratch.

All in all Griffith considered himself an unwilling recidivist and nothing more. He had been reduced to crime due to the unstoppable force of circumstances beyond his control. His spineless character and aversion to normal gainful employment of any kind had nothing to do with it. He lived on his wits and to date had done very well out of it. He didn't have to go begging to his father any more or to anybody else for that matter. He often felt that the cutting of his financial lifeline had probably been for the best after all. It had, no matter which way he looked at it, forced him to stand on his own two feet, even if his feet were immersed in a gutter of immorality and debauchery.

He had survived, which was more than could be said for his sister.

Of late Megan had become a nuisance She was forever demanding money from him. She never asked, she ordered. She had always been the stronger, more forceful of the two, and even at his age Griffith still found it difficult to defy his imperious sister.

Unlike Megan, he didn't feel cheated by the way his father had treated them both. He and Megan had been given every opportunity in life, so how could either of them complain? William Treharne had been a good father. It was their own fault that things had turned out the way they had and no one else's.

He finished his whisky, stubbed out the cigarette and got up. It was time to have a bath and get dressed. He had arranged to meet Megan later and he wasn't looking forward to it – neither was his pocket. This would have to be the last time he told himself, it simply couldn't go on. As he walked into the bathroom he tried to count the number of times this useless resolution had crossed his mind and gave up. The same thing invariably happened every New Year's Eve where the drink and cigarettes were concerned.

Megan and Griffith were different in many ways.

Megan was undoubtedly the harder and more intelligent of the two. She was also the most vindictive and concerned only with herself and self-preservation. Life evolved around her, not the other way around. Even as a child, she had always insisted on being at the centre of things. She had been bossy and precocious, always seeking attention. As the first-born, she had always assumed it her right to berate and cajole her two younger siblings to do her will.

Her domineering ways had been more successful with Griffith than her other brother Glyn. Megan had often felt that his early and heroic death had somehow seemed appropriate. Glyn was as near to a perfect human being as one could get. Too perfect to live in fact. As a child he had been blessed with physical perfection and intelligence. He was by far the brightest of the three. He would usually do Megan's bidding but it was always in a way that made her feel that he was simply humouring her, pacifying her like an adult with an irate child. He made her feel inferior by his calm and always correct manner. He never exercised the normal spitefulness of childhood or involved himself in the rivalry for adult approbation. Glyn was above puerile nastiness and competition.

He would often walk away from their games and infantile frustrations to find his own amusement, his own world, Glyn's world. He never seemed to need the companionship of other children, preferring to turn within himself for company. He was often found alone in his bedroom or in the garden reading. Even at a young age Glyn simply didn't need other people; they were, it seemed, a superfluous necessity in his life. Nobody ever really knew what was going on in his mind.

Adulthood struck and nothing changed. Glyn and Megan continued to be distant relatives. He was out there somewhere, but close contact was rare and to be avoided anyway.

There had never been any doubt in Megan's mind that Glyn was the favourite in her parents' eyes. Her father would pay more attention to him than his other children; her mother did likewise but would always attempt to hide her favouritism. It never worked; adults all too often underestimated the perception and understanding of children. Megan's hurt at minor rejection had flared into a cruel jealousy; a jealousy that grew and festered the longer Glyn lived. In everything he did he excelled. Academically he never obtained anything less than distinctions and honours. All those he came into contact with respected and liked him. Women adored him. The black hair, handsome face and huge blue eyes made certain that he was never without a girlfriend. It was so typical that he should have volunteered for the service of his country when war had broken out.

Even his death had not been without honours. A Victoria Cross had been awarded to him posthumously. It had all made Megan sick. Not content with supercilious righteousness in life her brother had managed to obtain all the laurels available even in death. She had decided long ago that her brother simply wasn't human. He was never destined to live. Like Jesus Christ he was simply too good for this world. His death certainly hadn't left any tearful void in her life; if anything, it brought an element of relief, relief from the constant comparison by her father of herself to the nauseating paragon of virtue that was her brother.

Glyn's death did leave a mark on Griffith. His older brother had always been kind to him and tolerant. He had never felt threatened by Glyn's achievements or goodness. As a child Griffith had never taken life too seriously; he certainly wasn't jealous of his brother. He couldn't be bothered with such emotive inconvenience. Griffith would always go wherever life dragged him. An easy life was his only aspiration, which he sought with a passion that would have shocked any of his most inventive and insatiable man pleasers.

Griffith still missed his brother. The safety.

Glyn always knew what to do in a crisis, and Griffith's life had been been one long laborious crisis. He often wondered if it would have turned out differently had Glyn survived the war. Although wonder was as far as his thoughts were prepared to go, anything more demanding disturbed him. Too much thinking was dangerous for Griffith as it usually led to unpleasant truths and conclusions. He preferred his world of abject ignorance – easier to live in and far less troublesome.

Today was all that mattered; the only words from the Bible he could vaguely remember was something about it being sufficient unto the day is the evil thereof and not taking any thought for tomorrow. These were the only scriptural pearls of wisdom that he abided by – the rest was tripe.

"Pull in here please if you would," Griffith asked the taxi driver politely. He was still a gentleman at heart, that was good breeding for you – always apparent no matter what. The taxi stopped outside Scott's restaurant in Mayfair. Trust his sister to pick an expensive restaurant for a 'quick lunch' as if her demanding another 'loan' wasn't enough. One of these new hamburger places would have been quite sufficient. Wimpy's or something they were called. Whatever they were, he had enjoyed the ones he had eaten a week before. They were addictive. He had eaten one then ordered three more, all with fried onions and loaded with tomato ketchup. Only cost a few bob too. Megan was such a bloody snob, an expensive one at that. He could just imagine the look on her face if he had said "Meet you in the Wimpy bar at 1.00 p.m." She probably wouldn't know what he was talking about and assume he was referring to some newly opened American cocktail bar.

The Americans were getting big in London these days; at least their national habits and institutions were. Post-war collateral damage, Griffith called it, God help us! During the war they had nigh on bankrupted us for a few buggered-up ships and supplies – not to mention taking bloody great chunks of our Empire off us – and now they were viewed as saviours of the free world. Bastards! This was one area that did actually inspire a reaction from Griffith – his hatred of Americans. "Never mind the Russians," he was often heard to rant, "it's the bloody Yanks who are after World domination!"

He always made sure American customers paid more for the goods he provided – Griffith looked on this exploitation as well-deserved compensation. They always came back for more too.

He entered the restaurant and spotted Megan by one of the tables nearest the entrance. This would have upset her for a start. She had been used to eating at one of the best tables.

Griffith hadn't seen his sister for quite a while and it showed. The usual groomed and superior demeanour looked a little worn. Hard times were dancing around her body and having a good laugh. Her clothes had lost the tailored look and her face had been given a few extra coats of makeup in a vain attempt to camouflage the wrinkles and lines that age refused to hide. Her double chin was becoming more pronounced too in spite of the cleverly tied scarf keeping it in place.

Megan was not a pleasant sight – she sure as hell wouldn't have ridden into his stable anyway. Naturally he failed to notice his own bulging suit and alcohol abused face. Physically there was not much between them. They were two of a kind.

"Hello, Megan, have you ordered yet?" He asked as he sat down opposite her.

"No, that would be stupid. Punctuality has never been one of your virtues – not that there are any others that immediately spring to mind either, although I have to say I'm surprised you even bothered to turn up."

"Your usual civil self I note." Griffith replied, ignoring the insults, he was used to them. "Anyway, how have you been?"

"Fine, just bloody fine. How the hell do you think I've been? No money to speak of, no decent clothes. I even have to get my make-up from Boots for God's sake."

"Dear oh dear Megan, it's a hard life isn't it? We all have our crosses to bear I suppose."

"Don't be sarcastic, Griffith, it doesn't become you. Besides you neither have the wit nor the intelligence to make it effective."

"Ah well, never mind Megan. Can't all have razor-sharp intellects like you, can we now? The world would be a boring place if that were the case wouldn't it?"

"Oh, do shut up!" Megan was definitely in a bad humour. Griffith always enjoyed antagonising her. It was his means of revenge for all the years of nasty, hurtful remarks. It was even sweeter now because she needed him. Not the other way around. She seemed quite desperate and this pleased him. He would take full advantage of the situation and wallow in every second of it.

They ordered their food. As usual Megan insisted on the best and most expensive items on the menu. She never asked if Griffith was willing to pay, but just assumed this would be the case. In her world men always paid. A handbag was for decoration only. For Megan money was a vulgar necessity; even in her present, financially distressed state she held on to her unreasonable principles. She would never learn; she was far too stubborn.

A huge plate of beef and Yorkshire pudding arrived. Scott's was famous for traditional English fare.

As Megan laid into her food with a ferocity that would have shamed a jackal, Griffith picked at his. Surprisingly he was not a great eater despite his considerable girth. A slow metabolism and far too much alcohol were responsible for his overweight bulk, not food. He watched his sister gorge herself, not bothering to hide the disgust on his face. He felt like a visitor in London Zoo at feeding time. He was going to really enjoy making life difficult for her. He had noticed a greater urgency in her this time; there was also more anger than usual. He remembered her phone call a few days ago. It had been almost desperate; her voice had been strained. Temper. He knew his sister. She had refused to discuss anything over the phone.

He carried on picking at the roast beef, knowing that Megan would get around to the purpose of their meeting soon enough. As with most things, even a crisis, for her, food came first. It was her reason for living. When she had finished off a double portion of apple pie with extra cream she was ready for business.

The coffee arrived and Griffith waited for the demands of money. She hadn't said a word during the meal and even now, as she took her first sip of coffee, she remained silent, thoughtful. Megan's silence always meant danger.

At last she spoke.

"Have you read the newspapers lately? No, on second thoughts that was a stupid question. You never read, well apart from the *Beano* now and again"

Megan was certainly on form.

"Daddy has remarried. To that Jacobson woman." She stared at Griffith. Waiting. Waiting for howls of indignation that never came. He remained still and said nothing.

"Did you hear what I just said, you fool? Daddy has married that Danish woman!" Her voice was rising now, the bitterness and contempt ever more apparent.

"Don't just sit there like a lemon, you moron! Daddy's married that young slut, he's years older than her for God's sake! Griffith, it's disgusting, obscene. He's an old man! People will be laughing at him all over Wales. What will it do to our name? We'll be a laughing stock!"

Her brother stared at her and said calmly, "So what?" His indifference detonated the bomb waiting to explode.

"So what!? So what!? You imbecile, don't you realise what this means? As his wife she and her son can inherit all the property and money. We'll be left destitute."

Griffith interrupted. "You might be, my dear sister, but I certainly won't. I could retire now if I wanted to." He was enjoying himself; the lunch had turned out better than expected. Watching Megan get into such a state was a joyous experience. Couldn't be doing her digestion much good either. She was beside herself with hatred, possessed even. He could see all this on her face. It made him shudder. The blackness of her soul and heart was there for all to see. Her poisoned spirit couldn't be hidden by clothes or even mounds of over-indulged fat.

Megan went quiet for a moment before starting to spit her words across the table. "You don't care, do you Griffith? You really don't care. Our birthright is being taken away from us, our good name. Mummy's memory is being corrupted and maligned – and you really don't give a damn, do you? Do you ever take anything in life seriously?"

"Megan, I really don't care what the old man does – with his love life or his money. God knows I've had enough money off him over the years. You haven't done so badly yourself either have you? Lise seemed a nice enough woman to me. Let the old boy have a bit of happiness in his old age. So what? I quite admire him really, must take a bit of doing at his age to keep a young woman happy between the sheets. Probably kill him in the end, but then that's one hell of a way to go. Heart attack whilst on the job, bloody marvellous!"

"Griffith, that's so typical of you. Everything is just one big joke for you isn't it? How would Mummy feel if she was still alive?"

"For heavens sake, Megan, stop bringing our mother into this. She's six foot under and probably wouldn't care less anyway as long as Dad was happy. You're using Mum and 'family name' as an excuse for your own greed. All you care about is money. You're broke and you need it, simple as that. Dad's getting married has just put your mercenary nose out of joint. Now you listen to me." Griffith's newfound financial independence was giving him strength and courage. Fear of his sister's dominance was rapidly ebbing away. "Dad is happy. He deserves it. You know how he grieved after Mum died. Took him bloody years to get over it, even I could see that. He gave everything to us, when did we ever go without? Don't forget either, Glyn's death nearly killed him. Jesus Megan, he's had enough tragedy in his life. Leave him alone, he's entitled to happiness like everybody else and he probably hasn't got long to go either. You're bitter Megan, and it shows on your face. For all your sophistication and worldly ways you still can't see that any bitterness we harbour in our hearts eventually poisons and perverts the rest of our bodies. Leave them alone; Lise and the child have done nothing to you. Don't be so cruel."

"Jesus Christ, Griffith! How very noble you've become!" Megan was angrier now than before. "Just listen to it. Since when have you become such a bloody saint?"

"Perhaps Megan, I've just finally grown up," he answered quietly.

"Well, that will be one of life's great mysteries won't it? Born again or something ridiculous like that are we? You make me sick. You sit there lecturing me on moral turpitude and when you leave here you'll be arranging orgies for well-healed old Yanks who can't get it up. God, you're a fucking joke, you know that?"

"Maybe I am, Megan. Life is one big joke after all. 'As flies to wanton schoolboys are we . . .' and all that."

"Dear God, am I hearing things? You must be drunk! When the hell did you start developing an appreciation of Shakespearean pathos! You probably don't even know which play the words are from. Got that little gem of erudition off a box of Bryant & May matches did we?"

"King Lear actually, not that it matters. Look, I don't have to sit here listening to your insults Megan. I'm off. I've had enough of you, you're giving me indigestion. I'll see to the bill on my way out." Megan looked panicked for a moment as Griffith stood up.

"Griffith, don't go . . ." she said in a softer voice, ". . . not for a minute anyway." The charm of days gone by had suddenly returned. "We must talk, Griffith. We really must. We have to do something to safeguard our inheritance don't you see? Be reasonable."

"All I see Megan is your greed. You have a decent enough allowance, which, I hasten to add, is generously supplemented by myself. Why can't you live within your means, get a job or something, it wouldn't kill you. Spend on things you can afford, not things you want."

"I don't believe I am hearing this!" The charm act didn't last for long, it never did. "Since when were you the thrifty, careful housekeeper? Now you really are being stupid! People like me – and even you for that matter – simply are not meant to work, it's as simple as that. On the other hand I suppose I could become your pimping partner."

"Thank you for the offer but the clients might think you were the goods on offer. That wouldn't do at all. Dear God I'd be out of business within the week!"

"Very amusing I'm sure. You really are becoming quite spirited Griffith, aren't you? Pimping must suit you."

"Megan, I'm not going to sit here exchanging childish insults with you. Know this though, that whatever evil little plan you have up your sleeve I won't have any part of it. I'm quite happy as I am. The old man's wife has done nothing to me, so why should I care or why should I want to hurt her? Good luck to them both."

"Very well," Megan said resignedly, "if that's what you want, there's nothing more to say is there?"

"No Megan, there isn't. Now if you don't mind I'm going."

"Hold on will you, there was another matter I wanted to discuss with you."

I bet there is Griffith thought. Her voice was visiting the past again – the tone was gentler, more humble. He looked at his sister and the eyes that begged and pleaded all at the same time. He was all she had. He couldn't turn away. He never could.

"I'll send you some cash in the post over the next day or so. Now I have an appointment, I have to go. I'll see you soon. Goodbye."

Megan watched his back move to the entrance. What's happened to him? she thought. Normally he agreed with everything she said. He had actually fought back, seemed sincere too and sincerity was not one of her brother's strong points. It was obvious now that she couldn't rely on Griffith for support of her plan. His own opinions aside he would make an untrustworthy ally; his loyalty was questionable. The destruction of her father's new wife and son would have to be carried out by she alone. It was just as well, she could only trust herself to do it properly.

Her plan would require money to execute. The allowance she received from her mother's trust fund would be enough to enable her to travel if she needed to, providing she cut back on a few things for a few months. This would be difficult though, her food, drinks and cigarettes were essential to the business of living and so were the weekly outings to good restaurants. The car was a constant drain on her resources so that would probably have to go too. She would have to suffer real poverty for a while but the benefits outweighed the hardship. She was determined to put her plan into action; nothing and no one was going to stand in her way. If she had to go to Denmark itself, then so be it.

Griffith arrived back at the flat he had bought outright with his own money. Situated overlooking Hyde Park, he was a short distance from the West End and near to London's main concentration of entertainment. It was convenient. He had employed one of his girls to do the furnishing and decorating, having accepted the fact that when it came to tasteful décor he was utterly useless.

The girl in question was one of his best. Malvern Ladies College educated, aristocratic family and a body that could run up a flag on even the most reluctant of erections. With her help he had managed to create an elegant and salubrious home for himself.

He walked into the sitting room, and after pouring himself a whisky sat down in one of the leather armchairs. The room always soothed. Zoe had hunted around numerous bookshops to fill some of the walls with books that would imply discreet learning on the part of their owner. Megan was at least right about something: he never read. Not since being expelled from school anyway, but he had gained a smattering of the classics whilst being incarcerated there. To compensate for his cultural inadequacies he did have a fine public-school accent which automatically verified his learning or lack of it, as the case may be. The floors were covered with antique Persian rugs – some of his father had rubbed off – bringing to an otherwise dour and masculine room a touch of colour. Zoe had selected prints and pictures on various subjects to decorate the rest of the room. Some of them were obscene in their eroticism but the various sexual acts on display seemed to mingle well with the Euro-Asiatic character of the room. The main conversation piece squawked every now and again at the offending and outrageously sized penises jutting up and out from various locations in the room.

'He' was a black minor bird who had been trained to say 'Fuck off!' every time somebody walked into the room. The bird made no distinction between class, colour or gender. He treated every human being with equal contempt and Griffith loved him. 'Hotspur', as he had been christened, would insult with impunity and provided his master with never-ending amusement.

Finishing a cigarette, Griffith played a Billie Holiday record in an attempt to calm his anxiety. The Lady's voice electrified the room. It was subversive, rebellious. No wonder so many would-be jazz singers tried to copy her, Griffith thought. She reminded him of Megan. Neither could handle money or men. There was no doubt his sister was up to something and that only trouble would come of it. He knew her only too well and he also knew how hateful she could be. If Megan could somehow hurt his father and stepmother she would, of that he was certain.

"Stepmother," he said aloud to himself, "Hell, I'm older than she is!"

Griffith was no philanthropist, but neither was he a nefarious individual who went out of his way to hurt others. He would readily admit to naivety and shallowness and he was sometimes remarkably stupid and insensitive to the feelings of others, a fault again without any basis where genuine intent was concerned. And if he was careless, negligent even, it was not because of any inherent tendency toward malice.

Middle age was bringing new and hitherto unknown dimensions to his thoughts. His mortality. Only that morning he had been told about a friend's sudden death. The man had been the same age as Griffith. They had avoided blackboard dusters together. He remembered the man's smile, his innocent giggles. He remembered the friendship. The knowing. He looked at a mirror facing him and was strong enough to see the flaws.

As he drank his glass of whisky an overwhelming desire came upon him to put things right with his father. They hadn't spoken with one another for some years and Griffith decided that the time had come to end this sad state of affairs. After all, what had his father really done to him? Nothing, except teach him to be independent and to stand on his own two feet. If anything, he should thank his father, not hate him. What would he have done with a son like himself? Probably exactly the same thing.

It was time to make his peace with his father; to do something decent in his life for a change. He would go to Swansea to see his father and Lise and also to warn them about Megan.

CHAPTER 16

Griffith drove his 3.8 Jaguar through the winding roads of Gower with surprising skill and nerve. For an oversized 'moron' his control of the car would have allowed him to compete at any of the great racing circuits of Europe. He was proud of his driving prowess. Behind the wheel he found his elusive self-respect. He liked himself. He liked the car too. It made him feel that he had achieved something in his otherwise wasteful life. The smell of tanned leather upholstery always gave him a feeling of well-being, of stability. He had chosen the bright red colour so that all could see the fruits of his success. It was also symbol of his self-reliance; the Jaguar had not been inherited or given.

He was not an ostentatious man by nature – he had always been taught that a crude display of wealth was an outrageous example of vulgarity. He could never bring himself to wear an outlandish sovereign ring or a gold bracelet. These things were the stuff of fairgrounds. An expensive wafer-thin watch and gold stud cufflinks were his only concession to bejewelled extravagance.

Griffith was a product of privilege; not all the alcohol or food in the world could ever diminish it. This gift from his father was priceless. It ensured survival. Griffith, unlike his sister, at least remained semiconscious of the fact.

He was feeling a little nervous at meeting his father for the first time in some years. Over the past two months he had made a supreme effort to improve his physical appearance. He had lost some of his excess weight and cut down on the alcohol and cigarettes. He dearly wanted to make a good impression on his father, but more importantly he wanted to prove to him that he could be a success with or without his help. The fact that his wealth had been nurtured from the impatient loins of male kind was irrelevant. He had made it. The money accumulated had been wisely invested and would ensure financial security for the rest of his life. To Griffith, the absolute beauty of being wealthy was the freedom it gave. The material gains were neither here nor there; possessions were only important for the length of time they amused, otherwise they were worthless when compared to the power of independence from others and total liberty that money allowed.

Griffith could stick two fingers up at the world and get away with it.

He was beholden to no one and answerable only to himself.

Despite this island mentality he wanted to be reconciled with his father. He had always loved him, even though he knew that Glyn had always been the favourite. In fairness to his father there had never been any overt displays of favouritism towards his elder son, but Griffith had always known it existed. His father had never been able to hide the difference in his eyes when look-ing at Glyn or the slight changes in tone of voice when speaking to him. Griffith had never been made to feel that he was second best. It was just there – not that he was ever particularly bothered by it; being slightly on the spineless side he was quite happy to let Glyn receive all the attention and laurels. His attitude was one of 'anything for a quiet life'.

Still was.

He pulled into the forecourt of the Cliffs and got out of the car. When he had telephoned the week before, the conversation had been brief but polite. His father had been guarded. As he stretched his legs a voice from behind him said, "Hello, Griffith." He turned around and saw his father standing by a rose bush. The scruffy clothes and battered hat distracted Griffith for a moment. He thought it was a gardener being polite, although using his Christian name was a bit off. He squinted at his father just to be sure then said, "Good God, Dad. I didn't recognise you for a moment." William walked up to his son removing one of his gloves as he did so. The two shook hands and looked at one another for a moment.

There were no hugs or kisses, no dramatic gestures, no words. In that brief moment of physical contact both men knew that the time had come to let the past die. They both wished to be father and son again.

At last William smiled and released his son's hand.

"Well, well. If the car is anything to go by you must be doing quite well. It's not on Hire Purchase is it?" Griffith laughed in reply, glad that his father had broken the ice with his typical caustic sense of humour.

"That's typical of you Dad, you haven't changed a bit have you? Suspicious as ever! As it so happens it isn't on HP. Bought it cash, on the nose, brand new out of the showroom." William poked his head inside the car, the interior redolent of aromatic leather and burnished walnut. He was not entirely convinced of his son's so-called 'cash' purchase; still, as Lise had said, people change. Who knows?

"Do you want to have a drive, Dad?"

"You know I haven't driven a car for years, boy. This monster looks a bit too fast for me. Another time maybe. Come on in and say hello to Lise."

They found Lise sitting in the gardens enjoying the sun. Griffith noted that the last few years had been extremely kind to her. She must be in her early thirties, he thought, and yet she still managed to look much younger. She could have been his father's granddaughter never mind daughter. She really was a joy to look at. She still wore little makeup and yet her lips were red and full. The summer sun had accentuated her tanned Scandinavian skin to a rich dark colour, making her hair look even more yellow and natural. By God, he thought, what he could charge for her services! She stood up from her chair and came to greet him.

"Hello, Griffith, it's good to see you again after all this time." She held out her hand and smiled. Griffith ignored the hand and instead held her shoulders and kissed her on the cheek. God, she even smelled good.

"Yes, I am sorry Lise, but then you know what families are like." She didn't really but said nothing. "I'm also busy these days. It's difficult to get away."

"Never mind, have a seat. Would you like some tea or coffee?" He could have killed a cold Campari but resisted the urge.

"A cup of tea will be fine, thank you."

Lise went off to the house and Griffith admired the elegant walk and mouth-watering figure.

"She is beautiful Dad, seems to have a kind nature too. I'm happy for you both, I really am." And he meant it. He was perfectly able to appreciate a handsome woman without having to genuinely desire her. She was his stepmother after all, and even Griffith sometimes maintained a sense of propriety.

"Yes, I am lucky Griffith and I know it, believe me. Sometimes I wonder what the hell she sees in me but there's no accounting for the female mind is there?"

"No, indeed not Dad. Oh, I forgot, I have a wedding present for you both in the car. Bit late I know but there we are. Do you want it now?"

"No, leave it for a minute. Give it to us both after dinner or something. It's very thoughtful of you."

"My pleasure. I just hope Lise will like it and you of course." William was beginning to be utterly amazed by the transformation of his son. He was actually behaving in a civilised manner – he was even drinking tea! Unthinkable. What the hell was going on, no one could change this much. He would have to dig a little to find out the truth. His son was just too good to be true and he had even lost weight.

William acknowledged that Griffith had never been particularly vindictive or malevolent. Although stupid in the extreme on occasions he had always possessed a degree of animal cunning and a penchant for survival, but he was basically a good man who had managed somehow to wander off the beaten track.

He determined to discover how genuine his new son was.

"Griffith, do you mind if I be frank with you for a moment?"

"Not at all Dad, fire away."

"What is the real purpose of your visit? I can't help saying that I'm simply not completely convinced of your sincerity, so perhaps you could throw some light on this. You must know that your past record makes me believe that you're after something. Is it money?"

Griffith didn't feel offended in any way by his father's question. In fact, he respected the old man for being direct and to the point.

"Dad, look I know I've been a total fool in the past. I'm the first to admit it but I had my reasons. Mark you, I'm still quite capable of being an idiot from time to time. I'm certainly no paragon of virtue, you know that and so do I. However, I've never wished you harm or unhappiness and I have, despite what you think, always loved you. I'm not here to scrounge or to ask for money, believe me. I'm quite well off thanks."

"What is it that you do exactly?" his father asked. Griffith had prepared himself for this question. His father went on, "You do seem rather affluent what with the car and the tailored clothes. Even I can tell a Savile Row suit when I see one, and hand-made shoes."

"Well that's probably where I get it from then, isn't it?" Griffith laughed, trying to distract his father from too detailed an investigation into his career. "Anyway, as for my status in life as it were, a couple of years ago I started a company that specialises in corporate entertaining."

"Corporate entertaining? What is that when it's at home?" William had never heard of it.

"Don't be daft Dad, you do it all the time, or at least used to."

"Did I? Do explain, I'm intrigued."

"Right then, let's say you have a particular product that you are trying to sell to various companies or customers. They come to London or wherever to discuss the terms and conditions of the contract. Obviously you want to impress them and make them happy. You want them to buy. So you soften them up a bit if you like. Well, all I do is arrange to make their stay as enjoyable as possible. I arrange transport from airports and so on. Make sure they stay in good hotels and have plenty of entertainment. I just make sure they're kept happy."

"And companies presumably pay you a sort of commission for these services?"

"Not quite. I charge a fee but my clients have the benefit of knowing that their clients are being well looked after and will arrive at any crucial meetings in a reasonable frame of mind – a . . . er . . . pliable frame of mind if you like. A mind that wants to buy."

"You could say then that it is a form of bribery, a subtle form I grant you." There was a note of suspicion in Williams voice.

"Yes, you could call it that I suppose, but really it's no different to handing out bottles of whisky to customers at Christmas or taking them out for lunch. It's just goodwill on a larger scale. From what my own clients tell me, it works well. For instance, if possible I can arrange for the punters to do well at a casino or at the races, nothing illegal mark you, my customers just pay any losses, the Arabs in particular are keen gamblers. Everybody's happy. Their oil fields can afford it! Business is going international Dad, commercial isolation is old hat. Europe is opening up, markets are becoming global."

William was having trouble taking all this in. What on earth had happened to his son? Good God, the boy was showing some commercial astuteness. He would never have believed it!

"Well, I must say you seem to have done well out of it. Do you still have a debt problem?"

"No, thank God. I don't owe a penny to anyone. Not even a mortgage. Life is good."

His son wasn't lying. William knew that, which made this sudden transformation even more shocking.

"I'm glad to hear it Griffith, I'm happy that you've finally managed to bring some semblance of order to your life, I really am. I'm quite proud of you in a grudging sort of way."

"Don't overdo it now, will you Dad?"

"Don't be sarcastic, that's my territory. No, I'm delighted you have made something of yourself. Well done." William meant it.

"Thanks Dad." Griffith smiled. He had at last achieved his father's approbation – he was surprised at how easy it had been. It now seemed an appropriate time to broach the main reason for his visit.

"Dad, there is something I need to talk to you about."

"Sounds ominous. I knew there had to be some ulterior motive for your visit."

"Now now Dad. Wait a minute before you jump to conclusions. Look, I'll come straight to the point. Megan is upset about your marriage to Lise."

"Is she now? And you?"

"God Dad, if I felt anything like that I wouldn't be here would I? I think Lise is lovely. She makes you happy and it's obvious to anyone that you love each other dearly. I'm very pleased for you I really am. It's because of that that I've come to warn you."

"Warn me? Warn me about what?"

"Dad, Megan is very bitter. She's obsessed with hatred toward Lise. She sees her as an enemy."

"But why for heaven's sake? Lise has done nothing to her."

"You know what Megan's like."

"Sadly I do." William thought for a moment as regret and contrition tried to outdo each other. "I don't suppose you surprise me in any way."

"She sees Lise and Kristian as a threat to her inheritance, her good name and all that crap," said Griffith, quickly adding, "Excuse the language." It was all right for the old man to swear like a drunken navvy on a Friday night but not his children.

"Idiot girl, what's the matter with her? She'll be taken care of, she is my daughter after all. Anyway what is she doing now, how is she?" William quickly changed the subject for some unknown reason. "I don't think I've spoken to her since she left here with her husband some years ago."

"She's fine. Although I have to say that she looks somewhat worn. Megan without substantial sums of money is rather like spotted dick without the custard. Dry and pretty damned tasteless."

"You still have a quaint way with words, Griffith. When you put your mind to it anyway. Megan still receives a reasonable allowance, certainly enough to live comfortably on."

"I know that Dad. But Megan likes the finer things in life. Fast cars, fast men and fast food. You know what she's like. She would never entertain cooking for herself when there's some fancy French restaurant around the corner. Likes her smokes and booze too."

"Booze? She never used to drink much. Not to excess anyway."

"She does now, believe me. Her 'solace' she calls it. I thought I was bad but Megan is drinking her way into serious problems."

"What about her husband? He seemed a quiet, unassuming sort of fellow."

"That's all over. He finally found the courage to leave her. She made his life a misery I can tell you. Poor devil lost any personality he had ever managed to culture – which wasn't much I grant you, but even he got fed up. The last straw apparently was when Megan smashed a full bottle of vodka over his head. The lost vodka made her even madder so she pushed an ashtray into his face. I saw him a few days later. Stitches everywhere. She was lucky not to have been charged by the police."

"Are you serious, Griffith?" William couldn't believe what he was hearing.

"Very. You know what drink is like. Makes some people violent, others mellow. Thank God I'm in the latter category. Megan is aggressive by nature; add a pint of vodka and even Molotov would be impressed by her volatility."

"Is she doing anything with her life? Working?"

"Working? Come off it Dad! The only physical exertion Megan has ever experienced was filling her nappies when she was a baby. No, you can definitely forget any thoughts along those lines. Megan is one of life's beautiful people; she coasts along in a world of her own making and fantasy.

"I still don't see why you feel you have to warn me." So William hadn't ignored the warning after all.

"Dad, Megan can be vindictive. I just have a feeling that she's up to something. I don't know what but I do know my sister. She will do everything in her power to harm the relationship between you and Lise. That's all I can tell you really. She's up to no good. Of that I am certain."

"I appreciate your concern Griffith, but what can she do?" At that moment a thought struck him with a force that made his stomach turn. He quickly composed himself.

"Well, if she wants to behave in this way there's not much I can do about it. Leave me her address and telephone number. I'll get in touch with her and find out what's the matter. Nothing else I can do. What the hell is wrong with her?"

"I don't know Dad, I really don't."

"Thank you anyway. One thing I can tell you though. If anyone hurts my wife or Kristian, God help them, and even His help might not be enough. Now then, let's go back into the house. We've made some improvements since you were last here."

"I can see that. The gardens are really quite something, you must have worked hard."

"Yes, the rose garden in particular is my pride and joy. It gives me endless hours of peace; allows me to lose myself in thought and retrospection – age does that and before you start laughing it will come to you one day. It's almost like going on a pilgrimage each time I go in there, and do you know, I never get bored with it. That's the wonderful power of nature, its inherent beauty rarely stays the same. It's always changing, always going through a process of metamorphosis. It's nature that almost convinces me that there must be a God, as who else could create in such a way? Man certainly couldn't, too much evil and corruption in us, too great an appetite for destruction . . . I'm rambling now, see what I mean, old age again. Come on I'll take you to see it, I feel like boring someone to tears for a bit. No doubt Lise gets fed up with being a victim, so you can take over for a while and see some of my attempts at cross-pollination. I'm really quite proud of the results."

Griffith followed his father.

At long last peace had been achieved between them both.

CHAPTER 17

Megan and a man who seemed to make the best out of his limited wardrobe were sitting at a table in a small café just off the King's Road in Chelsea.

The man's face was a mixture of opaque blankness and Chinese conundrum; he had had seen it all before, done it all before. He knew so well the lurid sewers of human kind. For him, human beings were not fascinating – they were simple, fickle and no better than the animals they so often despised, despite their so-called power of reason. His cynicism and jaded opinion of people was clear now in the expression on his face as Megan, a client, began to make his morning unpleasant.

"Is this it?" she asked with a well-practised sneer of derision as she pointed at the flimsy blue file sitting on the table in front of her.

"Yes, I am afraid so. Without having to actually go to the country of origin itself, that's all I've been able to acquire. Birth certificates, etc. are all obviously to be found in the Danish registries. Further information would require discreet questioning of other family members and friends both in Wales and Denmark."

"But there's nothing here to speak of – nothing of any help anyway. You're supposed to earn your money, you know."

"Madam, if you remember . . ." The private investigator disliked this woman intensely; her manner was offensive and insulting." You only retained my services on the basis of a preliminary enquiry," he continued. "That I have done to the best of my ability bearing in mind the scant number of facts you gave me."

"Dear God, all I have here is her place of birth and a bit about her businessman father who apparently died by drowning. Couldn't you have found out anything more?"

"If you mean anything more incriminating, then the answer must be no. Apart from the fact that there were questions over her father's death, a possible suicide, I discovered nothing untoward. It's all there in the file. As I have already said, in order to discover more information I will have to do some travelling. This I cannot do without your authority as it will be expensive."

"It would be, wouldn't it? I'm surprised you have the nerve to charge anything for this." She waved the file in the man's face. He had met all sorts in his line of work and wasn't easily intimidated. He did need the work however and the money.

"Do you want me to continue?"

"No, I certainly do not. Just send me your bill," Megan ordered.

"I would prefer to be paid now if you don't mind madam, and in cash." The man knew Megan's type – rich woman fallen on hard times. Hadn't lost the arrogance but couldn't afford it either. They usually used chequebooks issued by merchant banks – impressive, although the cheques weren't worth the posh paper they were written on.

"Cash! What do you mean cash? I never pay anything in cash. That form of payment is for those people who can't afford bank accounts." Megan took a chequebook out of her handbag. It was one courtesy of Coutt's Bank as expected.

She started writing.

"How much?"

"I said madam that I prefer cash. £30 in notes."

"And I said that I don't pay cash!"

"That's a pity then isn't it? I shall just have to write to your father for payment won't I? I'm sure he will oblige; a wealthy man I understand." He always made it a rule to check out his clients as rigorously as he did their requests.

"What? How do you know my father you obnoxious little man?" The man was far from little. He was huge, with hands like shovels, strangling hands. He stood up and leaned forward. His tone was non-negotiable. It grated with menace.

"Up until now madam, I have been polite. My manners though are inclined to get neglected when clients refuse to pay for my services. Now the money please, for the last time."

Megan, like most people who bully and shout a great deal, was basically a coward. She looked up at the man and for once knew her place. She rummaged around in her handbag for a second time and produced a wad of notes. She counted some out then handed the money to the man.

"Now away with you, you horrible little man. I don't want to see you again."

"Have no fear madam, in future and having met you I will be more discriminating when deciding whom I work for. Good luck with your investigation."

He threw a half-crown coin on the table saying, "For the coffees," and then left.

Megan ordered another coffee and wondered what to do next. She couldn't afford private investigators, that was certain. She would have to rely on her own devices and that's all there was to it. She looked at the file the man had left. The information in it told her of Lise Jacobson's birthplace and a brief history of her family background. Megan was surprised to learn that Lise was half Welsh.

In some ways the fact partly explained her appearance in Wales. To most people it would have seemed quite natural for the Welsh mother and daughter to return to Wales after the war. The file also told Megan of the father's lapse into bankruptcy and death, yet more good reason for the return to Wales. None of this however seemed right to Megan. Her obsession with the fact that there was something sinister in Lise's background wouldn't go away. There was no mention in the file of any marriage by Lise or the father of Kristian. It was odd, all of it.

The man had said that a detailed search needed to be made in Denmark to discover the true facts about Lise's so-called marriage and son. There was nothing else for it. Megan would have to go to Denmark herself, more precisely the small town of

Randers, Lise's birthplace, a possibility that had already been considered. Her car and some jewellery had been sold in anticipation of such a necessity. The private investigator had given her a location and this was all she needed. She was smart enough to work out the rest for herself. Without knowing it the horrible little man had given her a new lease of life. A reason for living. Hope even. Her thirst for revenge was insatiable. Her malice blinded her to the fact that sometimes those who plot the destruction of others often end up destroying themselves, but she was determined to enlighten her father about the poisonous viper he had taken into his bosom, and that was that. Megan would save him from the money-grabbing whore and her bastard son if it killed her. Denmark was the lock, Randers the key.

Megan paid the bill and left the coffee shop. She actually smiled at the waitress taking her money – her good spirits did not extend to a handsome tip though, in fact she gave no tip at all. Megan didn't believe in such gratuities. People should work for their money. She was not a charity after all. It was a servants place to be grateful not hers!

CHAPTER 18

Megan tended to avoid trains or any other form of public transport for that matter.

She hated being squeezed against unknown people and having to mix with the 'rabble' or the 'swinish multitude' as she called them. And if it was raining, dear God look out, the stench of wet peasant could truly overwhelm. It really was intolerable! Flying would have been her chosen mode of transport; these new jet aircraft took hours off an otherwise tedious journey. Unfortunately, financial considerations had forced her into the inconvenient world of mediocrity. The ferry from Harwich to Ejsberg had been comfortable enough she had to admit, but the trip had been long and dull. The train journey to Randers took her through countryside that seemed to be lost in a hiatus of bland indifference

She looked out of the carriage window.

Nothing.

No life.

No movement of sea or green mountain falling to the back of the train.

Megan had been brought up in Wales – a place where nature had abused its creativity. Its power to subdue. Yet it had retained a humility in its colour. A grace. A heart of warmth and benevolence. The land that now crossed her simmering eyes forbade and punished. There was only pleasure in its ability to offend. To affront. All that could be seen was Nature's neglect and an occasional brick or tree protruding from a veil of empty space. The whole landscape had been dusted and polished. It was violently clean and flat. Sterile.

The Danes were proud of their cleanliness, but as with all things 'clean' there was no humanity. The train compartment sparkled with blister upon blister of scrubbing hand and searching fingertip. There wasn't a single child's nose smudge on the windows nor a worthy excuse for debris anywhere to be found. There were no odours of life. No perspiration, no perfume, no stale and crusty underwear. Spring arrived every day at the stations too. Even a discarded cigarette butt didn't enjoy its freedom for long.

The Danes celebrated their spotless stations and spotlessly flat countryside.

They humoured the lack of chaos. It was safe.

Megan had no idea what Randers was like. Whether it was a city, a town or even a village. It was somewhere on the map and that's all she knew.

She was not a keen traveller and disliked anything foreign. She harboured the classic prejudices of Anglo-Saxon xenophobia toward all foreigners and anything foreign. God forbid that she should try and learn any language other than English. She still believed in the Empire and the fawning servitude of all those unfortunate souls who were not English, and plenty who were.

Megan had never considered herself to be Welsh. Indeed she was positively ashamed of her true antecedents. Her Celtic origins were kept secret from those who knew her. She had never forgotten the schoolgirl mocking of her barbaric Welsh accent and birthplace. At school she had made a supreme effort to annihilate any traces, however remote, of 'Welshness'. She had succeeded too, although the offending vegetable monopolising her mouth was more the size of a marrow than a potato. Her overstated airs and graces would have made Oscar Wilde titter in spite of the misery of Reading Gaol. Megan was not proud to be Welsh and was frequently astonished as to how anyone could be. What was so special about being Welsh anyway? It was all utterly beyond her. Her countrymen with their black faces, unintelligible speech and pitiful singing were an embarrassment and nothing more. As far as she was concerned the less said about them the better – they could die from leek poisoning or choke on their rugby balls for all she cared. Woollyback land was definitely not for her and neither, judging from her brief encounter so far, was Denmark. Why couldn't the people speak English? Why couldn't they speak properly? As bad as the damned Welsh! What kind of language was Danish anyway? It was nearly as incomprehensible as bloody Welsh.

As the train pulled into Randers station all Megan could mutter was "bloody foreigners." Her words were so completely English that no observer, even of the casual kind, could have doubted her adopted nationality. Had Gwyn been there to meet her he would probably have said "stupid cow" and tipped a plate of laverbread over her head.

She took a taxi to a small hotel just around the corner from the station. She was a great believer in making physical movement as economical as possible.

When the driver asked for his fare she just stared at him in disbelief.

"My man, we have come from the railway station not Copenhagen." The travel agents had warned her that Denmark was an expensive country but, as usual, she had taken no notice. "Your fare is daylight robbery. Robbery I tell you." To her surprise the taxi driver said in remarkably good English.

"Madam, I assure you the fare is correct. Please be so kind as to pay."

For once, feeling too tired to argue she paid, at the same time damning all taxi drivers to hell, no matter where you went in the world they were all the same – thieving swine. The man's English had caught her off guard; she had yet to realise that the British when compared to the rest of Europe, were incredibly unenlightened when it came to linguistic versatility and fluency.

The following day Megan decided to do some exploring in an attempt to familiarise herself with the town. Her efforts could hardly be described as 'sightseeing' as there were no particular sights to be seen. Randers was an unenthusiastic town with little of interest as Megan soon discovered. The place was a shrine to boredom, but this suited Megan as it allowed her time to sit in a bar and plan her stay.

Finding a bar had been difficult, probably due to the fact that most Danes drank at home – buying crates of beer from the supermarket was far cheaper than drinking the stuff over the counter. The alcoholic culture of the Danes fascinated Megan. Randers was a boozer's paradise. She couldn't believe the number of people wandering around drunk. The shops and stores seemed to be full of tumbling inebriates and no one seemed to give a damn. In this respect it was certainly Megan's kind of town. Mothers pushing prams loaded with beer seemed to be quite normal and didn't seem to merit a second glance from anyone. There were no restrictive licensing hours in the town either, which normally would have suited Megan down to the ground had she been more solvent, but much to her annoyance her limited finances prevented her from taking full advantage of this wonderful drinkers' paradise.

She walked into a newsagent in an attempt to find an English newspaper. Failing to find any English 'daily' her eyes fell on a magazine with an English title. She picked it up from the shelf and started to flip through it. After the first page a look of horror appeared on her face; she dropped the offending journal to the floor and ran out of the shop like a frightened rabbit with a barrel load of buckshot up its arse. *Animal Farm* had been the title of the magazine and Megan, in her ignorance and naivety, had assumed the title to be connected in some way to the George Orwell classic. Well, the magazine was definitely 'connected' if not in the way Megan had expected. No one had warned her about the Danes' libertarian philosophy and their burgeoning sexual enlightenment. Pornography was there on public display for all who wanted it. Where was the shame in sexual maturity, why should it be hidden?

That night Megan had a nightmare where she was being chased around a farmyard by a rampant old donkey and a horny pig. Even Megan's imagination could be prompted into graphic detail given the right stimulus.

In the morning she vowed never again to pick up a Danish publication of any description.

By a gradual process of elimination Megan had finally traced a relative of Lise's. Jacobson was a popular name in Denmark but fortunately Randers was a relatively small town. A telephone book, a creative story and a modicum of patience had provided her with the lead she sought: Karl Schriver. Apparently he was a cousin of Lise and only too happy to meet Megan. He had not seen his cousin for years and would be glad to help.

Megan had kept her story simple.

Following a family upset, Kristian had left home maintaining that he was going to go back to Denmark to find out about the family he had never known. He had been away for nearly a week now and his mother, Lise, was becoming concerned as they had only received a couple of phone calls from him to say he was all right. Nothing else, apart from the fact that he was taking a ferry to Denmark, the last one being two days ago. Megan, his stepsister, had been chosen to track down the boy as the police, as usual in these cases, had been found to be wanting.

She had not gone into much detail over the telephone, deciding that the less said the better. If this cousin discovered the true purpose of her visit he would no doubt have nothing to do with her. Schriver's English had been excellent and an appointment for her to see him had been made.

Megan rang the doorbell and waited. A man answered and stood before her. He held out his hand and said, "Ah, Megan Treharne, is it not? Do please come in."

Karl Schriver made Megan gulp.

She had rarely seen such an inspiring specimen of manhood.

He was well above six foot in height and bore classic Scandinavian features. His hair was almost white in colouring, his eyes deep blue and intelligent, his skin tanned and smooth. If he had worn a Viking helmet and carried a sword and shield he could have been another Nordic hero pillaging and raping the coasts of a Britain trying to come to terms with itself. His facial lines were uncertain; he could have been anything between twenty-five and forty. His body had been put together by Odin himself. His arms, legs, torso and head fitted together in a showdown of physical excellence. The man was a bloody masterpiece; even Wagner would have been impressed.

Megan was almost speechless as she took his hand and tried to refrain from drooling all over it. For a moment even *Animal Farm* didn't seem like such a bad idea providing this Karl chap was the farmer who owned the farm.

"How do you do Mr Schriver," she rasped, "thank you for seeing me, I hope it isn't too inconvenient."

"Not at all," he replied as led her into a large open-plan sitting room. The whole house seemed to be one great big lump of pine – floors, ceilings and even the furniture. The room was light, fresh and spacious; their footsteps echoed around the walls and their voices seemed to carry more volume. No children, no wife. Megan was certain.

"Please sit down Megan, you don't mind if I call you Megan do you?" Karl smiled and the whole world woke up. "We Danes are not as formal as you English."

"No, not at all. I agree with you, we English do tend to be a little too formal. Too stiff."

"Too stiff? I'm not sure I understand you. My English you see is not perfect."

Megan nearly blushed at the first translation that immediately came to mind but controlled herself. "Well, 'too stiff' really means too formal, too polite if you like."

"Ah, I see, now I understand. My English lets me down sometimes although I do have to use it quite a lot in my business. Most Danes can get by with it. We are taught languages at a very early age. Is that not so in England?"

"No, I'm afraid not," Megan replied, regretting now her ignorance of other languages.

"Never mind, would you like some coffee or tea perhaps?"

"Coffee will be fine, thank you." She watched this gorgeous man disappear into another room, presumably the kitchen. God, she thought, I haven't felt so attracted to a man in years. She was feeling sexually aroused just by looking at him. She was embarrassed by her own thoughts; perhaps it was just the country, its sexual freedom. Yes, that must be it, she decided. When Schriver returned with the coffee she was not convinced though. He sat down and gave her the coffee.

"Now then Megan, how can I help you. You said on the telephone that a relative of mine had gone missing. Lise Jacobson's son, is that right?"

"Yes."

"Could you explain how you are connected to this sad situation please?"

Megan had not expected him to be so direct and was a little taken aback; his intelligent eyes noted her reaction.

"I'm sorry, again my English, I do not mean to sound so . . . er . . . blunt."

"That's all right, Karl. Your English is excellent believe me . . . Well Lise, your cousin . . ."

"Distant cousin." Schriver interrupted.

"Distant cousin then seemed to think that Kristian, that's her son, would try and make his way to Randers. You see in the past few months the boy had been constantly questioning his mother about the Danish side of his family. I suppose really he was just curious. Anyway he kept threatening to come over here himself if Lise wouldn't bring him. She hasn't been too well recently and Kristian wouldn't wait. He's a big boy now you know. I can see the family resemblance in you. Anyway, he no doubt had enough money saved and a few days ago he disappeared, just like that. He left a letter saying he was going to Denmark. Lise had mentioned you to him on a number of occasions and so we naturally assumed that this is where he would be heading – if in fact he hadn't turned up on your doorstep already so to speak. It's all very distressing, but he's such a self-willed young man.

Lise wanted to stay by the telephone in case he rang and, as I say, she's not too well at the moment having just undergone some minor surgery. Nothing serious I must stress, but she does need a little time to recuperate and travelling is not a very good idea, so it fell to me to come over here and see if I could track him down."

"Yes, it must be very distressing. I have to say though that I am somewhat surprised that Lise should talk about me to her son." He looked at Megan for a moment and smiled – she nearly passed out. "We were childhood sweethearts for a time many years ago, but that's all. We don't really know each other and I haven't seen her for years. I heard she and her mother had gone to live in England."

"Wales actually," interrupted Megan.

"Wales then, it was all such a sad business you understand, but that's all I really know. However, I am interested to know why you have been elected to search for this boy."

Now Megan had to be careful; she couldn't raise any suspicions about her motives. At first she had tried to avoid the question but then realised that this man was no fool. She only hoped her act would be convincing. She must avoid too much detail in her deception; a sudden mistake and she would be found out. She really wanted to discover what Schriver meant when he had referred to a 'sad business'. Could it have been the dead husband or something else? She had to get to the truth but in as subtle a way as possible.

"Lise is my stepmother."

"Stepmother? But you are . . .?" He was lost for words as he tried to avoid being rude. Megan came to his rescue.

"Yes, I know, much older than she is."

"Well . . . um . . . yes."

"My father is much older than Lise. Much older."

"Really?" Schriver looked more closely at Megan and said, "He must be quite a man." Megan didn't know how to take this remark; was Schriver referring to her father's sexual prowess or was he looking at her wrinkles and concluding that her father must be in his dotage? She had already experienced the Danish tendency toward sexual freedom and openness. Thankfully Schriver continued without waiting for a reply. "Are they happy? I hope so, Lise was a lovely girl as I remember."

"Yes, they are. But both are worried about the boy as you can imagine. Well, beside themselves would be more like it."

"Yes, I understand. How old is he?"

"Oh sixteen, nearly seventeen now I think." Megan replied.

Schriver paused for a moment, thinking. He took a sip of his coffee as his mind seemed to be making some quick calculations.

"I still don't see why he should try and contact me. After all he doesn't even know where I live."

"I found you easily enough, Karl. Obviously after so much time Lise had no idea exactly where you lived, but if I managed it I'm sure Kristian will. He's a bright lad."

"Like his mother if I remember correctly." Schriver's eyes wandered to the floor, a pause, a reflection. When he looked up his whole face seemed to be concentrating on both happy memory and regret at lost opportunity, "I had to try very hard to kiss his mother you know, and even then I never truly succeeded." This time his lips smiled. "I am glad she is happy. She deserves it. That business at the end of the war was terrible you know." Megan had to find out to what he was referring. His face had now taken on a solemn expression mixed with sadness.

She decided to gamble. "You mean the Germans?"

"Yes, you know about it?"

"Lise did talk about it but not very much and who can blame her. It was awful." She had to be very careful now. If her ignorance of the facts became known Schriver might well clam up. He didn't seem the type to be extravagant with words. She kept quiet, waiting.

Schriver continued. "It was as well that she left the country with her mother. After her father died there was really nothing here for them both except hostility and hatred. War does that to people. They were ostracised from the community. These days Lise's 'offence' seems so trivial. But then, with the war about

157

to end, fraternising with the enemy was as bad as committing murder. Justice was quick and brutal. They never found the men who raped and beat Lise. She wasn't able to identify them. The authorities were not enthusiastic about discovering who the perpetrators were anyway. The criminals could have been German or Danish. In those days the whole of Europe was in a state of chaos and madness. You in England managed to escape the post-war violence, the revenge. Lise was punished simply because she had been seen walking with a young German soldier. It was crazy. Insane. I was so young myself I can hardly remember exactly what it was all about. I remember adult whispers and pointing fingers though. It was a bad time but Lise was brave, very brave. It destroyed her father of course and probably her mother."

Megan could not believe her ears, her luck was in! She decided to deceive a little more.

"You said it was only an innocent friendship Karl, so where was her family to protect her? No offence intended but you must admit it does all seem rather odd." Megan's voice carried a calculated edge of suppressed outrage. She was accusing – a little outrage can camouflage the most flagrant of lies. She continued. "Where were you, where were the rest of her family? She arrived in Wales penniless, she and her mother. They had to work as maids in a hotel in order to keep body and soul together." Megan was away now, her false sincerity and moral bluster in fine fettle. Schriver said little, his guilt all too apparent. Megan suddenly stopped her subtle verbal outrage, careful not to go too far. She didn't want to offend Schriver too much and she could see by his eyes that there was genuine remorse.

"What you say of course is quite right. I still regret how my own family treated them. But you must realise that I myself was young, powerless."

"Of course." Megan's voice softened. "I'm sorry, I shouldn't have criticised you. After all it was hardly your fault. Please forgive me."

"That's all right, Megan, I understand. It must all be very painful for you."

"Yes it is. You see I lost my own dear brother in the war and the memories are still raw." A few tears started to queue in the corners of her eyes; they were not going anywhere but they looked good. Megan's performance deserved three Oscars. Her face showed nothing of the elation she felt. She could not believe her good fortune, everything she wanted was now in her grasp. So that's where Kristian had come from – the end product of rape, the father possibly a German, unknown. Her own father would go mad – the Germans had killed his own beloved son for God's sake!

Schriver said nothing about this but he didn't need to. The look on his face was enough.

Megan finished her coffee.

"Well, I really must go now Karl. Thank you for being so helpful and kind."

"I haven't done anything really, I only wish I could have been more helpful."

"Never mind, I'll leave a contact telephone number for you. You can ring if Kristian shows up. He may well be back home by now. You know what teenagers are like."

"Well . . . not really, but please let me know that everything is well if you would." He looked at Megan, his eyes searching. "I can imagine the real reason for Lise not coming here herself. You have been very polite. No explanation is needed. I do understand, believe me."

"That's very considerate of you Karl. Raking up past hurts rarely brings any joy to anyone, does it?"

"No, indeed not. Send Lise my best wishes and tell her I still have fond memories of her."

"I will. Here's the number." She handed him a piece of paper with a fictitious telephone number on it. "Thank you again, you have been very helpful," – more than you know, she wanted to add – "Goodbye."

Karl Schriver stood in the doorway watching Megan leave. The previous smile had vanished. He was a suspicious man by nature and hadn't been totally convinced by the woman's story. He looked at the piece of paper in his hand, the past. He thought for a few moments. Some things were best left alone. He closed the door, went into the kitchen and threw the piece of paper into a bin. As he did so Lise's pretty face forced its way into his memory again.

She had been his first love, he would never, could never forget. He remembered his bungled attempts at trying to kiss her. The innocence. He remembered the constant desire to be close to her, the mystery of the unknown. Puberty celebrated and condemned in equal measure, but the memories remained the same. They could still hurt and still bring joy, they could still contradict in the most painful way. Lise had been the only one, the only real truth.

His family had eventually moved to another part of Randers – a part far away from Lise or so it seemed to his young mind. Their love had wilted but never quite died, her touch still remained. He wondered what she looked like now, had time been generous to her? Beauty was only just beginning to dawn all those years ago. Now . . .? He drew in a sharp intake of breath, hesitating to think.

Good looks ran in his family and he had never had any problems with the opposite sex. He had never had to chase them, they usually came to him. They wanted to mother him as well as bed him. He seemed so vulnerable and yet so strong, he fascinated and challenged. His quiet nature and modest character had merely enhanced his woman-killing power. They simply couldn't leave him alone. He had refused the lure of wedding bells on numerous occasions. He had nothing against it, neither did he feel that it held any threat to his freedom. For Schriver it was simply a question of finding the right one. At thirty-two he sometimes wondered if he would ever discover a woman who could actually capture his heart. Women passed through his life with a regularity that Casanova would have been proud of, and some he had loved – but never enough. He desperately wanted that one special woman, that one human being who could make him whole. There was no longer any novelty in sleeping with a different woman every night. His masculinity was well established. He had nothing to prove. Sex was enjoyable and necessary but it certainly wasn't everything.

Schriver wanted to settle down, to have children, but more than anything else he wanted stability in his life. He had played long and hard, now was the time to retire. If only he could find the right sort of woman he would be a happy man. He had wealth and financial security, he had looks, he had personality, he enjoyed good health. What he didn't have was the most important of all life's treasures – love.

He thought again of Lise, he couldn't help it. The memory wasn't so much of the girl herself but of the purity and undefiled emotion that he had had for her. His first experience of love had been one that was uncomplicated, new and fresh. A childish crush it might have been, but nevertheless he still sought the same depth of feeling, the same infatuation. This total oneness had escaped him, eluded him for all of his adult life. He felt empty, unfulfilled. Experience had taught him that the more he looked for the perfect mate the less he would find. He had loved, deeply and without reservation, but it had never come to complete fulfilment. The perfection he so strongly desired had never been there. He would never settle for second best and yet deep in his heart, one day, he knew that perhaps he might have to. It was a disquieting thought.

Before going to his office a possibility arose in his mind. He quickly realised the madness of it and berated himself out loud for being so crazy. The Danish language was sadly lacking where profanity was concerned so instead he swore in English. "Fuck it! You're out of your mind!"

Megan enjoyed the ferry trip back to Harwich. For the first time in a long while she was happy, or at least close to it. She sat at the bar and drank champagne cocktails – it was celebration time.

The prospect of revenge and satisfaction made her spirits soar. She was drunk on the elixir of hatred, the champagne was merely an accessory. "Karl Schriver," she whispered to herself, "you lovely, wonderful man." She ordered another drink; money would soon be no object. Once her father discovered the true and vile antecedents of his new wife, Megan would be back in favour. Dear God, his son had been killed by Germans, how would he react when he discovered that he had married a German lover, that Kristian was a bastard, father unknown and a rapist at that. Possibly even a German soldier! The fact that she had no actual proof to corroborate any of her fanciful conclusions was simply by the way. Lise would be ruined, and that was all that mattered.

As she drank more her mind began to think of ways she could best use her new knowledge. Ways that would cause the most damage and pain. Megan's mind had become more twisted in its vengeful intent and delusion. And it showed. Her face had become more contorted with the ugliness of corruption and revenge, her body more foul and worn out. The only sparkle of light in her eyes was one of intense hatred. She thrived on it, lived for it. It was her food, her very being. It consumed her. Her mental state was rapidly reaching a dangerous level. Her obsession had taken over; her mind was no longer functioning in a rational way. On the surface she appeared perfectly normal, but below this her mind raged and fought against the powerful armies of insanity. She now personified an awful vial of bitter, deadly poison. Alcohol was taking her on journeys of temporary elation and then it would commit treason and drop her into a mire of paranoia and irrationality. The woman needed help and quickly. She couldn't see what was happening to her and neither, tragically could anyone else. The combination of insidious alcohol with a mental imbalance created a mixture of terrifying strength and consequence. Megan was the unexploded bomb; a slight nudge in the wrong direction and she would explode, destroying herself and all those around her.

CHAPTER 19

"What's the matter, William?" Lise asked, a note of worry in her voice. It was three o'clock in the morning.

"Nothing dear, it's just my stomach playing up again. That daughter of mine wants to see me next week about something. I received a letter from her this morning. Well, she can wait for a reply. I was going to ring her but never got round to it. First time we've heard from her in years, so God knows what she wants. Trouble no doubt. Damned girl has set my stomach off." William was pacing the bedroom in obvious discomfort, unable to sleep.

"William, this is happening virtually every night. It's not just Megan, you must go and see a doctor."

"Don't be silly Lise. It's just a bit of indigestion that's all. Don't fuss."

"I'm not fussing. Look at you, I've noticed your appetite hasn't been its normal healthy self recently. You hardly touched your dinner last night. How can it be indigestion? You didn't eat anything. You must go and see a doctor William, I mean it!"

"No need to raise your voice my lovely. I've never been to see a doctor in my life and I'm not starting now. There's nothing wrong with me. Old age, that's all."

Lise was not going to give up. She knew how stubborn her husband could be. "Old age maybe William, but that isn't the point. You're in far more pain than you're letting on, so don't try and fool me, I know you too well. Doctors are not ogres you know, they are there to help you not hurt you."

"Really? Well tell that to the poor bugger on the operating table who's just had his guts butchered."

"Oh, for heavens sake. I do believe you're actually scared."

"Damn right I am, first to admit it too."

"Don't be such a baby. It's probably nothing that a change of diet won't cure. Now come back to bed and get some sleep. I'll arrange an appointment for you in the morning. The sooner the better."

"Good God! And you have the nerve to talk about me being stubborn! Hell, you're like a dog with a bone." He paused for a moment knowing that it would be hopeless arguing with Lise once she had made up her mind. "Very well, you win," he said grudgingly, "but remember that I'll be seeing a quack under duress. Right?"

"Right, now get into bed will you, you silly old man."

"Now look here Lise . . ." he didn't get any further before she stopped him.

"Oh, shut up and go to sleep will you? I'm tired." He did as he was told. Lise was worried but she knew that she dare not show anything to William. It would make him worse. For the past few months she had noticed a gradual deterioration in his health. It wasn't just his appetite. He had been losing weight slowly but surely – his shirt collars were no longer filled with flesh, and for such an energetic man his manner had become lethargic too, his movements lazy. All his energy seemed to be ebbing away. Lise had always expected the inevitable ravages of age. What she hadn't anticipated was its sudden acceleration.

Somehow the death of William had never seemed possible; he had always been so alive, so full of character and personality. She had always believed that he would defy time itself.

As she lay next to him with an arm around him she shuddered. What would her life be like without the only man she had ever loved and adored? The prospect filled her with terror and fear. She loved him so completely she simply wouldn't know what to do without him. She had never before considered the death of her man. Now, as she held him more tightly, she realised how short and brutal love could be.

The safety of sleep eluded her for most of the night.

After William had given a brief description of the pain and answered a few questions, the doctor prodded, pushed and pulled his prone body.

"How does that feel?" he asked.

"Fine." William replied.

"Are you sure?"

"Yes." William nearly said, "Yes, Dr. Bollocks" but quickly remembered the man's name was Horrocks, poor devil.

"Right, you can put your clothes back on now, Mr Treharne." William dressed and returned to the doctor's desk. He disliked medical men intensely. Their arrogance and pomposity knew no limitations. They were usually curt to the point of being downright rude and who the hell did they think they were anyway? As bad as bloody lawyers, all big fish in a bloody small pond. He couldn't stand them.

"So, what's the verdict?" William refused to display any fawning respect for the man by calling him 'Doctor'. He was a human being like everybody else, not Lord God Almighty.

"I would like you to have some tests at the hospital."

"What for?"

"Oh, just to check your stomach that's all."

"Won't a couple of horse pills do the trick?"

"They might Mr Treharne, but I cannot prescribe the correct treatment until I know exactly what's wrong with you. The tests will tell me that."

"I thought you were supposed to be the doctor, not tests." The doctor sighed. Here we go, he thought.

"Mr Treharne, I can't find anything obvious wrong with you but then a brief physical examination wouldn't tell me that much anyway. We have to have a look inside you. Don't worry, there's no surgery or pain. Believe me, it's the only way; we must discover what is causing you this abdominal pain. Now then, the hospital will be in touch with you over the next ten days. In the meantime try to exercise a little restraint on the tobacco and alcohol. Also avoid spicy foods."

"If you say so."

"I do. It's for your own good you know."

I'm sure it is, William thought, and the good of your pocket too. He was a paying patient. Private.

"I will let you know when I get the results back. Now good day, Mr Treharne."

That was that. William walked out of the surgery to the waiting car. Lise was behind the wheel.

"Well, how did it go darling?"

"He just prodded me around as if I was a plump chicken about to be put on a spit. Like all doctors, conversation is absent from his social repertoire as indeed are any informative comments. Didn't enlighten me in any way, you are as wise as I am I'm sorry to say. Have to go to the hospital for tests. That's all for now." He didn't tell Lise about the orders regarding his pipe and booze.

"He didn't say anything else? Didn't give you any hints as to what the trouble could be?"

"No Lise, he didn't. Hell you know what quacks are like. I'm sure half of 'em are illiterate. Have you seen their prescriptions? Bloody joke. As for intelligent conversation forget it; if it isn't about science then they're buggered. Unread cretins all of them." Lise said nothing; she didn't want to show too much concern although she was relieved that he had agreed to go to the doctor in the first place. At least when the tests had been done they would both know what was wrong. If indeed there was anything wrong at all. Lise would just have to hope and be patient.

"Can we go straight home now, Lise? I am feeling rather tired. No stopping off anywhere."

"Of course," Lise replied as she rested her hand on his. "Don't worry my darling, everything will be all right believe me."

"I hope so Lise, I really do hope so. I'm not ready to hand in my dinner cards yet. Apart from anything else I want to remain on this planet a while longer if only to annoy you!" William said with a smile.

Yet despite the manly show of bravado he was worried. Deep down he was frightened; he knew his body and he also knew that there was something seriously wrong with it. He had been experiencing pain for some time, far longer than Lise thought. He hadn't said anything, wishing to spare her any undue anxiety. He should have gone to the doctor a year ago when the symptoms first started. He now realised how foolish he had been. He had allowed his pride and fear to get the better of him – again.

Without showing anything to the woman he loved so much William started to prepare himself for the worse.

William was not the only man considering his options.

Gwyn was alone with the lawn mower and his thoughts.

He and Bronwyn had been involved with each other for some time now and they had grown close to one another. Nevertheless, Gwyn was troubled; he knew Bronwyn was deeply in love with him. She adored him and would do anything he asked. She even put up with his intermittent bouts of drinking. She never complained or castigated him. He knew that she was a treasure for any man and and yet for all her wonderful qualities something was missing in his heart. He was extremely fond of her, he enjoyed being with her, but despite this the love he had known in his life was absent. Passion simply wasn't there. He had known the tremendous emotion of simply holding the one you love. Pulling her to you in the dark and lonely hours of the night. Just wanting that one woman next to you, close and warm. He had known the surge of unqualified love when looking at a sleeping face. But with Bronwyn these things never happened. He wouldn't be without her and yet he knew that if she left him he wouldn't suffer the devastation that he had known in times gone by. He wondered whether he had used up all his reserves of love. His wife had left his heart deeply scarred. He had loved her in a way that he knew was never possible with Bronwyn. He also knew that deep down in his heart he still loved his wife. He damned this emotional imprisonment. His feelings were incarcerated, unable to wander at will. His wife had cauterised his liberty as surely as if she had used a red-hot iron. Bronwyn was the last person in the world he would hurt, he knew that she would marry him as soon as he gave the word and be a good wife too. Somehow he couldn't take that step – he was frozen by the past, paralysed, and there was nothing he could do about it. He had tried, *duw mun* he had tried, but memories contrived to assail and thwart him. It worried him that the longer he encouraged the relationship with Bronwyn the greater the pain should it ever end. As he tinkered with the lawn mower's engine he wished that life could be as simple as a few nuts and bolts. It was not and for a while his mind remained disturbed and intro-spective.

William sucked on his pipe. He took the pipe away from his mouth and said, "Look, no smoke, smokeless tobacco you know, amazing!" He stuck the pipe back in his mouth and cursed all medical receptionists. They were all the same – stuck up harri-dans. Somehow they always made you feel guilty about being in the doctor's surgery. It was like waiting outside the headmaster's study with a sound thrashing minutes away. And God help you if you had the temerity to telephone. Trumped-up turds the lot of them, doctors included. At last the finely honed hatchet face behind the counter told William he could have an audience with the doctor. He stood up and said, "Summoned into the Royal Chamber at last are we?" while he looked at his watch. It was twenty minutes past his appointment time and he was a paying customer. "If a man can't be on time then his life is in a bloody mess, and I object to paying for someone else's mess!" he added, glaring at the sourpuss receptionist. Then he then walked towards the consulting room, leaving her open mouthed and disabused of her royal authority.

"Sit down please, Mr Treharne." The doctor was doing his usual anything-but-eye-contact bit. The last patient's notes were more important apparently.

William didn't like it. There was no smile on the doctor's face and so far the man had refused to make eye contact. At last the medical man looked up. He removed his glasses and placed them on the file before him. He looked at William and said, "Well, Mr Treharne, I'm afraid the news is not good. We have had the results of the tests back." The doctor paused trying to find the appropriate words to use. It was never easy and constant practise made no difference. William helped him.

"Come on doctor, out with it. No need to try and spare my feelings. Just tell me what's wrong . . . in layman's terms please." The doctor took a deep breath and said, "You have advanced stomach cancer."

William looked at the man, his face told the whole story. Words were unnecessary. "Nothing can be done?" he asked quietly.

"No, I'm afraid not," came the answer, "the cancer is far too advanced. Surgery and drugs will have no effect."

"How long?"

The doctor hated this question. He wanted to say, 'Well don't go boiling an egg for breakfast', but thought better of it. "Three months, maybe a little more. I will prescribe some drugs to alleviate the pain."

William stood up.

His legs were shaking but he tried to hide it as he said, "Very well then. I trust the news will remain strictly confidential. I will deal with my family in my own way."

"Of course, Mr Treharne. Before you go I would like to see you again in a month's time. Sooner if the pain becomes intolerable."

"What then? Morphine and a hospital bed?" William knew the form, he had seen his friends die of cancer.

"Something like that. The pain will increase quite rapidly Mr Treharne. You must be a very strong man to have come this far."

"Perhaps, Doctor. However the point is now merely academic. The business of living is unpredictable at the most optimistic of times. Good day and thank you."

William walked away from his death sentence.

Gwyn was waiting in the car. As William sat in the passenger seat he asked, "Everything OK, Boss?"

"Yes, Gwyn, everything is fine. Stomach ulcer, that's all. It will go of its own accord providing I watch what I eat."

"That's good then. So home is it, Boss?"

"Yes please, Gwyn. You know the bullets of time punish with greater velocity as one gets older."

"What's that Boss? Didn't catch you"

"Nothing Gwyn, nothing," William answered quietly. He didn't say another word during the drive back to the Cliffs.

Lise was waiting for him in the hall when he returned. She helped him with his hat and coat. He had his back to her as she said, "What did the doctor have to say then? What were the test results?"

William couldn't look at her as he said, "Everything's fine Lise. Stomach ulcer that's all. Have to lay off the vinegar and pepper. Plenty of milk." He turned to her and kissed her on her forehead, "Now I must go to my study to sort out the mail. I have some letters to write, so don't disturb me."

She held him for a moment and said, "I'm so glad my darling. I've been so worried about you."

William stroked her hair. "I know. But there's nothing to worry about now." His soul was dying more quickly than his body; he could not look into the blue eyes that adored him. He went into his study and closed the door.

Lise never disturbed him whist he was in his study; the place was all his, a piece of hallowed territory that remained detached and apart from the rest of the house. She always waited until he emerged of his own volition.

William put Bruch's violin concerto No. 1 in G minor on the record player and sat down at his desk. The sad melody taught him once again how music could teach so much understanding and give so such comfort. Yet this time his mind would not respond. There was only turmoil. For the first time in his life he was unsure. The room began to smell of death. What was he to do? The finality of death itself disposed of any debate where he himself was concerned. His worry and indecision centred around Lise. Would he tell her the truth? His death, he knew, would devastate her and yet was he underestimating her resilience? He had always believed women to be emotionally stronger than men – tougher. They seemed to have a greater capacity to suffer and yet still survive. Women were more courageous than men. They were still the warrior queens of old. They were still the Boudiccas and the Elizabeths. Their strength lay in their hearts where it mattered, not in their muscles. He quickly realised that Lise would get by without him, of that he was now sure. She was still a young woman with a good deal of living before her. Financially, Lise and Kristian would be taken care of. His solicitors had seen to that.

His mind quickly changed from pragmatic thought as he shuddered at the memory of a friend who had died from cancer. The man had suffered excruciating pain for a long time. At the end, his friend lay in a hospital bed comatose and wasted while people sat around the bed just waiting for the cancer to finally raise its victory flag. The friend who used to be so virile and vital was now reduced to a pathetic, dribbling skeleton, not even knowing that death was imminent.

The memory turned William's stomach.

He would not die like that.

The degradation was too much to even contemplate. The drugs would perpetrate a deathly inertia on his mind and his body would decompose for all to see. His lovely Lise would have to witness the man she loved so dearly rot and disintegrate into a premature corpse of hanging skin and jutting bone. He would not allow his Lise to have that last memory of him.

When the violin had finished its tortuous journey through melancholia William decided to gorge himself on Rachmaninov's tortured depression. Not perhaps the most appropriate choice of music considering his present mood, but he had always found the Russian composer irresistible. His favourite. Romance, love, hope, they all colluded together in the composer's fingers to create a beauty that defied any definition. The piece William now played was performed by the genius himself. The modest, flattened piece of black plastic had become one of William's most treasured possessions. It was one small part of his true and real wealth.

He sat down and thought about his life. He had striven to find answers to all the great questions. What is life? Why are we here? What is beyond us? He had studied all the religions of the world in a quest to find a God, he had read all the philosophical complexities of thought and being in order to discover some sense. He had searched with the fanaticism and ardour of a hopeless, misguided convert. What a fool he'd been! Every time he had submerged his hands into the barrels of knowledge he had retrieved them holding nothing. Nirvana. For him religion and philosophy were ideological and misspent delusions, like sex they caused more mental illness than anything else. Man's creativity was extraordinary, his capacity to solve insane insecurity inventive to say the least. Religion had been his most profound masterpiece of all. He had constructed a fraud so complex, so devastatingly real as to make humanity for all its excruciating intellect, a sop, a gullible whipping boy.

Nobody knew what happened after death – the dead don't write letters or make annoying telephone calls in the middle of the night. One of the most hysterical ironies of the human condition lay in the fact that 'truth', whatever the hell that was anyway, could never be discovered until death collected you in its permanent arms and made damned certain you were never able to reveal the real purpose behind life's most disconcerting mystery. The whole business of birth and death just happened. Religion merely convinces us, or at least tries to, into thinking that we never die. Utter nonsense.

William had concluded many years ago that religion in particular was nothing more than a hopeful imagination making unrealistic demands upon pitiful human necessity and insecurity.

When the mind died, God died with it. After all, wasn't it the human mind that had created a God in the first place?

Death had been concentrating William's mind for some time now. Months. He had not needed a quack to tell him it was time to say, "Goodnight". He concluded that he did not fear Death. Fear of what? His own mind?

All his life he had exercised control. Not the control of a tyrant but the control over his own will. His mind, a God perhaps, was his power and his glory. His immortality, his hubris and nemesis. This unrepentant will would decide his fate. He and he alone would take charge, conclude and finish. He was not prepared to allow the cancer that was devouring him to have a damn good belch and a self-satisfied fart after the meal. He had been master of his destiny all his life; he would not betray this power to the lackeys and flunkies of the comedy and farce that was life, religion and philosophy.

As the sun began to set and hide itself behind the sea the calmness of Nature's hand began to settle itself on him. He was tired, tired even of living. Life he knew to be just a piss-pot of passing fancies and haunting memory. For all that his life had been long and full. He had known both pain and love, but thanks to his own God love had played the greater part in his life. Now, as he stood being washed by the last rays of light he knew that his life had been blessed. There was no bitterness in his heart, no hatred. His mind raced quickly through the years of his existence and the memories were mostly of good things. He knew as a fact that humankind naturally obliterated hurtful memories if it could. Time always gave a helping hand in this healing process, and yet he still knew what a lucky man he had been. He was grateful. He had cherished and received more love than any man deserved; love from his first wife and love from Lise. In his life he had perhaps not done as much as many, but probably more than most. His wealth and material gains were still as nothing when compared to the riches of love that his heart had received and given.

He knew now that he had worn out his Time and that he was beginning to trespass on eternity. He had no right.

He turned from the window and went back to his desk. Taking an old and cherished fountain pen from a drawer he began to write. An hour later William turned off the green banker's lamp on his desk and went to join Lise for supper.

William sat at the dinner table and chatted with Lise about all the mundane things that had happened during her day. She had no idea how intensely William was watching her. For him everything became an exaggerated and fantastic experience of his past and future. His senses seemed more acute and powerful then they had ever been. The touching of her knife and fork on her plate seemed to crush his eardrums. The deliberate movement of her fingers, the blinking of her eyelids, the idiosyncrasies of her expressions all seemed to him to be a finished collage of everything he had fallen in love with. All their years together, all the love they had enjoyed, overwhelmed him. Her loveliness and beauty could still leave him speechless. He listened. He couldn't take his eyes off her. He didn't want to.

His food remained untouched. His body didn't need or want it. He was too absorbed, self-contained, obsessed with the emotion in and before him. For the first time in his life he realised that the woman sitting in front of him personified everything he had ever sought. His years of searching were over. The answer was in front of him.

"You are not eating again, William," Lise chided, "are you all right?" She reached across the table and held his hand. Her devotion noticed that something profound had embraced her husband. She couldn't describe it. Couldn't touch it. She just knew. Their eyes locked and in those few brief seconds an understanding so deep, so inexplicable passed between them. Their mutual knowledge was beyond any verbal expression or explanation.

"I'm fine my lovely. My appetite tonight is just not up to much." He squeezed her hand, "I've just got a few more things to see to in my study. I won't be late coming to bed." He stood up and kissed her gently on the lips.

"I love you so much my Lise"

"I love you too William. So very, very much."

With that he left the room. Lise remained seated. She felt disturbed and unsettled. She didn't know exactly why.

William locked the door to his study and walked over to the open bay window. Moonlight struck the gardens and his roses. They all seemed to cower and submit. At this time Night ruled and the moon guided its power. Nature had created them all – William had just been an idle helper. The artist and moneymaker as one. He stood there for a while, oblivious to the passing of time. There was no fear inside him. No guilt. No recrimination. No blame. He would exercise his will to the end. The Fates, the Gods could all go to Hell on a bloody donkey – all malevolent con artists together. Not that any such place existed anyway except in the minds of those who would punish.

With a smile he turned from the window and sat at his desk.

He unlocked one of the drawers and withdrew his son's army issue Webley. It was in mint condition. William had cleaned it regularly over the years. The revolver was a fitting choice. It would keep death in the family as it were.

He looked at his favourite photograph of Lise and whispered, "Goodnight my lovely, forgive me."

He placed the barrel of the gun in his mouth and squeezed the trigger.

CHAPTER 20

The funeral, on William's instructions, had been a simple and modest affair.

He had made it clear that there was to be no hypocrisy, no religion, no dramatic tears and certainly no hollow words of condolence.

'Oven baked' had been his chosen method of disposal. The idea of worms gorging themselves on his flesh, lifeless though it may be, had always repelled him as indeed had the prospect of waking up six feet under. On one occasion he and Lise had been walking through a graveyard in Vienna when he had pointed out what looked like a small bell next to one of the gravestones. A piece of rusted, broken wire led from the bell into the ground.

"That's there to be rung for the butler," William had joked, "or more seriously if the deceased decides that he wants to return to the land of the living. A cataleptic fit can make any signs of life undetectable sometimes, you know. I sure as hell don't fancy coming round with a ton of earth on me. It's Hell's flames for me, and don't you forget it my lovely, cast my ashes over the cliffs and let the wind carry my soul wherever it wants to go."

When all the mourners had left the house, apart from Megan and Griffith, Lise carried William's ashes to the rose garden. His 'pride and his joy'. She was still numb from shock, time passing without any clarity or distinction. Day and night had become one, the ticking of a clock endless and excruciating. She was in a life, but it was somewhere else or passing through. Sudden death mutilated existence, it tore to shreds any sense of the real or now. Her words and sight belonged to another place, not the grief of love and loss. William was everywhere, in her mind and body. Acceptance was taking time, a lifetime even. Lise moved in a world of locked-up tears unable to free themselves from a prison drenched in fear and devastation. Her husband's death had been so fast, so quick and brutal.

She walked aimlessly through the gardens and at last came to William's favourite place.

A garden bench surrounded by rose bushes of all colours and description overlooked the cliffs and the sea. The view stopped Lise – it always did. The bold hostility of cliff and sea demanded immediate attention. The passion and violence of Welsh history rose from every wave and jutting stone, splashing and screaming at the Celtic legends of centuries gone by. Welsh voices sang their beauty from frontiers that could never be discovered as poetry swirled and eddied around her in words that could only be imagined. The playful mystery could not be seen, but it could be felt as the past and present joined together in a flagrant abuse of wonder, here in this one small place.

It had been William's refuge. His peace and his glory of life.

Lise sat on the bench. She felt his touch. He was still here.

She sat there for an hour feeling him close to her. His spirit would never die and would always remain deep in her heart.

At last she stood up and walked toward the edge of the cliff face. A fence had been constructed some three feet from the edge. She stopped. She looked out across the sea for a moment and then opened the urn containing her husband's ashes. She held it tightly in both hands for a brief moment then spilled its contents into the winds – as she did so saying gently, "We will be together again one day my darling William. I love you."

The ashes vanished in nature's grasp and at last the tears came.

Lise remained where she was and sobbed her heart out as she finally accepted that William, her man, was gone.

Now she could grieve and start to recover from her tragic loss.

She remained standing and dabbed at her eyes with a silk handkerchief, one of a set that William had bought her in Paris.

Everything she saw and touched would remind her of him. She knew that she must learn to live without him and accept the constant memories with joy and not pain.

She forced herself to think about the night of his death. She had to accept. She had to be strong.

She had been in bed reading when the noise of a loud bang had interrupted her concentration. At first she wasn't sure, then unbelievably the fright and horror of war returned with a terrible clarity. It was a gunshot – she knew the report of a firearm. She had jumped from the bed, thrown on a dressing gown and dashed downstairs. The noise had come from William's study, she was sure of it. In these brief moments, as confusion superseded fear, her thoughts were frozen. When she reached the study Gwyn was already trying the door.

It was locked.

Her voice was pitched with panic as she shouted, "What's happening Gwyn? Was that a gunshot I heard? Quickly open the door, break it down if you have to! Quickly Gwyn, oh quickly for God's sake!"

"Door's too solid Lise," Gwyn answered, "I'll go round to the window. Quicker. Wait here." He left Lise by the door shouting, "William! William! Answer me!"

Gwyn finally entered the study through the French doors. William had left them open. He saw his boss and friend face down on the desk. He ran to William and switched on the lamp next to his hand.

In one split second Gwyn knew what had happened. His eyes took in the revolver on the floor, there was blood everywhere. The back of William's head had disappeared. Instantly he knew that Lise must not see any of this. She was still shouting outside the door. He could hear Bronwyn's voice now as well.

He went to the door and took the key out of the lock. Instead of opening it he went back the way he had come. Locking the French doors from the outside.

Lise was beside herself, nearly hysterical. He ordered Bronwyn to get a doctor and ambulance fast and then to come back. He held Lise in his strong arms trying to control her. His words were some of the most terrible he had ever spoken, raw and impersonal as death didn't recognise courtesy.

"He's dead Lise. He's shot himself."

The wail of despair that echoed through the house nearly cut him in two.

Lise tried to open the door, she kicked it, punched it and screamed at Gwyn to let her in. He would not.

"Let me in Gwyn! Let me in! I must go to my husband. Let me in! He can't be dead! He can't be!"

His strength kept her at bay. He hated having to restrain her like this but there was nothing else for it. She couldn't see William in his present state; it would haunt her for the rest of her life. Lise kicked and punched him but he wouldn't let go. He dragged her screaming to another room.

Soon an ambulance arrived with a doctor. Gwyn gave a quick account of what had happened and demanded that the doctor see to Lise first.

The doctor immediately took in the scene and with Gwyn's help injected a strong sedative into Lise's arm. The drug acted quickly and Gwyn gently placed Lise on one of the chairs in the drawing room. He opened the study door. The two ambulance men looked from William's body to the doctor; there was nothing to be done. They were cool and detached having seen it all before. The doctor quickly felt for a pulse; there was none. He told Gwyn to take Lise to bed as the injection had knocked her out. Gwyn carried Lise upstairs to her bedroom and laid her on the bed. Bronwyn, tearful and shocked, sat next to her holding her hand.

"Stay here now Bron," Gwyn ordered, "she mustn't be left alone. Right?"

"Yes, of course," she mumbled in reply.

Gwyn stood in the doorway, heartbroken, "I must go now and see the doctor. I'll be back. Be strong, Bron. Lise is going to need you like never before." He quickly left the tragedy and the tears. The tragedy left for the living to suffer. The doctor was waiting for him in the study. William's body was still crumpled over the desk.

"Why is the Boss still here?" Gwyn asked with a note of anger in his voice. The two ambulance men hovered near the door, their embarrassment obvious.

"I'm sorry Mr . . .?" the doctor began . . .

"Evans," Gwyn responded gruffly, "now, what the 'ell is going on?"

"Well, Mr Evans, we can't remove the deceased until the police arrive."

"The police?" Gwyn shouted. "What the 'ell 'ave the police got to do with anythin'? Jesus, the man's shot 'imself, that's all there is to it!"

"Yes, I appreciate your concern, but in cases of suicide certain procedures have to be followed. Believe me, there's nothing I can do until the police give me the authority to remove the body." There was an uneasy pause until they heard the sound of tyres crunching the gravel outside. "That's probably the police now. They won't be long I assure you. Please don't touch anything until they have finished."

"Jesus, don't tell me you think someone night have murdered 'im? Gawd 'elp us!"

"Not at all Mr Evans. As I've said, it's just normal procedure in these matters. Please, if you would like to wait outside I'll come and see you as soon as I've spoken with the police."

Half an hour later a tall plainclothes man came out of the study and announced himself as Inspector Rees. Apart from the drab suit and twisted collar the only other conspicuous characteristic about the man were the huge eyebrows that seemed to cover the whole of his forehead.

"Are you Mr Evans?" the Inspector asked in the typically officious way of a policeman.

"Yes, I am Gwyn Evans." Gwyn had already taken an instant dislike to the man but then he had never taken to policemen full stop.

"You found the body did you not?" the Inspector stated in the same automaton voice.

"I did."

"It seems most likely that Mr Treharne committed suicide."

Gwyn couldn't contain himself, "Most likely? My arse! Who the 'ell are you trying to kid. Think somebody 'ere shot 'im do you? Better get Agatha Christie in to give you an 'and 'cos you'll have one 'ell of a job proving foul play. Coppers," he sneered, "you're all the bloody same."

"I'll ignore that outburst Mr Evans," Rees replied with the contempt endemic to those who have risen from humble origins and been given a slither of power.

"We will need statements from everybody in the house. There's no need for anyone to trouble themselves right now. An officer will call around tomorrow, so please make sure that everyone staying here at the time of Mr Treharne's death is available. Perhaps, Mr Evans, you can tell me who is here at the moment?"

Gwyn told him, not very politely either. He hated policemen. They had given him a load of aggravation over the years. As if pissing in bus shelters was anything to get upset about. Admittedly there had been one or two shopping bags that he had mistaken for the gutter but so what. He was drunk wasn't he?

When Rees had finished writing in the inevitable notebook he said, "Mrs Treharne is in bed you say? Perhaps I shall have a word with her."

"The 'ell you will. You leave 'er alone." Gwyn moved directly in front of Rees, his body ready to pounce. "She's in shock and sedated. Don't you bloody well go near 'er I'm telling you now."

"Is that a threat Mr Evans? I hope not for your sake."

"Look, just leave her alone will you please." The aggression in Gwyn's voice had suddenly disappeared. He was tired and drained. "She won't be able to tell you much. Like I say she's in shock. Ask the doctor for Gawd's sake. Right now she's out of it. Give 'er a bit of time will you, let things register?" At that moment the doctor intervened.

"Inspector, I couldn't help hearing your thoughts. Mr Evans is quite right. Any questioning of Mrs Treharne at present is simply out of the question. I will not allow it. I trust you will respect my wishes." He looked at the stretcher being carried out.

"Very well doctor," Rees conceded then looked back at Gwyn. "An officer will call tomorrow Mr Evans as I have said. Now then I shall take my leave. A sad business indeed Mr Evans. Goodnight." Rees started for the front door and then suddenly stopped and turned around. "Oh, you might want to give this to Mrs Treharne," he reached into his breast pocket and withdrew some paper, "suicide note, won't be needing it. Had to open it I'm afraid." Rees ignored the expression of total disgust on Gwyn's face. "Goodnight again then, Mr Evans."

"Thanks," Gwyn scowled, he just wanted to see the back of Rees. He saw the doctor sitting on one of the chairs in the hall. The man looked off colour and drawn. He seemed too young to be a doctor. Perhaps this was his first gory suicide.

"Would you like a drink doctor?" Gwyn asked.

"Yes, you know I think I would. Whisky? Large."

"Hold on there a minute, I'll get you one." He returned with a large tumbler of whisky and gave it to the doctor.

"I'm sorry about the police. They tend to be a little insensitive in these sort of matters."

"You can say that again. Never mind, not your fault doctor." The man took two gulps of his drink, coughed and said, "Thank you. This is the first violent suicide I've attended. I have to admit it has shaken me a little."

"That's to be expected doctor. No doubt you'll see a lot more of 'em before your career ends. How did 'ee do it, the Boss? I know he shot 'imself, but how? There's an 'ell of a mess."

"From what I could tell he shot himself through the mouth."

"Quick then, at least he didn't blunder it. Didn't try a shotgun or anything, knew what he was doing even at the end. The Boss always knew what he was doing. Thing I can't understand is why."

"You have no idea?" the doctor asked.

"None at all. Picked him up from his doctor's earlier today. He was a bit quiet coming back in the car. Didn't even swear at the other drivers, not like 'im at all. Perhaps that had something to do with it. I've got this letter he wrote to Lise, I haven't looked at it. None of my business, probably very personal too. Don't want to intrude if you know what I mean. Wish that bastard copper hadn't opened it."

"Yes, I understand Mr Evans. Well, I must go now. It's very late." He stood up and walked to the front door.

"Mr Treharne's own GP will be in touch as soon as possible. I'm just here as a locum. I will let him know as soon as I get back to the surgery. He was out on calls when you rang. He will take care of Mrs Treharne. Thank you for the drink. Goodnight." The doctor closed the door leaving Gwyn alone in the huge hall. He went into the kitchen to make a cup of tea. As he was pouring the boiling water into a pot Bronwyn came in. Her eyes were red from crying.

"Shouldn't you . . . ? Never mind. Sit down Bron, I'll bring you a nice cup of tea. How is Lise?"

Bronwyn looked at him and started crying again, "Sound asleep. That's why I've left her for a bit. Oh God, Gwyn! Why? Why?"

"I don't know love, I really don't. Here we are, drink this, it will do you good." He handed her a mug of tea. "The Boss had written a letter to Lise. I've got it. No point giving it to her just yet. Best to let her sleep. The letter probably explains it all. I'll give it to her when she's more herself."

Bronwyn started to calm down a little. "You've been very calm over all this, Gwyn. Don't know what any of us would have done without you. Pillar of strength you've been."

"Seen it all before Bron, friend of mine did himself in. Shotgun. I was the one that found 'im." He looked into his mug of tea, his thoughts apparently a hundred miles away.

"What's the matter, Gwyn?" Bronwyn asked.

"Nothing really, Bron. I suppose the Boss's death is beginning to get to me, that's all. 'Aven't had much chance to think about it till now. I'm really going to miss the old bugger you know. I was very fond of 'im. Good to me 'e was. A friend and you don't get many of 'em. Jesus, this place is going to seem bloody quiet without 'im. Wonder what will 'appen to everything now. The 'ouse and so on."

"We'll have to wait and see Gwyn."

He finished his tea with one long gulp.

"Look Bron, when you've finished your tea go and sit with Lise. I'm going to go and tidy up the study. There's a bit of a mess in there. Don't want you doing it."

"All right, I must be next to Lise when she wakes up."

"That's right. Give her this letter when you think the time's right."

"I will Gwyn," she kissed him on the cheek and hugged him, "I think this is the worst night of my life. I'm so glad you're here." He held her closely; her warmth giving him strength.

"Sometimes Bron, I don't know what I'd do without you too. Go on now, go and see to Lise. She could wake at any time. She'll need you."

As she left to go to Lise Gwyn noticed a slight but unmistakable change in his feelings toward Bronwyn.

Lise's mind came back to the present. That night would never leave her. It would leave a scar that would fade in time but always be there just the same, like that night in Denmark. An ache would announce itself every now and again if only to remind and make certain. Scars never truly healed; they merely hid for a while but in time they became less painful. She knew that the memories never died, they could always prickle and sting when they wanted to. All it took was the right word or expression, they never needed much. William had been the only man she had ever loved and she would never stop loving him. Never stop loving the memories that stray and then return. He would never die, not in the untouchable fantasies of her mind or the soft whims of her secret body. At least now she was starting to think clearly and by so doing purge herself of a grief that could never end.

William had been right in his estimate of her fortitude and courage. She was not, as he had once quoted to her from Gibbon, one of those 'females whose fortitude is commonly artificial, so it is seldom steady or consistent.' Still looking out at the sombre movement of the sea she reached into her pocket and withdrew William's last letter to her. She decided that this would be the last time she would read it. A healing must prevail. Parts of the paper were bloodstained; her hands shook slightly as she held the letter. The agony in her heart still struck and hurt but she couldn't resist the words her husband had written. She would cherish them and take them to her own death one day. She read and as she did so the numb hand of grief clutched her heart once more as tears started to fall to the ground.

"My darling Lise,

It is difficult for me to know where to begin. When you read this I shall be dead and in my very own Neverland. Barrie had something there you know. A true Prophet. We have enjoyed a time together of true happiness and fulfil-ment. You gave me life and love at a time when I thought enjoyment of either was impossible for me to ever recapture. You gave me yourself, completely and without reservation. You gave me a contentment and joy that per-haps I did not deserve. Lise my lovely, you are such a wonderful giver. I have never loved anyone in the way that I have loved you, believe me.

With all my heart forgive me for what I am about to do. This morning my doctor told me I have three months left to live, if that. I don't have a stomach ulcer my lovely, I have cancer. It broke my heart having to lie to you but I wanted to spare you the hurt. The awful anguish. Lise, I want your memories of me to be happy ones, I don't want you to remember me as a pathetic, wasted old man.

I couldn't bear to see your beautiful eyes tainted by tears and pain.

I beg of you Lise to understand why I am taking my own life.

I cannot put you or myself through a bitter crusade with no hope of success. I do what I do for both of us. Be strong my lovely. Be strong.

When I am gone I want you to take life by the throat, as you have done in the past. I want you to find love and happiness once again. You must not be the grieving widow in a black dress and carrying a black heart.

Live, my lovely, my woman, live and please be happy.

With everything that I am, I love you Lise and thank you. Thank you for everything that you are, everything that you have been and everything that you will continue to be.

One day we will fly together again.

Forgive me my darling darling girl.

My kisses will always be with you.

Your loving husband,

William

When she had finished reading Lise folded the letter and placed it back in her pocket. "I must be strong," she said to herself as she turned to go back into the house. She did not blame William for taking his own life. She understood.

"Are you all right Lise?" Gwyn was walking up to her, a concerned look on his face.

She sniffed and dabbed at her eyes with the now soaking wet handkerchief. "Yes, I'm fine Gwyn. Really. I'm glad the funeral is over. I just needed some time to be alone that's all."

"Of course," Gwyn replied, "I understand." He hated seeing Lise so distraught. In his private moments he wished he could have taken the pain for her.

Lise took his hand. "Gwyn, I haven't thanked you."

"No need for that *mun*." As he answered his eyes looked at the grass at his feet. An absurd bout of shyness always overcame him whenever he was alone or in close proximity to Lise. He always struggled to find the right words to say. Lise ignored his modest reply.

"There is need Gwyn. You have been a rock of support through all this. Particularly on the night William died. I do remember you know. You have been wonderful, a great help. Thank you Gwyn, I won't forget how good you've been."

"Don't be daft Lise, it's nothin'. You know I thought the world of the Boss. Would have done anything for 'im. You know at the time I couldn't figure out why he'd done it. Wasn't until you told me about his illness that I understood it all. Just like 'im you know. Very proud and 'ee loved you, you know."

"Yes, I know," Lise confirmed sadly. Gwyn went on, glad now that at last things could be brought out into the open.

"Don't mind me talking about it do you?" he asked.

"No Gwyn, I don't. We must remember William. He wouldn't have wanted any of us to stop living our normal lives. He certainly wouldn't want us to fall into a pit of despair or to mourn our lives away."

"Very true," Gwyn replied, "'ee wasn't the sort of man to be at the mercy of doctors. 'Ee could never 'ave 'andled waiting for death. As I said, just like 'im to get in first."

"Yes, Gwyn. You are certainly right about that. Now then, are Megan and Griffith still here?" 'Live', William had insisted, 'Live'.

"Yes, they are. They're 'aving a few drinks in the house. At least Megan is. Griffith seems to be behaving 'imself. Doesn't seem to have turned out too bad after all. Seems genuinely shocked at 'is father's passing away 'e does. The solicitor is 'ere as well, that's the reason I've come to look for you. I expect . . ." Gwyn began to feel awkward again but Lise came to the rescue.

"It's all right Gwyn, I know what you were going to say. They are waiting to find out what's in William's Will. They do have a right, they are his children. If I know William he will have been fair about his estate. Well then, I suppose we had better get on with it. I must admit I haven't given these practical matters much thought but I suppose now I will have to. I hope there won't be any trouble Gwyn, money always seems to bring out the worst in people." She took his arm. "Come on let's go and get it over and done with."

When Lise entered the drawing room Megan was sitting next to the drinks cabinet holding a large glass of gin and tonic. Kristian and Griffith were sitting together on a sofa.

Bernard John, an old and worn-out member of the legal profession, stood by the fireplace with a schooner of sherry in his wrinkled hand. The solicitor had attended their wedding. He was the only lawyer William had ever had any time for. The man was honest. He was really too old to be otherwise.

"Ah, Mrs Treharne. Firstly, may I offer you my deepest condolences. I attended the funeral but did not want to intrude. I did not feel the time was appropriate."

"Thank you, Mr John," Lise said politely, she had hardly spoken to him at the wedding but even after their brief conversation she had liked him. He was a refined man who bore one of those faces that shouted integrity and fair play.

"As my letter explained, I was your husband's solicitor for many years and I hope his friend. He was a good man. We will all miss him."

"Yes, Mr John. My husband spoke very highly of you." The old man nodded.

"Good of you to say so, Mrs Treharne. If you would like to sit down perhaps I can see to the business in hand. I do realise that you may feel that I am being somewhat insensitive by wishing to settle your husband's affairs so soon after his death. Sadly the law doesn't mourn, neither does it feel pain. I apologise sincerely if you find anything upsetting; if this be the case then please say, and perhaps we can arrange another meeting tomorrow. However, I would stress that the sooner probate on William's estate is granted, the better for all concerned."

"No, Mr John, please carry on. I appreciate that certain matters have to be dealt with."

"Too right they do," Megan interjected loudly causing everyone to turn their eyes on her. She had not been seen to shed one solitary tear since the death of her father. "I want to be back in London tonight. I have a dinner to attend, so let's just get on with it."

Griffith looked at his sister in disgust. "Megan," he said firmly, "do try and exercise a modicum of decorum for once in your sorry life will you?"

"Oh, shut up little brother. Come on Mr John get on with it. Let's hear what dear Daddy has done with all his lovely lolly."

The solicitor looked at her for a moment his eyes conveying utter contempt. He had witnessed the mercenary excesses of beneficiary greed many times during his long and distinguished time in private practice. Even so it still never failed to disgust him.

He ignored Megan, opened his briefcase and withdrew a thick wad of parchment paper tied together by pink ribbon. He sat down in an armchair, undid the ribbon and said carefully, "I have here the Last Will and Testament of my client, Mr William Treharne. As you can see it is a somewhat copious document in length. Indeed it would take some time for me to read it to you verbatim." He looked at Megan and sighed. "In view of the urgency for some to depart I shall read only those clauses particularly relevant to those present here today. I have had copies made, so each of you will be able to study Mr Treharne's Will in detail and at your leisure. I will be happy to answer any questions you may have now or later." He could see that this was a painful process for Lise, therefore he would do his job as gently as possible.

"As you all know, Mr Treharne was a wealthy man. His financial interests are legion and diverse. His Will is a complicated affair both legally and financially. I will endeavour to simplify his testamentary dispositions as best I can, obviously again please ask about anything you are unsure of. We lawyers do sometimes have a tendency to speak in esoteric language for which I apologise."

"Oh, just get on with it for God's sake!" Megan interrupted. "How much do we get? That's all I want to know." The solicitor ignored the objectionable outburst and continued.

"For tax reasons the bulk of my client's estate has been placed under various trusts. The two executors and trustees of his estate, that is the persons appointed to carry out the wishes of his Will, are myself and my partner Mr Simon Strachan. Mr Treharne has made various modest bequests to friends and employees, these you can all read for yourselves, they are straightforward enough." John paused for a moment, bracing himself for what was about to happen – he knew only too well how money corrupted family values and decency. Death tended to bring out the more unattractive and avaricious side of human nature, more particularly when there was money on the table. One of the main purposes of a Will was to avoid uncertainty and ensure that the testator's last wishes were carried out to the letter. Sometimes this wasn't to be, and John was anticipating such an occasion now. "The bulk of Mr Treharne's estate has been bequeathed to his wife, Lise Treharne. Various trust funds and annuities have been set up to ensure," he looked at Lise, "your comfortable existence for the rest of your life. You are also to receive all Mr Treharne's real property, that is bricks and mortar absolutely, along with various capital bequests."

"What? What?" Megan screeched. "I don't believe it, I . . ."

"Please be quiet," John snapped harshly, "I have not finished; adequate provision has been made for you if you will just be patient, now please." Megan shut her mouth and waited. The hatred flowing from her toward Lise could have set the whole room on fire. John continued. "Maintenance and advancement trusts have been set up for Mr Treharne's stepson Kristian and for any grandchildren that may be born in the future. These trusts basically allow an income and capital to be provided for general living expenses, but more specifically to assist and help the beneficiary in any educational pursuits or career that he or she may decide to undertake in the future. Upon reaching the age of twenty-five the beneficiary or beneficiaries will receive a capital sum. Now then, regarding you Megan Treharne and your brother Griffith, your father has provided you both with an immediate bequest of £100,000 each plus a generous income from capital for the rest of your lives. Perhaps you would like to turn to page seven of the Will for greater clarity." John had avoided reading out this clause preferring to sit back and wait.

"£100,000!" Megan shrieked, now beside herself with anger. Then suddenly the tirade stopped as she continued to read. Her eyes bulged, her three chins wobbled, her face turned white and her mouth dropped open.

"What . . . what's this? What's this for Christ's sake?" John knew what was coming. "My father . . ." Megan spluttered. "My mother . . . I don't . . . I just don't . . . how can . . . this is impossible!" By now everyone had turned to page seven and gone silent. The same could not be said for Megan who stood up in an apoplectic rage. "The bastard, the fucking bastard!" she screamed. "How can he say he's not my father? If he's not, who the hell is?!"

John tried to calm Megan down. "Please Miss Treharne, do sit down and calm yourself. I have a letter to give to you from Mr Treharne. It explains everything." Megan wasn't listening.

"£100,000! The bastard! He's worth millions!"

"Miss Treharne, please control yourself. You have been taken care of and need never have to worry about money again. You have been provided with a handsome yearly income plus an immediate bequest. You are a wealthy lady."

"Wealthy lady! Wealthy bastard more like! How could he? How could he do this to me?! My poor mother! The pig is saying that someone else fathered me, that my mother had an affair. I don't believe any of it. He's lying, he's just trying to humiliate me!"

John said quietly, "It's all in the letter Miss Treharne, with some documents of proof too. I beg you to calm down, please."

"Calm down!" Megan turned on Lise and pointed her finger at her. "That bitch! That slut! That German-loving whore twisted my father's mind. I'm going to fight this," Megan fumed, "I'm going to contest the Will! You won't get any of my father's money, you thieving bitch, I'll see to that! Neither will your bastard son!"

No one said a word while the tension exploded throughout the room.

Megan then pointed at Kristian. "Oh I know all about you don't you worry . . .! You, my little Danish friend are the offspring of a rapist – or worse, a German soldier!"

Griffith leapt up. "That's enough Megan!" He shouted and started to drag her out of the room. The virago in her was not to be quelled.

"You're a bastard, Kristian, like me, so join the club. Your mother never married, she was raped in Denmark, had to come over here to avoid the shame. She was screwing German soldiers, I know it all. Your father is either a rapist or a German. I know the truth. Your mother's a slut a . . .!" Griffith at last managed to push his sister through the drawing room door.

"Jesus Christ, Megan, you've gone too far this time! I'm taking you home . . . now!" With that he bundled her out of the hallway and through the front door. He didn't even stop to collect their luggage. He drove off at breakneck speed.

Back in the drawing room Lise couldn't move.

She couldn't even think.

So much tragedy.

So much pain.

It was unrelenting.

Why?

How did Megan know all this?

Lise felt cold.

She looked at Kristian. Her only child

She was at a loss for words.

Mr John sat still. He too could find no words. The War. Casualties. It went on. He recognised the agony and shock that clung like odious parasites to the two people left in the room. There could be no further discussion of his clients Estate.

True to his gentlemanly nature he said, "I am so very sorry, Mrs Treharne. It was not my intention to be the harbinger of such distressing and hateful conduct. I am truly sorry, but I had no choice but to reveal the contents of my client's will. It was my duty as your late husband's solicitor. Do forgive me."

Lise collected herself. "Oh, Mr John, please it is not your fault. There is no need to apologise. No need at all . . ."

"Well, I do not think it is the time now to pursue these matters further. I shall begin the process of applying for probate. Perhaps you would be so good as to arrange an appointment to see me in my office over the next few days. No rush. There are some papers you will need to sign. I will take my leave now. Again my sincere apologies for that appalling outburst . . . unforgivable, quite unforgivable. Please ring me at any time, day or night. Good day."

The solicitor left the room leaving Kristian and his mother alone. After a few minutes of total silence Kristian finally asked, "Mum, what was that all about?" There was no anger in his voice, only confusion. "Is that woman crazy, drunk or what?"

Lise rushed up to him and held him in her arms. Tears rushed from her eyes.

"Oh God, Kristian, I am so sorry, so terribly sorry." She pulled away and sat next to him; taking his hand she said, "Kristian, your father was not a German soldier. Neither was he killed in the War, as I have always led you to believe. It's true I never married in Denmark. You were born out of wedlock."

"So, I am a bastard then?" Kristian mumbled.

"If you must put it that way, yes you are. Just listen to me though please." Lise fought a desperate battle to find the right words. She knew that whatever she said now could lose her son forever. The prospect filled her with dread.

"The war was coming to an end. I was alone in your grandparent's house one evening. I'll never forget it. Winston Churchill was speaking on the radio. Two men broke in and well, you heard. They . . . er . . . they abused me . . . violently." Lise tried desperately to stop the tears that were drowning her eyes. ". . . You see, I had been seeing a German soldier, only a boy really, a year older than me, he was seventeen. We weren't sweethearts although I was beginning to become quite fond of him. We walked together a couple of times and that was all. There was nothing else I promise you." A sad smile passed her lips, "You must understand, Kristian, that the Germans were our enemies. They occupied our country against our will. There was hatred toward them, and of course fear. They weren't all bad though. My 'crime', if you like, was the fact that I had been friendly with one. You see this kind of thing wasn't done. To Danish eyes I was a traitor. I had betrayed my own blood, my own countrymen. My own people made sure that I was punished for my sin, my friendship. Its innocence was ignored. I was too young to understand war. Death. The two men beat me and cut all my hair away. Then they raped me without mercy. Out of that desperate evil God intervened and you were born."

"So, who is my father Mum, do you know?"

Lise took a deep breath. "No, my darling, I have no idea. Both men were masked."

Kristian's intelligent mind wanted more. "Why did you have me Mum? You must tell me, surely you could have . . . well, you know." Kristian was a young man now, she could not shelter him forever. The Sixties were demolishing all taboos.

"Abortion didn't happen in those days, at least not without danger. Besides I wanted you . . . desperately. Somehow I knew that your birth would cleanse me of the outrage committed upon my body. I felt that the goodness in my child would cleanse the evil of those men. It's so hard to explain Kristian, but you must believe me. I just knew that having you was the right thing to do. I just knew. I am telling you the truth."

Kristian looked at his mother. He saw the hurt in her eyes. The fear. The love. As if William wasn't enough.

"I believe you, Mum, I believe you." He put his arms around her. "I'm still a bit shocked though. How the hell did Megan find out about all this?"

"I don't know, I really don't. I know that she had wanted to see William. She had written to him a couple of weeks ago but I don't think he had replied. She has hated me since the first day we met, I suppose William's Will was the last straw. In a way I can understand her desire to hurt me and you, but we mustn't let her, Kristian, we really mustn't."

"Mum, I loved William, he's the only father I have ever known. I don't like seeing you like this, you've been through enough." He hugged his mother again. "I love you too – and what difference does it really make in the end, whether my father was some vicious Dane or not? I'll never know either way. The only memories I have of my childhood are happy ones with you, Bron, William and Gwyn. I'm not going to spoil those memories with some daft obsession about who my real father is. I don't think I really want to know anyway. Why should I? As far as I'm concerned the whole thing is best left dead and buried. You couldn't help what happened Mum, so please don't blame yourself. I love you and always will, that's all that matters." Kristian was having difficulty controlling his own tears but there was one last question he had to ask. "Would you ever have told me the truth?"

"Oh, yes, one day. I always felt that you should know eventually. You have a right to know, but I wanted you to mature a little more so that you would understand better. I knew one day I would have to tell you; it was just a question of finding the right time. I am sorry Kristian, I wish now I had had the courage to be honest with you sooner. All this could have been avoided. I have been rather a coward in some ways."

"Don't hurt yourself, Mum. I don't blame you for anything. I would have known sooner or later as you say." He looked at his mother again, the blue eyes seeing everything. He smiled, "You know, you must be a tough old bird underneath all that helpless woman bit."

"Enough of the 'old' please!"

CHAPTER 21

Megan's bitterness had turned into a furnace.

She was being burnt alive by hatred.

It had become her only reason for living.

She sat in her flat brooding and planning. She had become obsessed with Lise Jacobson and her bastard son. She wanted their lives ripped apart and the pieces thrown to rabid dogs.

She wanted them dead.

They were the cause of all her unhappiness. Her humiliation.

Her father would never have cheated her had it not been for their calculated invasion into his life. Her father? She was still unable to accept the fact that another man had created her. She had read the letters that John had given her.

Her mother had had some torrid little affair with a business associate of her father's. According to the letters, they were both very much in love. A real romance. Then it suddenly ended, the reasons unclear. The only certainty was Megan.

She didn't believe a word of it. The whole thing was merely an insane ploy by her father to cut her out of his fortune, a ploy instigated and planned by Lise. That woman, Megan knew, had coerced and pressed her poor, ageing father into doing something against his will. As she thought of this explanation her mind quickly changed tack. On second thoughts, perhaps it wasn't Lise after all. Her 'father' had always been a callous bastard, he had even spat on her by dying unexpectedly. She had planned to go and see him on the day of his death to tell him about the things she had learnt about Lise in Denmark. The inconsiderate fool had died before she could sow the seeds of calamity. So what if he wasn't her true father, he was a weak fool anyway. She was better off without his blood. She was strong, ruthless.

The more she thought about it the more grateful she was for not having William Treharne's blood in her.

Despite this, her twisted mind still seethed at the loss of her true inheritance. The Will had left more or less everything to Lise and her son. Her anger at this humiliation was beyond description, her parting scene at the Cliffs and the look of shock on Lise's face little compensation. Megan would never be fully sated until she exacted revenge. Millions of pounds had gone to a Danish whore and her offspring. Megan began to believe that Lise was some kind of supernatural being casting evil spells and drinking magic potions of every description. As she sat alone drinking more and more, her imagination ran riot. Of one thing she was certain: she had to contest the Will. She had rights, didn't she? She was William's only daughter; even if adopted, there must be some law that protected people like her from such perfidy and injustice. She had seen her own lawyers to find out about what she could do. The thought of all that money going to Lise was killing Megan. She stank of vengeance. She herself had now become a tool of lethal intent. She would never rest until full satisfaction had been given . . . and restitution.

True insanity was gradually beginning to tighten its devious grip on Megan's mind. She needed help urgently, but her mind was unable to perceive this. All she could think of was revenge. Her trip to Denmark, the elation of discovery, her plans of victory had all been devastated and now lay in ashes at her feet. Her father had defeated her, even in his dying moments. His suicide had taken away the perverted ecstasy she had hoped to experience when revealing the true antecedents of his wife. Her 'father' had pushed a knife in her and turned it around, he had abused and checked her ambitions. She would never forgive him for this. Had he remained alive her devious machinations would have ensured a proper inheritance, or so she believed. His death had infuriated her. Her frustration had become even more psychotic than before. Any grief over her adoptive father's death was obliterated by her mad notions of revenge. She felt nothing over his loss. She was the victim not him. She sat alone in her flat and mourned.

Tears fell as Megan grieved for Megan.

CHAPTER 22

"Thank you for coming in to see me, Mrs Treharne. Please sit down."

Lise sat opposite Mr John.

The old gentleman inspired confidence and well-being. He still wore the old detachable collars of his calling, brilliant white, starched and formal. His black suit and military tie gave a sense of efficient propriety. The man was in control.

"Firstly, Mrs Treharne—"

"Please, Lise will be fine. I know that William valued your friendship."

"Thank you, er . . . Lise. Well, firstly I am so very sorry for the unpleasantness that took place at your home after the funeral. It was so unnecessary. Unfortunately it was unavoidable. As I explained, all beneficiaries have a right to know the contents of a testator's Will. Sadly, there was nothing I could do to blunt your anguish. Again I apologise."

The man's sincerity touched Lise in spite of William's constant ire where lawyers were concerned – 'Pompous bastards who lied and cheated their way through other people's misfortunes' had always been his description of them. She kept her thoughts to herself but remembered that her late husband had always maintained that John was an exception to the rule and indeed a true friend.

The solicitor opened a file before him and glanced briefly at some papers it contained.

"Well, it seems that your stepdaughter intends to carry out her threat."

"I beg your pardon Mr John, threat?"

"Bernard, please. Yes, I'm sorry, you probably don't remember the exact tone of her virulent outburst after the funeral. She made it known that she intended to contest the Will of your husband. As you know we were good friends."

"Of course. Contest the Will? What exactly does that mean?"

"Put simply, she feels that she has been cheated out of her true inheritance. She will try and prevent probate, that is stop us administering your husband's estate until she has been granted what she considers to be a fair share as it were. She is proceeding on the grounds that William was of 'unsound mind' at the time he executed his Will."

"Unsound mind?" Lise asked, still somewhat mystified.

"In layman's language – insane."

"That's ridiculous," Lise objected calmly. "William was dying when he committed suicide. His last letter explained everything. There was nothing wrong with his mind at the time of his suicide or before. Megan is gravely mistaken Bernard I assure you. 'Unsound mind'," she repeated, "nonsense, total nonsense."

"Lise, I agree with you entirely. There is ample evidence to rebut such a claim. William anticipated, as indeed did I, problems over his Will particularly where the issue of his first marriage were concerned. Legal safeguards were initiated. Frankly, I do not feel there is anything serious to worry about. The actions of his adopted daughter will merely delay things for a while. They will create a little inconvenience but that is all. The end result will be the same. The terms of your husband's Last Will and Testament will be carried out to the letter, of that I can assure you. I do not feel there is any cause for you to worry, please trust me."

"Why Bernard? Why? William left her enough money, didn't he? He didn't cast her aside or anything."

John looked at Lise and for the first time saw why his client had adored this woman so much. His heart went out to her, the iciness of his profession was turning to water as he said softly, "Lise, believe me there is nothing unique in any of this. Whenever death opens the coffers of wealth there is invariably a rush for its appropriation. Relatives who had always loved one another, been civil to one another and so on suddenly adopt hatred and jealousy. Money corrupts and poisons, as you no doubt know. When a wealthy individual dies the vultures appear from nowhere, hovering and sniffing, waiting patiently for a chance of any scrap of money that may be left over. Your stepdaughter is a bitter woman, she feels cheated. Abused. She feels that she and her brother are entitled to most of the estate and she is going to fight for this. Your stepson is apparently uninterested in any of this. He seems quite content with his lot. Had William totally disinherited Megan, then perhaps her case would have merit. But this is not so. He was careful to provide generously for all his children. I do not think you need worry about anything at all. As for his being of 'unsound mind', that is preposterous. We have an abundance of witnesses who are prepared to swear affidavits to the contrary, his own doctor among them. No Lise, there is no need for concern. All Megan will do is lose some money paying expensive London solicitors. It will all be to no avail. She will reap a harvest of financial loss and sadness. That is all."

Lise looked pale and drawn. The solicitor could see that she was uncomfortable and upset. He said nothing and waited for her to respond.

"Bernard, I am no lawyer. I understand little of all this. The legalities anyway. All I really know is that the man I loved is dead. Not all the money in the world can ever change that. Somehow I feel unclean sitting here talking about my husband's wealth. It just doesn't seem right. I feel sickened by it all. Sickened. Let Megan have everything if that's what she wants. I'd rather that than drag William's memory through courtrooms and legal battles. I've survived through greater hardships in my life, and I can survive again. William meant more to me than any sum of money. Let her have it all please. I don't want any of this."

John was impressed by her total lack of venality and was struck yet again by her beauty and inherent goodness. He had no doubt that her words were genuine. He had only to look into her eyes to see that. He knew people. It was his profession and job to know.

"Lise, I cannot do that. William would not have wanted me to either. Let me carry out his wishes as I am legally bound to do. The whole purpose of a Will is to ensure certainty where the intentions of a testator are concerned. I am sure Lise that you would want to respect your husband's dying wishes. Your grief is still raw, so please allow some time to pass before doing anything rash. If at a later date you wish Megan to receive more, then you can always remedy this. For now, however, it remains my legal duty to carry out the terms of the Will, my duty as a solicitor and my duty as your husband's executor and friend. Leave everything to me and I shall try, as much as I am able, to avoid any upset or unpleasantness. Once we have obtained probate then we can take a more detailed look at your actual position. For now though trust me Lise, please."

She had listened to every word John had said and realised that the man was right. She was too drained to argue.

"Very well Bernard. Please do as William has instructed. You are right. His last wishes must be respected, and knowing my husband he never did anything without good reason."

"Good. Now then, please sign some of these papers and then you can go home. Forget about all this. Believe me Megan is more than looked after. You have nothing to feel remorse or guilt about."

Lise stood up after having signed the various documents.

"One last thing Bernard . . ."

"Yes."

"I have some savings, but the Cliffs does cost rather a lot of money to maintain. So at least whilst all this mess is being sorted out, I thought Kristian and I might move into something more modest. I . . ."

"Lise, believe me there is no need for you to consider anything quite so drastic at the moment – you are a wealthy woman.

Just carry on as normal. The bank will afford you overdraft facilities for the time being should that be necessary, there's nothing to worry about. I have already written to them advising of the situation. You will find them very helpful if you have any difficulties. If you have no other questions . . ."

"No, not at the moment anyway."

"Good. That's it then, thank you Lise. Leave everything to me. I shall keep you informed of any developments and please ring me or call if you need to."

"Thank you Bernard, you have been very kind."

"Not at all. Go home and get some rest. Try not to worry about anything."

"Goodbye then."

"Goodbye Lise. I'm here if you need me."

She closed the office door and left. John remained standing for a few moments and decided that his friend William had been a lucky man. A very lucky man indeed.

When Lise arrived home the house was quiet.

It would take her a long time to get used to the feeling of emptiness and isolation. William had always been there. If not in the house then in the gardens. He was always close by. Near. Normally at this time she would have been preparing his lunch. Now she didn't know what to do. The Cliffs seemed so big and useless without him, like some deathly mausoleum erected purely for memory and nothing else. Lise didn't need any reminding of his life. He would always be within her, a part of her, for as long as she lived. She went to his study and instinctively raised her hand to knock on the door. He had never liked being disturbed when he was in there. It was his private room; his 'thinking room' as he had called it. She opened the door and walked in. This was the first time she had gone into the room since his death. She walked toward the bookshelves and touched some of the books. Her fingers then travelled toward the elegant mahogany desk. Touching and feeling. A fountain pen, William's favourite, still lay on his desk next to a wad of writing paper. His collection of classical music remained where it had always been, the records untouched and unplayed. She took one record out of its sleeve and put it on the record player. It was Puccini's *La Boheme*, one of William's favourites. 'Ghe Gelida Manina' was an aria special to them both. As the tenor sang, Lise was taken back to a small café in Paris. Like the opera she now listened to, it had been called *The Rose*. They had drunk hot coffee and eaten croissants while they loved each other. Lise sat at his desk and toyed with the fountain pen. As the song continued its words of mourning and love it made her feel as if William was sitting right opposite her. She knew he would always be with her. He was with her now in this room. His spirit, his presence still lived in her. As she put his pen down she knew that William would never want her to grieve and cry her life away. She remembered the words of his letter again. There had been so many tears already. He had wanted her to live, to be happy and fulfilled. She looked around the room once more as the aria came to a poignant end. The song's end also marked the finishing of her apathy, her guilt, her reluctance to fight with the business of living. She went to the window and looked out across the rose garden. It was beginning to look neglected and unkempt. This wouldn't do at all. She looked around herself deep in thought. An idea was developing in her mind. She went back to the desk, and taking the fountain pen began to scribble some notes and draw some rough plans. At last she was returning to the land of the living. Her life was finding purpose again.

Her idea, provoked by some words William had said to her a long time ago, could be her saviour. She stayed in the study for another two hours, thinking and planning. When she had finished, she went into the kitchen and told Bronwyn to go and look for Gwyn, Kristian and the gardener. They were all to be present in the drawing room within five minutes. Bronwyn had received her orders and had immediately gone searching. She had noticed too the sudden difference in Lise. Her voice had become firm again and full of energy. Something was up, that's for certain, Bronwyn thought as she hunted around the house. For a moment she wondered if they were all about to be given the sack. Lise seemed determined, serious. No, she thought, Lise wasn't like that, must be something else, but what?

Five minutes later they were all assembled as requested. Lise walked in to the drawing room and told them all to sit down and make themselves comfortable. The decrepit gardener began rolling a cigarette, but Lise was too quick for his fingers or, for that matter, his matches.

"We'll have none of that Mr Jenkins, if you please. No smoking in the house." The wizened old man stared at her with a look of bemusement.

"The Boss always let me smoke in 'ere. Never said anything he didn't, smoked 'imself he did."

"Not in here he didn't Mr Jenkins, and Mr Treharne smoked a pipe and then only in his study"

"Well, I'll be buggered, but the Boss—" Before he could say anything more Gwyn stopped him, knowing what an unrestrained mouth Dai had.

"That's enough now Dai. Mrs Treharne 'ere is the boss now, so do as your told." The old man mumbled something against the whole female sex but stopped rolling his cigarette.

"Thank you, Mr Jenkins." Lise stood in front of the fireplace, facing them. Her whole demeanour had suddenly changed. She was no longer the pitiful grieving widow, but now the mistress of all she surveyed. This change hadn't gone unnoticed by the people in the room. Bronwyn looked at Gwyn with an expression that said 'Look out we're all in for the boot, she's selling up'. Lise spoke at last.

"Now then, this is a big house. Too many rooms and much too much space for three permanent residents and . . ." she looked at Gwyn with an amused glint in her eye, "one part-timer." She had known for some time that Bronwyn and Gwyn were sweethearts despite their efforts to hide the fact. Gwyn moved uncomfortably on his chair. That was the trouble with Lise he thought, never missed a bloody trick, she's getting back to her old self again, no doubt about it. "You are probably wondering what all this is about. I can see by your face, Bronwyn, that you are anticipating some kind of domestic upheaval. Well, you needn't worry. Upheaval there will be, changes there will be, but you can all stay on at the Cliffs if you want to. I will need your help more than ever. William would have wanted it this way. I have reached a decision, a decision which affects us all which is why I wanted to talk to you." She stopped for a moment and absorbed their expectant faces. For the first time since William's death she smiled, "I'm going to turn the Cliffs into the best hotel on the Gower Peninsula." For a moment no one said anything; this was one thing none of them had anticipated. Without giving anyone an opportunity to respond she continued. "Are you going to stay with me and help?" They all answered, "Yes," without hesitation. "Good. We can still remain as a family. This project will bring some purpose into my life, we will all have to work hard. There's a lot to do and I'm sure William would approve of our efforts. Right then, you can all go back to what you were doing now and Mr Jenkins, you can smoke your cigarette – not in here though, I repeat – disgusting habit that it is."

Gwyn was about to say something, but decided against it. He was going to ask when she intended to start all this but felt that Lise was no doubt sorting these details out herself. She was a capable woman he knew, always had been. As they left the room, more than anything else they were pleased that their mistress and now their employer was returning to her true character.

CHAPTER 23

"Well that's a turn-up for the books, isn't it Bron? A hotel, ay?" Gwyn said as he took another sip of his tea. Bronwyn sat opposite him at the kitchen table.

"Don't you think it's a good idea then?" she asked.

"Course I do. The place needs a bit of life. As Lise said, all these rooms going to waste. 'Ell of a lot of work though. Expensive too. Cost a bloody fortune and if I know Lise, she won't stint either. She's thrifty, always 'as been, but when it comes to doing something properly there's no beatin' 'er. She's a shrewd woman with no flies on 'er. It won't be your average little B&B that's for certain: Lise will do things in style. She's got the money for it too. Bet the Boss left her plenty and good luck to 'er I say."

"At least we know our jobs are safe too. I was a bit worried Gwyn."

"Shouldn't 'ave been girl. Lise would never do the dirty."

"It's a grand idea," Bronwyn enthused, "and did you notice Lise actually smiled? I'm so glad. She's looked so awful lately, not surprising. I know Mr Treharne's death coming like that must have been a terrible shock."

"Aye, well she'll get over it. She's strong. Building a hotel is just the thing. Give 'er something to do, something to occupy her mind. It's a good thing in many ways. Anyway, Bron, I best be off now. My Mam will be wanting her evening paper." He walked round the table, took a quick look over his shoulder to make sure no one was about and gave Bronwyn a kiss while making a quick assault on her heaving bosom.

"Get off Gwyn *mun*!" she shouted. "You randy old bugger, someone might come in!"

"Ah, shut up woman," he laughed, "might be back later tonight, so be ready for a boardin' party . . . God, I just love your tits!" he added as he attempted another squeeze.

"Gwyn, get out of here before I scream will you!"

"All right girl, don't get your draws in a twist. I'll untwist them later on though if you do." He gave a last squeeze for good measure and ran out of the kitchen shouting, "Lovely by God, best tits on the Gower coast."

He made his way back home, stopping off at the local stores to buy the *Evening Post*, a packet of cigarettes, and a bottle of sherry. He didn't get drunk on it, just mellow and lethargic. A good dose of the sweet wine always ensured a good night's sleep and a degree of armour against his mother's constant attacks. He walked into the cottage and there, as always, sat his mother. The television blasted out the early evening news.

"Here's the paper Mam, don't know why you bother," he said as he handed it to her, "load of rubbish, gossip and news about Mrs Jones' new toilet is all you get."

"What's that?" his mother squawked.

"Aren't you on the air *mun!*" Gwyn bellowed referring to her hearing aid and pointing to his own ear. She fiddled around with some plastic stuck in her ear, after which there was a loud buzzing sound.

"What was that you said?"

"Never mind, not important. What's for supper?" His mother's head was already buried in the newspaper and without looking up she said, "*Cawl* in the kitchen, on the stove." Her quick answer confirmed his suspicions that the hearing disability was another fraud, another weapon to be used against him. His mother was crafty enough to play on it, but he didn't quite know why she bothered. She only ever heard what she wanted to hear anyway. The hearing aid was simply a cosmetic accessory, a means of attracting sympathy – and in Gwyn's case, torment. He gave up trying to talk to her and went into the kitchen to have something to eat.

Cawl was a traditional Welsh stew of lamb and fresh vegetables. It was nourishing and tasty. Gwyn helped himself to a large bowl of the stew and a few chunks of bread. He remained in the kitchen to eat his food. He could never stand eating with his mother; she always made such a bloody din with her slurping, smacking of lips and cracking of false teeth. His appetite invariably waned when victim to such a cacophonous symphony of his mother's physical appreciation of food. A good belch and an odoriferous fart were not unknown as the encore. Understandably, when possible, he chose to eat alone. After he had finished his supper he went into the living room to join his mother.

"What's on TV Mam?" he asked.

"What's that?" Came the reply.

"What's on TV?" Gwyn shouted again, sometimes convinced that she made him repeat himself on purpose just to annoy.

"Nothing, as usual."

"There we are then." He didn't say anything more. Conversation with his mother was like trying to communicate with foreigners. All gestures and no sodding sense. For want of nothing better to do he started laying into his bottle of sherry.

"Drinkin' again are we? Can't you leave the stuff alone, you wicked swine?"

"Helps me sleep Mam."

"Sleep? That's a good one. Turn my house into a pub you do. Drink and smokin' is all you think about. And women. Waste all your money you do."

"I 'aven't got much in my life 'ave I? A little sherry and a fag don't do any 'arm," Gwyn replied. Her hearing always seemed to improve when a row was on the brew.

"A little sherry!" she shrieked, "whole bottle more like. You'll be dead before long if you carry on like this."

"Aye mam, but what a way to go."

"Bloody fool, what about the time last year when a policeman had to bring you 'ome? Fancy walking up to the off-licence to get more drink and forgetting to put your trousers on. Drunken bugger!"

Gwyn had heard this one every day for the past year and so had most of the village. He had to admit though that at the time he had already had a shed-full of booze, so God knows what made him decide to go out and get more, half dressed at that. Very embarrassing it had been, and his mother was not going to let him forget it. He was sick of hearing the same thing, but this time he decided not to rise to the bait.

"Yes, yes. Go on now watch the telly will you and give me a bit of peace for Gawd's sake. Make my life a bloody misery you do."

"Ungrateful wretch," his mother responded, "where would you be without me, ay? In the gutter that's where. In the gutter!"

He was not in the mood tonight to start a verbal war with his mother so he kept quiet while she watched 'Coronation Street'. At about midnight Gwyn had finished his bottle and was snoring away on the settee. His last thought before intoxicated sleep arrived was whom he would save if his wife and mother were both drowning at the same time in the same river. His mother probably, came the mentally slurred reply: you could always have another wife but never another mother. Suddenly his snoring stopped and his breathing became laboured. He started to gasp for air. His eyes opened as a sharp pain shot through his leg and flames tried to grab his feet.

"*Jesus!*" he shouted as he leapt up and nearly fell over. His head was still fuzzy from sleep and drink. Flames were eating the settee he had been sleeping on with a furious appetite. Smoke was filling the room. Smoke the killer. It was almost impossible to breathe. Gwyn's brain quickly went into gear. He lay on the floor where the smoke was less intense and started to crawl toward the telephone. He dialled 999, reported the fire, and then made a bolt for the stairs, shutting the living room door after him. His mother. So far the smoke had not started to reach the upstairs rooms. He arrived at her bedroom door and hammered on it, as he did so, he remembered that she always locked the door and never wore her hearing aid to bed. Smoke was starting to drift up the stairs.

"Shit and 'ell," he yelled, "Mam, open the bloody door will you, the 'ouse is on fire." Still no reply. "Ah, bugger it!" he shouted and gave the door a shove with his shoulder. The small lock gave way easily enough. His mother lay in bed sound asleep. He ran to her bed shouting and then started to push and shove her sleeping body. At last she woke up.

"What! What! What's goin' on?! What you doing *mun*?! There a fire or something?! You're drunk, drunk again you wicked devil. I'll give you waking me up!"

"Shut up *mun* will you, the 'ouse is on fire. Get up quick before we both get burnt alive!"

"Fire?" she finally realised the danger they were in but stayed clam.

"'Ave you called the fire brigade?"

"Yes Mam, they're on their way. Now come on before we get burnt to death. The old woman grabbed a dressing gown and following Gwyn made for the door. It was too late. Flames were engulfing the bottom of the stairs and the smoke was unbearable.

"Back into the bedroom quick!" Gwyn ordered. He slammed the door shut and ran to the window. A fire engine was just arriving."

"Lie down on the floor Mam!"

"What for, you bloody fool?"

"Just do as I say will you. Lie on the floor for pity's sake!" For once she did as she was told. Gwyn stuck his head out of the window.

"Up here! Up here!" he shouted, "can't get out any other way. Flames and smoke. Quick my Mam's dyin', dyin' I'm tellin' you!" He nearly added, take your time if you like, have a cuppa before you start, but thought better of it. His mother was calmer than he was, bloody typical. Not a scratch on her. His foot ached like hell though. A fireman soon appeared at the window.

"My Mam, quick get her first. She's an old woman!"

"Right you are sir, pass her to me then."

The fireman was all calm and efficiency. Gwyn lifted his mother up and dragged her to the window. She was in a swoon and not helping much. He started pushing her through the window to the waiting fireman but was having trouble with her rear end.

"*Iesu Mawr*, mam, never realised you had such a fat arse!" he exclaimed as he gave one last shove. Down the ladder she went with Gwyn in hot pursuit. It wasn't long before everything was brought under control. Most of the damage to the house was caused by smoke. There was very little on the structural side. The Chief Officer walked up to Gwyn's mother.

"Well, Mrs Evans, you have been fortunate. I have to say that if it hadn't been for the quick thinking of your son and his un-selfish courage you may not be with us now. A very brave man indeed."

"'Im?" she pointed at Gwyn who was having his burnt foot seen to by an ambulance man. "The old fool was drunk down-stairs. I know what 'appened. Probably dropped a cigarette down the side of the settee and fell asleep. Done it before 'ee 'as, wasn't so lucky this time was 'ee? Go and look at the settee if there's anything left of it, burn marks everywhere."

The fireman shifted around on his feet, an embarrassed look on his face.

"Well, that is possible Mrs Evans. We just don't know at the moment. Could have been an electrical fault. These old prop-erties you know. When did you last have the wiring checked?"

"Oh, I don't know. Ask that fool over there." The fireman didn't want to get involved in domestic blame seeking so instead changed the subject.

"You are insured?"

"What? With that bloody fool in the 'ouse? Course I am. Walkin' disaster 'ee is."

"That's all right then. I suggest you get in touch with the insurance company first thing. They will take care of everything."

"Pity they couldn't take care of 'im isn't it?" she answered pointing at Gwyn. "None of this would have 'appened if the fool hadn't got drunk."

"Not for me to comment Mrs Evans. Main thing is that you're both alive. A few more minutes and believe me, it could have been otherwise. You have a lot to thank your son for. He is a brave man," he repeated. With that he walked back to his men and started to order their departure.

"Brave man, my arse," she mumbled after him, but this time a slight smile invaded her lips – Gwyn came limping up to his mother.

"Electrical fault then was it? That's what the fireman told me."

"Don't give me that, you blackguard! You think I'm some kind of idiot. You were drunk and left a cigarette burning. I know what 'appened. You can't fool me."

"Nothin' of the sort Mam. I'm tellin' you it was electrical," Gwyn insisted.

"Gawd help us, what are we goin' to do now then? Ay? No home, no nothin'. Lucky we're here to talk about it. *Duw*, you and your sherry. Made us 'omeless now it 'as."

"Oh, don't take on so will you? Everything's insured, new for old. 'Ave everything replaced. All newly decorated. Could be a blessing in disguise. New carpets, decoration – everything. The place needed tartin' up."

"Tartin' up you say! Still got women on your mind after all this. I give up I do. Sent from 'ell you were to torment me. Sent from 'ell! The midwife gave your father a good lamping when you were born! All 'is fault, 'is side of the family 'ad all the drunks and wasters!"

Gwyn ignored his mother's overactive spleen. "Come on now Mam, I'll take you over to the Cliffs. We can stay there for a bit while things get sorted out."

"I'm not going anywhere!"

"Come on now will you, you can't stay here. Mrs Treharne will look after you until we get things sorted out."

Finally, after a great deal of persuasion, his mother finally saw sense and agreed to go with him.

The following day the local rag hailed Gwyn as a hero. He became the Welsh Achilles overnight. The minister of his mother's chapel turned up at the Cliffs full of admiration and new respect. He was heard to say, "You saved your mother's life Gwyn. Such devotion. Such courage. All of us at the chapel give thanks to the Lord for using you as His instrument in the saving of your dear mother from such a terrible death." Gwyn had stood in front of the minister, head down and shuffling from foot to foot. All humble and noble.

"'Twas nothing Doctor Edwards, nothing," he had replied. "What else could I do? She was my Mam."

"Yes, yes Gwyn, I understand. Even so, your bravery and total disregard for your own safety will be noted by the Good Lord. Believe me." Aye, Gwyn was thinking, if it hadn't been for my bloody foot and the fact that the only way out was up the stairs, things might have been different. The old crone might have cooked after all, well done at that. He kept his thoughts to himself as the minister continued to lionise him. He was a hero and enjoying every minute of it. Funny how things turn out, he thought, a forgotten fag and before you know it fame and fortune. The insurance company agreed to fork out for everything and were even paying for he and his mother to stay in a good hotel while all the work was being carried out. He had already thought out a way of fiddling the hotel account to ensure a constant supply of booze. The whole episode had turned into a pleasant holiday, although his big toe still ached. His mother was in fine shape, and despite not saying anything he knew she was quite happy to have the cottage redecorated and refurnished.

A bottle of sherry, a fag and all's well that ends well.

Grand.

CHAPTER 24

"Are you certain, Doctor?"

"Most assuredly, Mrs Treharne. There's no doubt about it."
Lise sat opposite the man in a state of flux and confusion.

"You seem perturbed, Mrs Treharne." The doctor continued,
"Understandably perhaps in view of your husband's recent death.
You are of course quite a mature woman and I must impress
upon you that there could be complications." He paused for a
moment choosing his words carefully, "We can prevent a pregnancy, if you wish. Your age is a factor . . ." Lise looked at him,
her eyes burning with fire.

"No! Definitely not. I won't even consider anything like that.
I will have the baby. Dear God, I want the baby!"

"Very well. It's your decision of course. There's nothing
more to be done for now except let nature take its course."

Lise stood up to go. She still couldn't quite believe she was
pregnant. She opened the door and looked back at the doctor.
Her face beamed, almost blinding him.

"Thank you doctor, that you so very much." As she walked
to her car she looked up at the skies and said, "William you old
devil. You damned rascal. Your life will continue in the little
baby inside my womb. Wherever you are, one day you will be
proud of your child. I promise you. My God William you still
manage to give me joy even in death. I will give our child enough
love for both of us, that I promise."

As she drove back home she knew now that life could be
lived again and could be happy. Her elation was without limit;
she laughed and cried at the same time.

PART II

1965

CHAPTER 25

Charlotte giggled and clapped her hands as she made a valiant effort to blow out the two candles on her birthday cake without quite succeeding. Lise, amused, gave a discreet helping hand and the candles at last went out. Everybody at the table sang 'Happy Birthday' and Charlotte giggled and smiled with absolute delight. This was her day. The child was a flawless little gem. Her head was covered by a vast density of naturally spiralling curls, their colour nearly auburn but not quite. It was more a mixture of gold and red, her father's colour. A small nose, slightly upturned announced a somewhat imperious nature, again another legacy of her father. Charlotte was William's child of that there could be no doubt. Sometimes Lise would look at her daughter and despair – where were her genes in the child's body and character? The little one was William all over, in looks and nature.

Lise couldn't help but cry a little as the cake was being passed around. It was at moments like this when she missed her husband so much. She wished with all her heart that he could have been with them to share these happy moments: to be with his daughter and to watch her growing up. He would have been so proud. Charlotte was already showing signs of wilfulness, and yet the child seemed to have a giving and unselfish inclination toward other children. She never cried or threw tantrums if her little friends took away one of her toys. She always shared and actually seemed to enjoy doing it. From her birth Lise, despite her wealth, had decided that Charlotte would never be spoilt. She would try and nurture her daughter in a way that William would have wanted. Charlotte would never turn into another Megan.

As Lise cut the cake her daughter banged her plate with a small spoon. Impatience. Another of William's not so endearing characteristics. Her eyes darted around the room, as if making a mental note of every detail for future reference. They were like William's – intense and sensitive, hazel with blue specks.

Cake flew everywhere until at last the child got to work with her spoon and her fingers. Fingers were far easier to manipulate than silly adult instruments designed to confound the young. Ophelia, the Rottweiler quickly cleared up the tasty debris lying on the floor, much to Charlotte's delight. Ophelia was her dog. Her friend and protector. They were both the same age, give or take a month or two, and were growing up together. Gwyn had advised Lise to buy a guard dog after William's death. He didn't like the idea of her being alone in the house. At first she had been against the idea, particularly with a baby on the way, but gradually her fear of lonely nights and Gwyn's persistent pestering had prevailed. Ophelia arrived and was named after the Shakespearean character – it was Lise's attempt to begin instilling some culture into her daughter at an early age. "Catch 'em young," William had always said and that's what she was doing. Charlotte of course had great difficulty calling her new companion 'Ophelia'. Time, Lise knew, would remedy the problem. 'Offy' was all her daughter could manage, but the dog didn't seem to mind. In two years the two had become inseparable. It never ceased to amaze Lise how gentle Ophelia was when around her little mistress. The dog was more tolerant than any adult, allowing Charlotte to kick, poke and abuse her in any way she chose. Lise had yet to witness any of the vicious aggression supposedly endemic to Ophelia's breed. The bitch was as soft and as dopey as a St Bernard, without the crass expression and overactive salivary fluids. It was impossible to walk the dog in public because every time she met a stranger she would roll onto her back, lift he legs in the air and plead with her huge brown eyes to have her tummy tickled. Despite her obvious docility Lise had noticed the fervour of a Rottie's inbred protectiveness. Ophelia was known to make threatening noises at any unknown entity who would invade her territory or, God forbid, make hostile movements toward her 'family'. The child would always be safe when Ophelia was around, which was most of the time.

Once the presents had been opened and the party food thrown about the room Lise left Charlotte and her small friends to their own devices, with Bronwyn keeping a watchful eye. Tomorrow was going to be a big day, the culmination of two years hard work, frustration, anger and at last satisfaction tinged with a hint of reticence and uncertainty. Lise needed reassuring so she went in search of Gwyn who, since William's death, she had come to depend on in more ways than she realised. She found him in a kitchen that bore no resemblance to its former self.

"Ah, Gwyn, I've found you. Good." She sat down at the long oak table placed in the middle of the room.

"Want a cup of tea Lise?" he asked.

"No thank you. I wanted to have a word with you."

"Oh yes, what's up then?" He could see Lise was agitated and wasn't surprised. Over the past two years he had become close to his employer. Sometimes he felt he knew her better than he could a wife.

"Party got a bit much 'as it?"

"No, not really . . . I'm nervous Gwyn, nervous about tomorrow night."

"Ach, don't be *mun*. Nothin' to be nervous about. Everything will go as planned, just you see. I've double checked everything, nothin' more to do."

"What would I do without you Gwyn, and how many times have I said that I wonder? You and Bronwyn."

"Don't be silly *mun*, you pay us don't you?"

"I get far more from you both than honest labour and you know it. Look how you've helped me over the past two years."

"Nothin' Lise, nothin'. The Boss looked after us didn't 'ee? Least we could do is return the compliment like, if you see what I mean. Anyway, now don't you go getting yourself in a tizz about tomorrow. Everythin' will be just grand, just you wait and see."

Lise smiled, grateful for the reassurance and support.

"God, I hope so Gwyn, I hope so."

"God 'as nothing to do with it. Have a cup of tea and relax now will you?"

"Go on then, it's nice to get away from screeching children for a while."

He put a mug of hot tea in front of Lise as cups and saucers were not quite his style.

"Kristian couldn't make it then?" he asked.

"No, I'm afraid not. I thought he might have made an effort though, what with his sister's birthday and everything. He would have moved quickly enough if Suzy had wanted him." 'Suzy' was Kristian's most recent conquest. There was a touch of anger in her voice.

"Now, now. Don't go blaming Suzy. He's young, full of it. You know what students are like."

"No, I don't Gwyn, I was never that fortunate."

"Neither was I come to think of it. Still you know what I mean, 'ee's a man now Lise, you just 'ave to accept it, 'ee 'as to spread his wings you know."

"Oh, no doubt he's doing plenty of that. I just hope he's as enthusiastic about his studies as he is about enjoying himself. University students are supposed to study aren't they? That's what they are there for isn't it?

"He's doin' fine. Now don't take on so. You've just got a bout of the old vapour's that's all."

"Yes, I suppose you're right," Lise conceded. "I feel a little irritable at the moment. I'll be glad when tomorrow is over."

"Won't we all, and Amen to that," Gwyn agreed.

Lise finished her tea, glad of the respite from demanding children.

"Thank you for the tea Gwyn, I had better get back to my other offspring. She and her friends are probably driving Bron-wyn to distraction."

"Bron can handle 'em, good with children she is."

222

"Yes indeed, no doubt about that," she looked at him, "I can't help feeling that she wants some of her own Gwyn."

"Is that a fact now?" He tried to ignore Lise's knowing eyes, she was always dropping certain hints where he and Bronwyn were concerned.

This time though Lise decided to be a little more direct. As she walked out of the kitchen she turned to Gwyn and said, "Why don't you make an honest woman of her Gwyn? You know she's besotted with you, always has been. Be fair to the girl for heaven's sake."

"Er . . . well . . . Lise, she's too good for the likes of me so . . ." Gwyn had been stalling marriage for years.

"Nonsense!" Lise interrupted before he could make any further excuses. "Do the decent thing and marry the girl, what's the matter with you? Men. You're all the same!"

Before he could say anything Lise was gone. She had a point though, he grudgingly admitted to himself. He was a good and decent man at heart and knew deep down that he wasn't doing the right thing by Bron. They had been close to one another for quite a few years now and he knew that Bron loved him dearly. The trouble was that he had never quite felt as strongly towards her. He wouldn't be without her that was for sure, but passionate and consuming love was absent. Perhaps Bron had always been too convenient for him. She was always there. He realised that he used her sometimes and often treated her feelings too lightly. A pang of guilt struck him as he thought about her. Lise was right, he ought to do the right thing and marry the girl. Maybe next year.

That night Lise lay in bed trying to read. She couldn't sleep and neither could she concentrate on the words she was trying to read. She hoped with all her heart that everything would go well later on that day.

The Ragged Cliffs Hotel was finally being born.

Two years of meticulous and painstaking planning were at last coming to fruition. Two years of hard labour, worry and consternation were at an end.

Later that day one hundred guests would arrive at the hotel for the grand opening of what was to be the finest hotel on the Gower Peninsula, or for that matter Lise liked to think, in the whole of Wales.

From the outset Lise had eschewed any resemblance to or influence derived from the contemporary method of hotel building, those huge, ugly blocks of concrete containing identical rooms and identical furnishings. Lise wanted a hotel that was full to the brim with character and warmth. Everything about her creation was to be steeped in Welsh history, culture and tradition. Overall, Wales had been kind to her and so had its people. She never wanted to forget this.

Following all the extensive building work, the Cliffs was now transformed into a forty-five room wonder. Her natural eye for design had helped her to maintain the main structure of the Cliffs and its character. From the front any onlooker would not have noticed any particular change. Lise had built onto the back of the house, trying as far as possible to give every room a view to the sea. She had constructed three wings to form a perfect rectangle with the main house. Within this rectangle she had preserved William's rose gardens and much of his creativity. Cobbled paths ran in all directions and would allow guests to stroll and enjoy summer evenings at their leisure. A swimming pool had been built along with a games room, a small nine-hole golf course and a second bar and restaurant, separate from the main building, for public use during the summer. Lise had spent a fortune putting her original idea into practise, but her shrewd mind was convinced that all the financial outlay would be returned with dividends.

The Cliffs was special: there was nothing like it in the whole of Wales. She had spent days and long nights designing all the rooms, each one invoking a particular period or incident in Welsh history. Prince Llewelyn, Lloyd George and Dylan Thomas were all immortalised by her imagination and skill with fabrics and décor. To the visitor it was a journey into the past, a rich, notorious and romantic past. She had spent hours with Bronwyn discussing menus and the type of food to be served. The post-war years of thriftiness and boredom where food was concerned had now passed. French, Italian and even American cuisine was becoming the norm. This tide of taste toward the new and exotic would never abate, Lise recognised this, but at the same time she believed people would always hanker after traditional, good honest food. Welsh food. Her menus were filled with laverbread, cockles, Welsh-cakes, stews, Welsh lamb and black beef, all cooked with the freshest vegetables and ingredients.

At last she dozed off to sleep, her thoughts were of William, they always were. She knew he would approve of everything she had done. In all her deliberations he had never been far away from her mind. He had always been her inspiration.

CHAPTER 26

"Well, I must say Lise you really have done a wonderful job. The old man would have been very proud of you."

"Thank you, Griffith. It has been quite trying sometimes, though I have to admit. I'm still nervous about opening later on."

Lise and Griffith were sitting on one of the sofas in the main foyer. He had just arrived from London and had been quick to absorb the transformation of the old hallway. Here Lise had really gone to town. Before, it had been a dark and intimidating area. Now tall windows had been built into some of the walls, decorated in an extravagance of swags and tails using rich contrasting colours to accentuate their folds and brightness. The marble floors and wood panelled walls had all been restored to their former glory. Oriental rugs met with leather sofas and easy chairs. Her taste was inspiring and yet his father still seemed to walk across the rugs. There was William's hand but Lise's touch wherever he looked. His father remained the Master of the house, but Lise had obviously intended it this way.

"Don't worry Lise, everything will be fine, have no fear."

"I hope so Griffith, I really do."

"Stop fretting, will you? Now then is there anything I can do to help?"

"No, not really. Thank you for offering though. You must be tired. It's a long drive from London."

"You can say that again. I might take a little nap before all the activity begins."

"Do that Griffith, because heaven knows how long the celebrations will go on."

"Right then." He stood up. "I'll settle myself into my room and see you later." He paused for a moment. "On second thoughts,

time enough for afternoon naps when I'm old and knackered."
Lise remained seated and seemed to experience some difficulty
in saying her next sentence.

"Er . . . Griffith, could you just stay a few minutes longer? I'd
just like a few words while it's quiet."

He noted her seriousness and sat back down. Lise and Griffith
had become quite close since his father's death, a sincere friendship having developed between them.

"Of course Lise, fire away."

"How is Megan?" she asked.

Griffith thought carefully before answering. The question
had been unexpected but he also knew that Lise had never borne
any animosity or ill will to either himself or his sister. Where his
sister was concerned Lise would have been fully entitled to
harbour bitterness and anger. Megan had given Lise a lot of pain
and anguish. Her vindictive and malicious nature had wreaked
havoc upon the lovely woman sitting next to him. Also she had
done everything possible to sabotage his father's Will and in
the end had got nowhere. All she had achieved was the full
and profitable employment of a London solicitor. Griffith had
always sympathised with Lise, he liked and respected her. Despite
his sister's constant attempts to create discord, Lise had remained
dignified and calm. He admired his father's widow. He had frequently been impressed by her strengths and magnanimity.

"She's not very good Lise, I'm afraid."

"Is she not? Oh dear."

"As you know, she's in and out of various clinics most of the
time."

"So, the drink problem is still going on?"

"Yes, I'm afraid so. It's not just the drink either, she abuses
drugs with equal enthusiasm."

"Drugs? I never knew . . ." Lise's voice was shocked.

"Oh, don't worry, not illegal drugs. Tranquillisers, sleeping
pills and so on. I sometimes wonder if the learned medical
profession knows what it's doing. Megan is like a walking dis-
pensary. Vallium, Mogodon, you name it. Now of course she's

been taking all these pills for so long she can't live without them. Put booze on top of drugs and you have one hell of a cocktail. Most of the time she's not really on this planet and God knows where she is. Her moods swing from sedated listlessness to downright anger and aggression. She was never the most subdued of individuals, but in recent months there has been a definite turn for the worse. She's become obsessive, paranoid if you like."

"About us?" Lise interrupted.

"Well . . . er . . . I suppose I have to say yes to that." Griffith replied cautiously, not wanting to cause any undue alarm. "You have to remember that most of the time she's not in her right mind. Her hatred and bitterness toward you is probably the only tangible emotion she has left to hold on to, as perverse as that may sound. You see there is nothing and nobody in her life. All she can do is make sure of a constant supply of booze and pills. It's her life's work. She has nothing better to do but brood and think of glorious times gone by."

"She blames me for it all no doubt," said Lise. Griffith hesitated. "Come on now Griffith," she continued, "there's no need to try and spare my feelings. I'm not stupid."

"I can't deny it I suppose," he admitted.

"I feel so sorry for her Griffith, I really do. What do the doctors say about it all?"

"Not much they can do. She's become quite violent now as well; two clinics had to ask her to leave, she caused havoc. You see there's not a great deal anyone can do for her until she decides to quit herself. Until she says 'no more booze and drugs, I want to get away from my addictions', there's no hope for her. She dries out, detoxes, leaves the clinic in reasonably good shape, but then her first stop is the off-licence. The drugs are on prescription and the doctors are wary of taking her off them for fear that the damage could worsen as opposed to improve. I must say though that they try and keep the dosage as low as possible, but Megan just compensates with alcohol."

"But Griffith, what exactly is wrong with her? I mean is she mentally ill or is it just drug and alcohol addiction?"

"Good question Lise, and I'm not entirely sure I know the answer. She apparently had some kind of breakdown after the old man's death. I must admit up to that point she seemed to be reasonably in control of herself. When Dad died and the revelation of her true paternity came to light she seemed to fall apart. I can't really imagine why, she was hardly the most dutiful or loving of daughters to be brutally frank about it. It's all a bit of a mystery. The words 'nervous breakdown' were bandied about by the doctors, but what the hell is a 'nervous breakdown' anyway? A load of psychoanalysis and meaningless tripe was talked but no informative conclusions were provided. As far as I can see the booze and drugs have unbalanced her. I don't think there's ever been any real mental problem to speak of, at least prior to the binges. Now however it's a different story, she's definitely ill. I've no doubts on that score. It does worry me Lise, she is after all my own flesh and blood. I don't like her very much, never have done, but even so I wouldn't want to see her come to any harm."

"I'm so sorry Griffith, I really am. I only wish there was something I could do to help. How is she managing financially? These private clinics are expensive, aren't they?"

"Oh no need to worry about that, that's precisely the damned trouble. Megan has plenty of money. Despite her bitterness the old man left us both comfortably provided for. Sometimes I wish he hadn't left Megan anything as she has plenty of money to feed her habits and pay the doctors who, in my book, help her addictions. Perhaps if she was broke she might get well – who knows?"

"Is there nothing we can do?"

"I don't think so Lise. As I've said, until Megan herself decides to pack it all in there's nothing anyone can do. She's not breaking the law after all. Sadly I have to say that, apart from Megan, everybody else is powerless, at least where the long term is concerned. At the end of the day all anybody can do is wait and hope. She's destroying herself Lise, and the tragedy is that no one can do anything to stop it – except Megan herself that is."

"Where is she now?"

"She's . . . er . . . well, believe it or not drying out again."

"Oh God, Griffith."

"Look Lise, I've tried everything under the sun but nothing seems to work." He sighed and changed the subject. "Now then let's forget Megan for the time being. At the end of the day she's the mistress of her own destiny . . . as I'm sure the old man would have confirmed." Griffith smiled, he was always smiling no matter what. "She'll survive Lise no doubt, she always does. So don't be too concerned, as admirable as your sentiments are bearing in mind Megan's conduct in the past. This is your big day, so don't spoil it." He took her hand. "Come on, you can give me an exclusive grand tour of the place. I haven't seen all of it yet. Give me a bit of the personal touch before the hordes arrive."

"I can't." Lise protested. "I'm too busy."

"Nonsense," he replied as he dragged her through the reception area. She knew it was no good trying to argue. Griffith was William's son underneath the all the swank and banter.

"Griffith, you're incorrigible you know, just like your father."

"Is that a fact?" he answered, adding, "And you don't know the half." She didn't say anything more. She was proud of the Ragged Cliffs Hotel and enjoyed showing off her achievement.

Whilst Lise and Griffith walked a road of calm sanity, Megan was in the process of tearing a young doctor to pieces. It was her way now; hostility had become the bread of her heaven.

"I'm telling you, these pills are not strong enough! They're not having any effect. Look at me, I'm a nervous wreck man!"

"Megan," the doctor began patiently, "we are trying to reduce the dosage gradually in an effort to lessen your dependency. You must understand that it's for your own good."

"My own good! Who says? A young doctor just out of medical school who probably doesn't know a corpse from a living human being? God, you people are killing me, do you know that? Get me a decent dose will you? Now!"

"I can't do that I'm afraid. Just try and relax, your anxieties will pass, trust me."

"Trust you?" Her mouth curled in an ugly message of contempt. "I wouldn't trust you with my fucking hamster. Another thing, why haven't I got my own room?"

"This is a national health clinic Megan, you know that. You will have to go privately if you want the privacy of your own room."

"Oh, damn you, damn the lot of you!"

She lay back on her bed resigned to defeat. This was the first time she had placed herself at the mercy of the National Health. That month her funds had started to run a little low and so had her bank manager's patience; her father's bequest had been spent a long time ago unbeknown to her little brother who still assumed that she was living a life of luxury. Her monthly allowance, though generous by anyone's standards, was still not enough to meet her personal needs and private clinic bills. She had been forced to mix with the rabble. For Megan this was an extremely unpleasant experience. After a particularly enthusiastic binge on alcohol and drugs both had taken their toll, with the result that she now found herself in the psychiatric unit at Friern Barnet. This was not her style at all. The bleak, challenging Victoria buildings left any casual observer little doubt as to their true purpose. As Megan frequently reminded the staff it was a 'nuthouse', a 'looney bin', a 'fruitcake's paradise'. She did not consider herself a mental case; she was there to 'dry out'. There was nothing wrong with her mind. She felt insulted by having to mix with people whose brains could only be compared to scrambled eggs, with even less substance. Once the vitamins had taken effect and the shakes had disappeared she would discharge herself. At the moment she felt too ill to move. By God though, while she was there she would give the staff a run for their money. The shrink had not improved her mood; they were all the same. As usual he had sat there like a constipated Buddha saying nothing apart from the occasional question that presumably was meant to stimulate some kind of meaningful response. Megan would ramble on about a perfectly happy childhood and a privileged one at that; this always confused the hell out of them, but then Megan was of the opinion that it didn't take much to confuse a psychiatrist. At the end of one of these sessions Megan would leave the room none the wiser, apart from feeling that she had just expounded her own detailed and occasionally amusing curriculum vitae. The whole session had been a complete waste of time and she didn't appreciate being treated like a moron either. She was above the rest of the inmates; her brains were still intact, or so she believed anyway.

The woman lying down in the bed next to her started rummaging around in her bedclothes. She was wearing day clothes like the rest of the patients; this was encouraged as a means to effect at least a veneer, no matter how false, of normality. Megan watched the woman with fascinated interest. What the on earth was she doing? The woman was quite obviously right off her bloody trolley; one look at her face was enough. The eyelids were half closed, leaving what could only be described as two murky pupils seeming to look at nothing. There was no Hungarian folk song being played in her eyes; it was more a funeral march. Her jaw dropped slightly and her tongue seemed to rest, exhausted, on her lower lip. A sudden fear gripped Megan as she looked at the woman. Had drugs committed such a glaring atrocity on the woman's face that was once, Megan was quite certain, remarkably pretty? The woman's clothes were of charitable origin with that aged, worn-out look about them. Faded knitted cardigan, stained skirt and a shirt five sizes too large. As Megan watched the woman's movements became more frantic, more intense. There was a tragic desperation in her face, a panic, as she started to throw the bedclothes around.

For once, a spark of humanity entered Megan's mind.

"What's the matter?" she asked warily. The woman stared at Megan with eyes that said nothing. "What's the matter?" Megan persisted. Maybe she saw herself in the twisted bedclothes. "Have you lost something?" At last her question seemed to penetrate the black sarcophagus of the woman's mind. She stopped rummaging.

"Fags, lost my fags," came the mumbled reply. The woman was distraught, about to breakdown. Her world was rapidly coming to an end. No 'fags', no sanity. Snarling black dogs were waiting at the bottom of the bed ready to pounce.

"Here, take these." Megan threw a half packet of cigarettes onto the woman's bed. For a moment the woman stared at the red and white packet. Her eyes seemed to be struggling to acknowledge whether this sudden gift was real or not. Slowly she touched the packet with her fingertips and then as truth finally dawned she grasped it with both hands. Tears began to spill from the sightless eyes; she looked at Megan and for the briefest of seconds a smiled moved her lips and her eyes seemed to dance a happy polka.

"Thank you," she said, "Thank you very much." Then the joy evaporated as quickly as it had arrived. The face changed from a vision of chaos to a veil of calm. The woman shuffled out of the room, her slippered feet dragging along the tiled floor. Megan whispered to herself, "Jesus Christ, I have to get out of here. As soon as possible."

She was a voluntary patient; her quick exit would not be difficult. This was not the case for the shuffling, smoking woman. Megan decided to go for a walk in the grounds of the hospital. She needed to get away from the covert tragedy of sedated insanity that threatened to suffocate her. With modern medicine and drugs there was none of the dramatic wailing and tearing of hair that was so characteristic of the true Bedlam of the 1800's. Instead, the modern-day lunatic asylums were populated by patients so heavily drugged that personality had become a thing of their pasts. An occasional outburst of violent rebellion would occur, but this was quickly put down with grievous bodily harm by a syringe. Not fatal, but enough. Mental patients were kept in a world of fantasy and unreal sleep. Time passed, and yet they were unaware of any hours or minutes ticking by. A day or even a week could pass without them knowing it or even wanting to.

Megan walked along the grass smoking a cigarette. She would stick it out another couple of days and then go home. Her trust monies would be through by then. As soon as this thought entered her mind the hatred returned. Why should she have to wait upon the discretion of trustees for her money? Why was she in this hellhole when she should be in an first-class clinic where discretion and privacy were assured? Why must she be contaminated by the ignorance and madness of a world that she considered dirty and uncouth? Her delicate inclinations were being swamped by the sordid hopelessness of crazy cigarette addicts and basket cases whose brains had emigrated to a gentler land.

She should not be here.

Her upbringing, her wealth, had not conditioned her for the companionship or even tolerance of the lower orders of society. They lived in one world, she in another. Her brief and transitory moment of compassion earlier was replaced once more by frustration and anger. Her own lifestyle of course had nothing to do with her present predicament. Her father's slut had caused it all; the desire to avenge never let go. It kept her alive. How many times had she heard people say, "Forget the past." "What's done is done." "The chapter is closed." She treated these 'nice' and unworldly platitudes with the seething derision they deserved.

Eventually Megan sat down on a bench donated by some liberated and grateful ex-patient. Griffith had told her about Lise's new venture and the creation of a hotel on the Gower coast. It was her hotel not Lise's. Her mind quickly returned to its favourite and obsessive pass-time. Planning and scheming was all the intellectual stimulation that Megan had left. She would never, ever close the door on Lise Treharne and revenge, no matter how many bottles or how many pills.

The past had become her present and her future.

CHAPTER 27

Lise's hand was beginning to ache, its bones rattling from the constant handshaking.

Swansea's best had not let her down.

No doubt a free dinner, champagne and natural curiosity had all helped to ensure a full turnout. Having greeted the last of her guests she retreated quickly to the kitchens for a strong cup of tea. The opening reception could do without her for a few minutes. Some of the handshakes had been less than sincere, at least those of the female variety. To some she was still a foreigner, an outsider, or worst of all a gold-digging harlot. All the same business was business, and at least the men were gracious and enjoyed touching her hand. Some of them couldn't stop touching.

Griffith had helped her to compile the list of people to be invited. He knew all the 'right' families, all the 'right' money. She and William had never bothered much with socialising or mixing with a particular social 'set'. All they had ever needed was each other. He had always been sceptical of friendship, believing that most of the time it was more an institution of dependency than genuine affection. Lise, he claimed, was his truest friend and with her he enjoyed all the friendship he needed. As she drank her tea she smiled at the thought of his reaction to all the people presently gathered at his house. He would have had a fit, gone red in the face with temper and cursed with a crudity that would have shamed a group of rugby players out on a stag night. She didn't know many of the guests, if any. The names of some were familiar but that was about it. Griffith was doing a fine job as the surrogate host and she had been quite happy to let him get on with it.

Before going back into the breach she straightened her hair and touched up the scant make-up that she wore. She was now past her mid thirties and yet her whole body seemed to challenge and mock the determined efforts of age. Time had somehow forgotten about her; discarded her even. She was still beautiful, and if anything the passing years had accentuated her natural beauty. It had become subtler, more delicate. Her blue eyes seemed more knowledgeable, more capable. They had matured like the rest of her face into a soft and gentle visage of kindness and tolerance. She had never espoused vanity, and now as she looked at herself in the mirror she realised only too sadly that beauty was merely a veneer, a cloak that hid the true character beneath. Nature had been generous; it had not penalised her body for the grief and pain she had suffered in her life. It had punished her heart, wounding and scarring it but making certain the lacerations could not be seen. Even nature had felt reluctant to inflict obvious damage upon such a lovely body.

Taking a deep breath Lise made her way toward the noise and clinking of cutlery and glass. She had laid on a buffet of traditional Welsh food with smatterings of Danish fare. It was a Welsh Smorgasbord, a unique creation for this part of Wales or for any other part for that matter. Hot and cold dishes had been prepared. For five days before the event she and Bronwyn had slaved away in the kitchens. Welsh lamb had been marinated in crushed peppercorns, shallots and sliced garlic before being cooked. Tarragon, thyme and rosemary had been added together with the zest of oranges and the tang of red wine. This had been served with roast parsnips. The guests had been given a further choice of traditional Welsh faggots and peas, cockles from the beds at Penclawdd and fresh oysters. The mussels had been cooked in butter and almonds; the cockles merely waited for generous helpings of pepper and vinegar. Local cheeses, some of Italian origin sat and glowered on another table. Laverbread had formed part of the ingredients of one of these. It was impossible to be more Welsh than laverbread; the pulped seaweed was unique. One quick glance told Lise that everyone was enjoying themselves. There were over one hundred people eating and drinking as if there was no tomorrow. Solicitors, doctors, businessmen, local government officials, all and sundry were present. It was Lise's intention to make her hotel the best in Wales. She wanted her guests to recommend Ragged Cliffs to friends and business associates alike. The food and drink had cost a fortune but she looked on it as an investment. The local press had been invited, along with various respected and influential commentators on the hotel and catering business. Lise exchanged polite pleasantries with these people but nothing more. She felt no need to seek their approval – the hotel itself was enough.

At 1.30 the following morning Lise said 'Goodbye' to the last of her guests.

It had been a long night and she was tired.

Despite her fatigue there were still the remnants of elation. The night had been a wonderful success. She had taken a substantial number of bookings for the coming summer season with numerous promises of more to come. All her previous misgivings and doubts had disappeared, but as always she still wished that William could have been there to share it all with her. She made her way up to her bedroom after making sure that Gwyn did all the locking up. He had been busy himself that night, particularly where Kristian was concerned. After the boy had drunk himself into a stupor thankfully Gwyn had put him to bed out of harm's way, so avoiding an inebriated embarrassment. He had left a bucket at the side of Kristian's bed in anticipation of a stomach expressing its outrage at such abuse. Before going to bed Lise looked out into the night. Even now the adrenaline was still flowing. She felt so alive, awake. The excitement still simmered.

It was a beautiful night; a full moon lit up the sea and mesmerised the waves and cliffs. Nature was in one of her passive moods, but Lise was only too aware of how erratic she could be – one minute benevolent and thoughtful the next vicious and destructive.

She sat down on a chair and began thinking about her conversation with Griffith. She looked at the empty double bed. Memories and a realisation of loneliness. She had material wealth, two lovely children and people around her whom she loved. Yet there was an unsettling gap in her life.

Lise needed to love.

She needed to give and to receive.

Before William and now after, her life seemed incomplete, unfinished. She was like some sturdy and apparently indestructible house built on a foundation of sand. Despite the people who were constantly in her life she was desperately lonely. There were times, as now, when despair would cut her to shreds. Loneliness was a disease; it gnawed at and worried the soul. Her body and mind were demanding a touch, a kiss. For the years since her husband's death she had tried to ignore her feelings or at least keep them deeply buried at the back of her mind, but every so often her isolation would remind her of them. Lise needed and wanted a man in her life again. She wanted more than anything else to adore and love; she wanted arms to hold her tight in the small hours of the morning, she wanted a hand to hold and cherish. She wanted to love and be loved.

She began undressing to get ready for bed. She had always slept naked and when she had removed all her clothes she stood in front of the full-length dressing mirror that had once checked William's immaculate suits. She studied her body with a critical and brutally detached eye. Her breasts were still firm and full and yet they appeared delicate, defying any callous bar-room desire. She was not big, but there was enough to satisfy the most enthusiastic touch. She gently stroked her belly and sighed. A slight stretch mark or two reminded her of the two little human beings she had brought into the world. Her children had left their mark and so they should. The rest of her body remained taut and trim, smooth soft skin and no hanging flesh or unsightly droops. Lise didn't look her age, she enjoyed the body of a twenty-year-old not a thirty-six-year-old.

Her hands moved from her hips to the inside of her thighs.

Her fingers began to search and explore.

It had been so long.

She lay down on the bed and continued to use her fingers.

Time ceased to exist.

She was no longer lying on her lonely bed.

Her fingers began to move more quickly as she let her body dictate their movements.

She was hot.

The wetness began to flood and soak the probing of her fingers.

Her eyes were shut tight, her mouth open.

She lost control of her body as the spasms of pleasure wreaked havoc on her muscles. Her mind jerked and pulled. She was unaware. Intensity occupied.

Her buttocks lifted as a gasp of sexual desperation and relief was ripped from her mouth.

She lay still. Her body twitched as it gradually gained control.

Her last thought before sleep was that her life was not a natural one.

She needed a man.

CHAPTER 28

Despite the opening of the new M4 motorway and the Severn Bridge, it still took Griffith over four hours to reach his flat in Lancaster Gate. He hated these new motorways; the stark paths of concrete that seemed to go on forever without respite took away any enjoyment of driving. With these new roads it was more or less just a question of pointing the car in the right direction and starting the engine. The monotony killed any creative or adventurous driving. Anyone could press a foot down on an accelerator. The motorways were fast and convenient he had to concede, but by God they added a new dimension to boredom.

Griffith parked his Jaguar in front of the block of flats that housed his own home; the parking was for 'Residents Only'. He sometimes wondered how many people actually lived there – it must be hundreds judging by the usual paucity of parking spaces. This evening he had been lucky; he paid a hell of a lot of money to have to rely on 'luck'.

He opened the door to his flat, dropped his suitcase on the mosaic-tiled floor of the spacious hallway and before going any further picked up the mail that lay in a pile on the doormat. He walked into his sitting room leaving the front door open; there were more things to collect from the car. Before he was able to glance at the post a voice announced his name. "Mr Treharne? Mr Griffith Treharne? There was a quiet formality to it that tended to allay any immediate threat. Two men were standing in the doorway to the sitting room. They were big, clean-shaven and dressed with as much imagination as the M4.

"Christ! Who the hell are you? And what the hell are you doing in my home?" Griffith demanded, his anger at the intrusion overwhelming any fear. If the two men were burglars they had no idea how to dress for the job. They walked up to him slowly. Griffith's outrage had no effect upon their blank, clean faces. One of them flashed a warrant card as the other began a litany of doom and destruction.

"Mr Treharne, we are arresting you . . ."

Griffith was unable to take it all in. One of the policemen handed him a search warrant as the other continued to make reference to the Sexual Offences Act 1956 section 30 and something about 'living wholly or in part on the earnings of prostitution'. He stood in front of the two men. He was unable to absorb exactly what was happening. Before he knew it he was being taken to the police station. So much for the minor bird, the bastard's insults had fallen on deaf ears. It's the taste of lead on the next pheasant shoot for him!

As Griffith waited in the police cells for his solicitor to arrive the shock of his predicament gradually began to wear off. He had no idea what type of punishment the courts meted out for this type of crime, but it didn't take him long to realise that any punishment by the court would be as nothing when compared to the odious publicity that would no doubt be shovelled upon his good and decent character. He was a well-known figure in London, and Wales for that matter. A few years earlier the Profumo scandal had shaken the Establishment to its very core. Griffith wasn't in that rarefied league of political infamy; on the other hand some of his clients were government ministers and senior judges. Oh Christ, the more he thought about it the more his stomach turned. Jesus, he wasn't a spy for God's sake or a KGB agent and he sure as hell wasn't about to kill himself either like that poor bugger Ward. Nothing was worth that . . . his old man notwithstanding.

As the hours passed while he was obviously being left to stew and pickle – he wasn't sure which – he began to adopt a more philosophical and realistic approach to his problem. He had plenty of money, more than enough to retire on. The police would have one devil of a job trying to find out where all his 'earnings' had gone and indeed exactly how much he had 'earned' over the years. Griffith had always been good with figures and arithmetic. The serious stuff was all in his head and the 'books', such as they were, were with one of his most trusted girls. His wealthy lifestyle was easily explained – his father's money and the perfectly legitimate private company he had set up whose activities were basically involved with the entertainment industry. The police would have found nothing incriminating in his flat, of that he was sure. The details of the various bank and building society accounts he had opened up in bogus names and addresses were kept safely tucked away in the bowels of a private bank vault; a place far more secure than his own home. He knew enough law to know that the burden of proof lay with the prosecution. Without evidence they were buggered. So, he wondered, what evidence did the police have and who had tipped them off in the first place? As he continued to consider this last question his eyes noticed a red button on the wall of his cell. Some wag had written beneath it, 'Ring For Butler'. Griffith couldn't help smiling – at least his sense of humour was still intact.

He tried to recall all the people with whom he had fallen out over the years and realised there were not many. But then if any of them had played a part in his present undoing, surely they would be running the risk of prosecution themselves? All Griffith's business arrangements had been two-sided. If a man wanted a high-class tart he paid for the privilege, and Griffith always vetted the clients first. He made sure he knew all of them, not for the purposes of any future blackmail but purely for self-protection. It had worked too – up until now. So whoever had pointed the finger at him obviously had nothing to lose. This was worrying.

Eventually his solicitor arrived. He was told 'to say nothing', duly charged with living off immoral earnings or something or other and released on police bail. Before leaving his solicitor on the steps of the police station he had asked what he could expect if the worse were to occur.

"Hard to say at the moment, Griffith, dear boy." They were on first-name terms, the solicitor having frequently required the discreet services that Griffith provided and at a discount! "Let's see what evidence they have first."

"Come on, Tom, cut the legal crap will you? What do I stand to get if I'm nobbled?"

"Well, depending on whether we go to magistrates or Crown Court anything from six months to seven years inside," the solicitor replied with a shrug of resignation.

Griffith's face went white, suddenly drained of all colour. "What? Seven years!" he muttered in disbelief.

"Now don't take on so, Griffith. It's early days yet. Seven years is extremely unlikely in these enlightened times"

"Early days? I just hope to God the late days aren't spent at Her Majesty's pleasure!"

"Don't worry now Griffith, let's see what they've got. You might just get away with a fine. We'll know more in a couple of weeks. I'll be in touch then. Give me a ring if there's anything you think I should know or be aware of."

Like most lawyers Griffith's solicitor was not particularly concerned about his client's guilt or innocence. It was his job to take his client's instructions and act accordingly. If Griffith wished to plead not guilty, so be it. Assuming the magistrates heard the case, Tom would go into court and basically say to the prosecution, 'prove it.' He would then try and demolish the evidence.

Thomas Valdane had known his client for a long time. He didn't say anything on the steps of the police station but he felt that a plea of guilty would be the advisable course. He wouldn't convey these thoughts however until he had perused the prosecution's evidence. Griffith had been walking a legal tightrope for some time, the inevitable outcome bound to happen sometime or another.

The two men shook hands.

"Go home Griffith, pour yourself a stiff drink and try to relax," Valdane said, and added reassuringly, "I wouldn't worry too much, our society is a little more liberal these days." As he walked away he couldn't resist saying. "And who knows, dear boy, you might find the judge has been one of your 'clients'."

"Very funny," Griffith shouted after him. He made his way home as advised.

For the rest of the day all he could do was think about the person who had informed on him to the police. Who could it be? As far as he was aware he had never made any real enemies in his life, at least none who would want to destroy him. He was too affable a character for that. He wracked his brains trying to think of someone who would want to do him harm and why. As usual, like all lawyers, Tom had refused to commit himself to any exact prognosis of his case. Lawyers never predicted on principle; it was bad for public relations and they knew only too well the capriciousness of the law, particularly the criminal law. He fell asleep that night still mystified and anxious His dreams were filled with slamming cell doors, echoing corridors and judges wearing the black caps of execution.

Three weeks went by.

"Have you ever heard of a Miss Sylvia Edmunds?" Thomas Valdane asked Griffith.

"No, should I have done?" His reply was quick and unequivocal. Griffith was sitting opposite his solicitor, who had both elbows resting on his desk. As usual the man was immaculately dressed. Starched white collar, hand-made red striped tunic shirt that fitted every nook and cranny of his body. Valdane straightened his arms, at the same time shooting his cuffs, which were again brilliant white and clasped together by discreet gold cufflinks. The solicitor had made a great success of his legal career and a lot of money. He was middle-aged and handsome. His slightly wrinkled face allowed authority to ambush his younger adversaries. Much to the dismay of many of his female clients, both young and old, he was also happily married, apart from the odd lecherous fling which kept boredom at bay.

"Are you sure you have never heard of this young lady, dear boy?"

"Positive. At least my memory has never heard of her. Good God Tom, have you any idea how many girls have worked for me over the years?"

"No, but I can imagine." Valdane looked again at the sheets of paper before him. "Well, she has certainly heard a lot about you – or should I say knows a lot about you. Her statement is very exact, detailed. She even gives exact times and dates." He handed Griffith copies of the statements. "Must be quite a diarist, Samuel Pepys would admire her. Have a read. I'll go and arrange some coffee."

Griffith began reading. As he did so, suddenly the secure atmosphere of leather upholstery, bookshelves stacked with law reports and legal authorities didn't seem so comforting. His eyes couldn't believe what he was reading. His stomach began to turn inside out as the consequences of what he was reading began to sink in. Valdane came back and placed a cup of coffee in front of Griffith. One look at his client told him something a little stronger was required. He walked along the expensive dark brown pile carpet to an oak filing cabinet in the corner of the room. He extracted a bottle of the best malt whisky and returned to his desk. He poured some into Griffith's cup without asking; his fine wrinkles edged this way and that as he poured. Such a good whisky. Sacrilegious waste.

At last Griffith finished reading.

"She's got me by the balls."

"I have to agree." Valdane said. "The point is Griffith, she can corroborate everything in her statement. I've done some discreet checking of my own and everything she alleges can be proved no doubt about it. She can call an army of witnesses. The police have got a winner and they know it."

Griffith took a long gulp of his coffee and said, "What I can't understand is why? I do remember the girl now . . . vaguely. Pretty little thing. If I remember, quite popular too. I don't recall there ever having been any problems with her or reasons if you like for her wanting to crucify me. Why has she gone to the police with all this? You say she can call witnesses. Who, for God's sake? I've always treated my girls well."

"Not this one it seems."

"Look Tom, will you stop being so bloody cryptic, what do you mean? Do you know something I don't?"

"As I said, I had some checking done myself. It seems, dear boy, that you are a father."

"A father?!" Griffith exploded. "A father?! For God's sake, when?"

"You have a four-year-old son. Charming little fellow apparently."

"But . . . but . . ." Griffith was dumbfounded. Speechless. He didn't know what to say. He kept his mouth shut for a long time as he tried to absorb the sudden and unexpected revelation of his fatherhood. "I never knew anything about this, and apart from anything else how the hell are you so certain the child is mine? Dear God, the boy could be anybody's! His mother was hardly the celibate type after all."

"Ah well, now there we have a slight problem. You see the mother is perfectly prepared to undergo any medical tests you require in order to prove your lack of paternity. Likewise of course, the converse could be the case. Miss Edmunds does seem absolutely certain who the father of her child is. Are you though Griffith likewise inclined? You really must consider the consequences here. Miss Edmunds is not seeking to find you responsible for her son, morally or financially. As I read the circumstances here, her whole motive is one of revenge. She wants only to er . . . 'crucify' you as you so succinctly put it. Whatever did you do to her, Griffith?"

"I told you, nothing! I knew nothing about any child and that, believe me, is the truth . . . unless . . ."

"Unless . . . Griffith?"

"The child is four years of age you say. Well about four years ago I moved, new address. That's the only explanation."

"If that is the case and I really can see no reason why you should lie about it, not to me anyway, then she is obviously out to do you as much damage as possible. She is apparently very bitter about what she sees as your desertion of she and the child. She's after your blood – hell hath no fury and so on. Sorry dear boy, but there's the rub of it."

Shakespeare again, Griffith thought.

"Hell Tom, if she had come to me and told me all about it of course I would have helped. I'm not that callous."

"Well, according to Miss Edmunds she did try and contact you. Wrote to you as well. However, all her efforts were to no avail. She quite obviously felt rejected and hurt. As far as she was concerned she was carrying your baby and you refused to have anything to do with her or the child. It appears that she is now attempting to redress the balance as it were. Woman can be vindictive, indeed from my experience – both personally and professionally – in this area they will outgun any of us amateur males. Bring children into the equation, Griffith, and you had better dive for cover."

"So Tom, what's your advice?" Griffith knew he wasn't going to like the answer.

"The final decision must, of course, rest with you. Put briefly the situation is this. 'Living wholly or in part on the earnings of prostitution' carries a maximum sentence of seven years, that is if you are tried by a judge and jury. If you elect for summary trial by the magistrates the maximum penalty they can impose is six months. Now then, the real question here is how good you feel your chances are of getting a 'not guilty' verdict. If you feel disposed toward this plea then I would advise that you place yourself at the mercy of a jury. They are more likely to be sympathetic to your case, particularly if we can ensure a strong male presence. The magistrates, however, are not so easily fooled by litigious eloquence and the charms of your defending advocate – in this instance, me. If you were to elect for Crown then obviously we shall have to brief counsel. An expensive business

I might add. The crux of your choice is this – if you plead not guilty and a jury finds otherwise you are likely to receive a hefty prison sentence. Seven years I doubt very much, but certainly more than six months. If, on the other hand, you plead guilty and place yourself at the mercy of our Worshipful Justices of the Peace then the most you will get is six months or a respectable fine. Either way, it's a gamble. You can, of course, plead not guilty to the magistrates, but I have to advise you that if they find against you they might well commit you to the Crown Court for sentencing, should they feel you deserve more than six months in clink. Perhaps the most important point you need to consider is the consequences of a not guilty plea. If you do this you could be opening a right royal can of worms. The prosecution will dig and facts may emerge that you would prefer to be kept quiet, more particularly facts that the Inland Revenue would be more interested in than the Courts." Griffith hadn't thought of this one; his stomach turned again. "It might be as well for you to go quietly, keep the damage to a minimum. Anyway, Griffith, don't make a decision yet. Go home, read the statements and then get back to me with your instructions."

"This is all very well Tom, but you still haven't really answered my question. You have told me the options and what can happen, but what the hell do you think I should do?" Griffith emphasised the word 'you'.

"Persistent fellow, aren't you? We lawyers don't enjoy taking decisions regarding the pleas of our clients. We are merely here to outline the pros and cons as it were of a given situation and then to act upon the instructions of our masters. At the end of the day the decision must be yours. However, as you are an old and valued client I will break my own rules for once."

"'Valuable' Tom would be a better description; you've been bleeding me dry for years, you old sod. Now come on, get to the point. What do I do?"

"Guilty. Go before those charming schoolteachers and pillars of our community and throw yourself at their mercy."

"A straight answer at last Tom. Well done." Griffith stood up and put his overcoat on. "I'll have a think about everything you have said and let you know."

"Very well dear boy, but don't take too long about it though. The law waits for no man you know, it expects us to wait for it."

CHAPTER 29

"Don't' walk so fast Gwyn, will you? I can't keep up with you *mun!*" Bronwyn shouted.

"Ach, come on girl, what's the matter wi' you. Young woman like you should be racin' ahead of me!"

"*Duw*, Gwyn, there are times when you annoy me. Don't be so thoughtless will you!"

"Alright Bron, alright." Gwyn started walking a little more slowly. Out of habit he took Bronwyn's arm in his.

"Lovely isn't it, Bron?" he said stopping on the brow of a huge sand dune. They were almost completely alone apart from the occasional man or woman walking a dog. "Come on Bron, let's sit down 'ere for a bit and enjoy the scenery."

It was late April. A time of resurrection. Of demand. Nature was hungry.

Bronwyn had nagged Gwyn to take her for a walk around Three Cliffs Bay. It was early evening and the sun was beginning to bed down for the night. Bronwyn cuddled up to Gwyn for warmth. The view before them quelled their usual banter and squabbling into silence. They both sat quietly saying nothing. They watched as the sun began to descend into its watery bed, its last rays of energy shooting here and there with the stubbornness of a young child being ordered to sleep. The waves and wind touched their faces and ordered them to be silent. Gwyn and Bronwyn clutched each other. They felt so small. For Gwyn, all the facets of the Welsh character were here at Three Cliffs. There was the mystery, romance and the vivid colour of Welsh folklore. There was the singing of the wind and sea as they gripped the air with passion and love. Shine and glow fell asleep together as the sun waved 'au revoir'. The view was always changing, the colours constantly packing up and leaving for others to take their place. The sunset had become an over-crowded bed and breakfast, a magician with no more tricks in his hat. Every human emotion was visible to those who could recognise them.

Nature ruled.

Bronwyn looked into Gwyn's eyes and kissed him on the lips. There was tenderness, love. She withdrew her lips from his and their eyes locked. Perhaps it was the natural drama that had silenced them, perhaps it was just the more benign side to Nature's capricious will, for in that moment Gwyn's heart went to Bronwyn. Her lovely green eyes and pretty face finally trapped him. At last he saw the true treasure within his grasp. His past reservations melted away completely. It was a moment of liberation as his emotions were at last free to run wild.

He put his arms around Bronwyn, returned her kiss and said, "Bron darlin', when you smile it's better than all this put together." He waved his arm at the scenery that spread out before them. "I love you, Bron, I really do. Let's get married."

"Oh . . . Oh, Gwyn," was all she said as she sank into his strong arms.

The silent sand dune became their premature honeymoon bed.

Nature had won yet again.

CHAPTER 30

"What are you going to do for the summer, Kristian?" Lise asked.

"I don't know really Mum, haven't thought about it," he answered warily. He knew his mother, and bone idleness was not one of her favourite occupations.

"Right, well I will think for you. You are not going to laze around here for three months living off your recent success. You may have passed your second year exams with flying colours but that does not give you an excuse to start getting blisters on your backside. Tomorrow morning you will be at this office 9 o'clock sharp." She handed him a piece of paper.

"What! It's a building company!"

"Correct, and you are going to work for it. I know the owner and he has a good honest labouring job for you. Bring you down to earth a bit. You're too cocky as it is."

"But . . .!" Kristian bleated.

"No 'buts' about it. Be there in the morning. I'll take you there myself if I have to!"

"Why can't I work here?" he protested.

"No possibility of that. You will make the staff uncomfortable. No more argument, just make sure you're there or heaven help you." Kristian made a loud sigh of resignation as he watched his mother walk off to see to hotel business. When she said 'no argument' she meant it. He could get around her on most things, but once she had made up her mind on something there was no going back. She was immovable, like a bloody great mountain. As he thought about the job he gradually decided that perhaps it wasn't such a bad idea after all. He hadn't done much physical exercise over the past few months and he was feeling a bit flabby. Kristian looked after his body, he was proud of it. Normally, during term time he would spend at least four sessions a week working out in the University gym. He also hammered himself on the squash courts and swam like a bionic fish. He was usually extremely fit; he had to be to sustain the social life he led. Yes, he thought, labouring on a building site wasn't such a bad idea after all. Do himself good with the added bonus of keeping his mother happy. The words *'mens sana in corpore sano'* (a healthy mind in a healthy body) came into his mind. Philosophy, Latin? He must be mad!

Every Monday morning Lise held a meeting with her manager and chef to discuss the previous week's business. The manager, Mr Pascoe, was a man who treated formality with respect and dressed accordingly – black morning jacket, grey pinstripe trousers with creases tough and sharp enough to cut cheese and always a red carnation in his lapel. He had worked in the hotel business for years and had come highly recommended. His dark curls, greying here and there, and tanned skin gave him a slightly Italian look, although his CV had indicated his place of birth to be Merthyr Tydfil. His voice was high, even effeminate and he did have a tendency to 'gambol' around the hotel. His body movements were a shade too graceful for the average man, leading Lise to suspect that he probably 'batted for the other side' as her son no doubt would have put it. She had picked this up at their first interview, but being a reasonably broadminded woman she had decided that Mr Pascoe's sexual preferences were his own affair – as long as he did the job to her satisfaction then he could lift as many shirts as he liked. Off the premises of course.

The chef, Honore Balzac as he called himself was a taciturn and neurotic perfectionist. His pretensions to connections with the famous French novelist were treated with amusement and good humour, at least by those familiar with the true Balzac's literary works. His French accent could never quite erase the powerful Welsh lilt of his place of birth – Llanelli – particularly when his voice started to rise in temper and frustration. For all the fantasy he was a wonderful cook – an artist.

The three of them were sitting in Lise's office. This was one room in the house that had hardly been touched. It remained in its original state. The room had been William's study.

"Right then, Mr Balzac, what menus have you prepared for the week?" Lise asked

"They are all here, madame, for your inspection."

She took the proffered sheets of paper and read them quickly. She never called any of her staff by their Christian names; she believed in keeping a sturdy wall between herself and those she employed. William had always fervently maintained the adage of 'familiarity breeding contempt' – except where Gwyn and Bronwyn were concerned of course. They had earned their 'familiarity'. She had absorbed his lesson well.

"You are prepared for the private party on Wednesday night, Mr Balzac?"

"Most certainly, everything is in hand."

"Good."

They discussed bookings and what the takings had been like in the previous week. This meeting provided an opportunity for improvement and a voicing of ideas. It also ensured that Lise was completely up to date on the day-to-day running of the hotel. She respected the two men's individual territories and rarely interfered with their judgement. She had always believed in keeping her staff happy and avoiding conflict where possible. Her system of management worked well; her employees seemed content and at ease and she certainly paid them over and above the going rate, which Lise looked upon as an investment. Happy staff were more productive and loyal. So much of her business acumen had been a result of William's teaching. Many times when alone she thanked him for his lessons. When everything had been discussed and finalised Lise ended the meeting.

As Mr Pascoe was leaving he said, "Oh by the way Mrs Treharne, a guest booked in last night by the name of Karl Schriver. From Denmark. He said you might know him."

Lise sat still.

Her breathing stopped.

Her eyes widened and she found it difficult to respond.

She collected herself.

"Karl . . . Karl Schriver you say. Are you sure?"

"Yes, Mrs Treharne. Positive." The manager noticed the shock on his employer's face.

"Are . . . are you all right Mrs Treharne?"

Lise still found it hard to speak. She had to try again to compose herself.

"Yes, yes, I'm fine . . . why didn't you tell me sooner Mr Pascoe?" There was a hint of recrimination in her voice.

"It didn't seem necessary. I did ask the gentleman if he wanted me to advise you of his arrival. It was very late. He simply said he would introduce himself sometime today and not to bother you."

"How long is he staying?" Lise's voice was tight with tension.

"He has booked his room for a week but said that he may be staying longer. He's here on business apparently. Have I done something wrong, Mrs Treharne?" Pascoe was genuinely alarmed, it was rare to see her so disconcerted.

"No Mr Pascoe, you haven't done anything wrong. I apologise for giving you that impression. You acted perfectly properly, now please if you will excuse me." As the manager was closing the study door he couldn't help but wonder what all the fuss was about. Who was this Schriver man and why had he put wind up Mrs Treharne? Being the discreet man that he was he decided to say nothing about the incident to any of the staff. Like Lise, he believed in maintaining barriers, besides he harboured a great deal of respect for Mrs Treharne and fondness. He would do nothing that may cause her embarrassment or harm.

Lise remained seated at her desk. Her mind was in turmoil. Could this man be her cousin? The name Schriver was common enough in Denmark as was Karl. She hadn't wished to question Mr Pascoe too thoroughly – this would only lead to greater suspicion. She tried to convince herself that the Schriver who was staying in the hotel could not possibly be the cousin she had known. Her brain was in a panic; she didn't know what to do. Dear God, it must be him – he had said she might know him!

She felt devastated and wanted to be sick.

Her cousin knew all about her life in Denmark – the tragedies, the horrors. He had the power to resurrect all the evil and agony of a past that had died long ago. She had to be decisive. There was no other way. Lise thought for a few moments then reached for her pen. She scribbled a few words and placed the note in an envelope noticing as she did so that her hands were trembling. The past: it never went away, it never would, it was what she had become.

She walked out of her office and into the foyer. She gave the receptionist the envelope.

"Gaynor, please make sure our guest, Mr Karl Schriver, receives this when he returns." She had noticed that his room key was behind the reception desk. The girl did as she was told, at the same time noticing the worried expression on her employer's face. Lise returned to her office. It was only 10.30 in the morning but she poured herself a large cognac. She sat down and drank it in one gulp.

Gradually the alcohol settled her and the jitters began to fade. "What's the matter with me?" she said aloud." I'm being paranoid. Karl can't possibly mean me any harm. We were good friends once."

She poured herself another drink and cast her mind back to the days when she and her cousin used to be so close. It had been such a different world then, a secure, loving world. There had been none of the hatred and horror that was to erupt with the onset of war. The two youngsters had been innocent and untouched by life. Lise suddenly blushed when she remembered their childish forays into the physical unknown. Doctors and nurses had prodded and giggled together behind bushes and wooded hiding places. Attempts at French kissing had led to embarrassment, laughter and failure. Karl had always protected her. Looked after her. He had become her own big brother.

Even after all these years her memories remained fond and affectionate. She had not seen him since the outbreak of war. Like so many families at that time his had moved to other, safer places. Her stomach fluttered at the prospect of seeing him again. What would he look like now? How had the years treated him? He was older than she by a couple of years. He was handsome even as a youngster. Had manhood been kind to him, she wondered?

As the brandy worked its soothing spell her anxiety subsided. It would be good to see someone from her country of birth and to be reminded that she still had some blood roots from the land that she had never stopped loving. For a while her mind wandered in Denmark as it struggled to ignore the bad and remember only the good. Her thoughts were interrupted by a knock on the door.

"Come in." She ordered.

The door opened.

Immediately Lise knew there could be no mistake.

Her cousin Karl Schriver stood before her.

For a few moments they just stared at each other.

Lise was paralysed for a few brief seconds.

Quickly she came to her senses and rushed up to her cousin, hugging him and giving him a kiss on the cheek.

"Karl! Oh Karl, it's been so long, so very long. Why didn't you write to let me know you were coming?" He returned her embrace. He too had been nervous about this meeting and yet now that it had happened he wondered at his own stupid apprehension. Time hadn't passed at all. They were children again, pure and unscathed. He returned her kiss.

"I didn't write because I wasn't sure that the Lise Treharne who owns this hotel was the lovely cousin of my childhood." His voice was deep and confident. He had spoken in Danish and the language immediately took Lise back to her mother country.

In his brief sentence she could once again taste, smell and feel the land of her birth. She replied in her mother tongue surprised at how fluent she could still be with her own language. In recent years she had tended to neglect her command of Danish. She would only converse in the language with Kristian from time to time.

"But how did you know I was here?"

"Well Lise, to be truthful I didn't really. I had to come to this part of the world on business. Then I remembered the visit from your sister-in-law or was it stepdaughter, I can't remember now, it was a few years ago."

"What! Megan?"

"Yes, that was the name, Megan Treharne. She told me you lived in Swansea and when I saw the name of the hotel's proprietor at the entrance I immediately thought of you. Quite a coincidence really." Lise was already unnerved by all this and remained quiet. What else had Megan said and done? Karl continued, "Anyway, I hope your son returned home well and in one piece. The lady was very worried. Obviously I never heard anything from your son though."

"Hold on a minute Karl, you say Megan my stepdaughter came to see you in Denmark?" It was taking Lise a little time to absorb all this.

"Yes. She told me you had a son who had suddenly decided to go and check out his Danish connection as it were or something. I remember that bit of the conversation. She asked me to get in touch if he appeared on my doorstep. I told her that I couldn't imagine why he would do such a thing. After all he didn't even know me or where I lived, but she seemed to think that it was a possibility. A resourceful boy apparently."

"Oh yes, you could say that." Lise mumbled, thinking of her son's 'resourcefulness' with young women and alcohol. So this was where Megan had managed to obtain her poison. Karl noticed her withdrawn expression.

"Lise?" he asked, "did I do anything wrong? You look upset."

"No Karl, you did nothing wrong. Please don't worry about anything."

Then it suddenly dawned on him. "Oh my God! Of course, I remember now. This Megan woman did ask me some very personal questions about you and our families. But please believe me Lise, I said very little. I'm not an indiscreet man."

"I believe you Karl. None of it was your fault."

"I had thought of trying to contact you, but well . . ." He seemed embarrassed, uncomfortable. Lise helped him.

"Karl, what happened then happened. War twists and corrupts everything it touches and more. We were both young, helpless."

"We did – the family that is – desert you though, didn't we?" Karl was serious now. Guilt. Shame. "In that respect we all have a lot to answer for, me included. I knew what had happened, what was going on."

"Perhaps," she replied, "but did you really know? You were too young Karl, too young to fully understand."

"Was I Lise? I wonder."

"Don't Karl. I know only too well how hard it is to keep a painful memory buried. No matter how hard one tries, sometimes it rears its stubborn head to taunt and dismay us. We endure I suppose, and try as best we can to suppress that which hurts us. We never fully succeed but we do learn to carry on. That's probably the best we can hope for. Leave it now, dear Karl. It's wonderful that you're here, that's all that matters."

"You knew nothing of this Megan woman's visit? I was a little suspicious at the time I have to tell you. Was your son's disappearance a fiction too?"

"Yes I'm afraid so, Karl. You were duped. However, what you have told me does explain a few things. Megan can be very convincing so I wouldn't feel too badly about it. No real harm came of anything, so just forget it."

"But why, Lise? Why all the subterfuge? I don't understand."

"Neither do I really, Karl. Believe me. Megan is not a well woman. It's a long story, one day maybe I'll tell you but now is not the time. This is a day to celebrate. We shall have a special lunch in the rose garden, just you and me. You can tell me all about yourself and about the people I once knew. You will probably make me feel terribly homesick."

"Have you never been back, Lise?"

She looked at him. Her eyes spoke their own sadness as she said quietly. "No, never."

Karl quickly realised that pursuing the question would be tactless. They arranged to have lunch together later that day. Before he left her office they embraced again as Lise said, "You know Karl, it really is good to see you. You've no idea how happy it makes me."

"It's the same for me Lise, we were childhood sweethearts once you know, remember?"

Before she could answer he was gone.

She walked through the French doors of William's study and out into his rose garden. It had always been William's favourite 'thinking' place as he had called it. Now it had become hers. The sudden meeting with Karl had been such a shock for her, but now the surprise of it all was melting away as quickly as it had arrived.

Unbelievably her cousin hadn't changed much.

He was taller of course, over six feet, and more muscular and broad. Smooth lines of determination and will had replaced the childish folds of youth on the tanned skin of his face. Wrinkles had yet to fully mature; it was as if they didn't dare. The shining blond hair of childhood remained, so much like her own and without a trace of middle-year grey or ageing resignation. His eyes were still the compelling deep blue of his race, still intense and demanding. The passing years between youth and mature adulthood had served Karl well, they had merely improved and refined. There were no rough and ready throws of a cynical dice on his face, no tucks and dips of bitter and disillusioned thought or angst.

Karl Schriver was a striking, handsome man.

Despite the years that had gone by, Lise would still have known him immediately. Memories, Lise thought; some can never be forgotten, nor perhaps should they be. She had told Karl to forget, but had she really meant it? For her, to cast aside the past created a possibility that maybe one day the memories of days gone by, even in some of their most hateful glory, could return with a sly finality to corrupt and attack the future. One of the dramatic realisations of middle age was that some memories could never be completely cauterised or ignored as they imprinted an indelible and permanent scar on one's psyche. They left a claim on your very being, on your soul. They could and did make you a prisoner of the past and experience. Perhaps memories were the keys to all the many doors that opened up an individual's character and nature. Such vulnerability was a little disconcerting – frightening even.

She remembered her first childish attempts at kissing with Karl; the crushing infatuation. She could only smile and feel warm. She was glad he had come back into her life. He was the exception to the darkness that had become Denmark.

Their lunch had been slow. On purpose. Both Karl and Lise were too absorbed with each other to even enjoy the extra special offerings of Balzac. Kristian and Charlotte had interrupted their intimate memories only briefly. When at last they realised that the coffee was beginning to get cold, Karl said, "Beautiful children, Lise. No doubt about who the mother is. Particularly Kristian, he has inherited your fine looks." Lise blushed. This was the first time since William's death that she had enjoyed anything remotely resembling intimacy with another man. Karl made her feel feminine again, desirable. It was simply his manner. Long-forgotten feelings slowly began to emerge.

"Yes, he is my son there is no doubt about that. Charlotte though is more like her father."

Karl looked at Lise directly in the eyes and said gently. "Lise, I don't wish to intrude but what happened to your husband?

"He died Karl, more than three years ago."

"Oh, I'm sorry, I truly am."

"Don't be. We had a wonderful life together. I have only happy memories."

"Tell me about them, Lise. Tell me about your life since leaving Denmark, I would really like to know."

For the second time in her life Lise felt that here was a man she could trust. She had known him as a child, known him as a victim of puberty. Childhood trust was everything.

Of course, he knew all about the reasons for her departure to Wales all those years ago but he seemed uninterested in that part of her life. He was obviously sensitive enough not to intrude and tear open old wounds. He showed a genuine interest and concern for her life in Wales. He wanted to know about Lise the person in the same way as she felt drawn to him, to his own life. She wanted to know everything about him. She hadn't felt this curious about a man since William.

They spent all afternoon talking. Gently prying into one another's lives, searching for detail and facts that would reveal the true character beneath the outward physical persona. They were like a man and woman who, meeting for the first time, could not resist an immediate onslaught of mutual attraction. They fenced with each other, thrusting and parrying. Treading cautiously, not wanting to offend in any way. As the hours passed they became more at ease with each other, more comfortable. It was almost as if the passing years had never intervened, as if time and space had never existed. They were absorbed with one another.

When ease and comfort had become fully established Karl pursued his earlier question about her returning one day.

"Have you never visited your old home . . .? I know what happened Lise, and God knows I don't want to cause any pain, but perhaps it would do you good. Help you in some way. Kill the ghosts once and for all." Lise looked down at the table, her thoughts her own.

"Perhaps, Karl. I'll have to think about it."

"You can always bring Charlotte with you. Stay with me in my house – it's big enough and hardly used. No one would know you now Lise, think about it."

"I will Karl . . . a big house? Hardly used? You haven't mentioned anything about a wife, children? I have been too polite to ask." Karl smiled.

"No children. No wife, not even an ex-wife. And before you ask, I don't fancy your manager either! Denmark has become more liberal I think than most European countries. The marriage ceremony seems to have less and less significance. I have had long relationships but somehow have never married." For a moment Lise detected whispers of loneliness. "I am not a father which, I have to say, bothers me sometimes. Never mind though, who knows . . . ?" He looked at Lise and smiled with mischief.

"Karl, Karl! Stop it will you?" She was blushing again. Time and practise was needed. It had been a long time. She had forgotten how to flirt, how to handle a man. In spite of the banter Lise knew that Karl was a sensitive man. He seemed as vulnerable as she. Her perceptive eye missed little. His masculinity sometimes ran away leaving a gentle and tactile human being behind.

"I must say you do seem to have a way with little ones. Lottie liked you."

"Yes, I know," he smiled. "That isn't really the problem, the problem is finding the right mother, the right wife." His eyes looked straight into Lise's again. She was stripped. Naked. The only man who had been able to affect her like this had been William. Karl made her feel so utterly female. Her own thoughts shocked her. What was happening to her? She had only been with the man for a few hours. She wanted to edge the conversation away from children and marriage; it was unsettling her.

"What are you doing over here anyway?" Lise asked bringing the conversation down to a safer, more banal level. "You haven't told me. I am one of very few Danes in Swansea as far as I know."

"Windmills." Karl replied.

"Windmills?" Lise repeated somewhat bemused.

"You know you look beautiful, Lise, when your face becomes all serious and curious."

"Now stop flirting Karl, will you, I know you of old, don't forget!" She couldn't help smiling, "Now will you just explain to me what on earth windmills have to do with you being in Wales? I mean it's hardly Holland is it."

"Quite," Karl laughed. "I'll explain. There is a lot of research going on at the moment into the generating of electricity by the use of wind power. It's all very technical so I won't bore you with the details. Basically, it's just the use of wind to make electricity, the medium being windmills. Of course, they are nothing like the windmills you have a picture of in your mind. It's early days of course and the technology needs to be refined, but there is a big future here and I want to be in on it at the beginning. The environmental implications are huge, the potential is enormous. Clean energy is the future, believe me. Anyway, I'm over here looking for possible manufacturers who might be prepared to construct some prototypes. One company in Swansea has shown an interest and that's why I'm here, checking things out."

"Wind power! What next? Still, if it keeps the air clean I suppose it has to be a good thing. Somewhat beyond me though I have to admit."

"It's a bit beyond most people at the moment. You are not alone, believe me. I do have other interests in Denmark of course, mainly property, importing and exporting. I can see a huge European market in the future way beyond the present situation and I want to be in at the beginning. I'm sure that in time and with the development of the EEC trade barriers and so on between European countries both east and west will vanish completely. I want to be prepared for all these advances in commercial trading."

Lise couldn't help but be impressed by the man's enthusiasm and foresight. He was obviously someone who liked to be in control of his life; a man who did not wait for things to happen but made them happen. They were very much alike in this respect. They were both strong and knew where they were going. Lise admired entrepreneurial aptitude in a man; she had always respected William for his business acumen and these same feelings were now being directed to the man sitting opposite her now.

They continued to talk with one another until Lise at last had to drag herself away to see to some hotel business. They had been sitting with one another for four hours – to Lise it seemed like four minutes. She couldn't get enough of the man. Her eyes rarely strayed from his and life no longer seemed to exist beyond their dining table. There were no other movements, sounds or voices but their own. They heard and saw nothing but themselves.

When she returned to her office, Lise sat behind her desk and couldn't stop smiling. She started to analyse – a condition that had troubled her for most of her adult life – and quickly gave up. Age was beginning to mature her wisdom. Often it was best to accept things and leave it at that. Whys and wherefores were not important. She was feeling a kind of release, elation even. The last time she had felt like this had been on her honeymoon. She knew without any shadow of doubt that Karl was moving her emotions into an area that had been unexplored since William's death. For a moment she felt fearful, even guilty, as if she was committing some kind of matrimonial offence. The word 'adultery' came to her mind, and then just as quickly she banished it from her thoughts; she was being stupid. William would have wanted her to be happy. His last letter to her had almost begged her to love again. No, she decided, there was nothing at all to feel guilty about, she was not betraying William or his memory. He would have given her his blessing.

Was she was falling in love? It seemed so silly. An infatuation perhaps? A childish crush? How could she? A few hours, some lunch? No, impossible . . . and yet. Since William's death love had become maternal only. Apart from this demanded love there was only her emotional relationship with the past. With death even. She had doubted that there was any man walking on earth who could compare to her late husband. She had fought off loneliness to the best of her ability; after all she had her children. She had resigned herself to a future life without the love of a man. Now though, everything had changed. Karl had walked into her life.

She thought about the man who was causing such a dramatic upheaval in her relatively uncomplicated life. He was so good looking, so attractive and yet the powerful physique belied the quiet, thoughtful man behind the muscle. His mind was sharp and perceptive, challenging; Lise could never love or respect any man who was unable to match her in intellect and intelligence. Karl knew his own mind but was not overbearing, and certainly not the type who could be bullied. He was master of his own life and destiny; he was in control. Lise found these attributes difficult to resist. She had never wanted a man that she could dominate – that would have made life extremely tedious and such a relationship she knew would never last. William and Karl were so very much alike in character. Physically they were both extremely attractive but in different ways. Lise had learnt a long time ago that physical attributes could never hold, could never be permanent. A love of the flesh was a fickle, shallow thing, to be enjoyed briefly and then forgotten. Her love needed to feed on much more; it needed sustenance from character and personality. Like William, Karl had both; his physical appearance was merely a bonus. Lise wanted to be with him; she wanted to touch and kiss him. She wanted his body as well as his mind.

They arranged to meet again that night.

Lise was counting the minutes.

Could this man from her past bring her the fulfilment she so desperately sought? She hoped with all her heart that he would. He seemed so right. She would have said perfect, had not her own sensible opinions believed in there being no such thing as perfection.

CHAPTER 31

"Well Mr Treharne, we have listened to your plea in mitigation and have to say that we do give you credit for at least providing us with an honest admission. Your occupation and means of earning a living however come within the parameters of the criminal law. By your own admission you have chosen to flout that law, and naturally this crime of yours must be punished."

Oh God, Griffith thought as he stood in the dock, I'm for the bloody high jump. The magistrate continued. "You are a man of previous good character and from an impeccable background. I have to say that it saddens the bench to see you here before us on such . . . er . . . tawdry charges. We may well be living in a new modern world of free love and expression. However, that is for the world and the people out there," the magistrate pointed to one of the windows of the courtroom, "not for the law-abiding world in here. You have broken the law and must therefore be punished. We fine you £1,000 and sentence you to three months imprisonment . . ." God almighty, Griffith thought as his legs nearly gave way, the £1,000 was nothing – but three months inside? The magistrate, having paused to enjoy the look of shock on Griffith's face, then continued, ". . . to be suspended for two years. That is all. The court is adjourned."

Griffith stood motionless, unable to think. Everyone stood up and bowed.

At last he came to his senses and walked out of the court a free man. He waited for Tom outside the courtroom. Eventually his solicitor turned up, all smiles and beaming.

"Well Griffith, you must be feeling very pleased."

"I'm still in shock, I thought they were going to put me away. Christ, it was touch and go in there."

"Not at all, I wasn't worried for a moment. All magistrates, and for that matter judges, pause when giving a suspended sentence. They do it for effect, naturally. It's a wonderful opportunity for them to vent their inherent sadism. Never mind though, I thought they were quite lenient."

"£1,000 worth of lenience, Tom. Don't forget that."

"Now now Griffith dear boy, don't be ungracious. You got off lightly all things considered. My plea in mitigation was a work of genius, don't you think? Marshall Hall would have been proud of me."

"Bullshit Tom, pure bullshit. Even I was embarrassed."

"Dear boy, that's my job. Without, as you put so succinctly 'bullshitters' like me, where would you be? In clink right now I shouldn't wonder."

"I suppose so." Griffith smiled. He had always liked Tom for all his 'bullshit'.

"So what are you going to do now, Griffith?" the solicitor asked.

"Wind up my business and go into early retirement, Tom, that's what I'm going to do. I've just had a good warning. Time to say goodbye and lead the life of a good honest citizen."

"Quite so, dear boy. A good idea if I may say so."

"I have plenty of money now, so the time has come. I might well move back to Wales. I don't know yet though."

"Yes, Wales is certainly quieter and less fraught than this panic-ridden metropolis I grant you. Well, no doubt you will do what is best. You will keep in touch?"

"Of course Tom. Besides I've still got your extortionate fees to pay, haven't I?"

"Now that's a point, Griffith. Yes, I must see to my fee note. Worry not, it will be as modest as ever."

"Modest? Like hell! That will be the day."

"Oh dear me Griffith, you really are a difficult man to retrieve funds from. Which reminds me, have you placated the Inland Revenue?"

"Yes, no problem there. We came to an arrangement."

"Good. Very good. Well, I'll be off. Keep in touch dear boy, and do take care now."

"And you Tom." The two men shook hands and left one another.

As Griffith walked to his car relief flooded through him, not only from the result of the hearing but because he was giving up his past lifestyle. No more worry about the police and possible arrest; no more worry about the Revenue. Before turning the ignition in his car the idea of Wales came back to him. Yes, it would indeed be good to go home. He would feel safer, less threatened.

CHAPTER 32

Karl parked his rented car in a side street by St Mary's church in Swansea's town centre. He had an appointment with the managing director of a manufacturing company that might be able to assist him with his latest business venture. He sometimes wondered why he was always searching for new opportunities to make money. He was a millionaire in his own right and really didn't need to create more wealth. He would often question his own motivation. Was it raw greed, an appetite for power, or simply the challenge? He was never quite certain. He didn't consider himself a greedy man and yet, if he was honest, he had to admit to nagging doubts where his covetous nature was concerned. He was human being after all. As for power, there was no doubt that he revelled in it. He gained a tremendous satisfaction from controlling the fates and lives of lesser mortals, although he always tried to avoid hurting unnecessarily. He could be ruthless, but only when circumstances left no other choice. As he walked into the town centre he decided in his mind that his true motivation for making money was the thrill of a challenge. He simply couldn't resist betting against the odds and winning. Lise was a challenge he thought, and he was determined to break her defences and win her. The woman was exquisite, each time she smiled it was like some glorious pyrotechnic display of colour and life.

It had been many years since any woman had had such an obliterating effect on him. He was not sure whether or not he was falling in love with her. He was unsure about the exact character of love, indeed he was uncertain as to whether he had ever truly experienced the emotion at all. He had known infatuation, fondness and lust that defied description. But love?

He wasn't at all certain about this most human of all emotions and perhaps the most lethal. One thing he did know without any shadow of doubt, he would have Lise if it killed him. He would have her. He wanted her more than anything else in the world, more than wealth, more than prestige, more than power. She had totally bewitched him. Each time he thought of her his heart seemed to tingle and his pulse quicken. It was ridiculous. She was the most beautiful woman he had ever met, so serene, so gentle and yet strong.

Karl normally slept with his women then forgot them. He rarely held any respect for them. With Lise it was different. She was a successful businesswoman, financially independent and confident in herself. He respected and admired her achievements. For Karl, respect was one of the most important attractions in a woman. If he could dominate, cajole and humiliate a woman he would tire and get bored. He needed a woman with spirit, a woman who would fight him.

Lise, he knew, was such a woman.

As he walked through Swansea market he stopped here and there fascinated by some of the foods on sale. There were stalls selling some kind of Welsh bread called 'Bara Brith', the words meaning nothing to him. Everywhere he looked he saw mounds of cockles, mussels and some black stuff that looked thoroughly revolting; laverbread it was called but he failed to see the connection between the fishy smelling ooze and bread. He stopped at one of the stalls and bought an apple. There was no such thing as a quick deal in Swansea market. The woman selling him the fruit wanted to know where he was from, how long he was staying and how many children he had. The strong Welsh accent made her questions difficult to understand even though Karl considered his English to be beyond reproach. He left the woman somewhat bewildered and none the wiser for their conversation. For all he knew she could have been speaking in Welsh, a mysterious tongue that even his talent for languages could never enable him to master.

He finally reached the exit to the market and left the symphonies of the Welsh language, Welsh curiosity and dawdling Welsh commerce to their own devices. Would such passionate chaos prevail in the more industrial areas of the town? he pondered. The thought was a disquieting one. As he reached his destination, some offices in the Kingsway, he decided to reserve judgement. His last thoughts as he entered the building were of Lise and the evening ahead.

If his feelings were a preamble to 'love' then he was all for it.

"How did your meeting go?" Lise asked, genuinely interested in Karl's answer. They were sitting in her private apartment drinking coffee and brandy, having finished an exquisite lobster supper prepared by Lise herself.

"Fine thank you, Lise. I think I may have to stay in Swansea a while longer. There's quite a lot to do." Lise wanted to say, 'Good, I'm glad', but didn't. She tried to avoid thinking of Karl's inevitable departure. They sat facing each other on a leather settee.

"I can't stay in Wales forever though," he continued, "I have so many commitments in Denmark that need my attention. That's the trouble with going away – how do the English put it, 'while the cat's away the mice will play'."

"I'm fortunate in that respect," Lise said. "No one here would probably notice if I disappeared for a year. The hotel would run itself. I do have good and trustworthy people though, which is a great help."

"Oh, I think you are being too modest Lise. That's the sign of a good manager you know – when no one realises that he or she is away. You run the show around here. I have noticed. Nothing moves without your say-so!" Lise smiled.

"Oh all right, I suppose I do tend to keep a watchful eye."

Karl looked into his glass for a moment and said, "Lise, I've been thinking about my earlier suggestion that you come and stay in Denmark for a holiday. Have you given it any thought?"

"Well . . . er . . . no, not really," she replied carefully, not wanting to appear rude.

"Don't say anything yet, let me finish." She remained silent. "You know Lise, you should put the ghosts to rest. No one will remember you now, it all happened so long ago. You could stay with me or in a hotel, it's up to you. I have a charming holiday cottage overlooking a lake, it's peaceful and beautiful in the summer. Do please come over and have a vacation, it will do you good. Exorcise all the unpleasant memories once and for all. Bring Charlotte and Kristian. It will be a wonderful holiday for them. Plenty of young female holidaymakers too for Kristian!" Lise looked at the man who had suddenly changed her life. Caution and reluctance vanished. Indecision had never been one of her strong points.

"All right, yes Karl I will, as you say enough time has gone by. They can manage here without me. There will probably be a great sigh of relief and it won't do me any harm to let go for a bit. Besides, I haven't had a proper holiday for years. I deserve one."

Karl leaned across the settee and took her hand, kissing it. No more words were spoken. They held each other and kissed. Karl's lips moved to her neck, his teeth gently biting her skin. He kissed her cheeks, her eyelids, her ears. Her mouth opened. She was lost and did not want to be found. The desire that had been subdued for so long exploded in her body. She was unable to think. All her senses were concentrated on the man holding her. She was being taken to another place. Another world. She couldn't speak. All she could do was respond. He picked her up and took her into the bedroom. He didn't turn any lights on knowing how sensitive some women could be about their nakedness, particularly when making love to a new man for the first time. He undressed her slowly. She was a wonderful gift; he wanted to drag out the unwrapping for as long as possible. His anticipation was to be savoured and then devoured. He laid her down on the bed. His tongue travelled from her neck to her feet.

He kissed and licked every inch of her. She was the only woman in the world. His tongue and teeth sucked and bit as he let his head spin with her most intimate aromas. Lise's pleasure made her body shudder and her hips strain and plead for Karl's tumescence. She held him tight with her legs and took his head in her hands. She kissed him. Passion overwhelmed. Her spirit joined Karl's. They soared and flew together. Male and female. At last Karl penetrated her. She cried out as if in terrible pain. Her body was on fire. Her wetness soaked him. His thrusting became faster. They both lost control. She clung to him and shook. Mutual orgasm ruined them. Lise's wouldn't stop. Her body kept going, it wasn't going to give in without a fight. Her throat had tightened making any sound impossible. She gasped for air.

At last the excruciating waves of pleasure subsided.

She lay her head back on the pillow.

She was exhausted.

Lost.

Karl withdrew from her and held her tightly to his chest. Neither of them spoke. After a while Lise stroked his chest and said, "I'm going to love you, Karl."

He kissed her on the lips and whispered. "Lise, you are the most beautiful creature I have ever known. God, how I want you . . . forever."

At last he had discovered the most mysterious and at the same time most painful emotion of the human condition – love.

CHAPTER 33

Megan sat on a bench staring at the wanton mess that was Swansea Bay.

A few cargo ships making their way to the docks could be seen on the grey horizon. This was not the place she had known in childhood. The once yellow, healthy sand and clear blue sea had been poisoned by pollution and man's own filth. Sewage pipes could be seen vomiting their frothy, bubbling fluid into what was once a natural haven for flora, fauna and the aquatic denizens of the sea. When the tides moved out all that was left was a sickening yellow sludge of processed urine and faeces. Megan remembered the name it had been called in later years: 'Granny's Custard'. She smiled at the recollection. But not for long; her face soon collapsed and crumbled. The skin was unused to the sudden movement of a smile.

For a few brief seconds her eyes had shone and her mind had become harmless. Happiness had delivered for once.

After a while she left the bench and returned to the small bed-and-breakfast hotel where she had booked a room for one night only. The hotel was one of many that lined the road facing the bay. They seemed quite content to ignore Granny, her stinking custard and the foul tankers that wallowed in it. Why the hell would anyone want a view of Swansea Bay? Megan thought as she arrived at her B&B. For a moment the latent anger that possessed her began to stir.

What was she doing in a place like this?

What had she come to?

Her father's bitch had forced her to this – she had ruined Megan's life. The only true daughter of William Treharne, the fact that she herself was adopted had been forgotten long ago.

The Danish whore had taken away everything that rightly belonged to her, her inheritance, her father, her life. Megan had heard about the birth of another girl but as far as she was concerned the child was a bastard and certainly no offspring of her father's. Lise had probably rutted with one of the servants, that's all the slut was capable of.

Megan seethed with bitterness as she looked around her small, modest room. My God she thought, that bitch has a luxurious hotel, my father's hotel and I'm here.

Tears began to spill from her eyes.

Tears of hatred, jealousy and pain.

She cried and cried.

The tears had become a part of her life. They were her only release.

Her body and her mind were both irredeemable wrecks. They were so shattered and distorted that any resemblance to the young Megan had become less than a faded memory. She lay down on the single bed and closed her raw eyes. Gradually sleep took her to a merciful blackness. Her sick mind rejected dreams, even nightmares.

Megan was here in Swansea finally to commit her permanent and lasting act of revenge. She was determined to be free from bitterness and hurt. She wanted her mind to be calm, free from the constant attacks of anxiety and fear. She desperately wanted peace and happiness – to begin again. To feel.

She wanted life.

Her alarm clock woke her at 2 a.m. the following morning. She quickly shut it off, not wishing the noise to be heard by any other guests. She dressed slowly. A calmness had seemed to take over her normally agitated mind and body. The knowledge of what she was going to do somehow brought a sense of relief. It also placated as her destination finally came into view. All was in sight. All was clear. For the first time in years her life had a solid purpose, a motive.

She left her room and made straight for the car she had hired the day before. Before setting off she opened the boot and made one last check of the items she had purchased the previous day. Everything seemed to be in order. Satisfied, she got into the car and drove off. The roads were quiet at this time in the morning. The peace and emptiness helped her resolve. She was used to being alone. Isolation had become a way of living; it was her natural habitat. Her loneliness had become a comfort – lately people had started to frighten and intimidate her, crowds to terrify and oppress. She craved the solitary hours of night, wishing the darkness to remain constant. Permanent. Here she was able to hide from herself and her mind. She felt safe and powerful, no longer afraid as her thought processes became more acute, more aware. She was as one with the mysteries and veils of blackness, the effortless nothings with their delusions and spells of emptiness. Black was perfection, with nothing to see, nothing to touch. It could only 'be'. Daytime and light brought sickening revelation, she could see who she was, who she had become. There was too much dread, too much fright. Too much Megan. Now as she drove, her natural confidence returned. She had purpose. Desire.

She knew with total certainty what must be done.

Lise couldn't sleep.

Karl's arm lay across her breasts as if protecting her from some unseen dangers. Even in sleep the man attempted to look after her. She smiled to herself and enjoyed listening to the deep, even breathing of the man she had fallen in love with, so hopelessly in love. Her emotions would not allow rest to come. It was as if she wanted to wallow in every minute that life could give. To stay awake meant she would miss nothing. She felt Karl's warmth next to her body, his strength and his love. She wanted this moment in time to last forever, never to succumb to death. Her joy was complete, her life full to the brim. For an instant a cold fear ran through her – what would happen to her if Karl were snatched away? Quickly she immobilised the thought; it was too horrific to even mentally glance at.

She gently lifted Karl's arm away from her and got up from the bed. He was sleeping soundly and she didn't want to disturb him. She put on a bathrobe and walked into her sitting room. There was only a half moon but it gave enough light for her to see what she was doing. She walked over to the window and looked out at the sea and stars. She felt at peace. Content.

Love did strange things to a human being, she thought. It could give all and take all, it could give happiness and also inflict mortal agony. To love was to undertake an unfathomable risk; the stakes were so critically high. She had known the depths of despair, the horrendous violation of her soul and spirit, the seething trauma of hopeless poverty. It was this knowledge, this experience, which made her realise how extremely kind the Fates, the Gods, were being to her.

Lise had never harboured any deep religious conviction; even so she respected spirituality. Where religion was concerned she was a confirmed libertarian. Her beliefs were a melting pot of this and that. Sometimes she was an ethical atheist, at other times a Buddhist Christian. She believed strongly in the Christian ethic, but not in the mythology. Dogma was anathema to her, as was the fiction of monotheism. She was content to mix and blend all the great frauds and apply what she needed at the time. Now as she looked out on the calm sea she thanked her indeterminate Power. She had been blessed with an adoring kind husband, two beautiful children and material well-being. Now there was Karl. No woman could ask for more. Humility made her feel so fragile as she looked at the stars. She gave thanks. The suffocating loneliness that she had known since William's death had dissipated. She felt whole again. Human. She trusted her faith.

"What are you thinking about?" Karl asked from the bedroom doorway. Before Lise could answer he walked up behind her and placed his arms around her waist. He kissed the back of her head.

"Oh, nothing really," she replied. "I was just thinking how lucky I am."

"Luck doesn't come into it, darling. We are together because our love is meant to be. That's all there is to it."

He turned her around to face him and kissed her softly on the lips. "Don't be sad Lise, we have years ahead of us."

"I'm not sad Karl, just a little humbled. It's sometimes difficult for me to comprehend how I could receive such good fortune. Sometimes it seems almost obscene, particularly when I think of all the human misery in the world. I feel so . . . so selfish somehow."

"Now now, Lise. You mustn't think like that. Perhaps your life has just gone through a process of balancing good with bad. You've had your tragedies. You've had your losses and grief, now the scales must tip in the opposite direction. You deserve every ounce of happiness you receive. God knows our lives are brief enough Lise, what we have now we must hold on to and cherish. People often say 'here today, gone tomorrow', it's not 'gone tomorrow', it's gone next second. That's how fickle our insignificant lives are. We have each other Lise, let's be gluttons with the love that is between us." He kissed her again. "Now come back to bed. We both need some sleep." He took her hand and led her back to the bedroom.

Megan stopped the car about two hundred yards from the main entrance to the Cliffs. The fact that the vehicle would obstruct the narrow lane was of no concern to her. At 3 o'clock in the morning it was highly unlikely that anyone would be using the narrow road anyway, hotel or not. The half moon provided her with all the light she needed. She had picked a good day for it. She opened the boot of the car and retrieved a holdall plus the items she required to carry out her plan. As she walked up to the main building she tried to remember the exact layout of the house. She noted there had been some changes, but nothing drastic; her father's house was more or less as she remembered it. She tried to avoid the main forecourt as her rubber-soled shoes would create a warning noise on the gravel. She headed for the series of steps that led to a basement beneath the east wing of the house. In her father's day the basement had been used purely for storage. She hoped that this was still the case. Turning a corner the moon was suddenly obscured and she found herself in total darkness. For once it wasn't her friend as she cursed quietly and reached into the holdall for a torch. Megan the organiser was still living, if only just. She had wanted to use it only as a last resort – there was a risk it could attract unwanted attention. She sighed and switched it on. About two yards in front of her were the steps leading down to a closed door. At least there was not much wrong with her memory, she thought. With the torch lighting her way she walked down the steps and studied the door. It was new and seemed secured by a substantial padlock. Megan was undeterred. She was prepared. She knelt down by the door, rummaged around in the holdall and found a sturdy screwdriver she had purchased the day before. Megan was not a professional burglar, but she did know that unscrewing the clasps that the padlock held together would be an easy-enough task. Taking care to make as little noise as possible she removed the clasps and soon gained entry to the basement.

Although Megan didn't know it luck was on her side this night. The basement door was the only door in the whole house that hadn't been fitted with intruder alarms. Lise hadn't bothered to wire the basement doors – there was rarely anything in there worth stealing. Once inside Megan shone the torch from one end of the room to the other. She was relieved. The basement was still being used for storage. There seemed to be all kinds of equipment, food and general merchandise boxed and neatly stacked. Without pausing for more than a few seconds, she set about the final execution of her plan. The two-gallon container she had brought was making her arm ache. She started pouring the paraffin it contained all over the contents of the underground warehouse and noticed that some boxes contained a similar liquid. She smiled at the irony. Lise was actually helping her! When she was satisfied that everything was saturated she looked up at the ceiling. Her memory told her that the main hallway to the house was above her, which meant that the fire should begin more or less in the middle of the Cliffs and spread outwards. She had planned well. Perspiring slightly from her efforts she took one last look at her work and dug in her pocket for a box of matches. Had her sense of smell been more sensitive and not dulled by the years of cigarettes, alcohol and drugs, she may have noticed that parts of her clothing had been splattered with the inflammable fluid she had been casually throwing around in her insane enthusiasm for destruction. The box of matches she had bought was a 'Safety' one. Even so, sometimes the combustible tips of these matches could fly off the stick and burn the striker. Megan had chosen one such rogue match from the box.

Her face twisted from the exertions of fury and euphoria.

Megan struck the match.

Flames consumed, flesh boiled and spat

No one heard the last agonised screams, no one heard the last desperate gurgles of despair. No one heard Megan Treharne

She died as she had lived – alone.

Alarm bells exploded all over the hotel. Lise and Karl leapt out of bed and threw on the nearest clothes that were to hand. This was no fire drill exercise. Lise had authorised no such activity. This was real. They both ran to the foyer and straight to the reception desk. There was no smoke or fire to be seen. Behind the reception desk was a fire alarm panel, a red light flashed underneath the word 'Basement'.

"The basement!" Lise shouted. Already guests were beginning to appear, half dressed, half drunk, half asleep and half annoyed. There was no panic. They all seemed to be following to the letter the 'In case of fire' instructions stuck to the back of their room doors.

Kristian came charging down the main stairway holding Charlotte.

"What the hell's going on?" he shouted, trying to outdo the piercing noise of the alarms.

"Fire!" Karl yelled back. "In the basement. Kristian, go and ring the fire brigade. Quickly!" Karl had never fully trusted alarm systems; he assumed Lise's was automatically connected to the local emergency services but he was taking no chances.

"Karl!" Lise shouted. "Grab some fire extinguishers and follow me!"

It was only when they arrived at the door that led from the kitchen to the basement that they realised the seriousness of the situation. Smoke was beginning to make its way under the door. Lise quickly took in the scene. "Outside, hurry. We must go in through the outside door. Don't go in here, the sudden surge of air and oxygen might cause an explosion. We don't know how long the fire has been smouldering. It must be starved of oxygen."

From the outside flames could be seen through the basement windows. Lise snatched an extinguisher from Karl's hand and started to make for the open door. Megan had not had the time or the inclination to close it. Karl, seeing the danger Lise was putting herself in, ran after her and dragged her back. He couldn't help but admire her tenacity and courage.

"No Lise, no!" He shouted, the heat was beginning to scorch their faces and hair. "You can't go in there, there's nothing you can do!" He roughly pulled her away, dragging her to safety. "Wait until the fire brigade comes!" He continued to shout. "They will be here in a minute!"

Lise struggled against Karl, she felt compelled to do something, anything. Her whole life was in Ragged Cliffs. She used her fists against him, thumping his chest in anger and frustration.

"Let me go! There must be something I can do. My hotel for God's sake – let me go!" Karl was not about to allow the woman he loved kill herself. He was about to manhandle her further away from the blaze when the fire engine sirens could be heard.

"Thank God! Now come on Lise, we must make certain all the guests are accounted for." Seeing professional firemen calmed her down a little. "Look Lise, leave it to the people who know what to do," he ordered. "We must see to the guests!"

A short time later all the guests had, as instructed, gathered in the forecourt and were remarkably calm. They were checked off against the visitors' book and appeared to be unharmed. Kristian and a bemused Charlotte stood next to their mother who was sitting on one of the garden chairs having almost fainted with relief. Karl knelt down in front of her and took both her hands in his.

"The fire people seem to have everything under control Lise, I don't think there's too much damage so don't be too upset. Fortunately the fire didn't have time to spread and no one has been hurt." He lifted her chin with his finger. "Come on my darling, the end of the world hasn't arrived yet, your insurance will cover all the damage so you have nothing to worry about."

"Oh Karl," Lise replied. "You've been so calm and collected, and all I've done is panic and be stupid. You're right though, the damage is nothing – but more importantly no one has been injured or, God forbid, killed. I don't know whether I could stand that." She reached out for the hands of her son and daughter.

"You were not stupid Lise, actually I thought you were rather brave. Another reason for me to love you more – if that's possible," he added.

A discreet cough made them both turn to the senior fireman who was hovering a couple of feet away.

"Mrs Treharne?" His voice seemed to have an edge of anxiety to it.

"Yes, I'm Mrs Treharne. What can I do for you officer? Is the fire under control?"

"Yes Mrs Treharne. The fire is out, you were lucky we caught it early. The only damage that we can see has been to the basement . . . er . . ." He looked at Kristian and the little girl. "Look Mrs Treharne, would it be possible to speak somewhere a little more private please?" Lise immediately realised something was wrong.

"Yes, yes of course." She replied a little nervously. "We can go into my office . . . um . . . you don't mind if Mr Schriver joins us do you? He is a close relative."

"No Mrs Treharne, of course not."

"Then follow me please."

The three of them walked into Lise's office. "Please sit down Mr . . .?"

"White, Mrs Treharne, White."

White sat down, removing his helmet as he did so. The man was nervous. On edge. He hated this part of the job.

"Would you like a drink Mr White? You probably need one after all this," Karl asked.

"No thank you, not just now. There's still a lot to do."

Lise was sitting behind her desk becoming more agitated by the minute.

"Mrs Treharne," the fireman began, "we experienced some difficulty getting to the hotel. A car, a blue Cortina, was parked – or rather left – in the lane leading to the hotel. There was no driver or passenger. Fortunately the keys were left in the ignition so we had no trouble moving it."

"A car? No driver? In the middle of the lane . . . but . . . who . . . what?" Lise could think of no reasonable explanation.

"Well, it naturally seemed odd to us. In any event our later discoveries may help with some kind of explanation." White lowered his head for a moment. He braced himself. For all he knew the charred body they had found could be this woman's daughter, sister or mother. The surname on the driving licence was Treharne.

"Mrs Treharne, we found a body in the basement – badly burned."

Oh Christ, White thought, how the hell can you ever be tact-ful about something like this. Karl immediately moved beside Lise and took her hand. White continued.

"We found some identification in the car; a handbag had been left lying on the passenger seat. There were various papers and documents in it naming a 'Megan Treharne' as its owner. Everyone living or staying at the hotel has now been accounted for except this one person. For the time being we must assume this person to be in fact the Megan Treharne named in the documents we found. I must also tell you that following our preliminary examinations of the scene we believe that it was she who deliberately started the fire. Paraffin was used. We found traces of paraffin in the boot of the car."

Lise's face had drained of all colour.

"You mean arson?" she asked.

"Yes, it certainly looks that way . . . I'm sorry."

"Are you sure that the person you found is Megan Treharne?"

"We cannot be wholly certain about anything at the moment Mrs Treharne, but all the evidence we have to hand at the moment would seem to indicate that the body is that of Megan Treharne."

"Oh, my God! And I was worried about the hotel! How could this have happened? How?"

White felt helpless. There was nothing he could do.

"Is she a relative, Mrs Treharne?"

"What . . .? Er . . . yes. She was my late husband's daughter by his first marriage. Oh, Karl. Poor Megan, it must have been horrible. Why should she want to do such a thing?"

Karl made no reply.

White stood up.

"I'm deeply sorry, Mrs Treharne. The police will be wanting to talk to you shortly I expect. Everything is in their hands now so I'll be leaving you." With that White walked out of the room, glad to get away from the misery that his job frequently encountered.

"Karl, I don't want to see anybody yet," Lise said, "Please keep them away for a while. I need a little time to absorb all this."

"Of course, you stay here. I'll get you a hot drink with a shot of brandy in it. I'll keep the dogs at bay, so just you stay where you are."

"Thank you, Karl, thank you." Once again Lise wondered how she would have managed without the man she loved. Soon after Karl had left there was a knock at the door and Kristian walked in.

"Are you alright, Mum?" he asked.

"Yes. I suppose so. You know about Megan?"

"Yes, if it's true that is, although there seems to be little doubt. There's nothing really I can say. I never knew the woman."

"No, I don't think I ever knew her either. You know she always hated me, she never wanted her father and I to marry you see. I've been thinking about it all. The fire was probably her way of exacting revenge, the same way she tried to hurt you. She must have finally snapped. I knew from Griffith that she was receiving psychiatric treatment and was having problems with alcohol and drugs. She must have finally slipped over the edge."

"Hell though Mum, what a way to go, it gives me the shivers."

"Me too, Kristian. I can't help feeling guilty somehow though – even responsible. At the moment I just don't know what to think . . . the stupid woman, oh God the stupid poor woman!"

Kristian went to his mother and put his arms around her. He always hated seeing her upset. He loved her and sometimes felt her pain. He said nothing but kept his arms tightly around the most important human being in his life.

CHAPTER 34

A few days later the hotel had returned to its normal hectic activity.

The damage caused by the fire had, as expected, been quite minimal and was quickly put right. During this time Lise had been saturated by reporters seeking sensational and deathly arson. She treated them all with the contempt they deserved and refused to make any comment. Even so, the press was forgiving and hailed Lise's bravery whilst at the same time hinting at some scandalous family feuding. The publicity had given bookings a boost and curiosity a tonic.

Lise would have preferred less sensational methods of improving business.

Kristian returned to university in his usual calm way, totally unaffected by it all. Karl, having satisfied himself that Lise was over the shock of everything, returned to Denmark for two weeks in order to check on his business commitments.

Love was making him neglectful.

The police had finished their investigations, concluding that Megan Treharne had, in the process of committing arson, accidentally killed herself.

The funeral was due to take place in two days time.

Every night since his departure Karl had telephoned Lise. They were both finding it hard being apart and each had determined to find some way to remedy the heartbreaking problem. As each day passed their love seemed to grow more intense and strong. The bond between them had become unbreakable. The shock of Megan's tragic death had waned, yet sometimes Lise felt that she had let William down in some way. There were moments of guilt but Karl helped to allay them. She always longed for his phone calls and always felt better when they had finished talking. He had become her rock, her priest and confessor. She needed him.

"I think we'd better wait a bit, Bron, before getting married, I mean what with Miss Megan and the fire and all." Gwyn and Bronwyn were sitting on one of the stone benches in the gardens, it was early evening and peaceful.

"Suppose you're right Gwyn." Bronwyn replied, although she wasn't happy about the delay. "How long though?"

"Oh, not long love, month or so. Won't 'arm will it? Must show a bit of respect like. The Boss was good to us don't forget, looked after us in 'is Will he did too. Few thousand quid each. Good start for us."

"Yes, you're right Gwyn." She snuggled up to him.

"'Ell of a way to go, mind. Burnt alive that Megan was. Perhaps it was just as well she snuffed it though, the judge would have 'ad her for 'arson around', ay!" Gwyn laughed at his own morbid sense of humour but Bronwyn was not amused; she poked his shoulder.

"Gwyn, that's a terrible thing to say!"

"Ach *mun*, the woman was a right cow, nutcase or not. Call a spade a spade that's me." Bronwyn ignored her man's truthful cruelty; she was more concerned about other things.

"You're not having doubts about us marrying now are you Gwyn?"

"What? Now don't be daft *mun*! We're only havin' a short delay girl." He kissed her on the cheek. "'Ell Bron, we got a lifetime together, few weeks 'aint goin' to make much difference now is it?"

"No." She answered reluctantly. "But oh Gwyn, I do so want to marry you. I just feel I've waited long enough."

"Aye you crafty bugger, been angling for me for a long time aven't you? And me, bloody old fool that I am, never even noticed. Never mind, we men can be a bit thick sometimes. Now

don't you take on so, everything will be fine, just be a bit patient."
They were both silent for a while, enjoying their closeness.

"It was kind of Lise to let us have the flat over the stable wasn't it Bron? Saved us a lot of trouble and money."

"You can say that again. Good woman is Lise and she seems so happy these days. Never did think it was right for a woman like her to be alone."

"Aye Bron, right enough. We all need somebody, the great human weakness it is."

"I don't know about that but Lise needs a man in her life. This Karl bloke seems to be just the ticket – handsome, plenty of money. Be good if they got married. They seem so much in love. Can't miss it. All in the eyes it is. You should see Lise's face when she talks to 'im on the phone. Like a different woman she is, like a child even. All smiles and blushes."

"I 'ave noticed Bron. All woman is Lise, criminal for her not to 'ave a man around. Every woman needs a good servicin' now and again, say what you like."

"Gwyn! You're so crude sometimes! All you think about is sex! Sometimes I think you fancy Lise."

He started smiling.

"Don't be silly love, you're the only woman I fancy, I'm only teasing you. I've always been fond of Lise since the first day I met 'er. She's a kind, lovely woman and made my boss a happy man. She's been good to me too, so I suppose I just feel very protective toward 'er. Don't want to see 'er 'urt or anythin'. I was so bloody annoyed at not being 'ere when the fire broke out. I could have 'elped if you know what I mean. Instead of that I was out cold at my mother's, useless sod that I am."

"Well Gwyn, all that's past now, so let's forget it. We have a future to think about. It will be so nice to have our own home," she smiled mischievously, "and our own big double bed, more room to move about!"

"Watch it girl, 'nough of that now. Too healthy by 'alf you are!"

"Oh, come on, you must admit my small bed is very uncomfortable. You're a big man after all and we never get any proper sleep."

"That's your fault, you never bloody well leave me alone, do you? You're sex mad you are, sex bloody mad!"

"Maybe, but you don't complain do you? Talking of which we have an hour or so before dinner, so why don't I go to my room and get ready? You can er . . . follow me up in five minutes. Make sure no one sees you."

She darted off, leaving Gwyn sitting on the bench smiling like a hysterical Cheshire cat. Don't know why she bothers trying to be discreet, he thought, everybody knew damn well they were rutting away like a couple of bloody bunny rabbits.

He lit a cigarette and enjoyed the evening.

He was at peace with the world – a nice little jump before dinner would make him feel even better. God though, that Bronwyn was a randy bugger. For a moment he wondered whether he would be able to stand the pace of marriage to her. He'd be dead after a month from exhaustion. But 'ell, those lovely tits . . . and her arse! Christ, her arse! His groin started to twitch. He stubbed out the cigarette, not finishing it. "Here we go," he said out loud, "at the trot and . . . charge!"

CHAPTER 35

The vicar seemed to be experiencing some difficulty in holding his Bible and umbrella at the same time. Rain spat down on the small group of people huddled together in contemplative grief or inconvenient respect. Funerals were like that, a mishmash of sincerity and insincerity. Some people cried, some people started to die for a smoke and some people just appeared in order to be seen. Death was never private; there were far too many people about – not that privacy was a concept likely to bother a corpse. Stiff eyes and ears didn't see or hear much, did they? The vicar mumbled some nonsense about the hereafter in an attempt to console Death, but the black hole, the grave-digger's shovel and the sodding rain were not about to wait much longer for God's prerogative. Bugger Him. A few hand-fuls of soaking mud, a few moments of certainty, a few moments of 'When will it be my turn I wonder?' and that was the end. Death could finally take over and everybody could go home. Bloody marvellous.

Megan's farewell was fast, furious and with no regrets.

She had peace at last.

Griffith walked Lise to the car. He had held her arm through-out the morbid deliberations and continued to do so.

"The funeral of my mother was like this," Lise said. "Rain and mud. At least there were a few more people this time."

"Not much of a turnout though," Griffith answered. "I have to say that I didn't really expect otherwise. Megan lost all her friends a long time ago, at the same time as she lost herself no doubt."

"I'm sorry Griffith, I truly am. It must be terrible for you."

"Not really." He paused before opening the car door for Lise, the rain having finally stopped. "In some ways perhaps Megan has at last found her place in the world. Or peace if you like. Anyway, God knows her life was unhappy and tragic enough. We all tried to help her but to no avail. She had decided on a voyage of self-destruction a long time ago, Lise. None of us have anything to feel guilty about, least of all you. Now let's get in the car and go home."

"Who was that man that stood away from the rest of us?" Lisa asked as they drove back to the Cliffs.

"What did he look like?"

"Middle-aged, distinguished. Well dressed."

"Ah yes, that would be James, Megan's first husband. I did notice him, but I could see that he obviously didn't want any happy reunions so I didn't approach him. He was a good man that one. Too soft and kind for Megan though. She walked all over him. In the end he couldn't take any more and he left her. Upset the old man that did, he liked him. The poor sod just wasn't strong enough to cope with my sister. He loved her too, adored her. In her younger days Megan was quite a looker you know. The less forgiving side of life – booze, drugs and money – changed all that as you know. Look Lise, Megan was one of life's tragedies, I just hope with all my heart that she has finally found peace. For all her faults, she was a human being and my sister. I will miss her. She was all the family I had left. The last of my own blood."

Lise could see that his eyes were smarting; tears were about to announce themselves. He took a hand off the steering wheel and quickly dived into his pocket for a handkerchief. After he had dabbed his eyes Lise took his hand in hers and held it tightly.

"You have us Griffith, you're not alone you know, don't ever think that. I am your stepmother after all." She smiled. "As ridiculous as that seems."

"God yes, you are too, aren't you *Mum*?"

They both laughed for the first time that day.

"Come on now Griffith, you have plenty of people around you who love you, so don't despair."

"Oh, I'm not despairing Lise. Don't worry."

The rest of the journey was given to thoughts of their own mortality. Funerals again. They confused life and death.

When they arrived at the Cliffs Griffith parked the car in the main forecourt. Before getting out Lise asked, "Shall we have dinner together tonight Griffith? On our own, as we haven't had much time to talk have we?"

"No, that's true. Sounds a grand idea. What time?"

"Eight o'clock in my apartment?"

"Fine. I'll see you then."

"That was delicious Lise, cooked to perfection. I haven't eaten any sewin for a long time. Did you do the cooking? Has your hallmark."

"Of course, I still like to keep my hand in. Genuine Welsh sea trout is getting more and more difficult to acquire these days, God knows why. Anyway I'm glad you enjoyed it. Would you like a brandy with your coffee?"

"Yes please, but just a small one. I'm still very cautious where alcohol is concerned. It frightens me when I think of what it did to Megan."

"Well, I must say Griffith moderating your more . . . um . . . intemperate inclinations has certainly had an effect. You're looking much better I must say. Dear me, when I first saw you looked an utter mess."

"Thank you Lise, nothing like a bit of candour. It's good for one's self-confidence." Griffith smiled. Over the years he and Lise had become close, he had always kept in touch and would stay the odd weekend. They were able to say what they liked to each other without any offence being taken.

"It's true Griffith! You were fat, sodden with drink and even at times obnoxious, although I concede that last bit was probably alcohol. Even your nose seems to have quietened down. It seems less livid. Less . . . irate."

"Hey! What is this, get at Griffith time or what? I note you still have a way with words. The old man's influence no doubt. Bloody foreigners!"

"Come on, you know it's true Anyway the main thing is that you managed to overcome things and get back on your feet. I'm proud of you, I really am."

"Thank you Lise, it hasn't always been easy."

"The past is gone now, so let's talk about the future. You mentioned very briefly that you had sold your business in London. Have you really retired?" Fortunately Griffith's minor scrape with the law had not reached this part of the world, or so he thought.

"I suppose I have really. To be honest with you, I don't quite know what I'm going to do at the moment. What with Megan's death I haven't had much time to think about it. Right now I'm just taking things slowly, there's no rush. Perhaps I'll open a hotel, give you some respectable competition. You seem to have Wales all sown up."

"Don't you dare!"

"Only joking. No, I'm really not sure what will happen next. I'm thinking about it."

"Why did you sell the business in London anyway? It made you a lot of money." There was a slight twinkle in Lise's eyes as she asked the question. She knows something, Griffith thought, knowing her as well as he did. Ah well, might as well come clean.

"Lise my girl, I get the distinct impression that you are teasing me."

"I'm sorry," she giggled, "but grave moral turpitude does reach even this part of the world."

"So you know about the court case?"

"Yes, there was a bit about it in the local paper. Don't forget you're from an old and well-known family." She omitted to mention that the local rags had done Griffith proud, front-page spread, the lot. He had been quite famous for a few days.

"You're quite right, of course. Shouldn't have expected anything else really. Thank God the old man had been spared, can you imagine it? I hope you are not going to judge me too harshly."

"Don't be silly Griffith. I must admit I found it rather amusing. You didn't hurt anyone and your 'girls' apparently enjoyed their jobs. The law is totally outdated in this country, it wouldn't have happened in Denmark." Lise giggled again. "After all you were only providing a service. Some service though, I have to say."

"I'm glad you find it so funny. The courtroom was not a barrel of laughs though I can tell you. At one point I thought they were going to put me away. Not my finest hour, that's for sure."

Lise stood up and kissed Griffith gently on the cheek. "Dear Griffith, you really are a scoundrel but a very loveable one! Now go and sit down on a more comfortable chair while I get us some more coffee."

When they were both seated Griffith said, "You know Lise, you've changed."

"What do you mean? I'm the same as I've always been."

"You're not you know. Over the years we've come to know each other pretty well. Something has happened in your life and I'm pretty certain I know what it is."

"Has someone been talking to you?" she asked coyly.

"No, no one. I've only been here since yesterday and haven't really had any chance to talk with anyone apart from you."

"How have I changed then?"

"You're happy, gay even, despite recent events. That can only mean one thing – you're in love. Don't deny it, it's me here you know and you can't fool me. If I'm right, and I think I am, then I'm delighted. You've still got plenty of living to do. You're a lovely woman and should not be on your own. The old man would want you to be happy as well. Come on then, spill the beans, who is it?"

Lise gave up. She told Griffith all about Karl and enjoyed every second of it. Up until now she hadn't been able to talk with anyone about her newfound love with Karl. Griffith listened and encouraged. When she had finished he said with a beaming grin on his face. "Good for you. Sounds a decent man, glad you told me, he's a wealthy bugger though, I might have put him down as a fortune hunter otherwise. You are a rich woman after all. I will look forward to meeting him, give him the once over as it were." Lise was flattered by Griffith's protectiveness and touched; she knew that he would always be there for her in times of trouble. "Are you going to marry him then?"

"Griffith! Always straight to the point, I'll say that for you. You're more like your father than you will ever realise. If you must know, neither of us has even thought about marriage. It's early days yet, and apart from anything else there are some practical problems with that."

"Such as?"

"Well, most of Karl's business is in Denmark so obviously he has to be there most of the time. There's the hotel here, which means I'm tied. I don't honestly know what is going to happen. Like you, things are a bit in limbo at the moment." She took a sip of her coffee and as she did so an idea struck her. "Griffith?"

"Yes, I can see you thinking. Now a woman thinking is dangerous."

"Be quiet a minute. I've just had an idea. Only an idea, so don't get all worked up."

"Go on."

"You have nothing much to do at present do you?"

"Hello, I know your devious little ways Lise. You're scheming."

"Oh, shut up and listen will you? Now then, you have time on your hands do you not?"

"Yes." Griffith replied cautiously. Christ he was back in the dock again.

"You're quite used to managing a business – even if it is of a dubious nature," she added.

"Yes, I'm as good as the next man or . . . woman. I think I know what you're driving at."

"You do know me, don't you dear Griffith?"

"I certainly do, my girl. Let me make it easy for you. Should you and Karl go the distance, it would mean you having to spend a lot of time in Denmark. Correct?" He did not wait for an answer. "Who then is going to look after Ragged Cliffs? You won't sell it, rightly so too, it's a goldmine. That leaves us with reformed Griffith to take over the reins in your absence. Correct?"

"Griffith, you would enjoy it! Give you something to do. I know I can trust you. You know the area, you know the people, you are the ideal candidate. I won't insult you by discussing money. I know you're a wealthy man but obviously you would receive generous remuneration for your efforts."

"No doubt I would, but running a hotel? I've run women faster than a racing car at Monte Carlo, but a hotel?"

"Griffith, you do know about food, comfort and people."

"You can say that again."

"Well then, that's all you need in this business and of course a shrewd eye for profit and loss. You wouldn't have to do much really, Mr Pascoe the manager sees to all the daily bits and pieces. He's excellent at it too. All you would have to do is just keep an eye on things and sign the cheques. You'd be a glorified babysitter really."

"Signing cheques, ay? Chancing your arm a bit there aren't you, darling Lise?"

"Don't be stupid Griffith, whatever else you might be you're not a thief! I trust you implicitly."

"Would I be allowed to provide 'special' executive services then? As a sideline you know. Keep my hand in. You know some of these businessmen get very lonely at night even in Wales."

"Griffith! No, definitely no 'sidelines' as you put it. We are a respectable establishment not a bawdy house."

"Pity." Griffith smiled. "The possibilities are endless."

"Very funny Griffith. Now will you at least think about it? There's no rush. Heavens, I don't even know what will happen between Karl and myself. He wants me to go over to Denmark for a holiday, and it would make me a lot more comfortable if I could leave you in charge."

"All right Lise, I'll think about it. That's all I'm going to say at the moment. When will you be wanting to leave?"

"Karl will be over here in a couple of days time. I'll know then."

"Fair enough. I shall enjoy meeting him. I'm not going anywhere for a while so I shall contemplate the prospects of becoming a hotelier. God, what next Lise, from high-class pimp to respectable innkeeper, life is full of surprises isn't it? You're not going to require references are you?"

They both laughed. The following day, laughter was the last thing on Lise's mind.

"Oh Karl! Another month? Does it have to be that long? Damn, I hate telephones they are so impersonal!" Lise was disappointed and angry.

"I'm afraid so Lise. I am sorry but there's nothing I can do about it. It's a lucrative contract but complicated; the negotiations are taking longer than I had anticipated. I really am sorry, darling, that I can't be with you sooner, as we had planned. You're a business woman, you know how it is."

"Yes I know," Lise sighed, her anger beginning to wane. "It can't be helped I suppose."

"Cheer up now Lise. I'll be with you soon. I don't like this anymore than you do, believe me. I miss you terribly and it's only my work that's keeping me sane. I love you my darling, so don't be too upset. I must go now, the meeting is starting up again. I'll ring tonight, same time. Don't be angry, I love you. Goodbye." He cut the connection leaving Lise a sad and dejected woman. She had been so looking forward to seeing him the following day and holding him in her arms again. When he was not with her she felt lonely and isolated. Most of the time she merely functioned.

She replaced the receiver in its cradle and thought, oh well, there's nothing to be done about it. Might as well get on with things. She then remembered her conversation with Griffith the night before. With Karl still in Denmark for the next month an ideal opportunity had arisen for her to show Griffith the general workings of the hotel – that's if he was agreeable of course. She had been deadly serious in her offer to him the night before. She knew in her heart that she and Karl would marry and this would involve her having to live in Denmark for a large part of the time. She hoped that Griffith would accept her offer; it would give her a secure freedom, if such a thing were possible. She went out to reception and asked Gaynor to call Griffith's room. After one ring he answered.

"Good morning Griffith. How are you?"

"Fine thanks. You're a bit sharp this morning aren't you Lise? It's not eight o'clock yet."

"Well, you know how it is, early bird and so on. Listen, would you like to have breakfast with me?"

"Delighted my girl."

"In my apartment 8.30?"

"Fine by me. You know we must stop meeting like this Lise, people will start talking."

Lise grinned. Speaking with her stepson always cheered her up.

"Let them talk, I'll see you later." A few minutes afterwards the telephone rang again. It was Karl.

Griffith arrived at Lise's private apartment. She greeted him with a kiss and a hug. "I must say Griffith, you really are look-ing the country squire this morning – very refined. Where are the dogs and guns? "

"Very amusing but thank you, I do try. I'm a great believer in Crombie tweeds and cavalry twills."

"They suit you. Now come and sit down and have some breakfast. Did you sleep well?"

"Fine, thank you." Which was of course an outright lie. His eyes absorbed Lise as they always did. Christ, she was beautiful – and for a brief second his earlier decision wavered. She seemed more full of life than usual this morning. Her lips seemed to have been sculptured into a permanent smile. Something was up.

"Now then, we have kippers or fruit juice to start and good old Welsh bacon, eggs and laverbread to follow, so what's it to be?"

"Go on Lise, I'll have some kippers, I haven't eaten them in years."

She glided over to the hotplate and started filling up their plates; even her feet seemed to have a bit more air in them. When she was seated she said, "Griffith, I had a phone call from Karl this morning. He won't be able to come over here for another month or so – business. Now I'm not pushing you Griffith, but I thought that the next few weeks would be an ideal time for me to show you everything there is to know about the hotel. It will give you the chance to reach a proper, well-informed decision, and of course you will have more time to consider my offer."

"Well Lise, to be honest with you I have already decided what to do. I'd like to give it a go; after all there's nothing else keeping me occupied. A reformed waster I may be, but I must confess the prospect of idle retirement has been troubling me somewhat. If everything's all right with you, let's give it a whirl."

"That's marvellous Griffith!" She rushed round the table and gave him another kiss on the cheek.

"Now then, steady on girl, no need to go over the top. What's up with you this morning anyway? Too lively for me this time of the day. This Karl fellow certainly has one hell of an effect on you. Good God you've only spoken to him over the telephone!"

"Can you keep a secret Griffith?"

"Of course I can." He answered.

"Karl didn't just make one phone call. He rang again just before you knocked on the door. He's asked me to marry him. Oh Griffith, I'm so happy!"

Griffith's kippers suddenly turned rancid. For a moment he didn't know what to say. Happiness for Lise seeing her joy, paradise lost once and for all. The final nail in the black coffin of his remote hope. All these thoughts filled his mind as they clashed together in a tempest of tragic resignation. Collecting himself he stood up and held out his arms to Lise. She came to him like a loving sister to her long-lost brother.

"Congratulations Lise. With all my heart I hope you both will be very happy." As she put her head on his shoulder, Lise's excitement never saw the one lonely tear that ran down Griffith's cheek to settle in the starched white collar of his shirt.

CHAPTER 36

Gwyn and Bronwyn were married in a tiny church not far from the Cliffs.

As the vicar pronounced them man and wife, Bronwyn couldn't help but let out a sigh of relief. She was two months pregnant.

It was a quiet affair with just close family and the contingent from the Cliffs. Karl had finally managed to leave Denmark and return to his beloved Lise. As a wedding present for the happy couple Lise had spent a great deal of money converting the old stables into a proper home. She even instructed the builders to make sure a small nursery was included in the conversion. Bronwyn had confided in her about the 'unplanned' pregnancy and at the time of the embarrassed confession both women had looked at each other with mischievous and twinkling eyes. Nothing further needed to be said. On discovering his impending fatherhood Gwyn had decided to give up the beer for good. During the wedding reception he was frequently heard to mumble 'Get thee behind me Satan!' His old Biblical day were returning with a vengeance, but if it kept him off the booze then as far as Bronwyn was concerned that was fine by her.

Later that night when all the nuptials were over Karl and Lise sat alone in her apartment drinking a nightcap before going to bed. Lampshades soothed the light around the sitting room as they demanded slowness in mood and movement.

"It's been a long day Lise. I must say I'm tired."

"Me too." Lise replied. They were sitting on the sofa holding each other. "You know I miss you so much when you're away, Karl. It's awful. I simply didn't know what to do with myself. I was walking around in my own little world most of the time. If it wasn't for Griffith I don't know what I would have done."

"I missed you too – desperately. I love you Lise, so very very deeply. We mustn't be parted for so long again. I like Griffith and he seems to be an admirable choice as someone to look after your interests here. We have already discussed your coming to Denmark to live and you seem quite happy and relaxed about it. Charlotte is young enough to adjust and Kristian seems determined to lead his own life. You can return to Wales as often as you like. Lise, I think we should get married as soon as possible, don't you? There is nothing stopping us after all."

"Oh yes Karl, most definitely." She lifted her face up to his and kissed him. Despite the tiredness in both of them love rescued passion from fatigue. Unable to reach the bedroom they fell to the floor and made love urgently and quickly. On this occasion there was no foreplay, no finesse. They had only removed the items of clothing necessary. Longing and desperation demanded urgency, so their lovemaking was fast and brutal. A few minutes later they kissed and touched more slowly. Breathing was deep and replete as they enjoyed the mixture and pleasure of each other's perspiration and love. Sex had moved on; now it was gentle intimacy with no barriers.

Recovering slightly Lise said, "That was quick Karl, what on earth happened?"

"I don't quite know but it was wonderful. Sometimes you know the short little 'quickies'– is that the word? – are the best." Lise laughed.

"Do you know this is the first time we have made love without being in total darkness."

"Really?" Karl murmured.

"Let me take your shirt off, you're very hot. You know I've never really had a proper look at your body, nor you at mine I suppose. Why don't we go and have a bath together?"

"Good idea, give me a minute though. You're an animal Lise Treharne soon-to-be Schriver, do you know that?"

"And don't you just love it!" She replied with a giggle. She undid the buttons of his shirt and gently removed it. As she pulled the sleeve from one arm Karl's right shoulder became visible. A table lamp shone directly on it.

Lise's hands stopped moving.

She gripped the material. Her knuckles turned white.

Her eyes opened wide.

Disbelief.

Horror.

Numbness.

Her whole body came to an absolute stop. She couldn't move. She couldn't think. There was no time, no life, there was nothing but the bare shoulder of the man she loved and a birthmark that bore an exact resemblance to a preying eagle.

Her throat tightened. She couldn't swallow. She couldn't speak. Her breathing almost stopped completely.

Karl opened his eyes and looked at her.

"What's the matter Lise . . . are you ill? Your face has turned white."

At first she made no response, then her senses partly returned.

"You!" She screamed. "You!"

She started to batter his face with her fists. She wanted to kill him. All the years of agony and pain returned in a deadly fury. She was in Denmark once again. Her body was being raped and violated.

"You!" she continued to scream as she tried to tear Karl's face with her nails. "You raped me, you nearly murdered me and all this time you knew it. You let me love you, how could you?! How could you?! Wasn't raping me enough?"

Karl managed to hold her wrists preventing her from doing any more damage. She had caught him totally by surprise.

Denial would be useless.

He knew he was guilty.

He tried to get away from her but she kept coming. He had never seen such rage in a human being before. Lise had gone completely out of her mind.

He started backing away toward the open French doors that led to the balcony. Lise blocked his way to the main door. Her eyes were on fire, the fire of hatred and revenge. She was sobbing. A great flood of tears gushed down her dress. Through the grief of her discovery all she could shout was "Why?!"

She rushed at Karl again all reason lost in her desire to punish. She raged for restitution. He backed onto the balcony knowing that he must physically abuse Lise again for her own good.

But she was too fast, too quick.

Her temper had given her the strength of two men; before he knew what was happening he was falling from the balcony into a pit of blackness.

Lise sank to the floor.

She sobbed and sobbed her beautiful heart out.

CHAPTER 37

"Can't you see Mrs Treharne is in shock for God's sake? Now is not the time!"

Griffith was standing in Lise's sitting room. His arm was around her. Protection. Lise was silent. Only her dried tears and empty eyes spoke.

"I am sorry Mr Treharne but we must establish exactly what has happened here." Chief Inspector Ian Hall spoke with the calm experience of a man who had seen it all before.

"It's pretty bloody obvious isn't it?" Griffith was annoyed at the involvement of the police. Who had called them anyway? As far as he was concerned 'police' meant trouble. "I have called our solicitor Bernard John. He is on his way."

"And why would you do that Mr Treharne? No one has suggested any foul play. We are merely investigating a serious accident. Is there something we should know?"

"Now don't start twisting my words Inspector. Sorry, 'Chief Inspector'. You know full well that there has been no 'foul play' as you put it. Karl must have fallen by accident. Full stop. What other reason could there be?!" Griffith was shouting now. Dear me, this was going to be one of those nights, Hall thought. If only his idiot wife hadn't picked up the damned telephone. He had just finished his last whisky and was on his way to bed.

"Please calm yourself Mr Treharne. Believe me, shouting will help no one – particularly the lady here." He looked at Lise. He had heard all about the Treharnes at Ragged Cliffs. A troubled family. A tragic one. Now this. Griffith Treharne had been a bit of a boy in his time too. Nothing serious though. At least running a brothel was hardly the crime of the century. Hall wished he could have afforded such luxuries. Had liked the booze and his old man's money too much so the story went. Changed man now apparently. He was certainly an angry man right now and very fond of his stepmother by the looks of it. Well well, 'Murder at Ragged Cliffs', Agatha Christie here we come. Hall could do without it. He wanted to get back into his warm untroubled bed. Untroubled that is when his wife wasn't in it. Hall's eyes travelled back to Lise Treharne. She was a truly beautiful woman, no doubt about it. She didn't look the type to kill, but then did any of them? He watched her sit down. Her movements were dignified even regal. That was serious money for you, the upper classes always kept their heads, no matter what. She hadn't said a word. Ah well, better get on with it Hall finally decided.

"Mrs Treharne, please tell me what happened?" He looked through the French doors; he had already examined the shredded safety rail on the balcony.

A handkerchief swept Lise's eye. She looked directly at him. Nothing. Before he could go any further Bernard John barged into the room. All dignity and reassurance. As usual. The old bastard should have retired years ago.

"Hello, Chief Inspector." They shook hands. They both knew each other. Freemasons were everywhere. John took in the scene. Griffith had already given him the bare facts. "May I have a word?"

"Yes of course, Mr John." They left the room. Outside in the corridor Hall spoke first.

"Not your thing this, Bernard. Criminal work."

"Who says it's criminal now Ian?"

"Could be. I have my suspicions. Your client not saying anything though doesn't help. Haven't been able to speak with this Schriver fellow yet either. Unconscious when he was taken to the hospital."

"You haven't got anything yet then to confirm your . . . er . . . suspicions?"

"No."

"How did you get involved anyway? I thought Swansea East was more your territory?"

"999. One of the residents. Didn't see anything though. Heard a crash and saw this Schriver fellow on the ground. Called an ambulance. They called us. Usual thing. My boss called me, thought the matter needed a bit of seniority. Wealthy family, well known etc., etc. He felt the delicate touch was needed."

"Quite so Ian, quite so. Thank you for the thought. You are obviously wondering whether Mr Schriver was pushed."

"The thought had crossed my mind."

"I would be extremely surprised if Lise Treharne was capable of such an act. They were very much in love. Engaged so I'm advised."

"That doesn't mean much Bernard, and you know it. Could be a domestic gone wrong. You know it happens. Won't be the first time. Have to see what this Schriver fellow has to say. That's if he lives."

"That serious?"

"Well, he didn't look too good going to the hospital. Not that I'm a doctor mind you. Still I know the signs. Hell of a height to take a dive from unless he had wings."

"Yes Ian, I take your point. I will have to advise my client to say nothing, for now anyway. You know the form."

"I do indeed Bernard. Wouldn't have expected anything less." He smiled. "Can't do much right now anyway, won't be dragging her off to the nick. The state of the guard rail does bother me though Bernard, so be prepared."

"Again, point taken. Thank you." They shook hands.

"Before you go Bernard, I have heard that Lise Treharne is a remarkable woman. She is certainly a real beauty."

"Ah Ian, even your policeman's ice doth melt. Smitten like the rest of us. Keep dreaming my boy, keep dreaming."

The middle-aged Chief Inspector thought about the trouble that lay in his bed snoring like a demented hog. Hair net, curlers and dribbling gob included. Going back to bed did not seem so attractive after all. He followed the solicitor into the sitting room. What a life. He wouldn't have minded throwing his wife off a balcony, bloody high balcony at that, wings or no wings!

CHAPTER 38

"Now then Chief Inspector, the patient has only just regained consciousness. Therefore be warned I will not tolerate any bullying. Is that clear?"

"Very, doctor." Hall mumbled.

"Good. Twenty-four hours haven't passed yet since the accident, so go gently."

"I will doc. I promise. Only a couple of questions. What's the damage anyway?"

"Bad."

"How bad doc?"

"Broken back. Doubtful he will walk again. Not all the tests have been completed and it's early days, but the prognosis isn't good. The fall would have killed a weaker man."

"He will live then?"

"Yes. His life is not in danger now. His quality of life in the future? . . . Well, that's another matter."

"Does he know?"

"We have told him what we can."

Hall looked through the glass panel and saw a handsome man. "A pity. A great pity."

"The patient is fully *compos mentis* but do bear in mind that he is receiving strong medication for the pain. He may seem a little drowsy. Be patient."

"Understood."

"Good. Well I'll leave you to it."

The doctor walked off. He had dealt with Hall in the past and knew he could trust the policeman to respect his wishes. Before he reached the end of the corridor he heard Hall calling him.

"Doctor, sorry to bother you again. Have there been any visitors?"

"No, none that I am aware of."

"Nobody at all?"

"Not unless the nursing staff have seen anyone. His next of kin has been given as his brother in Denmark I believe."

"Not Lise Treharne?"

"No."

"Thank you doctor, I won't trouble you again."

"So, you were dancing, Mr Schriver?"

"Yes."

"There was no aggression? You had not been quarrelling?"

"No. Definitely not. We were dancing. Enjoying ourselves. Celebrating. Celebrating our engagement. Our love. We were so happy. It had been a long time for both of us."

"A long time?"

Schriver sighed. "Yes Inspector. A long time without . . . love. We had both been living alone for some years. We were going to marry but now . . . well . . ."

" 'Going to marry?' you say. 'But'? You are talking as if the marriage is off Mr Schriver." Karl was quiet for a moment. Talking was difficult. He was fighting off sleep but he had to keep going. He had to. Hall persisted. "I said Mr Schriver that your words imply that the marriage is off. Could it be that you both had a violent quarrel resulting in you lying here?"

"That's nonsense!" Karl nearly shouted but his strength was draining fast. ". . . The marriage cannot go ahead. How can it? I am a cripple. I love Lise too much to inflict my broken body on her. I love her too much."

"Calm yourself Mr Schriver. I understand. Just let me get this right. You were both enjoying a celebratory drink. Maybe you were both a bit drunk. You started dancing together. Not much room on the balcony for a foxtrot is there?"

". . . For the last time, my fall was an accident. You are mad if you think otherwise. Mad. Now I am tired, please leave me alone." Hall did not give in easily.

"So you were enjoying a romantic dance under the stars I presume. Next thing you slip. You fall. You manage to smash through a solid oak guard rail. Is that right?"

"Yes, that's exactly what happened. I am a big man Inspector, the guard rail could not have resisted my weight."

"You are certain Mr Schriver."

"Certain."

Chief Inspector Hall looked at the face. The determination. The strength. For Karl Schriver the matter was closed. The questioning was over. No argument. No reasonable doubt.

Hall stood up. "Very well Mr Schriver. I will leave you my card in case you happen to remember something that you haven't told me." Before leaving the room Hall turned around. "Lise Treharne didn't push you?"

Schriver looked Hall straight in the eyes.

"No, she did not."

"Some residents heard shouting."

"Did they Inspector? I am not surprised. We were rather noisy. Laughing a lot. I expected a complaint or two. We were really being quite childish."

"Is that so, Mr Schriver? Except that children do not normally break each other's backs do they? You are a brave man Mr Schriver, a man who must also love very deeply. Goodbye."

The door closed.

It also closed on the years of guilt.

Karl's love for Lise had trapped and released him at the same time. It had also punished. No other woman had managed to capture all of him. He had known from the start that perhaps one day his secret would be revealed, its violence known. He had been prepared to take the risk. He had almost welcomed it – the secrecy and its revelation. His imprisonment and his liberation.

His back was broken. He would learn to live with this but his heart was broken too. This he would never learn to live with.

Lise's pain. Her agony. Her eyes of despair.

There was not a pain killer or medicine in the world that would soothe this memory or heal it.

EPILOGUE

Two years had passed.

Lise sat alone in William's floral kingdom.

She had picked a young yellow rose and was holding it carefully. Her small hand was incapable of inconsiderate grasp. The delicate petals demanded love and respect. They, their parents and their grandparents had been spoilt by William's touch.

Time had brought balance to her life in a strange accepted way. The strength beneath her loveliness had prevailed yet again, although there were times when an insidious despair ate its way into her lonelier moments. On these occasions she would search for Charlotte or Griffith and keep herself reminded of all the pure and innocent things in her life.

Despite all her efforts at recall she was unable to remember exactly what had happened on that disastrous night of discovery. She remembered only pain; the vicious slashing open of an old and mutilating wound. The intense agony had overcome her senses, her mind. She knew that all human beings could kill given enough provocation. Whether she had intended to kill or just wound she would never know.

There had been a police investigation, but Karl had resolutely maintained that his falling had been the result of drunken frolicking between two lovers. The police, though suspicious, had had to accept his explanation. Lise had been totally unresponsive to their questioning. She had given them nothing. She had been unable to.

Karl had returned to Denmark married to a wheelchair and a shattered spine.

Lise's basic humanity was still trying to come to terms with the man's tragedy. A tragedy entwined with her own. Her inherent capacity to forgive shone through the blackness of betrayal and deceit. Forgiveness though was so facile – it was the forgetting that seemed so unattainable. Karl would suffer for the rest of his life. He had paid for his crime. Lise had been his nemesis even though she had never wanted this. She could not help but feel a certain pity for the man. For her, revenge brought only corruption of the heart and bitterness. It served no one. His refusal to involve the police was perhaps an act of contrition. A redemption. His way of acknowledging his crime.

Whether he fell by accident or was pushed by her own hands she would never know. She comforted herself with the fact that she had lived with the unknown for many years of her life. Until, that is, Karl appeared. Not only had he solved the mystery of at least one of her attackers, he had also established his lack of paternity where Kristian was concerned. There was simply nothing of him in her son. Only a mother can reach such certain conclusions in respect of her own offspring. Kristian would never know the truth behind that night in Denmark. He, like Lise, would never know the identity of her other assailant.

Neither she nor Karl had exchanged one word since the night of his fall.

She thought of her son.

He had graduated with honours and was now finding his way in London. No doubt there would be girls, girls, girls for many years to come. He frequently brought them home. She feared for him as any mother would, but knew that he was now a man and that another would one day replace her in his heart. She also knew that there was no woman on earth who could love him as deeply as she did.

Ragged Cliffs continued to prosper. She and Griffith made a formidable management team, but she knew that he felt more for her than simple friendship. She was unable to respond in a way that he would have wanted so she kept a certain distance. There were times though when this distance narrowed. She would immediately take flight. Fear would win.

Perhaps one day.

Charlotte, her bundle of giggles and mischief continued to torment and delight everyone. The little one gave Lise enormous strength and joy. The child was so much like her father.

Gwyn and Bronwyn had carried on baby-making and were enjoying parenthood. Drunken battles were a thing of the past. Gwyn's mam still reached for the poker but it was never raised.

Lise looked out across the sea and felt, as she always did, the spirit of William. His touch never left the beauty of his gardens. He touched her now, the love and warmth of his fingertips reaching into her with a simplicity that was still overwhelming. She knew that her own fortitude combined with William's would see her through.

It had taken until now for her to find a just balance to all the appalling events in her life. The suffering. Her mind had never entered the pathetic, bleating realms of self-pity and excuse. Her determination and will concentrated her mind on only the good. Her children. Her love for William that had endured and remained pure. Her friends. She knew now that Karl could never have truly competed. Their passion had been too fast, too thoughtless.

She knew about love and was calm.

She knew its nature and its power.

At last she stood up and began the walk back to the house.

Before shutting the gate to the rose garden she looked again at William's pride and his joy. As she did so she kissed the yellow rose still held in her hand and whispered, "One day my darling we will fly together again. Just wait for me and I will be there."

THE END

Also by the same author . . .

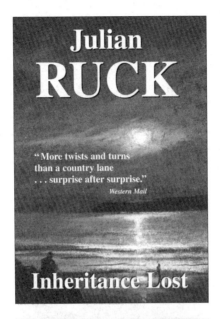

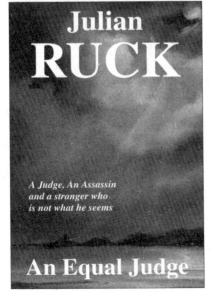

ABOUT THE AUTHOR

Julian Ruck trained as a lawyer in London before spending some time in both Denmark and Israel. On his eventual return he entered the world of Academia, lecturing law. This was not to be a lifelong commitment as some years later he found himself managing Legal Services Commission contracts in the Not For Profit Sector.

www.julianruck.co.uk